Arroyo of Shells

A Pueblo Tribal Police Mystery

Arroyo of Shells

A Pueblo Tribal Police Mystery

A Novel

Jack Matthews

Santa Fe

Sunstone books may be purchased for educational, business, or sales promotional use.
For information please write: Special Markets Department, Sunstone Press,
P.O. Box 2321, Santa Fe, New Mexico 87504-2321.

eBook: 978-1-61139-749-9

Library of Congress Cataloging-in-Publication Data

Names: Matthews, Jack, 1942- author.
Title: Arroyo of shells : a Pueblo tribal police mystery : a novel / Jack Matthews.
Description: Santa Fe : Sunstone Press, 2024. | Summary: "The search for stolen museum items, murder, pueblo ceremonialism, a bookshop, and an attempt at kiva revitalization from a prehistoric time form a contemporary novel set in the high country of the Sangre de Cristo Mountains of northern New Mexico"-- Provided by publisher.
Identifiers: LCCN 2024030953 | ISBN 9781632937476 (hardcover) | ISBN 9781632936745 (paperback) | ISBN 9781611397499 (epub)
Subjects: LCGFT: Detective and mystery fiction. | Novels.
Classification: LCC PS3613.A8483 A88 2024 | DDC 813/.6--dc23/eng/20240712 LC record available at https://lccn.loc.gov/2024030953

WWW.SUNSTONEPRESS.COM
SUNSTONE PRESS / POST OFFICE BOX 2321 / SANTA FE, NM 87504-2321 /USA
(505) 988-4418

I dedicate this book to my mother,
Gywn Parks Hollingshead, my first storyteller.

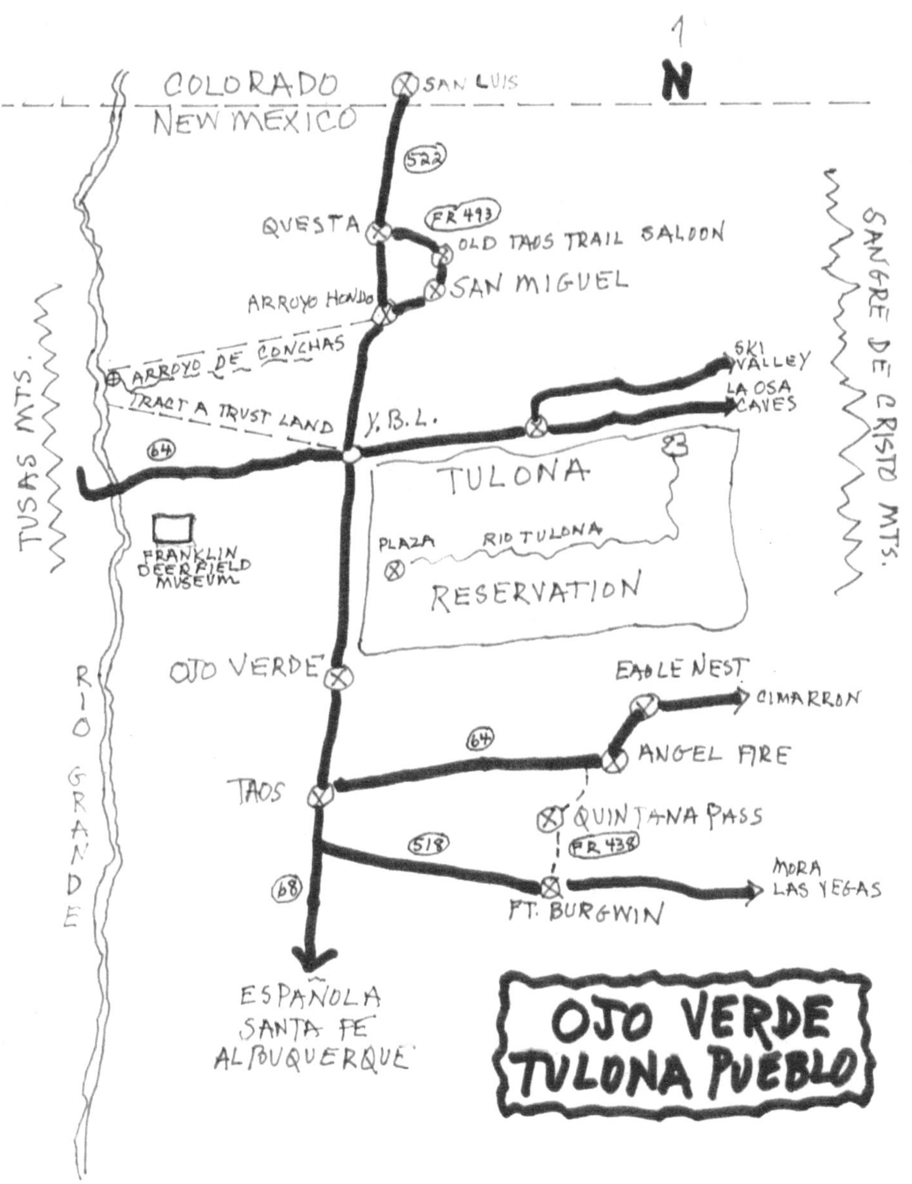

N
COLORADO
NEW MEXICO
SAN LUIS
522
QUESTA
FR 493
OLD TAOS TRAIL SALOON
SAN MIGUEL
ARROYO HONDO
ARROYO DE CONCHAS
TRACT A TRUST LAND
Y. B. L.
SKI VALLEY
LA OSA CAVES
TUSAS MTS.
SANGRE DE CRISTO MTS.
64
TULONA
83
PLAZA
RIO TULONA
RESERVATION
FRANKLIN DEERFIELD MUSEUM
RIO GRANDE
OJO VERDE
EAGLE NEST
CIMARRON
64
ANGEL FIRE
TAOS
QUINTANA PASS
518
FR 438
MORA
LAS VEGAS
68
FT. BURGWIN
ESPAÑOLA
SANTA FE
ALBUQUERQUE
OJO VERDE
TULONA PUEBLO

"They see no life / When they look / They see only objects…."
—Leslie Marmon Silko, *Ceremony*

"In the old days it was said that the shining fish would come up from the water just to partake of our faces as we washed. The wind played a song in the reeds just to draw us near."
—Linda Hogan, *Power*

Preface

Arroyo of Shells is a work of fiction and all characters are imaginary. Tulona Pueblo does not exist. Anthropological material used in this book is not intended to meet scholarly standards. This story is based on my field notes and relevant histories of northern New Mexico and the American Southwest, but it is not a work of scholarly history. I have neither sought nor used Indigenous informants in interpreting ceremonies that I consider living systems of spirituality. Furthermore, no Indigenous person has given me information, either freely or for payment. I have written *Arroyo of Shells* by standards of Article 31, United Nations Declaration on the Rights of Indigenous Peoples, 2007.

U.S. Geological Survey maps, particularly 7.5-Minute Series topographical maps, and U.S. Forest Service maps have been applied in writing *Arroyo of Shells*. Using this novel solely in navigating and orienting in forests, wilderness areas, highways, and backcountry is disclaimed. "The River Who Knows" and "Quintana Pass," however, do exist in Taos County, northern New Mexico.

List of Characters

Tulona Tribal Police and Law Enforcement

Richard Tafoya, tribal policeman

Janet Rael, U.S. Forest Service officer, liaison with tribal police, Isleta Puebloan

Tony Romero, sergeant, tribal police

Diane Parker, F.B.I. agent, Albuquerque

Franklin Deerfield Museum Staff

Jennifer Hornbuckle, director of museum

John McGinnis, curator

Martha Johnson, intern

Ray Tejada, Tulona curator

Puebloans

Leonard Bustamente (Bear Standing Fire), cacique of Tulona Pueblo

Medicine Wind (Ben Lovato)

Lion Walks Night, horseman

Quail Looks Away, wife of Medicine Wind (Ben Lovato)

Lance Bernal (Blue Sky Deer)

Alfredo Dominguez

Larry Armijo, computer expert

Villagers

Armando Ortega, sheepman, resident of San Miguel

Luis Ortega, son of Armando, sheepman, horseman, farrier

G. Armstrong Coe, bookshop owner

Jason Taylor, waiter at Tablita's Restaurant, avid skier

Father Jose Padilla, mission Catholic priest, Santa Fe

Santiago Majerus, Navajo medicine man

Equine

Star, gelding horse of Medicine Wind (Ben Lovato)

Sweet Hija, mare of Leonard Bustamente (Bear Standing Fire)

Buck or Bucephalus, gelding horse of Luis Ortega

Monte, gelding horse of Luis Ortega

Jess, mare of Medicine Wind (Ben Lovato)

I

Saturday, October 13, Day of Blessed Marie-Rose Durocher, Month of Leaves Falling Moon

A piñon jay cocked her head to one side as she saw the solitary Tulona puebloan trot-shuffle up the main trail from the pueblo. In the freezing chill, the man's breath came out in bluish-white clouds and ascended into the lower branches of ponderosa trees in the National Forest. It was first light, the gray light, before the sun rose over the Sangre de Cristo cordillera in northern New Mexico. The jay emitted a piñon jay note, then fell into nervous chatter as she flitted along the trail with the human. The Tulona puebloan glanced up at the bird and then looked back on the path to see if he was being followed; he was alone. Relieved, he adjusted his backpack whose contents were neither light nor heavy. Quickly diverting from the main trail, he angled deeper into the conifer forest as the sharp-billed, dull blue-gray jay flew curiously along, leaving her bowl-of-twigs nest far behind in more pleasant latitudes. She had no chicks.

Seeing the cliffside where he intended to stop, the man halted and looked around, verifying his bearings as to location: cliffside of granite behind him, Tusas Mountains toward the west, La Osa Caves to his north, and the pueblo and Ojo Verde far below to the south. Here was the spot. He dragged aside the brush that had covered a three-foot deep hole he had dug and chiseled a week before Tulona Feast Day on October 4. Slipping his backpack off, he checked the contents. "It's all here."

Taking the objects out of his backpack, he wrapped them in thick waterproof plastic and tied hemp rope, not acrylic rope, tightly around the items, creating one compact bundle. Stuffing the bundle back in the pack, he buried the pack, covering it up with mountain soil and stones. He smoothed topsoil over the hole, carefully placing twigs, leaves, and ponderosa needles on the surface. Dusting the dirt off his hands, he walked back ten paces and looked at the spot. He could not tell, nor could anyone else, where the pack and bundle had been buried.

Once again, he scanned through the trees and looked downward to Ojo Verde to determine he was alone and to emblaze the location firmly in his mind. Then he spoke in archaic melody and prayer.

"*Hey-yo, hey-yo, hey-yo! Yo!* Creator, I do this for the Tulona! The earth! The Hanging Shell people! *¡Bendiciones!*"

Finished, he returned to the trail and descended quickly away from the burial of the bundle and ran back to the pueblo.

The piñon jay floated down from her perch, as the man trotted away. Walking on the newly-covered hole, she cawed loudly and soon a flock of kinsmen, the jay people, briefly congregated on lower branches, then flew gracefully to the ground. Scratching impatiently, the jays scattered the ponderosa needles and leaves away from the Tulona man's careful placement concealing the backpack. Finding neither grubs nor seeds, the piñon jays rose as a flock and flew farther down the mountain to begin the new day in the sun's warmth among juniper and sage on New Mexico's mesas.

Several hours earlier...

Near Ojo Verde, overlooking the Rio Grande, the Franklin Deerfield Museum stood like an isolated adobe pueblo on an arid mesa west of the Tulona Pueblo. Its landscaped conifer and spruce trees softened the straight edges of puebloan architecture that the museum's benefactor loved. Before the sun rose above the Cristo Mountains in the east, the security guard made his rounds at far points of the museum, scanning the QR code location with the Security Lock app on his smart phone within the building and outside. The Detex mechanical watchclock had been replaced several years before. He paused at the southwest corner of the building and looked at the moon's sliver, a thin slice of sun in reflection, falling lower above the flat-topped peak of Pedernal Mountain in the southwest. He glanced at his field watch: 4:23 a.m. Shivering from the cold, he raised the protective flap for the QR code, caught the code with the phone, ensuring his presence on the southwest corner of the museum to satisfy his employer—and the insurance company. He noticed frost on the chamiso and fog rising above the Rio's gorge. If you listened closely, you could hear the river coursing below. But the wind had to be null; it was. He heard the Big River crashing on boulders below the lip of the mesa.

Movement in the distance tore the security guard's concentration away from the Rio's fog and sound. The security guard saw three human silhouettes running down the road away from the museum, their outline configured by the lights of Ojo Verde village in the distance. They were bareheaded or wore tight ski caps, he thought. The person leading the three had a headlamp that illuminated the road upon which they ran, its beam bouncing, growing dimmer, then disappearing where the road dipped down.

"Hmm," he uttered, "must be joggers. But this early in the morning? Odd."

When the security guard unlocked the side door to go back inside the museum to finish his reconnaissance, he noticed the hallway door to the inventory basement was wide open. Running to the basement door, he bounded down the steps. The inventory basement was huge, but a quick check revealed neither drawers nor cabinets open. The table of Native American objects the staff was working on the day before was exactly as he remembered when he made his round several hours before. Yet, the door was open to the basement and he knew, for certain, it had been closed—and locked. He ran up basement steps and walked quickly to the security office adjacent to the entrance and front desk. Entering his password on the computer, he quickly ran back the security video of the hallway outside the basement door to the inventory rooms.

The video was jerky, grainy, but fortunately in color. What the security guard saw scared him. He quickly lifted the telephone landline out of its cradle, called 911, and asked for law enforcement to come to his aid and assistance. He unbuckled his pistol scabbard and drew out his Walther PPK, making sure the clip was secure against the butt, and laid it on his desk in full sight. He felt confident a shell was in the chamber, but he re-chambered a shell, nonetheless. An ejected bullet fell with a thud on the floor and rolled around in a half-circle. He picked the bullet up and set it quickly back in the clip, resetting the clip firmly. The security guard was definitely not going back to the museum's inventory room until the troopers arrived; he prayed they came quickly.

2

The Tulona Pueblo, a Tiwa-speaking people, lay west of the Sangre de Cristo Mountains in northern New Mexico. North of Taos by ten miles or so, the village of Ojo Verde and the pueblo occupied the land between the Tulona and Taos Mountain ranges to the east and the Rio Grande and arid mesa-flatlands extending to the Tusas and Jemez Mountains to the west. North of Tulona Reservation and Ojo Verde were the village and town of San Miguel and Questa. From Ojo Verde south on the highway were Taos, Española, and Santa Fe, the state capital. A popular ski valley in the Cristo lay to the northeast of the reservation. The altitudes on the mesa floor and mountains varied from 6,000 to 13,000-plus feet. In the summer, tourists rafted the Rio Grande and, in the winter, skied the slopes above the pueblo.

The Tulona Pueblo had been settled before the Spanish conquest. Taos Pueblo to the south—also Tiwa-speaking—had been "settled" in about 1000 CE. The Rio Tulona or Cottonwood River bisected the Tulona main houses, one on the northside, the other on the southside. Taos County government oversaw the vicinity, but the Tulona, like other pueblos, had a tribal council, kivas, warchiefs, fisacales, and a cacique as major controlling factors in their lives.

Tulona Cacique Leonard Bustamente Bear Standing Fire held spiritual position for life. His voice was central in interpreting and remembering pueblo stories and ceremonial times. Though the council and warchiefs dominated the political aspects of the pueblo, Bustamente represented a spiritual voice and presence, extending back to the Fourth World, the world before the present Fifth.

Daily, standing on the rooftop of the highest pueblo house on the southside, Bustamente monitored the arc of sun and moon as they juxtaposed themselves with the Jemez and Tusas Mountains to the west and the Sangre de Cristo to the east. The arid mesas to the west were open and free. He often visited his Zuñi and Navajo friends and cousins west of the mesas. Bustamente, however, never traveled far nor spent many nights away from the Tulona Pueblo. His place was alongside Rio Tulona, not among the Zuñi or Navajo.

Earlier that morning, not long after the security guard at Franklin Deerfield panicked, Bustamente had watched the sun begin to shine on the treetops of Tulona Peak. As he meditated on past days and the present Month of Falling Leaves, he apprehended movement on the road to Earth Cloud Lake. A solitary figure trotted downward from the mountain and then disappeared behind the northside pueblo houses and ash pile.

"Who is this I see, Creator?" Bustamente said. "And what is occurring?"

A solitary magpie flew across the plaza, glided slowly upward, and landed on the adobe wall a few feet away from the cacique. The magpie turned around to face the running figure that had appeared again on Abalone Road, skirting past the ash pile, trotting away from the plaza.

Bustamente gazed at the solitary magpie, and then looked at the running man who grew smaller in size as he ran away from the pueblo. The north wind gusted and ruffled the blanket of Bustamente and the tail and wing feathers of the magpie, nearly pitching the black and white bird off the wall. The magpie, catching a cue it seemed, flew down to the ground and joined his brothers and sisters pecking at insects.

"A solitary magpie is not a good sign," Bustamente thought, as he saw the running man disappear around a curve on the road to Ojo Verde.

3

Tulona tribal policeman Richard Tafoya woke up when his landline phone rang at 4:44 a.m. On the other end of the line his superior, sergeant Tony Romero, quickly relayed that an emergency call came from the security guard at the Franklin Deerfield Museum.

"A possible theft has occurred, and the security guard has video of something strange. The Taos County sheriff's department is on its way there," Romero said. "We need to get out there fast!"

Tafoya dressed quickly, jumped in his police car parked outward from his home on the edge of pueblo land, turned on the flash bar, and sped to the museum. Sergeant Romero arrived at the same time. The security guard was opening the doors to the museum for the sheriff's deputies, as Tafoya slammed the door of his vehicle.

The tribal police and deputies secured the museum area from anyone tromping around outside and disturbing evidence. A quick reconnaissance outside the building revealed footprints near a side door on the opposite end of the building from the security guard's last QR code clocking at 4:23 a.m. Yellow security tape was stuck to the door on the outside and on the inside near the footprints. Taos County sheriff's deputy Chris Cordova discovered the footprints and radioed the deputies inside the museum to secure the door from the inside and isolate the hallway leading to the exit. Tafoya overheard the call from Cordova and walked down the hallway to the door leading to the outside.

Halting several feet from exit door, Tafoya squatted down and muted his flashlight so that only the indoor hall lights provided illumination. Gaining a visual on the floor relative to the door, he saw shoeprints. Shoeprints going out the door, not coming in. The prints were sports shoes, like running sneakers. That would, of course, be verified later, but the prints had a pattern of running shoes. Turning his flashlight on and off to see detail, Tafoya surmised there may have been more than one person exiting the museum through the side door. Re-attaching yellow crime scene tape blocking the hallway and exit door, Tafoya turned around and found his way to the security room.

"Does the cleaning staff mop down and polish the floors each evening?" he asked the security officer as he entered the security room. Several law enforcement personnel were huddled around a large monitor screen.

"The cleaning staff polishes floors every Monday and Friday evenings. They vacuum every evening," the security officer replied without looking up from the screen.

"Why do you ask?" Romero said, turning to Tafoya.

"We have a newly-vacuumed floor with footprints leading to the outside. If the cleaning staff did not go out that door, we may have shoeprints of the thieves...clear and pristine," Tafoya answered.

"We'll check it out, Tafoya.... Here, take a look at this security footage. Devils or angels or god-knows-what came out of the basement," Romero directed.

The officers cleared a space for Tafoya to view the monitor. They scrolled back the footage to the beginning. Tafoya bent closer to see.

Slowly, the basement inventory door swung open. A security camera was installed at one end of the hallway, and as the door swung outward it temporarily obscured the person coming out of the inventory room. The person turned quickly to his right and started in the direction of another hallway that angled left and led to the hallway door that Tafoya concluded was the escape door. The average-height male was dressed in black or dark gray clothing with dark running shoes. A mask completely covered his head, like a small barrel placed upside down, sitting on his shoulders. It was flimsier than a barrel, however. It obscured his face, but since he had turned away from the camera, the front of the mask was hidden. The mask imitated some personage or animal, strange and alien. Feathers appeared to sprout out of the mask and a fox fur collar encircled the neck. In both hands, the man held, what seemed to be, strips of buckskin with hair attached.

Another figure, shorter and frailer of body, emerged from the basement, and he, too, was dressed in black or dark gray. He looked up and down the hall when he came out the door. His face was covered with a ski mask, and a headlamp was ensconced around his head. He followed the masked person down the hallway and turned left, heading to the outside door. He wore a day pack bulging with items.

"Now, let's shift to the second security camera.... Here, I don't understand what the guy's doing," the security officer said.

In the second security footage recorded in the hallway near the exit door, the first person stopped and directly looked into the security camera at 4:12 a.m. The mask he wore was oval; it covered his face, forehead, chin, and neck. Holes had been cut out for the eyes. The predominant paint on the buckskin mask was brownish-red, a sienna red. The mouth was an oval hole like the eyes. The face had been painted black. Spaced in three semi-circle patterns on the facemask were closed "Xs," like hourglasses. The "Xs" were painted white. Some "Xs" were open at the top, not fully closed. Hawk feathers sprouted atop the mask with unidentifiable plumage. Tufts of eagle down were affixed randomly. Encircling the mask at the bottom, a fox fur collar gave off a wild, alien touch.

The masked man stared at the camera. Then, with the sweep of his arms, he opened his arms, then brought them close to his chest as if pulling the museum into his body. He opened and closed his arms seven times, jerking the strips of buckskin and hair. A private ritual performed?

Then, he stopped his antics, opened the door, and the two of them stepped out into the morning cold, their thievery complete. The time stamp on the security tape read: 4:13 a.m.

Tafoya tapped his forefinger on the screen monitor. "That's not buckskin and fur he's playing with. Those are scalps."

The room fell silent; only the sound of the heat ventilator could be heard.

"I didn't know we had scalps in our collections," the security officer said, a frission shaking his body. No one responded. After a moment, he broke the silence, "At this time, I was outside on the opposite side of the building, marking my time with the QR code. I turned around, looked in the direction of Ojo Verde, and I saw three figures running down the road. One had a headlamp. I thought it odd to be jogging so early in the morning. Then, when I came back in, I saw the door to the inventory room glaringly open. I ran to the security tape, saw this, and called for backup."

"You sure those are scalps, Officer?" the security officer said, turning to Tafoya.

"Yes, but they aren't fresh," Tafoya replied. Several officers groaned.

"Do you have any idea what else they took?" deputy sheriff Chris Cordova asked, getting off the subject of scalps.

"No, I have no idea. We will have to..." the security officer was interrupted.

The door to the security office swung open suddenly. Eyes wide open in anger and lips pursed, the director of the museum rushed through the door. Out of breath, an overweight middle-aged man followed her closely. The museum director stopped abruptly, scanning the law enforcement ensemble, trying to interpret the scene in her museum's security office.

"I'm Jennifer Hornbuckle, Director of Franklin Deerfield." Waving her hand, "This is John McGinnis, the Head Curator. What is going on? What's happened?" Hornbuckle stopped talking when she saw the image on the monitor. "And, who is that person with a god mask on the security footage?" she asked, staring at the still image on the monitor.

Tafoya and the security officer filled Hornbuckle and McGinnis in on the details. At about four thirty in the morning, the door to the basement inventory room was discovered open. It had not been opened at the last security check at two thirty. The security officer had seen three people running away or jogging on the road outside the museum at 4:23 a.m. as he time-stamped the QR code. When he came in, he discovered the basement door open. After briefly scanning the inventory room for unauthorized persons, he ran to the security camera video, backed up the footage a few minutes, and identified two men emerging from the basement, one carrying a backpack full of unknown items, and the other person wearing a mask. Two security cameras, one in the inventory hallway and the other at the exit door, captured their escape. The security officer, in his quick survey of the large inventory basement, had found nothing else askew.

"That's all we know at the moment," Tafoya summarized. His cell phone rang. He unholstered it and saw it was F.B.I. special agent Diane Parker. He squelched the ring, declining the call. Tafoya silently mouthed to Romero, "It's Parker." Romero shook his head and rolled his eyes.

Director Hornbuckle closed the museum for the day so the forensic team from the sheriff's department and tribal police could collect evidence: take photographs, dust for fingerprints, examine outside and inside footprints, and copy the security video from the servers from the previous twenty-four hours. The investigative team requested a list of museum employees with addresses and telephone numbers as well as cleaning staff personnel. The register book of visitors and receipts for Thursday and Friday were also collected for evidence. The museum would reopen the next day—Sunday afternoon.

Sergeant Romero headed the investigation; second-in-command was sheriff's deputy Chris Cordova. Tafoya would be on the team as well, but he left mid-morning to see F.B.I. agent Parker, who had called five times before he answered the phone, and said he was on his way for the Blue Lady Mine debriefing she requested.

The most tedious and time-consuming task fell in the hands of head curator McGinnis and his staff conducting an inventory of basement artifacts. Since there was no obvious break-in of cabinets, drawers, and files, the inventory investigation might take two or three days, perhaps more. Deputy Cordova and sergeant Romero had a specific order for the McGinnis and his staff.

"Two people will conduct the checking of artifacts, each cross-checking the other on the artifacts and lists. Two curators looking over the shoulder of each other, so there is no missing an item that was stolen. You understand that, don't you, Mr. McGinnis? Director Hornbuckle? Just to be clear," Romero stated.

McGinnis and Hornbuckle nodded their assent. "That may extend the inventory, Sergeant," McGinnis said. Romero said he understood the concern, but it was necessary for accuracy.

"Well, all right," huffed McGinnis.

"Don't begin the inventory until all of us meet later on today to finalize responsibilities. Director Hornbuckle, may we use the boardroom to have a meeting of principals and plan out the investigation?" Romero asked.

"Sure, Sergeant, it's available for whatever you need," she replied.

Romero and Cordova quietly knew there were reasons to watch the inventory closely. If any of the museum personnel were involved in the heist, they might try to obscure the stolen artifacts from the inventory. Consequently, there needed to be investigative redundancy of the inventory.

And, certainly to the experience of Romero, Tafoya, and the sheriff's office, the heist of Franklin Deerfield artifacts was, at least partially, an inside job.

4

In San Miguel, ten miles north of Ojo Verde and the Franklin Deerfield Museum, Armando Ortega rose from bed at five twenty in the morning's dark. His wife, Loretta, stirred under the quilts and woolen duvet that had been woven from their Churro sheep five years before.

"Stay put, Loretta, I'll turn up the stoves and start the coffee."

Armando rubbed his arms against the slight chill in their adobe home they had occupied since their marriage thirty years prior. The fire in the living room's conical fireplace had died out hours before. Yesterday's cold front was not going to lift on this Saturday, so Armando rekindled the fire. Armando opened the front door and walked out on the porch. He saw a sparkling clear sky above.

"Is that Orion's Belt I see?" already knowing the answer.

In the small village of San Miguel, a few house lights had come on. Despite the sun not breaking over Lobo Mountain for another two hours, a few San Miguelans, by a habit pattern formed long ago, arose around five o'clock in the morning and walked out on their porch to augur the weather. Inexplicably, walking out on the porch before sunup ignited their day. Standing on his porch, Armando felt good to be alive; he breathed deeply the sharp, cold air of the ebbing night into dawn. A bird, most likely a Steller Jay, quickly sang four notes. Armando looked in the direction of the song.

Glancing over at his son's house on the far side of the Ortega family compound, Armando saw Luis' kitchen lights on and smoke rising from the chimney in his living room. Luis was brewing coffee, too, but as was his morning custom, he would later walk over to his parent's house for breakfast and day planning. Armando was anxious to hear the story of the day before, when Luis inspected the Burned Mountain meadows for grazing their Churro sheep.

Luis had hastily told Armando the night before that Burned Mountain meadow could sustain a flock before winter, but they should avoid moving the sheep. Last week's explosion at the Blue Lady Mine, across the meadow in the granite crags on the southwest side of the mountain, had brought scores of law enforcement and Forest Service personnel that disturbed the grazing area. At the corrals, Armando heard Buck and Monte whinny and the Churro sheep bleat in their pen. He saw the shadow of Luis moving behind the curtains in his kitchen across the compound.

"Whew...," Armando shivered from the cold and stepped quickly back inside the house. Their sheep could be moved to Cimarron, across the mountains to the east. "Forget Burned Mountain meadows and the Forest Service teams. Cimarron for the Churro."

Dry, comforting heat rushed around Armando as he stepped inside the house. The baffles of the propane stoves popped loudly, expanding from the heat. Loretta ambled into the kitchen and checked the coffee maker that Armando had started before he stepped out on the porch to see Orion's Belt. The TV in the living room was turned on, but muted. Albuquerque TV stations were received by air, neither cable nor satellite for the Ortegas. Save money, stick to the budget. When the weather forecaster came on to sketch the highs and lows for the day, Armando unmuted the sound.

"Partly cloudy day for northern New Mexico, the Ojo Verde-Questa area. Temperatures in the upper forties, mid-fifties."

Luis knocked twice on the door and without hesitating, came inside. He carried his coffee mug; at his side, the Ortega's border collie, Zeke, bounded in and nuzzled Loretta and Armando for a scratch behind the ears. Setting his coffee mug down on the kitchen counter, Luis walked back outside to the stables to feed the geldings, Buck and Monte, before sunrise. Buck or Buc—a shortened nickname for Bucepalus, Alexander the Great's horse—was clamping his teeth on the feed bin, raising it, and then letting it fall to make a racket and show his impatience.

"You were a good war horse last week, Buck," Luis complimented, as he tossed in grain and hay. "If not for you, Burned Mountain would have claimed two more lives.... Rest today, you deserve it." His cell phone rang. It was the F.B.I. special agent Diane Parker asking for another interview about Burned Mountain explosion. She said her agents would drive out to San Miguel to interview him. Luis replied assertively that he would drive into Ojo Verde to the Taos County sheriff's department substation after breakfast. "I'll talk to you there."

Parker did not immediately respond, seeing no point in arguing the matter, "See that you do, Mr. Ortega. I need to make a powerpoint presentation by noon today, and your interview is vital." Parker hung up without saying goodbye, farewell, check you later, or *adíos*, *vaya con díos*, or by-your-leave.

Luis had no chance to say, "Goodbye."

Looking at his cell phone as if F.B.I. agent Parker was still on the line, Luis said, "I think I'll saddle Buck, put him in the trailer, and make you do the interview with me in the horse trailer."

5

Janet Rael, M.S., Biology Science Technician, U.S. Forest Service, was awake and stirring by six o'clock. She walked out on her second-story back porch apartment on Calle Zacate Verde in Ojo Verde to sip coffee, get a bracing blast of cold air, and start her day. It was still dark. Her cell phone rang. Stepping back into her casita apartment facing Tulona Mountain, she looked down at the caller's name. It was blocked, but Janet answered it, nonetheless, for it was early and probably important. It was the F.B.I.

F.B.I. special agent Diane Parker, with a minimum of small talk, requested Janet to be present for an interview later that morning at the sheriff's department substation in Ojo Verde concerning the Blue Lady Mine explosion last week.

"Be prepared to spend a couple of hours with us."

"Will Richard Tafoya be there?" Janet asked. "He was at the mine with me, as well as Luis Ortega." Parker replied that Ortega would be there later in the morning. As for the tribal policeman, he was next on her list to call and set up the interview.

None of the three to be interviewed were suspects in the closed case of Andreas Saltwater at the Blue Lady Mine near Burned Mountain. The interviews were routine in closing the case. Richard Tafoya, Luis Ortega, and Janet Rael were to give detailed statements about the event and resolve minor issues as to chronology and conversations. The future opening of the mine would require a large cash outlay, heavy machinery, and lawsuits as to ownership. The Blue Lady Mine might lie dormant for years before unearthing. Most likely, it would never be exploited again.

Janet showered and dressed for work at the Forest Service. She cleaned the gash on the right side of her head and lightly covered the wound with Vaseline and a skin-colored band-aid. With another week's healing, the gash would not be noticeable. She pulled a watch cap lightly over the wound to hide the band-aid. She looked at herself in the mirror.

"Like my ancestors before me, I *was* brave in the face of my enemies," she asserted at her reflection in the bathroom mirror. Janet's stoicism came, in part, from her Isleta Pueblo heritage, handed down in hundreds of lessons from her grandfather and grandmother.

She packed her field bag for the day in case there was any activity needing her skills in the one-and-a-half-million acres of the National Forest. As an afterthought, she threw in her pilot's logbook and several Visual Flight Rules aviation maps for northern New Mexico. No tasks had been assigned to her for the day. She rechecked her business emails for orders on her cell phone. None were scheduled, but her supervisor would find something for her to do. As to flying for the Forest Service, she was not assigned in her job description for any commercial activity. It was merely precautionary to take her aviation stuff along.

"Besides, Tulona tribal policeman Tafoya might need me to rescue him from harm's way," she chuckled to herself. Thinking of Tafoya, Janet smiled and looked forward to meeting him later. She started her red Subaru with a wind-eroded hood and drove to a local restaurant for breakfast. Leaving the restaurant, the sun had risen and she saw red and yellow colors among the aspen groves on the side of Tulona Mountain. Tourists were flocking to Ojo Verde to see the leaves change, returning for ski season later in the year that she hoped would be better than last year.

F.B.I. special agent Diane Parker called tribal policeman Richard Tafoya and was sent immediately to voice mail: "You have reached Tafoya's cell phone of the Tulona Pueblo. Please leave a message at the 'beep' and I'll get back to you as soon as possible. You may also try and reach me at the Tulona Tribal Police Headquarters. That number is…." Parker hung up without listening to the rest of message. She quickly called the police headquarters at the pueblo.

"I need to speak to Officer Tafoya! Right now!" Parker reconsidered the tone of her voice to the administrative assistant.

"I'm sorry. Let me start over. I'm F.B.I. Agent Diane Parker. I need to speak to Tafoya as soon as possible. I need to interview him about the Blue Lady event last week. Just wrapping up a final report."

"He's out on a case, Ms. Parker," Delores Rafael, the admin and officer said. "Been gone since about five this morning. Tafoya's at the Franklin Deerfield Museum. There may have been a theft...or something worse."

"I need more in his report about last week's mine explosion. It's just a wrap-up," Parker exclaimed.

"Agent, I'm really sorry, but he is out at the museum, and so is Romero and the Taos County sheriff's department."

"The museum is not under Tulona police jurisdiction, so why is he there? And, Romero, too?" Parker said, exasperated.

"That's not correct, Ms. Parker," the admin shot back. "The Franklin Deerfield Museum and the Tulona Pueblo Council have a signed *bona fide* contract to work together in collecting, assessing, and displaying Tulona Pueblo artifacts. The pueblo is to make sure there is no exploitation or vandalizing going on with Tulona sacred sites or artifacts."

"But...," Parker stammered.

"Furthermore," the admin continued, "the Franklin Deerfield Museum's founder, Franklin Deerfield, leased the pueblo land upon which the museum sits from the Tulona in the 1940s. He hunted and fished with Tulona guides, back up in the far reaches of the reservation. The lease is a ninety-nine-year lease, and I don't see it being challenged anytime soon."

"I didn't know any of that," Parker softened.

"Agent Parker, my name is Delores Rafael, or Morning Comes Snow. Visit us during ceremonial times...I'll show you around if you care to understand us. For now, tribal policeman Tafoya is where he belongs: helping the museum unravel the theft. I'll leave a message you called."

"But I need to compose a powerpoint, and he said he would submit his report by noon today," Parker lamented.

"Good luck on that, Agent," Morning Comes Snow replied.

6

Luis Ortega drove his pickup to the Taos County sheriff's department substation at Ojo Verde, ten miles north of Taos. Although Luis would not insist on his interview being conducted in his horse trailer, he, nevertheless, hooked up the horse trailer to his pickup and loaded Buck, unsaddled, into the trailer. Buck's saddles and tack were in an enclosed compartment at the front of the trailer in case he decided to ride. Luis frequently towed horse trailer and Buck when he ran chores in Ojo Verde. Buck enjoyed the travel and the people that came up to the trailer when it was parked to see him. Luis liked talking to the people that admired his horse, particularly the women with whom he flirted.

But serious flirtation was in Luis's past; now his focus was on Flowers Dancing, the sister to Quail Looks Away of the Tulona Pueblo. The week before, at the Saint Francis Day Festival at the pueblo, he became enamored with Flowers Dancing while sharing a meal with her family. Flowers Dancing blotted out Luis's attention to any other woman, whether they liked Buck or not. Nonetheless, any person close to him had to like horses. And that included Flowers Dancing.

By the time Luis and Buck pulled up to the sheriff's parking lot in Ojo Verde, Janet and Tafoya were inside the department getting debriefed by F.B.I. personnel. Since the Blue Lady incident began with a murder on Tulona reservation land, but then extended to National Forest land between Tres Piedras and Tierra Amarilla, the F.B.I. was authoritatively in control although they shared jurisdiction with other entities: county sheriff's departments, state police, game and fish department, and U.S. Forest Service law enforcement. In northern New Mexico where Hispano and puebloan historic interests overlapped government's authority, confrontations occurred. Some, but not all conflicts, simmered from centuries-old land conflict of European *entradas*.

Luis had wanted to participate in one such standoff many years before on the Humphries Wildlife Area, but he was too young, said his father, Amando, to participate in risky affairs. Nonetheless, Luis regretted his absence.

The standoff Luis Ortega missed had occurred in August 1989. In the middle of the night, sheepherders on horseback and foot in the Chama Valley had driven a thousand ewes with lambs onto the Humphries Wildlife Area. The government had denied and constricted grazing permits gradually over the years. Attempts of sheepherders to extend and maintain leasing rights for grazing on Jicarilla Apache Nation land had failed.

Ignoring local grass-roots objections, government and wildlife interests had sought to limit foraging by sustainable Hispano communities who traced their land use back for decades. The sheepherders in desperation drove their flocks ten miles into the Humphries Wildlife Area and stayed put with their flocks. Armed forest rangers said they were trespassing and could not stay, and if they did, the government would load up the sheep and truck them away. Wildlife areas were for wildlife only, so intoned the State Game Commission.

Sheepherders, in response to the threat by the government to take their sheep away, replied forcefully, "Don't even touch the fiber!"

Fortunately, the Land Commissioner of New Mexico intervened and found state park land nearby for the sheep to be herded off the wildlife area. But the sheepherders could only stay for three weeks.

The Blue Lady Mine incident was minor compared to the Humphries conflict in 1989. The Blue Lady incident was concluded, but conflicts between sustainable human communities adjacent to and on federal land were far from over. The conflict—an old, old story—was the pitting of traditional communities to conserve their way of life, and the rise of outside interests to change a way of life. More civil disobedience loomed in the future.

Luis promised himself he would participate in future protests. "I am in with the sheepherders."

Horseman Luis Ortega, Forest Service biology specialist Janet Rael, and tribal policeman Richard Tafoya wrote their reports and discussed the Blue Lady incident with the F.B.I. at the Taos County sheriff's department. Their reports were informative, but terse and brief. In sum, they agreed on the facts: a confrontation occurred at Burned Mountain with an individual who confessed to killing someone. There was a mine explosion burying the murderer and any other stories derived from his greed and rapacity.

F.B.I. agent Parker, by early afternoon, had enough information to write a report to F.B.I. headquarters in Albuquerque and create a powerpoint for a briefing that evening when she returned to Albuquerque. Parker wanted more detail, but she had to settle for what Luis, Janet, and Tafoya gave—not a lot, sparse as always. She had asked for a powerpoint from Tafoya, but he declined and gave her a lesson in pueblo mindset.

"From what I wrote in my first report and my interview this morning," Tafoya said, "I see no need to compose a powerpoint for the F.B.I. Besides, you never know when the Dancing Rock Power Cooperative will lose power in Ojo Verde, and you'll need to orally brief the audience without electricity. No electricity, no powerpoint magnified on the screen.

"It's like Tulona Pueblo stories of the trickster and the Fourth World. You don't go to Google or the library to look up emergence narratives, you go to an elder. He or she will always have power to brief an audience, if they choose to do so—until they die. The elders! *they* are powerpoints; the briefing is always retrievable in their heads. I wrote down what happened, and that can burn up in a fire. But as long as I am alive, I will tell you orally what happen. But no powerpoint, Ms. Parker. Dancing Rock Power Cooperative may cut the power, but I'll be around, and I don't need to be plugged in to brief you or repeat the narrative."

F.B.I. special agent Parker sighed and shook her head. She had been stationed among reservations all of her career, and she knew that she had hit a rock wall with Tafoya-the-Tulona, who was kiva educated and probably a sacred clown, warchief, or cacique-to-be. There would be no powerpoint. Funny, she thought, I think I see the what he's talking about.

"All right, Officer Tafoya," Parker said. "I appreciate your cooperation. Congratulations on your work last week at the Blue Lady. The case is closed. If there is anything I, or the F.B.I., can do to help in the Franklin Deerfield Museum case, let me know. I'll do all I can."

Tafoya was caught off-guard by Parker's offer of assistance.

Not knowing where the Franklin Deerfield case might go, Tafoya replied, "Thanks, Parker, I'm sure something will come up. We may need your laboratories. We don't have state-of-the-art technology here in Ojo Verde."

Tafoya paused, thought he might regret what he was going to say, but went ahead anyway: "By the way, if you come up for Feast Day next year at the pueblo, I invite you to my parents' home for a meal. I'll be around either policing or in the ceremony."

Parker smiled, straightened her back, and said she would attend Feast Day. She now had two invitations for Feast Day: Tafoya's and Delores Rafael's. Her stomach would be full that day.

When Tafoya walked out of the meeting with Parker, the administrative assistant handed him a note from Janet. "Sorry I missed you, Richard. The Forest Service reported a fire up near Peñasco and Rio Santa Barbara. I was ordered to go up with a crew to monitor and supervise. I'll let you know when I get back to Ojo Verde."

Disappointed, Tafoya started his police car and drove to Franklin Deerfield.

7

Saturday, midmorning, G. Armstrong Coe unlocked the door to his bookshop on Paseo del Norte in Ojo Verde. Fenster, the guard cat, rubbed up against his leg, then walked out the door and around the building to reconnoiter the night's activities. Coe's Bookshop was one of two bookstores in Ojo Verde: the Ojo Verde Bookshop and Coe's shop. A third bookstore, down the road in the direction of Taos, had lately started up, called The Three Sisters.

Having started his business twenty years before, Coe had built up a regular clientele and collected a large section of puebloan and Tulona esoterica he secured in back of his store, hidden from browsers, only available to scholars and puebloans. Being Saturday, and near the height of fall foliage in the high country of the Cristo Mountains, Coe anticipated brisk tourist business during the day. He double-checked the book section on local natural history and biographies of Kit Carson, Mabel Dodge Luhan, and regional artists such as Couse, Sharp, Phillips, and Blumenschein. The D.H. Lawrence section was not selling like it used to, but it should, he thought to himself.

"The blood consciousness of Lorenzo's writing should be read by the bourgeoisie and the up-tight tourists that come here. That'll shake up their repressions."

Turning on the radio to the local FM station KTULO, Coe heard the weather forecast. He turned up the heat in the bookshop. The news stated that the law enforcement departments, including the Tulona Tribal Police, were at the Franklin Deerfield Museum investigating a possible theft. Coe perked up at the newsflash. He was on the museum's board of directors, and they had paid beaucoup amount of money for upgrading their security system the past summer. Figuring he would hear all about it later, Coe proceeded to dust down the shelves, put money in the cash register, and let Fenster back in the shop to go in the storeroom for her kibbles. He made sure there were fresh copies of coffee-table art books on the center table of the store. Behind the front counter, he dusted the out-of-print and rare books that book collectors avidly sought.

"Today will be the day I sell the out-of-print Mabel Dodge Luhan, *Winter in Taos*, I just know it."

Coe had been trying to sell the book for fifteen years; but when people looked at the price—500 dollars—they put it back, even though it had a handwritten note and spring of sage within from Mabel herself. He was not about to lower the price; in fact, he was considering raising it to 750 dollars for the Christmas tourists flocking to Ojo Verde in December.

"If I raise the price and I value it that much, perhaps I should take it off the shelf and keep it myself?" he reflected.

Clouds, off and on, obscured the sun, and Paseo del Norte traffic picked up in front of Coe's Bookshop. Several logging trucks, hauling ponderosa pine, loudly drove by, one them using their engine as a brake. Coe stepped outside under the portico and watched jeeps, pickups, logging trucks, and cars drive past. License plates from New Mexico dominated, but there was an abundance of Texas and Colorado plates. Probably next to New Mexico, the Texas plates came in second, Colorado third. He glanced into his friend's shop next to his.

The shop was Cecilia's Boutique, a woman's shop of southwestern wear, upscale and moderate in price. It had a full gamut of fine clothing: scarves, dresses, hats, blouses, necklaces, bracelets, and a reasonably good inventory of little girl's clothing. Cecilia and her assistant were shifting stock to winter clothing—The Ripe and Quiet Times.

Cecilia noticed Coe standing inside the door. "I'm finally getting all the felt hats out for fall and winter," Cecilia said. "Prissy ought to come in and browse." Prissy was Coe's wife of forty years.

Coe remarked how pleasant it always smelled inside her shop. "It's room freshener. The lavender scent, Coe. Here, I've got an extra bottle. Take it. I think it improves sales," she laughed heartily.

"Between the smell of new books and lavender, how can my customers *not* buy a book?" Coe said.

"And, then, you direct them to come next door and buy a scarf...." Cecilia adjusted the winter coats on a rack. "Say, Coe, what's this I hear on the news about a theft out at the Franklin Deerfield? Aren't you on the Board of Trustees?"

News travels fast with only one radio station in the village, Coe thought.

"Cecilia, you know as much as I do, right now. We overhauled the security system a few months ago with a firm out of Santa Fe. They installed the same system that the School of American Research has. If I get a break today, I'll call Hornbuckle. So far as I know, it's still a crime scene out there."

A customer went into Coe's shop, and he broke off the conversation with Cecilia to assist the man. "Talk at you later, Cecilia, *adíos*.

8

After breakfast that Saturday morning, Bustamente and Ben Lovato Medicine Wind huddled close to the conical fireplace in the corner of Bustamente's backroom on the Summer House side of Tulona Pueblo. The piñon wood fire cast wavering, lambent light on their faces.

Bustamente was the cacique of the pueblo, a position held for life. In his seventies, Bustamente's arc of life had been full, but more was to come. Medicine Wind, also Tulona, had been one of the fastest runners on Saint Francis Feast Day, October 4. Thirty years old, he was a new father to Dezba, or Blue Flowers Springing. His wife Quail Looks Away had dressed in a yellow Pendleton blanket on race day at the pueblo, and with Dezba in her arms, they had seen Medicine Wind run with a magpie feather floating from his leather armband, his body flying along the racecourse on the northside of the pueblo. Fittingly, his Tulona name, Medicine Wind, matched his running speed and spiritual power.

The news of the break-in at Franklin Deerfield spread fast through the pueblo. Sacred objects from surrounding archaeological sites were held in the museum, and from time to time, pueblo ceremonial participants borrowed material from the museum. As a part of the covenant and original lease agreement with Franklin Deerfield, a Tulona would always be a part of the museum's curating staff, and a significant number of Tulona would be on payroll.

The break-in was alarming. What, if any, Tulona objects had been stolen? The theft worried Bustamente, Medicine Wind, and the rest of the pueblo community. The most sacred objects remained within the pueblo, fortunately, heavily guarded and revered. However, in the Tulona Pueblo religious world the most sacred things were the Tiwa oral narratives—not material things—and those narratives were not in the museum's inventory. Elders handed spirituality down; it could not be checked out and returned.

Medicine Wind fed three split-piñon logs to the fire. He sat back on several blankets with Bustamente. Hanging from Bustamente's wall were a large calendar with spaces for each day on which to write, a medicine bundle, and a crucifix. In the corner of the room were a Spanish working saddle and tack. In his earlier years, Bustamente worked on cattle ranches over in the Tusas near Burned Mountain. In an adjoining room, melodious conversation sounds of his wife and cousins were heard, discussing plans for the day. Bustamente drew close to Medicine Wind, so that his words could be heard distinctively.

"I am concerned about the break-in at Franklin Deerfield," Bustamente began. "You are an Old Bow kiva member. I would like for you to be the one to observe the inventory, but I know you have a new baby, and there are other things you must need to do."

"You are correct, Grandfather, I do have much to do, and I had put off my chores until after Feast Day ceremonies, but I will perform this errand, if you believe it important," Medicine Wind volunteered.

Bustamente stared into the piñon fire. "Medicine Wind, your senses are sharp and you are old enough to know the significant from trivial. I saw you run on Feast Day. I have observed your behavior fashioned by our traditional ways. If you do this for us, I will direct younger men to help gather firewood for your family and attend to chores as Quail Looks Away shall order them. You will be home each evening, and the inventory should not last more than a few days. Will you do this for me, for the Tulona?"

"I will, Grandfather. I will do this for the Tulona at Franklin Deerfield."

Leaning back from the fire, Bustamente breathed more easily, for he knew another pair of Tulona keen eyes were urgently needed on the investigation.

Bustamente turned directly to face Medicine Wind.

"One more thing, Medicine Wind. Be aware of any references in what they ae doing over at Franklin Deerfield to 'Hanging Shell'. I feel we are entering a dangerous time."

9

Later that Saturday afternoon, Medicine Wind drove to the museum and asked to see tribal policeman Richard Tafoya. They met in the courtyard outside the museum. Leaves from red willow trees lining the courtyard drifted down. Medicine Wind scraped them away with his boot and looked up at the trees. Magpies were fussing in the lower branches. Medicine Wind knew Tafoya as a kiva member, although not of his Old Bow kiva group. Tafoya was Blue Stone.

"Tafoya, Cacique Bustamente wants another Tulona looking in on the investigation, especially as to what objects were stolen. So, I accepted. He wanted me to be aware of any references to 'Hanging Shell,' whatever that means. He didn't explain, I didn't ask any more from the cacique. You know how he is."

"Hanging Shell? What is that about?"

"I have no idea, Richard."

"Did Bustamente have any suspicions about Tejada, the Tulona curator who's working here? Is that why he asked you?" Tafoya asked, puzzled.

"No, nothing brought up about Tejada. Just Hanging Shell."

"I can't think of any Hanging Shell stories in our background."

"Me, neither, brother. But that was what Bustamente wanted me to be on watch for," Medicine Wind added.

"I see no problem in you being present during the inventory," Tafoya said.

The magpies flew away, chattering as they fled the museum courtyard. They did not leave as a flock but in solitary escape, then by twos and threes. Tafoya and Medicine Wind talked about the parameters of the investigation. Tafoya said he would share what he could with him, but much of the evidence had to remain confidential.

"But for the moment, Medicine Wind, there's not much to go on, I can tell you that."

Tribal policeman Tafoya and Medicine Wind were admitted into the museum. Director Hornbuckle invited them into her office. Hornbuckle looked at Medicine Wind, then Tafoya. "What is he doing here?" referring to Medicine Wind. He wore his hair in two braided strands with buckskin and colored ribbons interwoven in the braids, hanging down on the front of his broad chest.

"At the request of Cacique Bustamente of the Tulona Pueblo, Medicine Wind will be observing the inventory count along with Ray Tejada, the Tulona curator," Tafoya replied.

"I don't see that as necessary...," Hornbuckle said.

"Director Hornbuckle, that's not your decision. This is a police investigation. Medicine Wind is here at the cacique's request, and if necessary, I may have to deputize him."

Medicine Wind looked at Tafoya. He had been a warchief, but not a policeman. Tafoya continued talking to Hornbuckle, ignoring him.

"Let me explain further. The Tulona and Franklin Deerfield Museum have a long-standing agreement about leasing Tulona land and preserving Native American artifacts. We want to ensure the security of the museum and our material inheritance. Medicine Wind is here at pueblo request. And, by the authority of the Tulona Tribal Police. Considering the fact there has been a break-in, I should think you would welcome all the skilled help you can get."

"Of course, of course," Hornbuckle quickly answered. "We have, or had, the state-of-the-art security system, and I am so embarrassed by this turn of events. I welcome anything you can do to solve this case."

"I will use the F.B.I. science and forensics labs and teams, if necessary," Tafoya said. "I've already been in contact with them." He thought of his invitation to Parker for next year's Feast Day. Why did I invite her?

Director Hornbuckle sighed deeply and rose from her chair. "Well, then, let's get on with it. Romero has called a conference in the board of trustees' room."

The principals for the Franklin Deerfield case assembled in the trustees' room of the museum: Jennifer Hornbuckle, Head Curator John McGinnis, Tulona Curator Ray Tejada, Taos Deputy Sheriff Chris Cordova, Sergeant Tony Romero, Richard Tafoya, and Medicine Wind, the Old Bow kiva member as requested by Bustamente. Sergeant Romero gave orders and rules of the investigation.

"At all times, a law enforcement officer from the Tulona tribal police or the Taos County sheriff's department will be present during the inventory. When a law enforcement officer cannot be present, the inventory will stop and everyone leaves the basement and the door will be secured. Medicine Wind of the Tulona Pueblo will observe and ask questions and be permitted to examine inventory records. Head Curator John McGinnis will direct the inventory operations with Tulona Curator Tejada assisting as directed. McGinnis, Tejada, and Hornbuckle have the most intimate knowledge of the holdings here, so they will determine where to look and in what order. All items will be inventoried in the basement sections. The focus is on the basement since we have the security footage of the two individuals emerging from the room. They didn't step out of the museum's display cases with stolen goods, so that's not a focal point." Romero paused and looked around the table for questions or comments.

"How many items are we looking at, to be inventoried?" deputy sheriff Cordova asked.

"Approximately 50,000 items, but a lot of them are grouped into box collections so that a quick count and inspection can be made," Hornbuckle replied.

"What do you mean 'grouped into box collections?" Medicine Wind asked.

"We group similar things together," Hornbuckle answered. "Pottery by pueblo, rings in a collection, squash-blossom necklaces in a collection, paleolithic tools in a collection, and so on. These groupings are placed together in drawers, cabinets, and shelves. Often, they are set in a storage box that can be opened and perused quickly. Each item has a special number. When you open a drawer or cabinet or lift the lid off a box, you can see if anything is missing quickly. I estimate two to three days of inventory. It will be quick, but accurate, I promise. The check-off will be fast, once we get started. We only have to inspect the inventory room. Display items can be left alone."

"When was the last inventory taken?" sergeant Romero asked.

"Last January, middle of the month. We had time to inventory and make comments on material decomposition or quality of the item from previous inventories," McGinnis answered.

"What is the method of recording the data?" Tafoya asked.

"We enter the data on laptop computers. We switched to that method in nineteen ninety-eight. Before that we entered information on standard inventory, hard-copy sheets, according to strict anthropological attribution standards," McGinnis replied. "The same attributions are applied in computer data entry."

"Did you keep hard copies made prior to nineteen ninety-eight? Or, did you microfilm the hard copies and destroy the paper records?" Tafoya inquired.

McGinnis looked at Hornbuckle. She smiled.

"Actually, Officer Tafoya, we did both. We have the paper records microfilmed, and we archived the hard-copies in our off-site warehouse," Hornbuckle said, pridefully.

Medicine Wind spoke up. "Do you store archeological material in the off-site warehouse as well, Director?"

"Not as a general rule", she replied. All archeological material is brought here to the museum and held until unpacked, sorted, and given an accession number. The off-site warehouse is for extra furniture, that kind of stuff."

No other questions were raised and Romero closed the meeting, appointing Tafoya to handle the first shift of law enforcement oversight. Tafoya had asked for the initial shift so he could be done with the museum and on to other cases.

Tafoya, Medicine Wind, McGinnis, and Tejada walked to the basement door and Tafoya took off the yellow tape, "Do Not Cross. Crime Scene." The four of them descended the stairs, Tafoya going first. He asked Medicine Wind and McGinnis to commence their inventory, but motioned Tejada aside.

"Where is the broom closet or maintenance room down here for the basement?" Tafoya said assertively.

"Why do you want to know?" Tejada asked.

"Just show me the room, Tejada," Tafoya ordered without answering Tejada's question.

10

At lunch shift on Saturday, the waiter at Tablita's Restaurant in the historic Ojo Verde Inn on Paseo del Norte, Jason Taylor, cleared the center table that had been occupied by two older, retired couples that had come to the village to see the turning of the aspens in the Sangre de Cristo Mountains. The October turning of the leaves was at its zenith in the Month of Leaves Falling Moon. After clearing the table, Jason went to the point-of-sale computer and ran a split check for Table 5 in the middle of the room for two couples visiting from Mesilla in southern New Mexico. Each couple had given him a twenty-five percent tip.

Quickly adding up his lunchtime tips to a fifty-dollar total for his shift, he said to himself, "Yes! More tips like these, and I can get the seasonal pass to the ski valley!"

Jason had been saving money for a seasonal ski pass since last season. Last year's ski season had been pitiful on the slopes. Some trails had never been open, and several lifts had not turned the whole season.

Jason had moved to Ojo Verde from San Antonio, Texas, mostly for the ski slopes north of the village, but also to get away from the hustle and bustle of San Antonio and Austin areas. For three years, he had lived in the Ojo Verde area, and he was not planning to leave. Out of the thirty-dollar tip from Table 5, half of the dollars was going for his seasonal pass, and that amount had put his savings for the season's pass near the top.

In addition, he was going to make money as a ski instructor. Sergeant Romero had asked Jason to teach his sixteen-year-old son, Alexander, to ski. The encounter of Romero and Jason occurred when Jason had strayed accidentally onto the Tulona Reservation in September. Jason had been briefly detained by sergeant Romero to clear up trespassing during the

Earth Cloud Lake ceremonies. When Jason's trespassing was determined to be unintentional, Romero had asked him to instruct his son.

Jason and other staff members at Tablita's cleaned Table 5 with a ponderosa-scented spray and wiped the tables with paper towels that they threw away in a recycle bin. They reset the table with flatware wrapped in yellow-cloth napkins, reflecting the changing of leaves in the Cristo. Jason looked up and saw the hostess set two middle-aged couples at Table 2, beside the windows looking out on the Paseo del Norte where eighteen-wheel trucks carried fresh-cut timber from the Tusas Mountains beyond Tres Piedras.

Table 2 had four positions. Position 1 was nestled up to the window with position 2 sitting next to 1 on the outside next to the aisle. Position 3 was also next to the window facing Paseo del Norte. Position 4 sat across from position 2 alongside the aisle. The two couples were married. Jason checked wedding bands, and they all had them; the women flashed big diamonds.

The husband sitting at position 2, on the outside away from the window, had a large black Patagonia knapsack he placed beside his chair. The man's attire was haute sports clothing—Polo shirt, Eddie Bauer cargo pants, and Filson hiking boots. He wore an Omega Sportsmaster Moon watch.

His wife was a toucher. She kept putting her hand on his leg, shoulder, and occasionally snuggling closer by leaning her head on his shoulder. Her behavior was a little shy of too much public display of affection. All at the table ordered cocktails except the knapsack man. Chardonnay for knapsack man's wife at position 1, pinot grigio for the woman at position 3 next to the window, and a Santa Fe Pale Ale for the man at position 4 across from knapsack man. Knapsack man order iced tea.

Table 2's menu choices were without special requests: The Kale Salad for position 1, knapsack man requested Beef Carpaccio with extra creamy chevre dressing, position 3 requested the Grilled Portobello Sandwich, and the Santa Fe Pale Ale man ordered a burger with toppings of green chile and sautéed mushrooms, "*Por Nuevo México*," he joked. Okay, I get it, Jason smiled. Table 2 ate haply and ordered a second round of drinks, but no dessert. The two couples split the check evenly, and as they started to leave the table, Jason spoke to knapsack man who had the affectionate wife.

"That's a nice backpack. Going on a hike?"

"Thanks, but no, not hiking I'm afraid. I have to carry this pack around because I am waiting for a heart transplant, and this pack contains my meds and a radio transmitter that is linked to my heart rate. It's a thoracic inductance belt." He lifted up his polo shirt and showed a black four-inch band wrapped around his lower chest that seemed like an insulated compress to Jason. That explained his wife paying more than usual physical attention to her husband. Each day may be their last together.

A couple at a nearby table overheard the knapsack man explain his inductance belt to Jason. The little-more-than-tipsy man raised his wine glass and said, "Cheers, old buddy! Good luck. I admire your spirit to wander up here to Ojo Verde."

"Thanks," knapsack man replied. "Cheers back at ya and your wife as well."

Jason stood and watched the party of four at Table 2 walk out of the room, the knapsack man hefting his pack and holding the hand of his wife. Jason starred into space.

"Touch all you want," Jason thought.

"As soon as snow comes and lifts open, I'm skiing," Jason thought. "And I'm going to ski hard and fast. I want the powder up to my knees and blue skies above."

Like knapsack man, Jason knew, despite his young age and love of life, "I cannot stay. But I will ski as long as I can."

II

Ray Tejada, the Tulona curator at Franklin Deerfield, had thought long and hard about the theft. Who among the people he knew at the pueblo might be involved? Tejada had graduated from the University of New Mexico with a degree in anthropology and was working on a Master's thesis dealing with eastern Puebloan pre-contact trails and pathways connecting pueblo communities. Being Tulona, he had been advised by cacique Bustamente and the tribal council to stay away from research and writing about kivas and ceremonials. Tejada had been kiva educated and knew the foundational secrets and narratives of the Tulona.

Tejada obeyed the cacique's advice and had never imparted secrets to his professors or classmates at UNM. Several Anglo classmates had asked him inquiring questions about Tulona mysticism, but he had put them off.

"Friend, I'm not going there. I'll never write down what I know, so don't ask me again.... Let me explain," he often expanded, "if I do tell you or write a paper on what I know, the tribal council will banish me and I won't be able to go visit my parents or kinsmen at the pueblo. So, I'm researching topics other than kiva things."

Tejada's choice of a thesis topic, "Pre-contact Roads Among Eastern Puebloan Communities in New Mexico, 1000–1540 CE," satisfied his promise to the tribal council and his interest in anthropology. But he knew some Tulona had been behaving badly, talking to non-natives about ceremonies, and ridiculing traditional ways with their addiction to smart phones, Facebook, Instagram—the Techno Imperium. Tejada's research on pre-contact trade routes among Eastern Pueblos kept him miles away from violating his promise not to write of kiva matters. For that, he felt good.

As a consequence of his anthropology background and being Tulona, twenty-six-year-old Ray Tejada would be appointed a permanent curator to the Franklin Deerfield Museum after he finished his coursework at UNM for the master's. He had a good-paying position at the museum, time off to conduct research in the field and write his thesis, and he felt like he was helping the Tulona maintain their material culture for posterity. But, now, the theft of at least one artifact—the god mask as Director Hornbuckle called it—was upending his work at the museum and, perhaps, bringing to light Tulona puebloans that disrespected traditional ways and might have committed a crime.

Tribal policeman Tafoya had asked Tejada, "Show me the broom closet or maintenance room." Tejada led Tafoya to the inventory room's cleaning closet and storage place for brooms, mops, boxes, paper goods, and cleaning supplies.

"Hold off, Ray," Tafoya said, "I want to go in first and look around. You stand aside."

Somewhat chagrined, Tejada stood aside. "As you wish, Officer."

Medicine Wind walked over to the broom closet and stood beside Tejada, looking at Tafoya who had taken one step inside the closet and stopped.

Tafoya took his flashlight out and used it to flip on the light switch. He stood at the entrance of the door and looked around. The room was bigger than he thought it would be. Approximately ten-by-ten feet, it held the nominal brooms, cleaning supplies, and paper products. A large dolly with a wastebasket and brooms and cleaning supplies was in the middle of the room and not in its proper place near the backwall.

"What do we have here?" Tafoya said. He walked over to the back wall and found two stools that may have been resting places of the thieves. "Evidently, the two guys took a break in here as they rifled through cabinets and drawers." Bending down and looking at a shelf nearby, he found two empty soft-drink bottles, one filled with a yellow liquid.

"Urine. I'll get this to forensics," Tafoya said, not touching the bottles.

"Ugh," Medicine Wind said from the doorway. He walked away from the broom closet.

"Yeah, ugh! We also need to make sure forensics has dusted the doorknob for fingerprints,"Tafoya said.

He paused and stared off in space, thinking. The thieves must have had some idea of where they could find what they wanted, or they took things at random, a theft of opportunity; then, exited with the goods. But it could have been focused and random.

"What time do the curators down here leave work, Tejada?" Tafoya asked.

"Let's see, that was yesterday, Friday...so we left work earlier than usual, say about five o'clock?"Tejada replied.

"Is the door to the inventory room always locked?"Tafoya asked.

"Yes,"Tejada answered. "It is a standard protocol to lock the door, regardless of how brief a person is absent from the room. The door is locked by the staff, even to go to the bathroom which is just down the hallway."

Tafoya continued to scan the broom closet. He would write up a report later, but he was already analyzing the facts. The two thieves gained access to the museum, then the basement. How so? Duplicate key, inside help from museum staff or the cleaning crew? Did they have an accession list of artifacts with locations? How did they gain the code to the digital locks on the front door?

"Does the cleaning crew have access to the keys?" Tafoya asked Tejada. Better to start simple with a key to the basement.

"The cleaning crew checks keys out at the security office,"Tejada replied.

"Okay,"Tafoya uttered. He made a mental note to ask about vetting cleaning crews. Since the security video was activated around the clock, an investigator needed to go through the video and determine who went into the basement. His list of tasks now included viewing video for several hours. Boring, but necessary.

"Let's close the broom closet until I check with forensics that they have scoured the closet,"Tafoya ordered.

Placing yellow tape across the door, Tafoya stepped out into the main inventory work room and saw Medicine Wind and McGinnis engaged in animated conversation. Tafoya and Tejada walked quickly over to the two men.

"What's the problem?" Tafoya said. Tejada walked over to the inventory cabinet that was open and two drawers were pulled out.

"McGinnis started the count of items while we were at the broom closet. That's not what we agreed upon," Medicine Wind said loudly.

McGinnis shot back, "Look here, I just started with the paleolithic axes and tools we had. The Tulona came a long time after early paleolithic people, and we only have one drawer full of early-paleo tools. There can't have been anything they wanted from that collection. I was getting an early start."

Tafoya brokered the argument tactfully, but plainly spoke to McGinnis. "We don't know what they wanted, or what they took other than masks and scalps. Perform the inventory of paleo tools again, and Medicine Wind will assist you this time. Start again, and do it by our agreed-upon protocol."

Tafoya gave a nod of the head to Medicine Wind to stand beside McGinnis and oversee. McGinnis slightly bowed and with a waiter's sweep of the arm invited Medicine Wind to stand beside him.

Tafoya looked at deputy sheriff Cordova, and said he wanted to talk to him in the hall. They took the steps up and out of the basement, while Tejada, McGinnis, and Medicine Wind proceeded swiftly to count paleolithic and prehistoric lithic tools. Tejada held the checklist and read off the items while McGinnis checked the collections. Medicine Wind looked on.

Outside in the hallway, Tafoya said to Cordova, "You think there's anything suspicious about McGinnis prematurely starting the inventory?"

"No, I don't think so, Richard, but I will look into his background. We need to talk to Hornbuckle and a few others about McGinnis. He seems a bit on the arrogant side, but maybe that's just his elitism," Cordova answered. "I think he's okay."

"Probably so, deputy," Tafoya replied, not entirely convinced. "Look, Cordova, I'm going back to the pueblo. Can you stick around until the next officer comes on duty?"

"Sure, I'll handle the inventory, Tafoya, you go on."

In the museum parking lot, Tafoya stepped up into his patrol vehicle and sat for a moment while he scrolled through his messages. There was no message from Janet who had gone up the Rio Santa Barbara near Peñasco to help with the fire. Tafoya had wanted to talk to her before he pursued a domestic violence case at the pueblo. Although the domestic violence case did not involve the National Forest, Tafoya wanted to broach the subject with Janet that she become a liaison officer with the tribal police. She had the smarts to work in situations with the tribal police, for she had handled the stress of the Burned Mountain-Blue Lady Mine explosion and help close the case.

"I wonder how she is with a pistol?" Tafoya questioned aloud as he started his vehicle and headed to the pueblo. He looked down at his messages again before he turned on the highway to drive to the yellow blinking light intersection and turn onto pueblo land. Regretfully, no messages, no emoji, nothing from Janet.

12

Janet Rael, the biology wildlife specialist with the Forest Service, had been stationed in Ojo Verde for three years. Previously, she had worked with the Forest Service out of Albuquerque, conducting field surveys in the Cibola National Forest of the Sandia Mountain range and in the San Mateo Peak area of the forest.

If she could get away with it, she never used the name, "Mount Taylor," to identify San Mateo Peak near Grants, New Mexico, west of Albuquerque. In honor of First Nations, she called San Mateo Peak, "*Tsótsĭl*," the Navajo name for the mountain. *Tsótsĭl* was the sacred mountain of the south for the Navajo, representing the female, the direction of south, and the color blue. To Janet, the Spanish and Anglo renaming of the 11,306-foot peak exposed the issue of power and conquest in Indigenous history.

Tsótsĭl was the first designation, but when the Spanish came, they called it San Mateo for the saint. San Mateo became Mount Taylor after the American annexation in 1848, following the war between Mexico and the United States. A conqueror's name. It's their privilege, she thought, but holding onto a cherished name is the right of a people that lived under a different government or social group.

To Janet, San Mateo Peak would always be San Mateo Peak or *Tsótsĭl*—never Mount Taylor! She had researched the name, *Tsótsĭl,* and discovered a link with the Mayan Indigenous people inhabiting central Chiapas in southeastern Mexico. So, the word, *Tsótsĭl*, was probably Mayan, predating even the Navajo, she reasoned. Of course, she knew how important it was to relate amicably with government officials and the topographical department of the Forest Service, so Janet would say, "Oh, yes, the mountain north of Grants is Mount Taylor, but I prefer to call it, 'San Mateo,' like the locals do." She wanted to, hopefully, leave it at that.

Janet had been ordered to the Carson National Forest north of Peñasco soon after her interview with the F.B.I. that morning, missing an opportunity to see Tafoya. Her orders were to monitor the fire crews' reports of game scattering because of the fire. By mid-afternoon, the Middle Fork Santa Barbara fire was fifty percent contained.

Monitoring the radio dispatches of fire captains and helicopter crews dropping water, Janet had logged mule deer, bighorn sheep, a small herd of elk, as well as upland birds like grouse and ptarmigans fleeing Middle Fork. She and a coworker from the Tres Piedras Ranger District, Jeremy, drove the ATV on back roads and trails, staying well away from the fire and maintaining radio contact with the command center for shifts in wind and direction the fire was moving. When returning from the east fork of the Pecos Wilderness Trail, they spotted a female bear and two juvenile bears sauntering away from the fire line.

"They don't look terribly frightened do they, Jeremy?" Janet said.

"No, they don't. They are taking their good time running away from the fire," Jeremy responded, as he drove in the opposite direction from the bears.

Janet and Jeremy watched the three bears until they disappeared into the forest below them. After entering the sighting and location of bear on data sheets, Jeremy turned the ATV around and headed for the command center. Infrequently, even in the National Forest, a clear view to Peñasco or Picuris Pueblo occurred, enabling Janet to use cell towers near the settlements. When Jeremy steered the ATV through one of those clear spots, Janet checked her cell phone. A voicemail from Tafoya popped up. Opening the message, Tafoya had sent her a request she wanted to respond to, but the cell service dropped out—no signal bars. She had to wait to reply until another clear view opened up, or she returned to Peñasco Ranger Station.

Tafoya's voicemail said, "Can we meet for dinner somewhere? I have a couple of things I want to talk to you about. Let me know if you will be available. Be safe." Tafoya said. The message was longer than usual, Janet thought.

Back at the command center, Janet and Jeremy were informed that the fire was now seventy-five percent contained, and they were relieved of duty since sundown was less than an hour away. When she arrived at the ranger station in Peñasco, she called Tafoya. Her call went directly to voicemail. She left a message.

"Hi, Richard. I am leaving Peñasco and driving by way of the U.S. Hill Pass over the Picuris range. I'll check my messages when I arrive at the Forest Service headquarters in Ojo Verde… I've been in the field all day. I need a shower. It'll be late when I get back… Maybe we can meet for breakfast in the morning? I want to see you and hear what's going on. I'll check back when I reach my apartment."

As Janet ascended the U.S. Hill Pass over the Picuris range, she thought how much better their relationship might be if they lived in the same apartment complex, but then she remembered Tafoya had put down roots long ago at the Tulona reservation, and he wouldn't budge from his territorial-style home. Janet then thought, "Is there an apartment closer to the pueblo I can rent?"

She carefully drove over U.S. Hill, then descended by multiple switchbacks to Talpa. Before she turned northward to Taos and on to Ojo Verde, she glanced over at the Spanish colonial defensive fortress, the *torreón*, that she saw dimly in the dark.

Tafoya checked his cell phone for messages and saw Janet had called him. He listened to her voicemail message. Disappointed they would not have dinner, he waited for her call-back when she reached her apartment on Zacate Verde. When she called, they agreed to meet for breakfast the next morning. Leaving his house on the edge of the reservation, he drove the backroads to the pueblo to eat dinner with his family. Their talk over dinner turned to Janet, and his mother had an opinion.

"She is good for you, Richard," his mother opined. "Being employed by the Forest Service brings good benefits. Besides, my grandchildren will be beautiful!"

Tafoya had usually responded to his mother's opinion about Janet with a shaking of his head or rolling his eyes. He did neither this time, but only smiled and put another piece of split piñon on the fire.

13

On the Winter House side or northside of the Tulona Pueblo, bisected by Rio Cottonwood, several fires were lit late Saturday afternoon, just before sundown. Young Tulona men were assigned as fire tenders. Several men carried a large drum, four feet in diameter, from John Sun Song's home and placed it near the fires and pueblo homes, so the north wind streamed like an invisible river above the heads of puebloans who gathered close to the drummers and fires.

The drum circle included six drummers who wielded long percussion sticks to fast beats, as first one singer began and others followed in chorus. The songs were high in pitch, joyous in Tiwa expression, as dozens of puebloans gathered around. There was no dancing, just drumming and singing. Some elders stood in back of John Sun Song, the principal singer, and added their voices, the stanzas swelling to full-throated volume of tenor, falsetto, and baritone.

As one song ended, drummers and participants spoke, "That was really good, Bro. Really good." A few slaps on the back in joy and musicians sipped Gatorade or coke to freshen their vocal cords. They sat catching their breath in fold-up chairs and camper seats without backrests.

Smiles all around, and then one drummer picked up a slightly different beat and began a solo percussion and song. Other drummers picked up the cue and, soon, six musicians beat furiously on the moose-hide drum stretched over a hollowed-out cottonwood tube four feet in diameter. Though it had been only two days since Saint Francis Day activities, the singers had recovered their strained voices from Feast Day by drinking specially brewed tea from herbs gathered in the forests and mountains overlooking their pueblo.

At times, the ferocious beating of the drum seemed so passionate the moose-hide skin might split. But the drumhead did not tear.

Tribal policeman Tafoya, dressed in mufti, stood with his mother and father who had come out to attend a few songs. Sergeant Romero and his son, Alexander, stood across the fire from Tafoya and nodded in recognition, as if saying, "It is this singing, Tafoya, we have sworn to protect and to sustain." Cacique Bustamente stood as an elder behind the drummers and sang fully. Medicine Wind and his wife and new daughter, Dezba, stood against one of the adobe homes, huddling for warmth and familial comfort. Quail Looks Away wore her yellow Pendleton blanket.

Several Tulona men stood tall and talked with one another a few feet from one of the fires near the arbors in front of the northside homes. One of the Tulona joked less, spoke few words, lost in rumination, self-contained, serious. The smoke from the fire drifted quickly to his introspection, as if a smudge of sage was being blown over a sick patient for purification. He closed his eyes and turned his back to the fire and smoke.

When the singing stopped, he said goodbye to his companions and drove back to his home near the Ojo Verde city limits to rest and go to sleep, for it had been a long day, an early day for him. Elders and young drummers continued singing for another hour, stopping only to drink tea specially prepared by cooks at the Senior Citizens Center on Abalone Road, north of the plaza. The pensive man, after building a fire in his corner fireplace, lay in bed next to his wife, listening to high-pitched refrains and drumming in the distance. Neither his anxiety nor fear lessened.

Before he fell asleep and dreamed, he whispered to himself, not wanting to disturb his wife, "Was my action this morning at the museum good, Creator? Or, have I upset the balance, a harmony within my pueblo?"

He heard nothing, only the north wind picking up speed, soughing across the roof.

"Is that an answer, Creator?" He fell asleep, not knowing.

14

Sunday, October 14, Day of Saint Callistus I, Month of Leaves Falling Moon

Rather than meet for breakfast at Tablita's Restaurant, Tafoya and Janet agreed to meet at a newly-opened café on the edge of the Tulona reservation, a café started by a young Tulona couple, featuring New Mexican and native dishes. Tafoya ordered over-easy eggs, bacon, pickled jalapeños, and tortillas. Janet ordered huevos rancheros with red chile sauce. She was still hungry from field work the day before. Fresh-squeezed orange juice and coffee rounded out their breakfast. Sopapillas with real butter and honey came last.

After listening to Janet rave about her field day in the Santa Barbara watershed and the Middle Fork fire, Tafoya told her the museum inventory had begun with a conflict between Medicine Wind and John McGinnis.

"Curator McGinnis began the inventory at the paleolithic end of the collection without Medicine Wind's oversight. He got mad and objected to McGinnis's way of conducting the inventory."

"Not a good start, is it, Richard?" Janet said.

"No, it's not. Sergeant Romero and I were talking about inventory yesterday. The beginning of the inventory should have started with the mask collection…not paleolithic tools." Tafoya set down his coffee and looked out the window toward the mountains.

Janet wiped her mouth with a paper napkin, took a sip of orange juice, and reached over and laid her hand on Tafoya's.

"What was it you wanted to talk to me about, Richard?" she asked, withdrawing her hand.

Tafoya turned away from the mountain view and smiled at Janet. "Have you seen the job opening for Liaison Officer of the Forest Service with the Tulona Tribal Police?"

"Nooo…," Janet said slowly.

"Well, the job originated with us, the Tribal Police Department, after the failed Saltwater raid up at the old Taos Trail Saloon a couple of weeks ago. In a post-mortem dissection of the failed Saltwater operation, the department recommended a special liaison officer from the Forest Service be appointed so we could work more closely with the Forest Service in field operations."

Tafoya paused and looked at Janet.

"Okay, so?" Janet smiled. Her eyes gleamed.

"I think you should apply for it, Janet. You would be the ideal liaison with us. You helped catch the killer at Burned Mountain."

One of the owners of the café came by and cleared the table, asking how they liked their breakfast. Janet was complimentary of the red chile sauce, and Tafoya said they would be back again, adding, "I need to bring my mother over here for lunch."

Clearing of the table gave Janet time to phrase her answer carefully.

"Richard, I like my research as a wildlife biologist, going into the field, evaluating the flora and fauna, and even writing reports about my work. Putting the laptop on the hood of the Forest Service vehicle as I work in *plein aire* in high country is what I like. I can't give that up."

Tafoya's face darkened slightly, preparing for a rejection.

"I say that to be open and honest with you, Richard. If I could be the liaison officer on a part-time basis, with say, seventy percent wildlife biologist, thirty percent liaison officer, I would do it in a minute. Do you think that possible?"

Tafoya nodded his head, yes.

Janet continued, "Could the tribal police and the Forest Service work out such a deal for me? I see myself able to do both jobs and since the Saltwater case, I want to engage in law enforcement work."

Relieved that she had not turned down the proposition, Tafoya smiled, his face lighter, not shaded.

"I'm sure we could amend the job description to fit your demands. There will be other applicants. But with your conduct in the Saltwater case, you'll fly right at the top of the list."

"I might add, Richard," Janet said, "I have a commercial pilot's license, and I can see flying for law enforcement. I was going to ask for flying activities in the Forest Service to utilize my license."

Tafoya had thought about asking her if she had a commercial pilot's license before. She had offered to fly him out to the Navajo Reservation on an assignment to interview a silversmith near Sheep Springs, New Mexico. But she had offered the flight in a half-serious way—there were no airports near Sheep Springs.

"I think that would be an addition...," Tafoya stopped when his cell phone chimed a text message.

"It's a message from Romero, I've got to go to the museum. Are you finished with breakfast, Janet? We'll talk later about liaising."

Paying out quickly, Tafoya and Janet walked to their vehicles—she in her red Subaru, he in his tribal police vehicle—and they departed pueblo land. Janet was elated with the prospect of broadening her career with the tribal police. Tafoya was happy Janet might work with the police department. But, otherwise, he was frustrated. Sergeant Romero had texted him to hurry up and get the day started, "But no rush."

"*Aii*," Tafoya said, turning on the flash bar to speed around tourist traffic.

15

Looking westward from the pueblo, Ben Lovato Medicine Wind did not see the Tusas nor Jemez Mountain ranges; they were completed obscured by low-hanging clouds. Cobalt-blue clouds, rounded and congregating together, also obscured the tops of Tulona and Taos Mountain ranges to the east. The forecast high for Sunday was in the mid-forties, and the chance of rain—snow in the higher elevations—forced Tulona and Ojo Verde residents to check their woodpiles and carry split-piñon logs inside their homes for fuel. The morning low temperature was below freezing and would not rise above icing until late morning. Going back inside his home—really the home of his wife, Quail Looks Away—Medicine Wind poured another cup of coffee and turned the battery-powered radio on again for the weather. He increased the volume.

The forecast was the same, "Chance of rain in the afternoon, winds turning southwest to twenty-five miles per hour, overcast throughout the day, highs in the mid-forties." Another cold day, Medicine Wind reflected.

He heard church bells at Mission Saint Francis del Monte, signaling the first Mass was concluded at the pueblo. Glancing at the clock, it was eight in the morning, and he was supposed to be at the Franklin Deerfield Museum by nine. He would make it on time. Quail Looks Away ambled from the backroom with Dezba cradled in her arms and sat down beside him at the table covered with a red-checked oil tablecloth. Dezba was still asleep, but would wake up soon to be fed.

Quail's mother had already risen and prepared coffee and a light breakfast. She turned up the gaslight in the big room with the cookstove in one corner, and then went to the conical fireplace to add more piñon to the fire for warmth. Electricity was banned from the pueblo around the main plaza and its two big houses and dwellings. Propane cannisters for cooking and heating had been approved by the Tribal Council, but electricity was forbidden.

The Tribal Council had spoken a hundred years ago, "With electricity comes the refrigerator, toasters, lights, phonographs. Things that bring debt upon the family. And, paying that debt requires wage work. That forces people away from the pueblo and the kiva." The prohibition of electricity still was tribal rule into the twenty-first century. Outside of the pueblo plaza, at other places on the reservation, electricity was permitted.

"The forecast is for cold and rain, today, Medicine Wind?" Quail Looks Away asked.

"Yes, Quail, that's what he said."

"Since you will be at Franklin Deerfield today, will one of our cousins help me change out the propane tank?" Quail inquired.

"They will. Bustamente has asked our kinsmen to stop during the day to help you with chores.... I hope this counting of old things is over soon. I have duties with the Old Bow kiva across the river. The harvest of crops has been completed, and we have a duty to give thanks...the Harvest Thanks Ceremony to the Creator."

Quail Looks Away attended to a restless Dezba who had awakened to the conversation around the kitchen table. Dezba's Tulona name, Blue Flowers Springing, had come from the Blue Lady legend of the Spanish. Legend had it that wherever the Blue Lady stepped on the earth, blue flowers sprang up in her footsteps. The Blue Lady was a Madonna, an angel, a helper to those in need.

Cradling Dezba in her arms, Quail Looks Away told the emergence story to soothe her restlessness. "In this Fifth World to which we came," Quail said quietly to Dezba, "we have soft earth and rain. The Black Eyes came up from the Fourth World several times in search of a home, and finally they found light, this place, this World. We are blessed." Dezba had stopped fussing, as much as from Quail's words, as the milk she suckled.

Quail's mother, at the other end of the table, added, "That is why the Harvest Thanks Ceremony in Old Bow and Blue Stone kivas is so important. To show our appreciation to the Old Ones, the Faceless Ones, the grandmothers and grandfathers before us."

"*Aii*," uttered Medicine Wind, overhearing Quail and his mother-in-law.

At the kitchen table, Medicine Wind lapsed in thinking about the long ladders that rose out of the kivas, pointing upward to the sky. He thought of stepping down each rung-step into the kiva, a sacred going under the surface. Medicine Wind pondered the fire in the kiva for warmth and the feeling in his body of drum beat within kiva walls.

The previous Fourth World was recreated with drum-rhythm and singing; an ecstatic state growing within each participant, flinging consciousness into boundless spaciousness. That was the reality behind appearances—a loss of self in rhythm, ending in people talking to spruce and deer and wind spirits. That was a reaching out, a feeling.

Within his reverie, Medicine Wind murmured, "Yes, we once conversed with the animals, and we still can talk with them, if we listen closely enough."

Dreamlike, he saw the kiva's long ladders as pathways to and from the previous World, when trees and animals talked to humans—and humans understood. In his thinking, Medicine Wind lapsed back to the old tales told in the Quiet Time of winter. Reflecting on these things, he felt an expansion, an enlarging, palpable spaciousness within himself. This state of mind and emotions had happened many times before. And, other Tulona had shared the same experience.

Medicine Wind's expansion of self in his reflections at the kitchen table, scared him.

"What's happening to me?" he questioned, suddenly back in his kitchen. No answer surfaced. He heard the silence of the kitchen, the hiss of gaslight, the popping of resin in wood burning, and saw the red-checked tablecloth.

Shaking his head, he stood up quickly. "I must go, Quail."

Medicine Wind kissed Dezba on the forehead, hugged Quail, smiled at his mother-in-law, and hurried out the turquoise-painted door of his home onto the plaza and faced the tasks before him in the Fifth World. He paused and looked at the long ladder emanating from Blue Stone kiva before he drove to Franklin Deerfield. He nervously questioned, "Where are we, as Tulona on that ladder? Another World coming? This World ending? Maybe I need an animal or bird to talk to."

16

At the museum, Sergeant Romero ordered Head Curator McGinnis and Tejada to focus on their inventory dealing with masks, whether Zuñi, Navajo, or any Indigenous community within their museum. "See if your inventory is missing a mask, and, if so, is the mask the thieves stole the same one we saw in the video?" Romero directed McGinnis. "Find that out first, then get back to the rest of the artifacts."

At the museum, Tafoya turned his attention to looking at digital video of Friday from noon forward through the night into the next morning when the thieves escaped the building. His immediate task was to finish watching the digital video for Friday afternoon, October 12. The museum closed at five in the afternoon throughout the year, its standard hours ten in the morning to five. Ray Tejada, the Tulona curator for Franklin Deerfield, had informed him that on Fridays the curating staff usually left mid-afternoon to go for drinks at a local bar. That was the case on last Friday, October12, when the curating staff, including McGinnis and the interns, had gone to a happy hour at Chanson Restaurant on Arroyo Luz Road. Tejada had been a part of the group at Chanson as well.

Before he went back to the boardroom where monitors had been set up for the investigation, Tafoya stopped by Hornbuckle's office and asked Adela, Hornbuckle's administrative assistant, to help identify staff members on the digital video. Adela, a graduate of New Mexico Highlands University in Las Vegas, had been with the museum for twenty-five years. She was medium in height, graying strands in her brunette hair, dark eyes, and a pleasant oval face. She had "broken in" Hornbuckle and two other directors of the museum over the years, and probably knew, Tafoya surmised, a lot of secrets concerning the politics and personal affairs of Franklin Deerfield Museum. As a girl, she had met Franklin Deerfield when her parents went to artist receptions in Ojo Verde.

Adela settled in a chair next to Tafoya. He scrolled the video back to two o'clock in the afternoon, picking up where he had left off. Tafoya saw a large crowd of school children come through shortly after two o'clock; a steady stream of senior citizens, most of whom appeared to be married; solitary people who were apparently doing research; and staff members that left the building at three forty. Tafoya identified Tejada leaving the building. Adela named the curating interns, two docents, and a clerk at the souvenir and jewelry shop that departed the front entrance. McGinnis had been a part of the happy-hour crowd at Chanson, but he had not yet left the building, according to the time stamp of the video.

Tafoya made a note on his yellow-sheeted legal pad, "3:50 p.m., McGinnis not yet appearing on video, nor left the building." Turning back to the video, he scrolled carefully. Several other couples, including a bored teenage boy who followed his parents reluctantly and never looked up from his cell phone, came in the front entrance. Still no McGinnis leaving.

"Is there another door to the museum used for coming and going, Adela?" Tafoya asked.

"Yes, we have three other doors: the exit door the thieves went through, another exit door on the opposite side of the building from that one, and a delivery door on the south side. The rules are that those doors are not to be used for leaving the building. They are also locked and stabilized from the inside. Unless the locks are undone from the inside, you cannot come into the museum from the outside. McGinnis observed the rules, so far as I know, Tafoya."

"So, McGinnis would have left through the front door...by the rules?"

"Yes," Adela said.

Suddenly, the monitor screen went dark for two seconds. "What's this about?" Tafoya said. The screen came back on. He looked at the time stamp on the video: 4:32 p.m. He scrolled back to the spot before the screen went black and looked at the time stamp: 3:56 p.m.

"Uh-oh. We have no digital video for thirty-six minutes," Tafoya said.

Tafoya re-checked the hiatus. Same results, no digital video from 3:56 to 4:32 p.m. He switched cameras to the hallway camera outside the basement inventory room, then to three other cameras in the museum. The security video on all of the cameras, from 3:56 to 4:32 p.m., was blank.

When the digital video from security cameras restarted at 4:32 p.m., visitors were ambling toward the entry door. The cleaning staff arrived shortly before five o'clock. McGinnis failed to show up as exiting. "Yet, I know from Tejada that McGinnis did attend the Chanson happy hour, so, presumably, he departed during the blackout of the video record," Tafoya said to Adela.

Tafoya and Adela began to scroll through the video after the blackout ended at 4:32 p.m. They paused when the Tulona curator, Tejada, knocked at the door and came in.

"McGinnis and I have found a mask missing, Tafoya. It's Navajo. The museum has possessed it since the 1950s, along with some other Navajo artifacts. Come see what we have." Tafoya shut down the monitors, and told Adela he would be calling on her later to get details about the cleaning staff.

When Tafoya opened the door to the basement, he saw McGinnis and Medicine Wind staring at the large monitor, looking at photographs of the Navajo mask and reading the acquisition notes on the mask. Two interns also crowded around the screen.

One of the interns spoke, "We've checked the storage cabinet for the mask. It is gone—it's the one stolen, and so are a kilt and two wooden cylinders associated with the mask. We ran a keyword search on our artifacts for 'masks' and found three masks we've curated."

"This one," said the intern pointing at the screen, "was the only one of the three masks missing, and its attributes in the anthropological field notes correspond exactly with the security video. We performed a quick-and-dirty analysis between the field-note photograph and the security video. It is a match." McGinnis and Medicine Wind nodded their heads in agreement.

McGinnis added his two cents, "The lab notes and anthropological research about the mask is thin. About all is known, so say the notes, is that it's a Navajo mask used in ritual chantways. That's all. We need more data."

State the obvious, why don't you, Tafoya thought to himself. "How did the museum acquire the material?" he asked McGinnis.

McGinnis scanned the acquisition notes quickly. "It says here in the notes, 'Acquired from estate of Roland McCluskey, Albuquerque, New

Mexico, April 16, 1953.' It has never been exhibited. The museum has been in contact with the Navajo Nation to see if they might want it for their tribal artifacts in a museum they recommend. A letter was written to them in 2015, but we have not received a reply back from them."

Tejada added, "That's not all. The two wooden cylinders also came from the McCluskey estate. Those were in association with the kilt and the mask. We don't know what they represent, or how they figure into Navaho ritual."

"I know who would know about the mask and cylinders," Tafoya said.

"Who might that be?" McGinnis asked, jealously thinking he was going to be the one to analyze the mask.

"Santiago Majerus in Arroyo Luz. He's the only Navajo medicine man around here and a singer for the Red Antway ceremony," Tafoya replied.

"Oh, yes, the rumored, 'Sleep Maker,' the witch," Tejada said.

"I worked with him on the Saltwater case. Majerus isn't a witch," Tafoya asserted. "I'll give him a call to see if he can come to the museum tomorrow morning to interpret the mask."

For the rest of Sunday, the curators conducted the inventory with interns. Medicine Wind observed quietly. The team proceeded carefully. McGinnis recommended the inventory proceed by specific collections: jewelry, tools, artifacts of all types that could be stuffed in a daypack. Items bigger than a daypack, such as Death Carts, furniture, were bypassed. When five o'clock came, the inventory stopped, the door to the basement locked, and yellow tape secured to the door. The inventory count would resume Monday morning at nine.

Tafoya drove slowly back to the tribal police station to write up a report of the day's activities and visit with his family at the pueblo. Nearly two days had been devoted to inventory, and the team was over two-thirds finished in completing the count. Surely, Tafoya thought, they could wrap this up by Tuesday evening, even completing the scan on the security camera data. After he conferred with Santiago Majerus in the morning, another Tulona officer could be assigned to keep watch in the basement. Tafoya had other cases to work. Being stuck in a museum basement for hours was not his idea of police work.

When Tafoya called Majerus, Majerus did not answer his phone. "I'll call him in the morning," Tafoya concluded.

Filing his report at the station, Tafoya drove to his house on the edge of pueblo land and changed into civilian clothes. At his house, while changing clothes to go visit his parents, he thought of Janet and wondered what she was doing on a Sunday evening before work the next day.

"If she was with me, we could go to the pueblo together and have dinner with my family," he thought.

Tafoya felt lonely. After changing clothes, he drove faster than usual to reach the plaza from his home. He looked up at the mountains. The clouds had scattered, but remained close to the mountain tops. Aspen leaves were brilliant yellow, splashed with red. The red aspen leaves triggered the memory of Janet on Saint Francis Feast Day a week ago, when his mother gave her red aspen branches from the decorated bower shading the priest. Janet told him that she had placed them on the fireplace mantle of her apartment on Ojo Zacate.

Tafoya sighed loudly at the thought of Feast Day and the red aspen. Quietly, to himself, he spoke softly, slowing down on the dirt road to the pueblo.

"I want to see the red aspen on her mantle…I want to see her." He lingered for a moment thinking of Janet's thick, brunette hair, falling to her shoulders.

He burst out, "Yes! like mother said, 'She will have beautiful grandchildren.' And *I will* have beautiful children." Tafoya shook his head to dispel the thought and increased his speed to the plaza. A jack rabbit ran alongside his car for a hundred yards, then darted away into sagebrush and chamiso.

17

Monday, October 15, Day of Saint Teresa of Avila, Month of Leaves Falling Moon

Early morning, seven o'clock. John McGinnis, Head Curator of Franklin Deerfield Museum, fifty-two years old, and a bit overweight from consuming too many Full-Moon burgers, toddled, eyes half-closed, to his coffee machine in his kitchen—a model kitchen built in his pueblo-style home—and stumbled in the low light. He had a bit of a hangover from quaffing a bottle of red Bordeaux with his steak the previous evening. He tripped over his red Ganado rug that mysteriously that been partially rolled up.

"What the hey!" he shouted. He righted himself quickly, grasping the backside of the sofa.

McGinnis looked down at the Ganado red that had been rolled up by a third of its eight-foot length. That was *not* how he left the open-kitchen space the night before. He looked around to see if anyone was in the room. No one was, but he saw the patio-door screen only half closed. And that was *not* how he left the screen the night before. He walked over to the patio door and saw that it was unlocked. McGinnis surmised he had failed to double-check the doors before he went to bed. He could not remember if he had checked the doors or not. Too much red Bordeaux.

He quickly locked the door and glanced around at his pottery collection to see if any pieces were missing. None were. Walking to his living room adjacent to his kitchen area, McGinnis saw all his paintings were still attached to the wall. The flint collection of tools under glass was untouched. He looked closely at his paleolithic tools; the Alibates axe collection—he had three axes—were still there. He stood there, trying to make sense of things.

Then, it hit him. Someone had come into his home while he slept. What did they want? If there was nothing taken, why had they broken in?

Walking back into the open-living space, he unrolled the Ganado red rug and out spilled a manila envelope and two wooden cylinders: one cedar cylinder painted red and a second cylinder of piñon painted black, each about a foot long. He untied the manila envelope. The metal fastener had been removed and the envelope was tied with buckskin string; the knots were knots used by Navajo medicine men to tie sacred objects—he knew at least that much about Navajo ritual.

McGinnis unwound the buckskin string around the manila envelope, but left the knots untied. One sheet of paper was in the envelope and on it was a message in black ink, all caps.

"THE GOD ROAMS THE FOOTHILLS FOR XXXXXXX OF HIS ENEMIES."

He took the red cedar stick and the black piñon stick along with the message to his kitchen-counter island. Carefully turning the wooden cylinders over in his hand, he assessed their age as being old, maybe even prehistoric. Splotched randomly on the sticks were fresh red ochre and charcoal, but the cylinders were carved long ago. Their length was approximately twelve inches and two inches in diameter. The piñon stick was black; the cedar stick red, both stolen from the Franklin Deerfield Museum.

It dawned on him: the person that invaded his space must know him. McGinnis read the message aloud, "The god roams the foothills for XXXXXXX of his enemies." The more he thought about the message, the more frightened he became. "A god roaming the foothills for his enemies?" he shivered. "And what is 'XXXXXXX'?"

McGinnis dressed quickly, carefully wrapped the cylinders in a towel, hurried to his car, and sped to the museum. Cylinders and cryptic messages definitely had something to do with the museum theft. But, more importantly, what did any of this have to do with him?

For a second time, Sergeant Romero called the principals of the museum and investigative team to a meeting in the boardroom after McGinnis brought the cylinders to the museum. As soon as Tafoya sat in place at nine o'clock, Romero opened the meeting. Present at the large boardroom table were Hornbuckle, McGinnis, Ray Tejada the Tulona curator, Medicine Wind, and Tafoya. Sheriff's deputy Cordova was in route.

Sergeant Romero called the group to order, "Quiet!" and brought out a digital voice recorder from his field satchel and turned it on. Speaking to the voice recorder, he listed those present, the location, and the time.

Then he said, "The purpose of this meeting is to assess new findings in the Franklin Deerfield robbery case and assign different responsibilities to the principals." He paused, and for emphasis, reached over and pulled the wooden cylinders closer to his tape recorder and notes. McGinnis frowned. Romero didn't care if McGinnis frowned or frothed at the mouth.

Tafoya leaned back in his chair, and thought to himself, "This is going to be interesting," noting that his sergeant rarely pushed his authority so strongly. It was not normal puebloan behavior to be so assertive; but this museum case was anything, but ordinary.

Romero started again. "At this moment, three minutes after nine a.m., there exists two crime scenes. *Two* scenes: one here at the museum and the other at curator McGinnis's home in Ranchos de Ojo Verde. These two scenes are sealed off, and until the sheriff's department declares them open, no one, not even you, McGinnis, are to go into the crime scene area. Period."

McGinnis said, "But it's my home you are sealing off, you can't do that."

"I can and I have," the sergeant answered back. "The sheriff's department is on standby to get your keys to the house so they can get in and process the scene. They should be completed by mid-afternoon. If not, you'll have to get a motel room. You need to be out there with them after this meeting is concluded to help them process the evidence. Your home is sealed off for the time being, McGinnis."

"But...," McGinnis blurted. Romero ignored him and talked over his whining.

"So, my first point is, crime scenes are sealed off. Only the tribal police or the sheriff's department can authorize entry."

Deputy sheriff Chris Cordova came through the door into the boardroom. "Sorry, Sergeant, but I was finishing up an accident scene up on the ski valley road." He sat down beside Hornbuckle who politely nodded, scooting over to give him room.

Romero paused, stalling to give more bad news to McGinnis. "I am appointing Tejada to direct this inventory." McGinnis looked up at Romero and then at Hornbuckle. Hornbuckle avoided his stare. "Hornbuckle and McGinnis will help get the inventory accomplished as soon as possible, but Tejada is in charge. Call in as many interns as you think you need, Tejada. Medicine Wind will be looking over your shoulders as you count and mark off the items."

Then, Romero spoke to McGinnis, whose cheeks were rosy red with frustration. "John, you've got to help the sheriff's department at your home, and Tejada will direct things here. That's basically why the shift in responsibility. I've no issue with how you've handled the inventory thus far."

Tafoya isolated the word, "basically," from Romero's explanation, and knew there were other causes to sideline the head curator, but Romero took the polite way out of moving McGinnis out of the way. McGinnis had clashed with Medicine Wind and had started the inventory by focusing on chronology and accession dates, not masks. Now it was some unidentified person dropping stolen museum property at McGinnis's home that needed explanation.

McGinnis interrupted. "The cylinders were rolled up in a rug with a message," McGinnis explained. "'The god roams the foothills for XXXXXXX of his enemies,'" he repeated from memory.

Yeah, right, a god roaming our foothills, thought Tafoya.

But Tafoya saw a threat in the message. Someone is going to be killed, and we need to stop it from happening. Inwardly, he was alarmed.

Again, Romero outlined the protocol for entering and leaving the basement inventory room, and asked Hornbuckle if she had an intern to assist the investigation in going through the list of visitors on Friday. Hornbuckle said she would loan out an intern to the police. Dismissing the meeting, Romero asked McGinnis to stay behind for a minute with Cordova and Tafoya. The rest of the group departed.

When only McGinnis, Cordova, and Tafoya remained in the room, Romero asked McGinnis, "Why didn't you call the tribal police or the sheriff's department when you found the cylinders, and that someone had broken into your home? You came here to the museum instead. Why?"

"I wasn't thinking straight. It all came apart as I read the note and held the cylinders in my hands...I got scared. The message talks about a 'god taking his enemies.' I wasn't about to stay at the house any longer. I panicked."

Romero considered McGinnis's answer. McGinnis was definitely scared. No doubt about that. Coming to the museum was his safe place. McGinnis was escaping a frightening discovery.

"Okay, John, I understand. Now get out to your house and help the forensic team," Romero ordered. McGinnis left immediately.

Tafoya stood up to leave. "I'll call Santiago Majerus again and convince him to help us interpret the mask, Romero," Tafoya said. "I tried to call him last night, and he was not answering his phone."

18

At nine o'clock in the morning, G. Armstrong Coe opened the door to his bookshop and let his resident gray-tabby cat, Fenster, out the door, so she could conduct a reconnaissance about the caterwauling around his shop the night before. Fenster would come back after a search, feast on some kibbles, and then find a place either on the coffee table holding art books or underneath the counter to help Coe sell books. She had been the resident cat for three years, ever since Coe had befriended her on a cold winter morning at Thanksgiving, when she huddled for shelter at his door.

In the past year, *The Taos News* had sent a reporter to write an article on the resident dogs, cats, and parrots, taking up with business owners in Ojo Verde and Taos. Coe and Fenster received good coverage.

"Every bookstore needs a cat, it seems," the reporter wrote, "and Fenster greets customers, keeps mice in check, and is an all-around moveable art piece for Coe's Bookshop. It is untrue G. Armstrong Coe ejects customers that don't like cats. I asked Coe directly that question, as he stocked books in the local geology and natural history section.

"Coe said, 'It's entirely false I toss customers out that don't like cats. I just add a ten percent annoyance tax to their bill and give them a free pamphlet on the virtues of feline companionship. No, I don't throw them out.'"

The morning clouds obscured the Cristo Mountains in the east and the Tusas Mountains in the west. The clouds were moving fast. Coe, having been an Ojo Verdean for almost forty years, knew the winds would shift to the southwest by the afternoon, taking the wind chill down into the thirties. The wind shift to the west and southwest occurred with regularity. Opening the front door for Fenster, Coe inhaled a scent of rain.

Checking to make sure his bell worked when a customer came

through the front door, Coe gently slapped the bell. It rang with a high-toned tingle. "Good enough," he judged.

Coe walked to the back of his store, and parted a heavy purple curtain blocking entry to the stock room. The stock room held a special collection of ethnologies and archaeological texts concerning the Tulona and Eastern Pueblos of northern New Mexico. This was an area of printed sources he kept off the shelves from browsing shoppers. Over the years, the books behind the curtain had stirred controversy among the Tulona and Taos Pueblo people. Coe shelved them in back of his shop, and would only show them to serious scholars and writers. If customers insisted on buying a book that revealed puebloan ways, Coe sold them, Alfonso Ortiz's *The Tewa World: Space, Time, Being, and Becoming in a Pueblo Society*, knowing the reader would not make it past the first two chapters because of its complexity.

Coe sat down at a library table in the stock room and opened a file folder labeled, "Franklin Deerfield Museum." He had taken it out of the filing cabinet on Sunday, but had no time to read it. Jennifer Hornbuckle had telephoned Coe on Saturday evening. He was a trustee of Franklin Deerfield. Being a trustee of the museum, he was entitled to know details about the theft and what had happened. Hornbuckle had filled him in on as much detail as she knew: the heist had taken place early Saturday morning, three people were likely involved, and an inventory was being conducted to determine what had been stolen. She invited him to see the video of the two men that emerged from the basement. Coe declined, saying he would leave the details up to law enforcement. Hornbuckle said that the Tulona tribal police and the Taos County sheriff's office were in charge. Coe knew about the lease-contract the museum had with the pueblo. He read carefully the details of the museum's security.

Coe and the trustee board had recently upgraded security for the museum. They had hired a security firm, Southwest Security Services, or SSS, based in Santa Fe, that the School of American Research and the New Mexico History Museum had employed for their display and collections. Museums, like Franklin Deerfield, required a special web of protective protocols because museums have displays of valuable artifacts the public wishes to see. That was categorically different from securing valuable paintings or bonds in a vault that would never be displayed to the public. Museum artifacts were to be seen, not hidden.

The basic principle, as SSS advised the trustee board, was to create a redundant system that when one system failed, another system would take its place. Depending upon how much a museum wanted to spend, SSS could establish alarm technology, on-the-ground human surveillance, laser detectors, motion-detection devices, wireless vibration sensors, and CCTV cameras. In addition, SSS had classified methods of security, and you had to join the security industry to learn about them.

It all depended on how much a museum wanted to spend, SSS advised. Coe and the museum board decided to install SSS's Level 1 security, the most basic level. Franklin Deerfield was neither the Louvre nor the Smithsonian, but a regional museum that had been established by a local wealthy mentor and donors, so Level 1, the least expensive, seemed appropriate. Level 1 SSS security included new video cameras scanning hallways and entrances, but not the interior of workspaces or the curating department in the basement. Level 1 established checkpoints for human surveillance and security rounds inside and outside the building. SSS recommended a more secure system for key and lock management which was adopted within the building. SSS inspected the roof for weak points, and suggested door reinforcement for the entrances. The alarm system was upgraded. As a caveat to their evaluation of security, SSS stated thefts that took less than two minutes could probably not be prevented, as well as internal thefts from the staff.

SSS wrote, "Inside jobs of theft are difficult to prevent, so the vetting process for employees needed to be as thorough as possible."

The bell jingled at the front door. Coe closed the file, tucked it under his arm and walked to the front bookstacks to greet customers.

"Just browsing," a couple said.

Coe stood behind the front counter and, again, opened the file to Franklin Deerfield. He concluded, after reading the file, that the museum had protected itself as best it could with their limited budget. Once the couple left the shop, after purchasing a book on the Day of the Dead rituals and cultural practices in New Mexico, Coe telephoned Director Hornbuckle.

Once patched through to the director, Hornbuckle brought Coe up to speed on Romero's briefing and orders that morning at the museum.

"Tejada is going to direct the inventory. But get this," Hornbuckle said, exasperated. "McGinnis's home was broken into last night. Burglars stole nothing, but left two wooden cylinders that may be ritual objects connected to the mask stolen here."

"That's odd," said Coe.

"It is," Hornbuckle said. "I've never heard of thieves returning stolen goods."

After a few seconds, Coe asked, "What's up next in solving the robbery at the museum? Any idea what you're going to do?"

"The focus is finding data on the mask and continue the inventory for stolen items. Officer Tafoya of the tribal police is going to talk to Santiago Majerus from Arroyo Luz. He's a Navajo medicine man, and he will help us interpret the wooden cylinders and mask. We don't have a Navajo specialist on staff," Hornbuckle replied.

"Ms. Hornbuckle...," Coe said, cautiously.

"Yes, Mr. Coe..."

"I'm not an investigator, but I suspect this is, at least partially, an inside job."

For a few seconds, both Hornbuckle and Coe were quiet.

Then, Hornbuckle sighed loudly, "I'm afraid you are right, Coe...I wish you weren't."

19

At nine thirty in the morning, Singer of the Red Antway ritual, Santiago Majerus of Arroyo Luz, heard his landline phone ring. His hearing was still good, for he heard the phone ring while outside visiting with his neighbor, Johnny Sisneros. Majerus and Sisneros each owned a long lot, a *suerte*, about two acres each, two-hundred-feet wide. Their lots bordered Arroyo Luz-La Osa Road. Each had a fruit orchard and a garden of mixed vegetables, especially onions, garlic, and corn.

Sisneros had an adobe home; Majerus lived in a trailer house. At the higher end of their long lots, the Acequia Arroyo Luz flowed east to west, diverting water flowing down from high-country streams. Hearing the phone ring, Majerus broke his conversation with Sisneros to walk up to his trailer house and answer the landline. His friends knew to let the phone ring at least ten times and to call again right after the ten rings or so, if he did not answer on the first try.

"*¡Diga!* Majerus here," he answered on the second callback.

"Mr. Majerus, this is Officer Tafoya. How are you, sir?"

"I'm doing well, Richard. "*¿Y usted?*"

"I'm fine, Mr. Majerus. I need to ask you a favor."

"What's that, Richard? Something to do with the Blue Lady-Saltwater case? I thought that was concluded."

"That case is closed, Santiago. Nothing more on that. This is a different case. There was a break-in at the Franklin Deerfield Museum early Saturday morning. One of the items stolen was a mask, a Navajo mask. I want you come in and look at the video of the mask and tell us what you know about the mask. The museum has no one on the staff with Navajo expertise. I know you have experience with these things. I'll hire you as a consultant. Can you see your way to help us, Mr. Majerus?"

Majerus quickly thought it over. Being a consultant brought in sorely-needed income. His woodpile was fairly high for the coming winter, so he would not have to cut wood for another two weeks. And, he thought, delving back into Navajo ceremonialism reconnected him with his past—a past that included learning and singing the Red Antway ceremony. He looked out his front window. Most leaves on his cottonwood trees had fallen.

The wind gusted outside his trailer, rattling an old wash tub that hung on the outside wall. Majerus attended the wind, the rattling of the tub.

"Believe the wind," Majerus thought.

He looked down at the whorls on the end of his fingers. Whorls were residual traces of wind when his ancestors were created. The wind appeared to be summoning him to work with spiritual forces again. The wind rattling the wash tub settled it. Majerus spoke into the phone.

"Sure, Richard. When can I start?"

"Drive to the museum as soon as you can, Santiago. We need movement in this case."

"I'll be there within an hour, Richard."

After hanging up his phone, Santiago Majerus placed his medicine bundle and sage in a small backpack. He had come to utilize daypacks that became popular with young people in the 1970s to carry books and personal items. Within his medicine bundle were objects from Navajo sacred mountains, colored earth containers of ochre and charcoal, parrot feathers, bison horn, nightshade-family tobacco leaves, and herbs. He had sewn ordinary tourist patches on the daypack as a frivolous touch to the sacred contents within. One room in his trailer house contained his medicine paraphernalia, and an outdoor shed held medicinal plants and spruce cuttings. Zipping the daypack securely, he closed the door to his trailer house and climbed into his pickup.

Waving goodbye to his neighbor, Johnny Sisneros, Majerus paused at his property line before he turned onto the Arroyo Luz-La Osa Road and looked closely at the cottonwood trees bordering his long lot with Sisneros. More leaves had fallen from the branches, but enough brittle leaves remained on the tree to rattle with the wind.

"Come another hard rain and wind, most of you will fall," Majerus said to the tree.

Tafoya met Majerus at the Franklin Deerfield front entrance and escorted him to the trustees' boardroom that had been designated as the investigative conference room for the duration of the inventory. Majerus saw the portrait of Franklin Deerfield on the boardroom wall.

"I knew Franklin, Tafoya. I was young and he was older, but we used to talk at the acequia association meetings. He and I were on the same acequia, the Acequia Arroyo Luz. I think one year or two, he was the *mayordomo* of the ditch. It was a wet year, and he handled our need for water fairly.... Yes, he was a good man," Majerus reflected.

"I never met him, though I've heard good things about him," Tafoya responded, anxious to get started.

The technical division of the museum had set up a hardwired connection to the security office, so investigators could see archival footage of the cameras. Tafoya had the monitors turned on. The footage of the two thieves coming out of the inventory room were frozen at the beginning. Tafoya took a chair beside Majerus to operate the mouse and keyboard for the monitor.

"Are you ready to begin, Santiago?"

"Yes, let's start," Majerus said, adjusting his chair to get a closer look at the screen.

Tafoya clicked on the footage as the basement door opened. One man emerged and quickly turned to the right, avoiding a frontal view of the mask to the camera.

"We will get a better view of this man on the next camera angle, Santiago," Tafoya said.

The second man emerged from the basement, wearing a backpack. Majerus saw quickly the pack was larger than the daypack he brought from home.

"Hmm," Majerus uttered.

"What is it?" Tafoya asked.

"Nothing, just the size of the pack is much bigger than commonly carried," Majerus answered. "There must be large objects carried in that pack…it looks heavy."

As the video flickered forward, Tafoya and Majerus saw the two men walking rapidly down the hallway, then turning left at the end of the hall toward the exit door on the opposite side of the building from where the security officer was clocking in.

"Here is the second camera footage of the men and the mask," Tafoya said to Majerus, as he clicked on the footage from the second camera.

The first man wearing the mask stopped at the exit door and looked directly at the camera. The mask had eyeholes and a hole for the mouth. The eyeholes were large enough so that the whites of his eyes could be seen as they moved. The mask was dark red, constructed of buckskin it appeared, with hanging shells dangling from underneath the eyes and mouth. Fur and feathers encircled the top of the mask. Painted in semi-circular patterns around the mask were closed "Xs," like hourglasses. Some "Xs" were only half-closed at the top.

The second man stood away from the masked man. The masked man opened his arms and swept them seven times back to his chest, holding skin and hair strips in his hands. The skin strips were stiff, the hair long in length. The man stomped his right foot. No sound was on the video, but Majerus and Tafoya noticed his mouth moving within the mouth hole. After sweeping the air with his arms, the man exited the side door, followed quickly by the second.

Majerus stood up, pushing back his chair abruptly. He walked to the far edge of the boardroom, shaking his head and running his hand through his hair. Tafoya had questions, but held his tongue until Majerus was ready to speak. Tafoya pulled out his notebook to take notes.

Majerus sat back down in his chair, squelched his lips together, and shook his head. As Majerus started to speak, someone knocked on the door and began to open it. Tafoya rose from his chair and went to the door. Director Hornbuckle entered the boardroom.

"I heard your Navajo friend is here and I wanted to meet him," she said.

"I'll introduce you, but we're in the middle of an interview, and it's private," Tafoya asserted. Hornbuckle smiled faintly at the rebuff. Tafoya made the introduction and shooed the director outside. He locked the door. "Sorry about that, Santiago, but she is the director."

Majerus understood.

"Let's start over, Santiago," Tafoya said, "what do you make of the mask and the man that wore it?"

"I know the mask. I've seen it many times. It's the Child of Water mask, also known remotely as He Scalps Around. It is a god mask, one of the gods of our Origin Legend. I'll explain later. Those "Xs" on the mask are hair queues, representing scalps. The open "Xs" are scalps yet to be taken. But Child of Water is the most used name, not He Scalps Around."

"That doesn't sound good," Tafoya sighed, scribbling notes.

Majerus continued. "The dance at the door by the masked man, or whatever it was, has no meaning...just silly. But in his hands are..."

"Scalps," Tafoya finished the sentence.

"Yes," Majerus answered sadly.

Santiago Majerus asked Tafoya to run back the video back so he could see the person dance, "Or stomp around in a mescal-induced antic, having no meaning whatsoever," he said sullenly.

Tafoya ran back the video to the place where the two men went out the side door of the museum. Majerus looked carefully at the man wearing the mask. "Stop it there, where I can see the mask plainly, please, Tafoya."

Tafoya stopped the video as Majerus looked closer. Tafoya enlarged the image so that details stood out.

"It's definitely the *To'badzistsíni* god mask, the Child of Water," Majerus said. "The sweeping of the arms seven times I think is an occult attempt to bring power into the thief, the spirit of Indigenous objects within the museum. That's not going to happen. The number seven may indicate the seven directions: north, south, east, west, up, down, and the center. The steps of the dance are non-sensical, lacking precision."

"Any significance to stealing scalps?" Tafoya asked. "Other than selling them on the black market with the mask?"

"No more significant for us, the Navajo, than for you puebloans, Tafoya. Scalps are trophies of battle. However, when it comes to our Origin Legends, the Child of Water or *To'badzistsíni* and his brother, Slayer of Enemy Gods, are both involved in destroying alien gods that harm the people. They help warriors in battle and those individuals that suffer from witchcraft sickness. Child of Water is a slayer of alien gods that roam the foothills. His brother, Slayer of Enemy Gods, is more prominent and also hikes among mountain peaks in search of alien gods. The mask taken by the thief is decorated with scalp symbols, the closed 'Xs' that are painted on the mask. Our most revered deity is Changing Woman and she gave birth to Slayer of Enemy Gods. White Shell Woman is the mother of Child of Water..."

Suddenly, Tafoya interrupted Majerus. "Did you say Child of Water roams the foothills? And is a slayer of alien gods?"

"Yes," Majerus said. "What about it?"

Tafoya opened a file on the other monitor, showing the digital image of the message McGinnis had brought from his home. "Check this out, Santiago," Tafoya pointed at the black-lettered message.

"THE GOD ROAMS THE FOOTHILLS FOR XXXXXXX OF HIS ENEMIES."

Majerus raised his eyebrows, "Where was this found?" Tafoya replied that it was a message accompanying the two wooden cylinders of red-painted cedar and black-painted piñon that had been left at McGinnis's home during the night.

"That message," Majerus interpreted, "is a direct reference to Child of Water looking for enemies to slay and take scalps among the lower mountains or foothills. Show me the wooden cylinders, Tafoya."

Tafoya opened another digital image that showed the wooden cylinders. Majerus leaned closer to the monitor screen to see the detail. He looked at the cylinders and the mask on the two monitors carefully for a minute. Then he sat back in his chair and faced Tafoya.

"Yes, those are cylinders symbolizing lightning bolts in our rituals. Child of Water holds the red cedar in in his left hand, the black piñon in his right. Child of Water follows Slayer of Enemy Gods in the Night Chant of the Navajo, my people. Child of Water is the brother of Slayer of Enemy Gods, but lesser in the hallway of gods. The message, 'The god roams the foothills for scalps of his enemies,' is associated with White Shell Woman's offspring, Child of Water."

Tafoya made no immediate reply, but looked at the monitors, focusing on the mask, then the cylinders. Finally, Tafoya spoke.

"I do not see good in this. Not that I was thinking I would see any good, but I definitely see bad consequences." Majerus stared at the stilled image of the two men as they paused at the exit door.

Speaking grimly, Tafoya said, "We have a theft of property from the museum. That's bad enough, but now we have a person or persons having spiritual knowledge of what they stole—a god mask of the Navajo. In addition, they have a knowledge of Child of Water's legendary behavior to slay alien gods. The message left behind at McGinnis says so. If the thief or thieves conjures up a real scenario about 'roaming the foothills and taking scalps,' then persons in our community considered 'alien gods' are at risk. That's really bad, scary, the worse-case scenario."

"I agree, Tafoya," Majerus concurred.

Tafoya continued, "The inventory has confirmed the theft of the mask from the museum's collections, but needs to find out what the thieves carried in the backpack. Must have been the cylinders, but there were other items there, for the pack seemed heavy. Those wooden cylinders do not weigh much, so there are other things in that pack.... Also, the theft of the Navajo items could have been a theft of opportunity. But I'm really not sure what their intent was. Too early to tell. I'm not eliminating any possibility at this time. We've got to find what else was stolen."

"Which means, Richard," Majerus said, "the thieves either were working in the museum or have worked here, or they had help, wittingly or not, from museum personnel. They had knowledge of what the museum held."

Tafoya looked at Majerus and smiled, "I may have to put you on the tribal police force if you continue to think that way, Santiago."

"Just my honorarium for the day will be good enough, Richard. I have two acres to farm in Arroyo Luz. That's good enough for me."

Before Majerus left the Franklin Deerfield Museum, he retrieved his daypack from the pickup. He walked around the building to the exit door where the thieves had escaped. He set his daypack beside the door, and turned facing the mountains in the east.

Darkening rain clouds tumbled down from the mountain tops, and as he turned toward the north and Colorado, he saw lightning strike the lower foothills. Rain had been forecast for the day; now rain was here.

Unzipping his daypack, Majerus opened a snuff container of soil from *Tsotsĭl*, the Navajo sacred mountain of the south. Specks of turquoise flakes were mixed in with the soil. He faced the east, then the north. Acknowledging in his prayer the south and west, Majerus took two steps away from the porch and door and scattered the turquoise-flaked soil on the ground. Then he took from his daypack several pinches of sacred tobacco, not the cheap chemical-laced tobacco of stores, but the sacred nightshade-family tobacco gathered in the wild. Again, stepping off the porch and away from the door, Majerus flung the tobacco in the air. Quietly, under his breath so no one could hear, Majerus uttered a prayer.

Beauty all around us! Child of Water! Slayer of Enemy Gods! Help us stop the perversion of these thieves! Help us always see beauty above, beauty below, the beauty all around us! Child of Water! Hear my plea! Creator, hear me!

Singer of the Antway, Majerus sought to stop the men from traveling the bad road. Yet, Majerus knew his limitations: stopping the outcome of perverting power for evil ends was now in the hands of law enforcement. Zipping up his daypack of medicines and good things for the world, Majerus said, aloud and not caring who heard, *Child of Water! Make it so!*

Dark cobalt-blue clouds passed swiftly over Franklin Deerfield Museum. Nearer the ground, winds became light, rain softly fell, and though cold, Majerus and the tourists visiting the museum inhaled scents of sagebrush and chamiso, a perfume of the air not reserved merely for spring. Light rain patted the mesas and high country, and all living things became attuned to their senses, understanding the munificence of Earth, the Changing Woman of the Navajo. To the puebloans, the season of Ripe Time was giving way to the Still Time of winter. Navajo Changing Woman was to rest before spring, the Beginning Time.

20

At nine o'clock, the same Monday morning of Majerus' visit to the museum, and before north winds shifted to the southwest and clouds materialized, Armando Ortega loaded his chainsaw, a container of diesel with injector-cleaner additive, protective chaps, and chainsaw oil in the bed of his pickup. The pickup's wooden siderails enabled him to stack a cord of wood neatly.

Loretta shouted at him from the porch, "Husband! Say a prayer before you fire up that monster machine," Armando knew she fretted about him, until he safely returned with his two arms and two legs—intact.

"I will, Loretta. Don't fret."

"Why don't you wait and cut wood with Luis?" she shouted.

"I'll be fine, *esposa*, don't worry, I'm taking Zeke, he'll help!" Loretta did not laugh.

He whistled for Zeke, their border collie, to hop in the pickup cab. Armando's son, Luis, had departed the family compound earlier in the morning. He had loaded Buck in the horse trailer to go to the Tulona Pueblo to give a farrier lesson to his friend, Lion Walks Night. No matter. As was usually the case, Armando cut wood by himself in the forest.

Before Armando headed northward on Forest Road 493, toward the Columbine-Hondo Forest reserve, he turned into the parking lot at the Chapel of Our Lady of Sorrows in San Miguel village.

Aged Armando was; aged he felt.

In his seventies, aches and pains, especially his knees, intensified. But the cutting of wood in the forest strengthened him, for the exercise pushed out pain and by the end of his chore, Armando felt invigorated, younger, and in less pain. In the forest, vegetation and dense stands of conifers muted the sounds of industry—except when he fired up "the monster." Piñon jays, juncos, and magpies kept him company. The forest was his church, and he was reminded of John Muir who had written that he had rather be in nature thinking of God, than in church thinking of nature.

Yet, for all that nature and piñon jays gave him, he wanted to pray in the chapel before he started to cut wood. Armando rolled down the windows of the pickup for Zeke to have fresh air while he was inside.

Ascending three steps in front of the large wooden chapel doors, he reverently rubbed a hand across the door carvings that had been chiseled by Antonio Zima, a Peñasco woodcarver, whose artistic skill had been acquired with the Works Progress Administration apprentice program in the 1930s. Armando and Loretta had hired the aged Zima, in his eighties a few years before, to construct and carve new doors when the hundred-year-old chapel doors needed replacement.

With the assistance of two young apprentices, Zima had completed the task within a year of hire, and in so doing passed his techniques to his apprentices. The newly-carved and constructed doors for Our Lady of Sorrows Chapel were works of art, not merely doors for the separation of profane and sacred space. The Zima doors were works to be honored, and the whole community and surrounding settlements believed so, too. Once Zima and his apprentices had completed their work, a celebration seemed necessary. What better time to celebrate the doors than on Christmas?

On Christmas Eve, before midnight Mass, the doors were consecrated in a special celebration. Eschewing the comfort of Santa Fe on Christmas Eve, a visiting priest traveled to San Miguel to consecrate the doors and conduct a special Mass. The priest was only twenty-eight years old and freshly ordained from a Mexico City Jesuit seminary. Parishioners from Questa, Ojo Verde, and Rio Hondo attended and filled the pews for the dedication that had been widely publicized in church bulletins. A heavy snow began to fall in the afternoon of the dedication; the church's community hall opened for shelter and food service. No mind; people braved the weather and snowy roads. Armando and Loretta had provided a room overnight for the visiting Jesuit.

Armando shook his head to dispel the memory, though he thought he smelled the fresh carvings of the wood—even still. He put his hand on the large bronze latch and squeezed the entry handle. The "Zima Doors" were unlocked, and he stepped inside. The chapel was warm; votive candles flickered in front of the altar. Dipping his fingers in holy water, Armando crossed himself and walked to the front of the chapel, scooted into a pew, and adjusted the padded knee rest for prayer.

"Thank goodness for small favors," he thought, easing himself down on the knee rest.

He looked up at the altar cross, but what always absorbed his attention were the *reredos*, the altarpiece. The backdrop of the altar held familiar symbols of Mary and Christ. On the outer margins of the iconography, wildlife forms emerged: deer, elk, rabbit, hawks, and eagles in placement with sagebrush in the foreground and blue sky above. At the feet of Mary, who radiated a blue aura, lay several sheep, Churro sheep from the shape of their horns and abundant fleece.

Armando closed his eyes and prayed for his family and friends. After praying he opened his eyes and gazed at the *reredos*.

In the *reredos'* background of wildlife, thick stands of spruce and ponderosa appeared deep-forest green in luminescent color. Armando, after all the years of sitting at Mass beside Loretta, had not seen the stands of spruce so bright and shiny. Years past, he had focused on the *reredos'* wildlife and Churro sheep. But not today; today was different. The trees captured his attention.

Why are the shining trees drawing me in? Armando had no answer.

Armando shook his head free of the question, stood up, and with his foot lifted the kneeling pad back in place. Crossing himself as he stepped into the aisle, he turned around and walked out of church alone, touching the Zima Doors as he exited.

Armando spent most of the day in the National Forest sawing wood, axing wood, and stacking logs in his pickup. True to his promise to his wife, he uttered a short prayer before he ignited the chainsaw. Zeke explored holes for critters and slept on pine-needle beds, staying within earshot of Armando's whistles and calls for him.

As Armando worked during the day, he noticed three men cutting wood on the downslope from where he labored. Their cutting wood was not firewood for burning, but shaping logs for large vigas, the supporting timber for ceilings and roofs. The men had lowered the tailgate of their F-250 pickup so that vigas extended two or three feet beyond the gate. The men, two young, the third an older man, worked intently, hardly acknowledging Armando's friendly wave from a distance. Armando's permit for woodcutting was in order, but he was not sure the viga-cutting men had permits.

Armando finished his work mid-afternoon, feeling invigorated as he thought he would but tired and ready to go home. Securing his equipment with rope to the headache rack of his pickup, he started the engine and drove downslope, mostly coasting on the unnumbered forest road, the mass weight of wood adding momentum, causing Armando to ride the brakes. He waved at the three men as he passed by them, but they ignored him, barely glancing in his direction.

"Not very friendly are they, Zeke?" Armando said. He drove home to San Miguel and decided to wait until the next day, a Tuesday, to unload the wood. Loretta said she would help him unload the wood, if he needed help.

"No, it's okay...I'll tend to it tomorrow...I'm tired and want to take a shower and rest." Armando's invigoration from woodcutting in the forest had dissipated. Uncharacteristically, Armando laid down on the sofa after he showered and went to sleep. Loretta covered him with a Churro-woven blanket as he slept—the wool from their own flock.

21

Five years before the theft at Franklin Deerfield...

The years had fallen hard on him. In his fifth decade, he regretted choices he had made: marriage to a woman who in her drunken states, cursed his Tulano heritage and ridiculed his body, "Too short, face ugly, and long hair in braids!" Their relationship had centered around partying, drinking mescal. Their differences flared into violence; but she was gone—he did not know where, nor did he care. Then there was his choice to drop out of technical school in Española and go on a road trip to California, where he ended up hawking the milk-bottle-knockdown game on Santa Monica pier. Sure, he saw the Pacific Ocean every day he worked, but the ocean was never blue, but gray, and the ocean stank. Bad choice to run away from the desert mesas and mountains of New Mexico.

Yet, he corrected his bad choices and decided to return to the Tulona Pueblo. His return journey back to the pueblo was slower than he intended. He stopped to visit his cousins at Heart Rock, near Crownpoint, New Mexico. He remained a hogan guest of his cousins for over a year, working at the Navajo Technical University as a veterinary assistant. He attended Navajo healing ceremonies where he became knowledgeable of Navajo customs. His cousins admired his ability to learn Navajo quickly, particularly one distant female cousin with whom he partied. Her father intervened in the relationship, forcing him to leave Heart Rock sooner than he wanted. Although his girlfriend wanted to leave with him, he told her bluntly, "I travel alone."

He returned to New Mexico, settling into working with a construction crew based in Ojo Verde. He installed floors and stone walkways, put up stucco walls, laid brick, learned the art of making kiva-style fireplaces. It was a good choice to return. He re-established his friendships with kiva brothers. He did not perform ceremonies, and for that he was criticized and often banned from being a participant in rituals. His friendship with cacique Bustamente waned after the cacique lectured him on social responsibilities to the pueblo.

"I'll not be told what to do, Bustamente!" he had responded, bluntly.

Bustamente was equally strong in response, "Then, you must find a place to live outside the pueblo, off the reservation, until you truly see the value of cooperation and respect for your people. Do not stay away long from us, but think about what you can do for the people, not always what the puebloans can do for you. *Go up into the trees*. Talk to them. I will advise the council you will be relocating."

He made another bad choice moving off the reservation. He rented a one-bedroom house in Ojo Verde, continuing to lay stone walkways and porches and build fireplaces.

"At least I am not banished," he said, comforting himself with his relocation. "I can visit in the pueblo and talk with my friends."

He was a member of the Old Bow kiva. An elder of his kiva, Looking Elk, had told him a story of a disused and abandoned kiva on a remote mesa, not far away from the Tulona Plaza, on the east side of the Rio Grande. The story intrigued him for he thought the lessons of the people that abandoned the settlement might be a passageway to personal power and his reinstatement to the Tulona Pueblo. He did not come to that insight quickly, for he was still going up into the trees, as Bustamente had advised. He did not talk to the trees, nor did he hear them speak. The trees were silent to him.

He brooded about the old pueblo near the Big River. The abandoned settlement was not in the high country of ponderosa or spruce, but situated among juniper and piñon trees, cholla cactus, sagebrush and chamiso, its ground arid with stones and arroyos. Only five miles from Tulona Plaza, in the distant past the old pueblo people and the Tulona intermarried and were considered as one people. The outlier settlement looked west and guarded the western edge of the Tulona when the settlement was populated. From Looking Elk, he had listened intently to the story of Hanging Shell.

The story of Hanging Shell…

One day, Looking Elk captured him with the story of the abandoned pueblo. It was a mild summer's day like many in New Mexico's high country. The wind was gentle and had turned from the north to the west-southwest in the afternoon, as was the prevailing change of direction during the day for Ojo Verde. Being light winds, no dust stirred from the plaza. He and Looking Elk sat on a large split log on the northside of the plaza under an arbor; the arbor vigas and *latillas* providing a lattice shade blocking the sun's rays. Looking Elk was in the mood to talk. And, to teach.

"Do you have time to hear a story?" Looking Elk asked him.

"I do. I finished laying stone this morning. I have the afternoon free."

Looking Elk wrapped his thin brown blanket more tightly around himself and leaned against an arbor post that abutted the split-log bench. "Sit on the opposite bench so you can see my face as I tell you the story," he instructed him.

No one else sat under the arbor. Tourists avoided the two men, but one tourist prepped his camera to take a picture. "No pictures. We're talking," Looking Elk rebuffed.

"Sorry," said the young man apologetically.

Most visitors meandered in and out of shops on the plaza. A few dogs lay sleeping in the sun. Looking Elk stared across the plaza at the river and cottonwoods along its bank and started to tell his story, but stopped suddenly. He seemed pensive, having second thoughts about verbalizing the story…. But then Looking Elk straightened up and cleared his throat.

He spoke, saying, "I think it good to tell you this story, so that you might learn and teach others of the good path to follow and the bad road to shun. Words have power; stories have power. Not talking about them erases them from memory. And the Tulona have wished to erase, to forget about the Hanging Shell Pueblo across the way," as he gestured to the west and the Big River and Tusas Range. "To talk about Hanging Shell brings its spirit back. Be careful, that can be dangerous."

Looking Elk paused, reflecting. Then with an affirmative nod of his head, he spoke, "But it has been such a long time ago, and the people at Hanging Shell no longer pose a danger…I think it permissible to tell you." Looking Elk took a deep breath, and exhaled. "I am like the old cottonwood you see east of our wall, along the racetrack." He nodded his head in the direction of the cottonwood. Looking Elk did not point, for that would embarrass the tree.

"That cottonwood has lived longer than I have. It is brittle and stiff and leaves do not sprout from its tallest branches anymore. When I fall away from dancing on this earth—like the cottonwood—the story of Hanging Shell Pueblo dies, like the cottonwood tree that will no longer shade the river's edge… But it has been such a long time ago, and they no longer pose a danger…" he said, repeating his concerns, his voice trailing off. He stopped, then he started again. His acolyte, sitting on the bench, did not stir, but sat transfixed.

"Our Puebloan Ancestors came at the time of the Third Light, the brilliant star that lasted for a few years, then disappeared, its brilliance less than the moon but much brighter than other stars combined. When the moon was slender at night, we could read animal track by the Third Light. When drought occurred our Puebloan Ancestors from Chaco and Mesa Verde came for wood and water here to the Cristo Mountains. The Tulona settled in many places as did the Taos People. Hanging Shell, across the way, was one of many villages. The Navajo were not here, but soon walked here.

"The people of the settlement over there," Looking Elk nodded in its direction, "fished in the river—it was much wetter then—and hunted with their kinsmen in the mountains for deer and elk. They did not have the taboo against eating fish as many of us have. The Tulona that lived there were exceptionally skilled in rabbit hunts. They were artful and traded in turquoise with the Chaco people. Their turquoise beads and shellwork have been found in places as far away as central Mexico and among the Mound Builders in the east. They were vibrant and joyous."

"What became of them, Grandfather? I have never heard of them," he asked in puzzlement.

"Be patient," Looking Elk admonished.

"Close to the river, the river from the north where snow never melts on the mountains, they came and built houses," he began solemnly. "There were pit houses at first, but as the people grew in number, they built houses of several rooms, some stacked one on top of the other, like our Winter side and Summer side houses. Their settlement came to be known as Hanging Shell. They fished from the Big River that flowed from the north. The people saved the shells from mussel or mollusk people. They drilled holes in their shells and strung them together to hang in their homes and in the trees where they rattled like the leaves of Tulona Pueblo cottonwoods. They built tower pueblitos that were round and served as defensive positions from their enemies. The Hanging Shell constructed only one kiva. Their members interacted with our Old Bow and Blue Stone kivas. The time was hard. The Hanging Shell were keen traders. They walked trade routes to Chaco in the west, Cerrillos mines to the south, and Manassa mines to the north.

"They were a good people, but evil times fell on them.

"A holy man by the name of Sun Shield emerged as a powerful Hanging Shell healer, knowing the ways of medicine plants and their curative properties. Sun Shield was a good, kind man. Another person came to challenge Sun Shield. He was a man of jealousy, envy, spite, and revenge. His name was Wood Quiver. Knowing the magic of witchcraft, he sickened Sun Shield. To do this, Wood Quiver performed the rite of the Ball of Thorns, customarily used against enemies, not against one's own people. Sun Shield fell sick and died. The people suspected Wood Quiver of witchcraft, but did not challenge him. Wood Quiver became the cacique of the Hanging Shell, but because he did not have widespread knowledge of medicine plants, he was never respected as like Sun Shield. Wood Quiver was knowledgeable of good magic for the Hanging Shell, and performed ceremonies with distinction, but beneath his appearance lay a brutal, ambitious man. He was a witch, a Sleep Maker."

Looking Elk paused in telling the story and closed his eyes. His listener, sitting on the bench opposite from him, looked at him and saw his lips moving, as if in a silent prayer.

After a minute of pause, Looking Elk opened his eyes and continued. "The Hanging Shell Pueblo became a place of disunity and argument. Wood

Quiver controlled the medicine bundle of the kiva and objects of power crucial to the pueblo's tranquility. Under his control were several sacred objects. One was a painted wooden panel symbolizing rainbows and bird figures. He possessed Corn Mother stone effigies, turquoise necklaces, a folded world straightener, and a ceremonial bowl. Within the sacred space of the kiva, a necklace of mollusks hung from the retablo panels. Wood Quiver kept the powerful objects wrapped in buckskin, except for a ceremonial bowl, openly displayed on a high shelf in the kiva.

"Wood Quiver knew good magic and learned much about plant medicine to help the Hanging Shell people. But magic can go in two directions, and eventually Wood Quiver was deprived of his role as cacique because he used his power to hurt people that he thought bedeviled him. Pressure grew within the Hanging Shell Pueblo to push him out of the pueblo.

"As the story goes, Wood Quiver, under pressure and threats, departed Hanging Shell and went to live with people out West. He returned to Hanging Shell after a few years and seemed to have reformed to follow the good road again. His changed behavior did not last long. After his return, he was accused of witchcraft again, even responsible for the death of several Tulona here at Cottonwood River.

"Because of Tulona deaths, the Tulona people of Cottonwood River formed a band of warriors and attacked the Hanging Shell Pueblo. They spared the innocents, but killed Wood Quiver as he sought to escape near the Big River crossing. When his pueblo room and the kiva were searched, the Corn Mother effigies, mollusk necklaces, wooden panels, and world straightener were not found. We have never found the relics. The ceremonial bowl was found in the kiva, but eventually it, too, disappeared. The Hanging Shell people gave up their village and migrated here to Cottonwood River. The Hanging Shell story faded from our memory by not being retold."

Looking Elk turned directly to him. "I am one of the last Tulonas that knows of the Hanging Shell.... Now, you know. Learn from this story... and put its lessons in your heart, Grandson."

The story finished, neither Looking Elk nor his acolyte said anything. The wind remained calm. Tourists walked around the arbor where they sat, looking back at the two men after they passed. A dog came over to the arbor and laid down in the shade. Finally, the man broke the silence.

"What do you think the lesson is to be learned, Looking Elk?" he asked earnestly.

Looking Elk said nothing at first. He looked all around the plaza, fixing his gaze upon the mountains in the background, the racing path going east, and the mission church at the edge of the plaza. A serious look came on his face.... Then, he spoke.

"The good path and the bad road are choices humans make. Sacred knowledge can be used to unify and bring people together, but knowledge can be turned around and used for evil purposes. Choose and train yourself and others to stifle envy, jealousy, excessive pride. Those chosen within our pueblo to lead must be those who handle power carefully and for the good of all the people. The same is true for all human communities.... And one more thing, my son."

"Yes, Grandfather?"

"Ceremonial objects are sacred and to be respected. Do not fool around with them...I hope the Hanging Shell kiva objects are forever lost, for they were very powerful at one time. If intact, they still are powerful."

Looking Elk exhaled and sat down on the bench beside his acolyte. The story had straightened his body and brought fire to his cheeks. Telling the story, even to one person, invigorated him, as it does all storytellers. Now the telling was over, and Looking Elk wanted to be alone.

The audience of one walked away from the arbor and Looking Elk. The story lingered and encamped within him. He shielded his eyes from the sun's glare and looked at Blue Stone kiva, on the southside of the plaza. The slender ladder poles of the kiva soared into the sky.

He walked across the bridge to a disused kiva, no longer serving any ceremonial purpose, its members long dead. Its vigas slumped; a few rungs of the ladder were broken. The disused kiva had had a history, but now, no one knew it.

"Perhaps it is time this kiva comes to life again?" He looked down into the darkness of the old kiva's room. Clouds obscured the sun from shining directly into the vacant, ancient structure.

He thought deeply, then decided, "No, not this kiva. I shall bring life back to the Hanging Shell kiva, the sacred place near the river where mollusks used to live. But I must have their bundle of ceremonial objects. Where can they be?"

The listener to Looking Elk's story, the estranged man from Tulona Pueblo, the craftsman of laying stone, and former barker at the Santa Monica fun pier felt called to power. He turned away from the disused kiva and walked to the parking lot, started his pickup, and drove to his rental house in Ojo Verde. He felt strong, even excited, for he had a vision of spiritual leadership for a good path. He would not be swayed to the bad road, he thought. So, he hoped, so he prayed....

On the night of the theft at Franklin Deerfield...

He ran fast behind the two younger men. He was in good shape, but it was hard to keep up their fast pace. The headlamp of the point man wavered up and down with each running step, causing him, the oldest of the three, to stumble and stub his running shoes on a protruding stone from the dirt road. They had barely escaped the museum guard's detection when they came out the side door, one carrying the backpack with the bundle and corn mothers, his wearing the god mask and under his hoodie, two sticks of wood stuck in his belt, the thunderbolts of Navajo *Yeibichai*—the gods. They had made good their escape from the museum.

The third man had met them at the intersection of the road to Franklin Deerfield Museum and led them, running, to their pickup. The three men jumped in and drove to the pueblo, taking the road to Earth Cloud Lake beyond the ash pile. At the first turnabout on the road, the youngest of the three jumped out of the pickup, and with the backpack containing the medicine bundle, began to trot up the road and, after a time, entered the dense forest. The older man turned the pickup around, and after dropping his companion at his home on the edge of the reservation, drove to his own house in Ojo Verde. He was tired, but excited and relished the success of the heist.

"*To'badzistsíni*! Walk among us, be a power Now! Among us!" he exclaimed, driving home.

But three days later, in the Month of Leaves Falling, their excitement had died, and despite their commitment, one of them returned the two thunderbolts of *To'badzistsíni* to the man of the museum with a warning message.

"A minor setback to give the thunderbolts back, but I must stop this man's thinking. And, if his thinking is not reversed, then I will choke off his weakness." So thought the older man, the former barker at Santa Monica fun pier, who had listened to Looking Elk's story.

He had listened but not understood.

22

Thursday, October 18, Day of Saint Luke, Month of Leaves Falling Moon

Richard Tafoya, Tulona tribal policeman, sipped coffee at the police station before he opened up the Franklin Deerfield Museum case file on the computer to begin his day. Early morning it was, winds light from the north. But by late morning, the forecast was for winds and increasing clouds. The winds were to shift later that afternoon to the west-southwest, and that meant dust blowing across the plaza.

Not wanting to start analyzing, he rose from his chair and walked down the hall to the front of the station. Tafoya paused at the front window of the station and looked up at Tulona Peak. Clouds obscured the top of the peak. Tafoya looked across the plaza and saw his kinsmen stacking firewood against their walls. Two of his cousins had set up a table to display jewelry to tourists. Taking another sip of coffee, Tafoya grimaced at its taste. He wondered if the department could change the coffee beans to something richer, like Sumatra. Bessie Talbot, at the Bureau of Land Management in Ojo Verde, next door to Janet Rael's Forest Service offices, purchased Sumatra Roast at Café Mundo in Española.

"Bessie needs to buy Sumatra Café Mundo for us. This coffee is terrible," Tafoya thought. He continued to drink it, for it was all the station had.

Tafoya walked back to his office and opened up the Franklin Deerfield case file on the theft, last Saturday, October 13. Tafoya had three components or silos of documentation: the department's computer files that linked up with the F.B.I. and Taos County sheriff's department's reports; hard copies of evidence in the Tulona stationhouse filing cabinets and material evidence lockers; and his personal field notebooks and yellow legal pad notes he kept locked away in his desk.

These silos of information were his primary sources. Further, in his office and in the conference room of the stationhouse, Tafoya depended on white boards for visualizing and posting photos and notes on evidence. Currently, there were few white-board graphics; the case was at an impasse.

Tafoya opened the station's digital files on the Franklin Deerfield case. He scanned through the data items: security video, guest register for the museum, footprints, urine samples from the broom closet, fingerprints, accession records for the mask and cylinders, and interviews with Hornbuckle, McGinnis, interns, and Tejada. The sheriff's department investigation of McGinnis's home revealed that his patio door had been jimmied open making the case one of breaking *and* entering. The message that "'The god roams the foothills for XXXXXXX of his enemies" was printed with a sharpie-like pen on ordinary white paper.

Tafoya pulled out his yellow legal pad. He made a note to complete the viewing of the security video. He heard someone come in the front door of the station.

"Hey, Tafoya, good morning!" Romero shouted from the front.

Tafoya answered Romero back and went on analyzing the evidence. Looking at the guest register for the museum on Friday, October 12, Tafoya focused on the time frame, 3:56-4:32 p.m., the time frame blacked out on the security video. Seven people had signed in during that interval: Arthur Goodwin, Doris Goodwin ("probably husband and wife," he thought), Mary Orlinger, Moses Ortiz, Jennifer Woodall, Jim Gonzales, and Frank Tolerance. None had criminal records. Dead end there. But why the video blackout at that time?

Tafoya looked at the forensics on the footprints leading out the exit door. The footprints on the newly-vacuumed floor and in soft dirt outside the museum were from running shoes. What brand they were, the forensic team had no idea, but the two sets of running shoes were different. The urine samples from the soft-drink bottles in the broom closet revealed that one of the men had diabetes. The other sample was normal. Diabetes usually indicates an older person, but not always. Tafoya looked at fingerprint analysis. Fingerprints on the urine bottles were lifted, but there was no record in state and federal data files for either of the two sets. Those prints, however, were found on the door leading out of the museum where they escaped. Tafoya signed off on his computer.

"Enough for now," he said. Tafoya stood up from his desk and walked to the breakroom and poured another cup of coffee. He looked at his watch: a quarter after nine. He walked to the front of the stationhouse where the administrative assistant, Delores Rafael, was sitting at her desk, entering data on the computer regarding welfare checks on two Tulona senior citizens—both were doing well—and a domestic disturbance at the edge of reservation at the casino.

"This time Romero got to the casino parking lot before a fight broke out," Delores said, "and he gave the married couple advice to share their winnings and not squabble. The husband wanted to gamble more; she wanted to go eat." Tafoya frowned and shook his head.

"I don't know if the money we get from the casino is worth all the trouble we have to deal with there," Tafoya said. "How did the squabble turn out?"

"Romero convinced the husband to take his wife to eat. She would drive and choose the café. Situation resolved! Ha!" Delores answered. Tafoya chuckled.

Again, Tafoya walked to the window looking on the plaza. Shallow snow drifts on the northside of cottonwood trees lingered from the light snow three days before. "Most of the snow has melted," he said to Delores. "Wasn't much of a snow anyway."

Delores stopped her data entry and looked at Tafoya. "How's the museum case coming along? You seem nervous about it. Or, is something else bothering you, Richard?"

Tafoya turned away from the window. "The museum inventory should be over today. I've been going over the information we have so far. It's not much." Tafoya paused… "I know there must have been a connection with someone inside the museum."

"Any promising leads, Richard?"

"No, none at all. We've got to drill down further and that's going to take time…. But the thing is, Delores, this is just a museum theft. No blood was spilled, no one murdered. Maybe time to move on to other things…."

"That's probably the way to go, Richard. As you say, 'no blood spilled.'"

Suddenly, a loud radio dispatch squawked from the Taos County sheriff's department, "There's a house fire out near Arroyo Luz. Volunteer fire department in route."

Static came on, and Delores reached over and squelched the frequency and turned down the volume. Romero came down the hallway and said, "I'll take the house fire call. Tafoya, you stay here and continue the museum probe. If it's bad at Arroyo Luz, I'll call you."

Tafoya shrugged, "I'll be at my desk," he replied. As he started down the hall back to his desk, he stopped, turned around, and went back to Delores. "Oh, by the way, I'm going to contact Bessie Talbot over at the BLM to get her to pick up a different brand of coffee at Café Mundo in Espa for us. You think you can contribute to a station effort to get some roasted Sumatra for our office?"

"Oh, yes! Where's the contribution jar?" She reached down in her desk drawer, opened her purse, and pulled out five dollars. "Here, Tafoya, I'm all in for better coffee! I'll get a contribution jar and take charge of it." Tafoya gave her five dollars to go with her five. Better coffee was on its way.

23

Tafoya went back to his office and sat down. He opened up the case file again on the computer and began to speed-read the accession notes for the mask and cylinders. Then, he stopped and wondered how he had missed it.

"Scalps! There are no accession notes or numbers or even comments about scalps. Plus, a thief dumped the cylinders at McGinnis's with a note, 'The god roams the foothills for scalps of his enemies'!"

He lifted the landline phone from its cradle and called Museum Director Jennifer Hornbuckle. He had pen and yellow legal pad ready to take notes. The museum phone rang.

"Franklin Deerfield Museum, Adela Montoya speaking, how may I help you?" answering on the third ring.

Tafoya pictured Adela behind the desk in the outer office of Hornbuckle's suite at the museum. Tafoya wrote her name down on his legal pad and put an asterisk beside her name to interview later. This was the second time he felt compelled to talk to her. Working at the museum for twenty-five years, she knew about skeletons in the closet.

"I need to talk with Director Hornbuckle, Adela. This is Richard Tafoya, Tulona Tribal Police."

"Sure, Richard." She put her hand over the phone, muffling the sound. "Director, it's Tafoya on the phone. Can you take the call?" probably shouting through an open door to the director's office. Tafoya heard a faint, "Yes," over the phone.

Adela told him to hold and then rang through to the director's office. Hornbuckle came on line after one ring, her voice calm and measured. After an exchange of pleasantries, Tafoya came to the point of the call.

"Director, I was going over the accession records."

"Yes," she said. "What about them?"

"I'm interested as to why there has been no mention of the scalps? There's no accession record listed for them. What's going on with that?"

"Scalps?"

"Yes, scalps. Trophies taken in battle. The man wearing the masks carried two scalps as he emerged from the inventory basement and fled out the side door. Why has the museum not listed them as artifacts stolen from the collection?"

"Just a second, officer." Tafoya heard her put the phone down and shut the door. He heard her chair squeak as she sat down again.

"Sorry about that, Tafoya, I did not want Adela to hear what I had to say."

"Okay, director, what is it?" This is not going to be good, Tafoya thought.

Hornbuckle exhaled loudly. "Human remains and archaeological excavations are handled with great respect and care, officer..."

Tafoya interrupted. "I know that, director. I am Tulona. I know how our remains have been mishandled in the past by conquering armies, filibustering troops, private collectors, even museums," Tafoya replied, irritated at the didactic attitude of Hornbuckle. "Go on, director," he said, exasperated.

"Sorry, officer, no offense intended," she replied apologetically. "In the case of the two scalps taken, the accession records are neither online, nor publicly available. In fact, we have restricted subsets of records at our museum dealing with human remains of which, by the way, we have very few items."

Tafoya made no reply.

Hornbuckle continued, her voice slightly higher in tone, "We do not collect scalps, nor skeletal remains. Our policy has been to contact tribal authorities for them to take control of such material and bury them in a manner consistent with their ceremonies. If our archaeology crews come across human remains, we stop the dig and get in contact with local tribal authorities and proper state authorities."

Tafoya ignored her explanation, continuing on point, "How many items, in this secret subset of records, does the museum have?" Tafoya asked. He was busy scribbling notes.

"Currently, we have three items, the two scalps and a clavicle."

"Currently?" Tafoya exclaimed, thinking there may be a lot more going on than he had imagined.

"Yes, currently," Hornbuckle replied. "Over the history of our museum, we have had one hundred and twenty-seven items associated with human remains. All but three have been returned to tribes. Now, after the burglary, we only have one item that remains in our possession, and we are in contact with the Kiowa to return those remains.

"Franklin Deerfield, from the beginning of our history, has respected the human form and the dignity of tribal customs. We were working with Native American lineal descendants and Indian tribes long before the 1990 Native American Graves Protection and Repatriation Act. Franklin Deerfield Museum has an excellent record. We do get funds from the federal government and must comply with the Graves Protection Act." Hornbuckle paused, waiting for a response. She heard Tafoya sip his coffee.

She's giving me a lecture, he thought.

Tafoya spoke impatiently, "For the second time, why did you not list the scalps as stolen? That is the question I want you to answer, Director Hornbuckle."

He waited for her answer. She did not immediately respond.

24

On Thursday morning at her apartment, Janet opened up the Forest Service online page and saw the job description for the liaison officer with the Tulona tribal police: "Part-time liaison duties with the tribal police entails a weekly conferencing with the Tulona department and, when necessary, extended hours for investigative purposes. The Liaison Officer must come from full-time Forest Service personnel that have at least five-years full-time employment with the U.S. Forest Service Department or Bureau of Land Management."

She closed the Forest Service Employment Opportunity page and opened up the link to the Tulona tribal police page to employment opportunities and found a similar job description. Janet bookmarked the link to the online application. She would fill it out later. In her native Tiwa tongue, she said, "*Hą*! I say, *hą*!" The "*hą*" was an emphatic English, "Yes."

From a cultural perspective, personal affection, and business sense, Janet knew she would not say, "No."

"I will move in harmony with both the Forest Service and the tribal police."

Thursday was forecast to be cold and cloudy, so Janet dressed in warm clothing, including a quilted coat that came down below her hips, black watch cap, and 12-ounce cotton canvas work pants with cargo pockets. She pulled on a base layer to give her additional warmth.

Driving to the Forest Service headquarters in Ojo Verde, she thought about Tafoya and if she was the liaison officer, how often she would work alongside him? Since the tribal police department had fourteen employees, she might not see him as much as she wished. But she saw him socially; so, whether she worked with him in liaison operations or not, they would have time together. Despite all that, even if Tafoya was not in the picture, she liked investigative work.

At Janet's office, her supervisor outlined tasks for biologists that day: wildlife count along the forest roads near Angel Fire, particularly focusing on the movement of elk herds; assisting the Tres Piedras ranger district in counting wild horse remudas southward toward Petaca Mesa and Comanche Rim; and an assessment of grassland and vegetation on Tract A Tulona Trust Land along the Rio Grande. The supervisor had no volunteers for the tasks, so he began with Janet who sat at the table to his left.

"You look appropriately dressed for winds blowing across the Trust Land, Janet. Why don't you take that assignment and drive the roads on the mesa? I've already cleared our grassland assessment with the Tulona Council," her supervisor asked, but his intonation indicated, "Take this."

Mulling the "suggestion" over, Janet did not want to drive all the way to the Angel Fire area, navigating hairpin turns and construction vehicles on the two-lane U.S. 64 highway; and she wanted to avoid the Comanche Rim area that lay in the Tusas Ridge area where the Blue Lady Mine had been located. "I'll go back to Blue Lady later, just not today," she thought. She assented to the grassland assessment.

"Sure, sir, I'll take the Tract A assignment." Then, as an afterthought, Janet said, "I need to take the Suburban with the high clearance. I need it crossing arroyos."

Her supervisor consented to checking out the Suburban for her field survey with a cautionary note. "We had rain and light snow a few days ago. Be careful crossing muddy pools of standing water in those arroyos, Janet."

After the meeting, she briefed herself on departmental notices of Forest Road and trail closings. She checked out a field-grade laptop that fit in the Suburban's cradle, retrieved topographical maps from the map room, and departed for Tract A. The forecast was correct. Clouds aggregated overhead as far as she could see. The Jemez Mountains were obscured as was San Antonio Mountain near the Colorado border, and it appeared to be raining in the mountains above the 8,000-foot level. The rains dissipated below that altitude and did not threaten Tract A of the

Tulona Trust Land where she would do the assessment. The temperature was in the forties, but the brisk wind took the wind chill down into the thirties.

Janet filled up the dual gas tanks of the Forest Service vehicle. Whoever had the vehicle last had failed to top the tanks when they returned to the headquarters. Janet performed a walkaround of the Suburban. Tires were inflated properly and all lights were working. She was glad the vehicle had a winch in case she bogged down in an arroyo. All looked well in her "preflight" check, as she liked to call it. She threw her field bag in the back seat, fit the field laptop snuggly in its cradle, and drove out of the Forest Service compound. She looked across the street at the Taos County sheriff's office Ojo Verde substation—their main station being in Taos—and did not see Tulona tribal police vehicles. "Tafoya is probably at the pueblo or Franklin Deerfield," she surmised.

She turned north on Paseo del Pueblo Sur, drove past the plaza, and continued on Paseo del Norte. A "Vacancy" neon sigh blinked at the Ojo Verde Inn and Tablita's Restaurant. "Turning-of-the-aspens tourists have gone back to the cities," she thought. G. Armstrong Coe was opening up his bookshop, and she saw Fenster amble around the building to investigate the night's activities. She waved at Coe; he waved back and for some reason, flashed a power fist sign. Janet smiled and made the same sign in response.

Janet continued north on Paseo, past the Tulona pueblo, and caught a green light at the "Yellow Blinking Light" intersection. The old blinking light had been replaced twenty years before with an elaborate red-light intersection and crosswalks, but the locals had continued to call it the "Yellow Blinking Light" intersection, or some derivative of "blinking light." She continued northward on SH 522 for two miles, slowed down near Tract A and waited for logging trucks speeding south to pass by, their displacement of air buffeting her Suburban. Then she turned across the highway and stopped at the gate to Tract A Tulona Land Trust.

At the gate, warning signs were posted: "Tulona Tribal Reservation, Unauthorized Persons Not Permitted Entry, Violators Subject to Arrest and Fines Up to $20,000."

She turned the tumblers on the heavy-duty lock, unsnapped the lock from the chain, opened the gate, and drove through. She redialed the lock to other numbers when she shut the gate so it would fasten securely. "I wonder if the code is shared widely?" she thought. The fencing on both sides of the gate was taut—a six-strand barbed wire fence with t-posts and large stabilizing posts at frequent intervals down the fence line. Janet turned around, facing west toward the Tusas Mountains and the Big River. She sharply inhaled and held her breath at the immensity of beauty all around her.

25

Janet's view from the gate was wide and expansive, the clouds obscuring the tops of mountains still, but she saw the hazy outline of all the mountain ranges—the Taos Mountains to the south, the Jemez and Tusas to the west, and less clearly, the Pedernal in the far distance. Looking northward, San Antonio Peak continued to fade in and out of sight with shifting clouds and low fog, like a ship at sea. For three miles westward, the mesa gradually sloped down to the Rio Grande, a drop in altitude of two hundred feet from SH 522 to the canyon rim. Cold winds remained brisk from the west. She inhaled the scents of sagebrush and chamiso with pungent dollops of juniper—bracing and wild to her senses. Janet radioed the Forest Service base station that she was on Tract A pueblo land and would call back when she departed. When she set the microphone back on its hook, she felt a pang of hunger and found an energy bar in her field bag to eat.

Once Janet ate the energy bar, she opened up her laptop to the satellite map of her location. Tract A was wedged shaped. The base part of the wedge or triangle fronted SH 522, narrowing downward to the Rio Grande, a total acreage of 7,326 acres or approximately eleven sections. No outlier homes for the Tulona had been constructed on the tract.

By satellite map, she identified four roads crisscrossing Tract A. Most prominently, Janet saw a wide arroyo, angling and meandering from SH 522 to a sloping drop-off into the Big River. Other arroyos, narrower in width, eroded the terrain. Janet decided to travel the dirt roads beginning with the southernmost roads, crisscrossing Tract A until she intersected the wide arroyo. Janet fetched her topographical map from her field bag to identify by name the wide arroyo and its water flow during heavy rains. With her forefinger, Janet traced the name on the topo map: it was called, "Arroyo de Conchas," translated "Arroyo of Shells."

Janet puzzled over the name of Arroyo of Shells. "Mysterious name for a semi-arid desert grassland segment," she thought to herself, rolling up her map.

She drove carefully onto Tract A. The banks of the arroyos no longer reflected abundant green grasses. Since the nineteenth century, "true" native grass had diminished significantly. Human grasp, domestic and native animal grazing, and fire altered the habitat. Drought took its toll. Two species of grasses were especially diminished: the black grama and bush muhly. Janet, in her field observations of shrubby mesa zones, always looked for rare species of true native grasses like the black grama. She never saw the grama, although she had read historic reports of its abundance. Farther east, over the Cristo cordillera, on plains approaching the Rockies, travelers in the nineteenth century reported grama grasses "as high as a horse's belly."

"I would have liked to have seen that, especially the gramma waving with the wind," she had thought when she first read J. R. Bartlett's personal narrative of 1854, as he surveyed the U.S.-Mexico boundary in 1850. At a botany workshop for Forest Service specialists, she had learned there were 125 genera and 435 species of grasses in New Mexico.

Despite Bartlett's narrative and the botany workshop, Janet was *now* traversing a plains-mesa grassland on Tract A; if she had surveyed grasses up toward the Cristo, Janet would have been in the mountain grasslands at 8,000 feet or more. To Janet, it made no difference; she was outdoors in the wild under cloudy skies with a cold wind from the west.

"No better place to be." She meant it.

Though she liked plains-mesa grassland, Janet preferred the montane zone, like the Rio Santa Barbara above Peñasco, flourishing with green dales and conifers. But her task today was to view Tract A, despite its aridity. Besides, the vistas all around were incomprehensibly beautiful. Tract A varied in elevation from 7,200 to 6,900 feet, the sloping mesa ending abruptly with steep drop-offs to the Big River. Though Janet saw the Cristo Mountains to the east and north with its ponderosas and firs, she was working that day in a desert-like, shrubby environment, the sagebrush and chamiso predominant, along with juniper and cottonwood bosques along arroyos.

As the morning progressed, clouds endured with cold wind chill. Driving the Suburban along the dirt roads on Tract A, Janet charted the landscape, stopping intermittently to write field notes. Predominantly, sagebrush grew. Its leaves were lime-green with gray-black woody trunks that had weathered the seasons. After a rain, the leaves were vibrantly green, the woody trunks blacker. She noticed black fire stumps from years, decades ago. Janet carefully crossed arroyos, avoiding the muddy places, as per her supervisor's advice.

On northern slopes of the mesa, snow lay in the shade. Gambel quail and jack rabbits were the only wildlife she identified; small, darting birds flew out of the brush, never rising more than five feet from the surface as they found shelter in other brush. Janet made a note to consult her Peterson for bird typing when she was back at headquarters. She crisscrossed the southern part of Tract A, driving on rougher roads. Sun shone through breaks in the clouds, but toward the middle of the afternoon, clouds thickened and the sun retired from spotlighting patches of shrubby landscape.

Janet stopped her vehicle at the rim of the canyon overlooking the river. The Rio Grande lay five hundred feet below the rim, flowing from her right to her left, north to south. Not the longest river in North America, but it was "*grande*," nonetheless, flowing from the Conejos in Colorado to the Gulf of Mexico in extreme south Texas. She looked across the canyon to the mesas, stretching toward the Tusas Mountains and the Jemez. Clouds had lowered so that tops of the mountains were obscured; haze blurred their edges. Janet unholstered her smart phone and took pictures of the river below, the mesas extending to the Tusas. Janet absorbed all she saw, stunned at the sheer power of the earth at this place. The cold wind chilled her face, checking her reverie of the Big River and mesas. Time to turn back to the road and find the big arroyo, write her notes, and drive back to the gate on SH 522.

Janet drove through shrubby habitats. She stopped at the crossing on the Arroyo of Shells. Janet disembarked from her Suburban and walked across the road that dipped down onto the arroyo stream bed; it tested solid. Satisfied, she drove the Suburban across the stream bed; the four-wheel drive gripped sand and rock, safely crossing the arroyo.

Ascending the steep arroyo bank, Janet gained level ground, stopped, and looked around. Alongside the north bank of the arroyo she noticed grassy vegetation, tinged green, in an area about the size of a small backyard in town. Junipers grew on either side of the patch, and a small cottonwood bosque flourished downstream, a hundred yards away from the green patch. Setting her vehicle in park, she alighted from the Suburban and walked over to the vegetation.

Various grasses had grown in the sheltered patch. Janet noted some clumps of black grama grasses growing healthily, having for some reason evaded fire and overgrazing over the years. She quickly noted in her field journal the GPS coordinates for the patch. She took photographs with her smart phone. "This will impress botanists at headquarters, for sure!"

Recording all that was necessary, Janet decided to follow the Arroyo of Shells side bank down to the cottonwood bosque, perhaps discovering other grassy surprises. As she came closer to the bosque, she saw fresh tire tracks, perhaps two-days old. Debris had drifted into the tracks. The tire tracks had cut a path to the bosque and stopped. She walked closer to the bosque.

Then, Janet stopped dead in her tracks. Above her, emerging from level ground above the bosque's side bank, an architectural structure took shape. She walked up the bank to get a closer look. The structure was prehistoric. The stones appeared to have been quarried from the basalt cliffs overlooking the Rio Grande.

The structure was circular. "This is a kiva," she said aloud. Janet then noticed other stones jutting up from the ground, appearing to be rectangular edges of ancient walls. But the kiva was the most prominent.

Janet took photographs of the kiva, noting that digging had been done within the circle of basalt walls. Were those diggings test plots of archaeologists or pothunters? Tract A was Trust Land of the Tulona, and the Tulona Council tightly controlled and regulated any archaeological digging. "Do they know about this digging?" She knew of no archaeological surveys or excavations currently taking place. In fact, there had been none for years. Pothunters? Not likely, risking imprisonment and a $20,000 fine.

Upon closer examination, Janet concluded the digging as

reconstructive, not destructive. In her field report to the Forest Service, she would send a copy to the Tulona Council and advise a follow-up visit and periodic inspection of the site along the Arroyo of Shells. Another task for Tulona warchiefs; they would not be thrilled. Looking at the black grama patch of grass one more time, she climbed in her vehicle and headed for the exit gate on SH 522.

At the kiva, Janet had not seen the fresh sign of human activity a few yards away toward the Big River. Obscured from Janet's view were vigas, freshly cut and carried from the Columbine-Hondo forests. Three men had cut the timber without a permit to harvest National Forest wood. They had cut vigas, unlawfully, for a kiva roof. Their goal was to construct a roof and have it finished by All Souls' Day or Day of the Dead, the second of November. On the Day of the Dead, a kiva, the Hanging Shell Kiva, would rise from the past, no longer dead. Three Tulona puebloans were determined to revitalize what was ancient history to present time.

26

"But the scalps, why did you not list them on the sheet of missing items, director?" Tafoya had asked Hornbuckle, for a second time.

Over the phone, Hornbuckle paused, exhaling loudly. Tafoya could tell she was nervous, but Hornbuckle pulled herself together and answered.

"Those scalps were part of a personal collection we were originally given by Franklin Deerfield, our founder, after his death. Where he acquired them, he never left a record. We will never know the provenance of the material. When he died in 1981, it took us several months to integrate his private collection into the museum. The scalps were in a wooden box with Indigenous symbols painted on the outside. The thieves left the box behind; they took the scalps." Hornbuckle stopped talking.

"You still have not answered my question, director," Tafoya pushed. "Why were the scalps left off the museum's accession list?" He waited for her answer.

Hornbuckle, after a long pause, finally admitted, "The director at the time of Franklin Deerfield's death put the scalps on a secret accession list. It was my idea to continue to leave them off the public accession list when I became director," Hornbuckle said, in a confessional tone. "Possessing the scalps would have reflected badly on the museum. The publicity that, 'Franklin Deerfield Museum has scalps originally owned by white benefactor,' would damage our reputation, perhaps even result in losing our lease with the Tulona."

Tafoya said nothing in response to Hornbuckle for a few seconds; then he recovered. "I think you underestimate the tolerance we Tulona have for the Anglo community-at-large, and what Franklin Deerfield has done to protect our Tulona heritage. So far as I know, the museum never exhibited the scalps, did they?"

"Heavens no, officer! We kept those on the secret list of accessions. The Museum never exhibited them." Hornbuckle began to plead. "Can you keep this scalp business out of the newspapers, Mr. Tafoya? I really don't want this to get out and offend anyone, especially Native American communities. I hope we can keep this part of the robbery discreet and out of the papers. Please."

Tafoya agreed to do his best to keep scalps out of the news. He ended the conversation quickly and hung up the phone, disgusted with the interchange.

27

Monday, October 22, Day of Saint John Paul II, Month of Leaves Falling Moon

Monday morning was starting off with good, strong coffee. After making a fresh pot of Sumatra Roast coffee purchased from Café Mundo in Espa, Tafoya poured a cup. Delores had purchased the coffee on her way back from a shopping trip in Santa Fe on Saturday. With coffee in hand, he walked back to his desk to go over the details of the Franklin Deerfield case.

Issues of the theft remained and Tafoya was ready to put the museum case on the backburner if no movement was achieved quickly. He sat down at his desk and began to go over the details of the case. The mysterious return of the red and black cylinders nagged at him.

"Why return the cylinders? Maybe there's another angle for the heist? Someone remorseful? Internal squabbling among the thieves?" The phone call with Hornbuckle about the scalps had occurred several days earlier, and it was now Monday morning and time to move to other elements of the case.

The inventory, ending last Thursday, had uncovered several additional items missing from the museum's collection. The full list included the Child of Water mask, a medicine bundle wrapped in reeds and secured with belts of shells, and, of course, the two scalps. The two wooden cylinders associated with Navajo ritual had been returned, along with the strange message, "The god roams the foothills for scalps of his enemies." Navajo medicine man, Santiago Majerus, had confirmed the ominous correlation with the Child of Water mask.

"Are the Tulona facing a future killing?" Tafoya thought, fearfully.

Despite the message, no blood had been spilled, so Tafoya wondered if he was spending too much time on the case. What kept him focused on the case was the most likely involvement of museum employees or administration in the theft. If the thieves could not be apprehended, what might keep them from stealing in the future, using inside help? The next time, Tulona artifacts might be stolen. Jewelry perhaps?

Tafoya leaned back in his chair. "Let's look deeper into the medicine bundle," he thought. He opened up the file on the medicine bundle; an accession form was attached. He opened the .pdf file. One photograph was attached. He read carefully the accession notes.

1) ID: Number (BLM) Not applicable
2) Accession/Cat. ID Franklin Deerfield 1950-3789-55
3) Depository: Franklin Deerfield Museum; Ojo Verde, New Mexico
4) Description of Artifact, Cultural Data, Narrative: Medicine bundle, 2.5 feet long, 15 inches circumference, 12 lbs. approximate weight. Marsh reeds encircling contents. Dried buckskin wrapping of contents. Artifacts within dried buckskin: two stone Corn Mothers, two turquoise necklaces, dried corn cobs with kernels loose (blue, yellow, white), colored and folded wooden "world straightener," retablo of rainbow, retablo of bird figures (eagle, magpie, chokecherry bird). Belted shells encompassing reed bundle: 24 shells sewn on leather belt. See one appended b/w photograph. **Cultural Data:** Bundle is medicine bundle of shaman or cacique, most likely associated with kiva ritual. World straightener is puebloan as are bird figures, stone effigies, and retablos. Further pueblo typing is uncertain, but most likely Eastern Pueblo. Turquoise has been typed as Chaco (n.d.). Shells are freshwater, possibly Rio Grande.
Narrative: Original provenance of bundle is unknown. Bundle was in possession of Tulona resident and given to Franklin Deerfield Museum in 1950. Leroy Walhuime was the donor. Mr. Walhuime died in 2001. Mr. Walhuime stated that the bundle had been in the possession of his family "for as long as I can remember" and was never used in any Tulona ceremonies. (Recorder, Robert Ellis, 12/15/1950; updated 2010 by John McGinnis.) Form ADO-6231-4

Tafoya ran off a copy of the PDF file. With a pen, he encircled in red ink the words: world straightener, Leroy Walhuime, and John McGinnis. "What is a world straightener?" he pondered. He made a note on his legal pad to talk to the descendants of the Leroy Walhuime family. "Maybe they have more information of the bundle than what Leroy gave Robert Ellis, the original recorder?" He also jotted a note to ask McGinnis about the updating in 2010. "Why did McGinnis feel necessary to update the accession material?"

Setting aside the focus on McGinnis, Tafoya drew up a list of questions not connected with McGinnis. A major question had always lurked about in the case: "Who blanked out the thirty-six minutes of security video? Or, was the blanking out of the security video a glitch in the system? Did the thieves have the bundle *and* god mask in mind to steal, or was it opportunistic? Why were the wooden cylinders returned to McGinnis? Who broke into his house to return them? Why steal artifacts in the first place?"

"We need more people on this case!" Tafoya said aloud, slamming his pencil down on the desk, breaking the sharp point.

As he reached over to sharpen the pencil, Tafoya heard the main phone ring in the stationhouse. He heard sergeant Romero pick up the phone. Romero's voice rose in pitch. Tafoya did not understand what Romero said. Tafoya quickly stood up from his desk and walked to the front of the stationhouse to see what the call was about.

Delores looked grim as Tafoya walked in the front office. She shook her head, grimaced.

"There's been a body found, Tafoya," Romero said, as he put down the phone.

"Where, who?" Tafoya asked.

"Quintana Pass, south of Valle Escondido, off of U.S. 64, headed to Angel Fire."

"Why were we called, Romero, that's off pueblo land, it's even outside the Red Willow people's reservation?"

"Taos County sheriff's department is at the scene. The male's driver's license says he is Lance Bernal, Blue Sky Deer, your Tulona kiva brother. So, we are in this, whether Taos County likes it or not."

28

Lance Bernal lay on his back, splayed like an "X," twenty-five yards off the rutted Quintana Pass dirt road, toward the aspen grove, spruces, and fir trees, 9,600 feet high in Carson National Forest. The aspens had shed their leaves in conjunction with early morning frosts in the high altitude. The Quintana Pass dirt road rose higher to the east, eventually climbing to a ridgeline, then downward into Colfax County and the Mora Land Grant. The dirt road followed a middle route into the Quintana Canyon, switch backing downward on the other side of the ridgeline. Quintana Pass was one of several passes in the area that crossed over the eastern ridgeline of the Sangre de Cristo.

Four young men from Taos, riding in a Jeep Wrangler with high clearance, had found Lance Bernal. They had intended to take the Quintana Pass Road into the forest, but had seen the body at a distance and stopped their Jeep to investigate. The driver of the Wrangler and one other man had driven back to U.S. 64 to catch a cell tower signal, calling 911 who quickly dispatched the Taos County sheriff's department to Quintana Pass. Authorities from Angel Fire had also been called. The young men's day expedition ended abruptly; they had no further desire to explore.

Sergeant Romero and Officer Tafoya arrived in less than an hour after the sheriff's department informed them of the Bernal's identity. Driving on U.S. 64 with the flash bar activated made only a slight difference in speed since the road was narrow and few turnouts had been constructed for slower traffic. Tafoya drove, his hands firmly clutching the steering wheel.

"U.S. 64 is dicey, but since I drove a Humvee in Afghanistan, this is a walk in the park," Tafoya remarked as he passed a dump truck on a wide road in Shady Brook, a small village east of FR 437 that intersected Quintana Pass.

GPS coordinates on their field laptop cradled in the tribal police vehicle directed Tafoya and Romero to turn south off U.S. 64 onto FR 437, then FR 438 until it intersected the Quintana Pass Road. Immediately, they saw the assembly of patrol cars from the sheriff's department, Angel Fire police, an ambulance from Taos, five U.S. Forest Service vehicles, and two New Mexico State Highway Trooper cars. Tafoya and Romero pulled to a stop next to a Forest Service Suburban. Tafoya thought of Janet. A hundred yards away, they drudged to the tent shading Lance Bernal and investigators.

The discovery had been made two hours earlier. The forensic team of the Taos County sheriff's department had already begun to process the scene: photographs taken, situational maps drawn, GPS coordinates registered, and hypotheses advanced. The medical examiner, Eli Rosenbaum, had arrived earlier. He had taken liver temperature, but had not moved the body. Rosenbaum, knowing the identity of Lance Bernal, and being informed Tulona tribal police were on the way, deferred to move the body until Bernal's tribal brothers arrived. Tafoya and Romero stepped inside the tent covering Bernal from the elements.

"I am sorry, Richard...Tony," Rosenbaum said, placing his thin, long doctor's hands on each of their shoulders. "Deputy sheriff Cordova told us that the deceased, I mean Lance, was a kiva brother. I will use all my powers to determine what went on here. It doesn't look good at first glance. Cordova, you can tell them what you theorize happened here."

Cordova sighed and began to explain. "Lance was shot. Shot twice. Entry wound on the front left side, heart level. Powder burns indicate close range. There is an *exit* wound also on the front of Lance. We don't know for sure if there are powder burns on his back until Eli turns the body over. He bled out here...died here."

"What was the time of death, Eli?" Romero asked.

"In the afternoon, between three and nine in the evening yesterday, I estimate. Lance was here overnight. Fortunately, no scavenging by animals. There are unusual cuts and tears on the right side of the cranium."

"The god roams the foothills for scalps of his enemies,"Tafoya said to Romero, in a sidelong look at his sergeant. Romero's face blanched white.

"Ambient temperature in the afternoon," Rosenbaum continued, “never rose above forty-five degrees yesterday, and there was a hard frost last night. Angel Fire registered twenty-five degrees. It was probably colder up here in the mountains. Since you two are here, we can turn the body over.”

Rosenbaum and Tafoya turned the body over. The entry wound on the back had no powder burns. “Shot at a distance,” Tafoya said. “Then the murderer came up and finished his nasty business.”

After the Taos County ambulance service removed the body to the morgue in Taos, the forensic team began to dig into the ground underneath where the body had lain, searching for the bullet they presumed had passed through Lance’s body. They unearthed a slug three-inches in the ground. Although the slug was slightly damaged, it was concluded to be a high-caliber type, perhaps from a deer rifle. Further lab work might reveal the precise caliber. Both bullets had passed through Lance and had not ricocheted within the cavity. One bullet went into the ground, the other bullet passed through Lance, and it had not been recovered.

“How far have you searched toward the tree line and back down on Quintana Pass Road, Cordova?” Tafoya inquired of the sheriff’s deputy.

Cordova replied they had searched for a quarter mile in each direction from where the body had lain. No trace of a recent camp had been found nor off-road tire tracks. The tire tracks on FR 438 and the Quintana Pass Road were inconsequential, but they had taken photographs and casts nonetheless. There were no tire tracks from the road into the meadow where Lance had fallen.

The wind picked up, beginning to upslope to higher altitudes for the day, swaying the aspen trees whose slender white trunks waved like a choir of arms emerging from the earth. Though the upsloping wind was warm, the air settled cold when the wind died. Clouds moved rapidly over Lance Bernal’s death scene and on toward Black Lake on the leeside of the Sangre de Cristo and then onto the plains of eastern New Mexico.

Tafoya turned and faced the upsloping wind from the west. Only yesterday afternoon, he thought, Lance Bernal had been alive, breathing, inhaling mountain scents, the fresh sharp air of higher altitudes. “Why was he here? So far from our pueblo?” Tafoya was silent, staring into distance. Then, squaring his jaw, he said, “I need answers.”

Tafoya turned to face Romero and deputy sheriff Cordova. "I'm going to walk from this spot where Lance was killed and track in the direction of the forest. There is probably nothing there, but I'm going to do it anyway." One last time, Tafoya looked at where Blue Sky Deer had lain on the ground and noticed aspen leaves, red and yellow, had blown onto the scene, covering the ground, obliterating the Bernal's bloody spot.

To the trees, Tafoya walked. The forest floor was soft from conifer needles and leaves from The Month of Leaves Falling Moon. The forest, forever a part of Tulona life, attended the people to Earth Cloud Lake, the forest holding sacred places all around. "Was Blue Sky Deer on a sacred visit?" Tafoya thought. The wind soughed. Below in the Fourth World, Old Ones emerged to find another world and they found the earth soft and the Old Ones returned to lead the people and animals to the Fifth World. The earth was soft in the Fifth World yes but Tafoya believed and he had told Bustamente that the Old Ones found the earth soft but it was the soughing of the wind in the trees that the Old Ones heard in the midst of a clear meadow with sun shining, the air cold and crisp, holding moans of sound in the trees, the soughing bringing them upward. The Old Ones went back to the Fourth World and brought people and animals and birds and fish to the Fifth World because of wind soughing through trees, the meadow clean, the sun warm, and the earth soft. "Was Blue Sky Deer on a sacred visit?" Yes, Blue Sky Deer, all of us, are on a sacred visit in nature and the visit has no beginning and no end, endless, infinite. To the trees Tafoya walked, believing the soughing of trees, the wind, were sounds the Old Ones heard leading them to the Fifth World.

Tulona tribal policeman sergeant Romero saw Tafoya disappear into the woods. The high altitude shortened Romero's breath, but he trotted to the trees to accompany Tafoya and make it less lonely for his friend, and, pragmatically, four eyes looking for clues were better than two.

"Wait up, Richard," he shouted as he reached the edge of the tree line.

Tafoya heard him, stopped, and waved him up alongside. The two tribal policemen, adept in tracking, keenly observant of broken twigs, and crushed leaves found nothing related to the crime. Windfall timber littered the ground. They scared up two grouse. They came across shed elk and deer antlers and evidence of cougar scratches on trees, some as high as six feet.

"When we are off-duty, we need to come back up here and harvest antlers, Richard," Romero said. "They make good knife handles."

After hiking back in the forest for a quarter mile, they turned around and walked back downhill toward the vehicles. They paused at the tree line before they reentered the meadow. The sun was high, the wind blew hard, and the cumulus clouds continued to race across the cordillera, skipping like children going home after school. The world seemed sharper, harsher, clearer at 9,800 feet.

At the tree line, to get a broader perspective, Tafoya and Romero separated, fifty yards from each other. They stood still and looked at the meadow. The tent that covered the body had been struck, affording a better view. Tafoya squatted down and looked into the meadow, trying to catch anything out of place, strange, an item dropped, grass flattened.

Nothing.

No answers in sight—for the moment. Nodding to one another, they descended to their patrol car and departed Quintana Pass. They said nothing to one another. Romero drove U.S. 64, the narrow single-laned highway, back to Ojo Verde.

The traffic became lighter. Tafoya turned in his seat, facing Romero, "Tony, all we have is the body and a crime scene. We don't know where Blue Sky Deer came from. He could've come from out of the forest and been shot; he could have been walking or running away; he could have come from the high pass from Angel Fire. We know next to nothing." Tafoya paused, "But that's the way it is in the beginning of any investigation."

Romero looked ahead, saying nothing. Tafoya continued, "Was Bernal shot intentionally? Was it an accident? Of course, it wasn't! Otherwise, the shooter would have gone for help or quenched the wound, not given the kill shot.... We don't have much to go on, but we have to go on what we have." Tafoya twisted in his seat, then turned back, facing Romero. "Why was he so far away from the pueblo? What is it? Fifty miles from here? It's not deer season either. Poaching? And there is not a vehicle associated with Bernal.... He didn't just fly out here." Tafoya sat back, disgusted.

Romero let Tafoya run out of speed in his speculations. Then,

Romero said, "We have to go back to the pueblo and start running down information. I've already given the order to station a patrol car at his house on the edge of the reservation until we get there and talk to the wife. We'll interview his friends...find out his movements the last couple of days. Like, who has he been hanging out with lately?"

A pickup and stock trailer full of sheep slowed them down. Romero passed them on a straightaway, prompting Tafoya, "Didn't Lance hire out as a sheepherder one time? This area is well-used territory for grazing in the summer. Let's try and find out if Lance herded sheep last season, and who has grazing permits up here at Quintana Canyon. Maybe that'll give us a lead."

The radio came on, "Dispatch to any available unit. Car accident at Talpa and highway sixty-eight intersection. Who can take the call?" A state trooper responded he was nearby and would take the call. Taos County deputy Chris Cordova came on the radio, stating he was also enroute.

"That's not for us today, Tony," Tafoya said. "We have a murder. Our kiva brother has been shot!" Romero sped up to get back to the reservation. Tafoya reached over to the dashboard and aggressively flipped the flash bar switch to clear the traffic and get back fast to the pueblo.

Tafoya pushed his reasoning for answers, but there were none...for now. He brooded, "The god roams the foothills for scalps of his enemies."

29

Tuesday, October 23, Day of Saint John of Capistrano, Month of Leaves Falling Moon

For bookseller G. Armstrong Coe, Tuesday had been good for sales. Although the tourist trade had begun to slacken because high-country aspen trees had lost most of their yellow and red leaves, many out-of-towners had decided to extend their vacation in Ojo Verde and shop for books and enjoy local cuisine for a few more days.

He sold six books to a researcher from the University of Arizona who had found several out-of-print books on the New Mexican and Pueblo insurrection of 1847, Kit Carson, and U.S. Army occupation in the Taos area, 1847-1852. Two separate customers bought R. C. Gorman's coffee-table books, one of them also purchasing a biography of Georgia O'Keeffe.

Toward the end of the afternoon, Coe took Mabel Dodge Luhan's *Winter in Taos* off the shelf behind the counter, deciding to take it home and put her memoir in his and Prissy's personal library. The signed book, along with an inserted note and stem of sage from Mabel, was a treasure he had decided to keep. He had acquired the book in an estate sale in Taos. The estate managers failed to notice the book's contents, and when he called their attention to the note and sage, they merely raised the price by twenty dollars, so he bought it. Feeling guilty for buying it so cheaply, Coe had called the descendants of the estate, but they had a bad opinion of Mabel and were not interested in keeping anything related to her. That was the end of that.

"I was fated to keep you, Mabel," he chuckled, as he put *Winter in Taos* snugly in his briefcase to go home.

Sales had been good during the day, but had slacken off around four o'clock, so Coe decided to close shop early and stop by Tablita's for a drink before heading home. Jason Taylor, his favorite waiter, would be on duty and Coe could order an appetizer and drink before heading home to Prissy. Since the day had been good in sales, he would give a good tip, helping supplement Jason's bankroll for the ski season. Scratching Fenster behind the ears and checking on her kibbles and water for the night, he closed shop and walked down Paseo del Norte, crossed in the pedestrian lane—the eighteen-wheelers with Ponderosa logs stopped for him—and entered Tablita's.

Jason saw him and waved him over to his preferred table overlooking Paseo del Norte traffic. As Coe sat down, he saw two of his customers that had purchased books. He acknowledged them and nodded to the rest of the patrons in the dining room—a French-custom of café behavior he had learned while in Cherbourg with the U.S. military.

"Prissy joining you?" Jason said, as he brought a glass of water and set down a paper cocktail coaster.

"No, I texted her and she's in for the day. I'm just here for a glass of wine, chips and salsa, Jason. I'll join her later for dinner."

"Say, 'Hello,' to her, Coe, won't you?"

"I will, Jason." Coe looked at the wine side of the menu, but already knew what he wanted.

Looking at Tablita's wine list was merely perfunctory, nothing more.

"You want the lizard, Coe?" Jason smiled, already knowing the answer.

"You know me well, Jason. Yes…the lizard."

The lizard was the brand icon on the bottle of Alzania's Gardacho, a red wine from the Navarra area of Spain. Gardacho had been so named from the lizards that climbed around on the trellises in the vineyard. It was a dry, bold red. Ojo Verde Inn, the home of Tablita's Restaurant, made sure Spanish wines were always on the list. It fit well with the image the inn wished to advertise, a blend of the Old World with frontier-northern New Mexico.

Jason brought a sparkling, non-stained, wine glass to Coe's table along with the bottle of Gardacho, the "lizard," and poured a glass directly from the bottle, adding a tipple over four ounces, the customary pour. Another server brought chips and salsa.

Coe performed the requisite protocol for tasting the wine: twirling, looking, sniffing, tasting carefully, including the finish, and then a nod of approval. Jason had already walked away to serve another table, knowing Coe would call him back if the Gardacho had turned "plonky lizard."

Of course, the "lizard" was healthy and running over vineyard trellises. No plonky slow lizards.

Suddenly the wind buffeted the windows looking out over Paseo del Norte. Large raindrops splattered the panes. Coe had not been paying attention to the weather with all the bookshop business of the day. The wind shifted to the east and rain fell from the directions of the Tulona Mountains.

Coe looked out the window onto Paseo del Norte and saw the rain shower darken the late afternoon, turning the street to a darkened, shiny, gray-slate slab. He smelled fresh rain even from inside, as the rear of the dining room faced an overhanging porch where one of Tablita's windows opened to a patio bordered in blossom-less hollyhocks. A cold breeze moved through the dining area.

"Nothing better than this," Coe said, as he sipped his wine, "except I wish Prissy was here." Jason closed the window.

The two-lane road in front of the restaurant bore heavy traffic: SUVs, eighteen-wheelers, logging trucks, old pickups, new pickups, and even Volkswagen vans from the seventies. The rain was moderate, neither light nor heavy in gray-white sheets. Coe realized he would have to make a run for the parking lot next to his bookshop to get his car.

Finishing his lizard, he tipped Jason twenty-five percent and ran across the street in the rain and back to the parking lot near his bookshop. He had left his briefcase in his car with *Winter in Taos.* He glanced at the front door of his bookshop and saw two blanketed men standing at the door, one of them shading his eyes, trying to see if anyone was inside. The man tried the door and it was locked. Coe recognized him. It was Bustamente, the cacique of the Tulona Pueblo. Coe looked at his wristwatch—five o'clock. He did not recognize the second man.

"What was Bustamente doing here now?"

Coe hollered at Bustamente, "Bustamente, wait a minute. It's me, Coe." Bustamente turned and saw him, smiled, and waved.

Coe had met Bustamente several weeks ago at the pueblo when Lion Walks Night had been in the bookshop and heard a prank call by Tulona adolescents to Coe. Lion and Coe had gone out to the pueblo to resolve the issue amicably. The adolescents had apologized to Coe, and he had made friends with Bustamente.

"I'm closed, but I'll open it up for you, Mr. Bustamente," Coe shouted as he darted under the shop's porch to get out of the rain.

"Thank you, Mr. Coe." The cacique turned around, facing Paseo del Norte where the rain continued to fall. He looked up at the tall cottonwoods along the paseo whose limbs swayed with the east wind. He pulled his thin, brown-striped blanket tight around him.

"Nice rain, Mr. Coe."

Coe locked the door behind the three of them. Fenster had taken a resting spot on the front counter, looking inquisitively at Coe's return and the two Tulona. She did not move.

Bustamente introduced his companion, "Ben Lovato Medicine Wind." Coe thought it late for Bustamente to be cavorting in town, but that was none of his business. Bustamente glanced around the shop and looked at the main display table in the middle of the room, focusing on a Bert Geer Phillips art book. "My cousin down at Taos Pueblo posed for some of his paintings," Bustamente said.

Knowing that Phillips was one of the earliest Anglo artists in Taos and had been dead over fifty years, Coe wondered if the, "cousin down at Taos," was still alive. Probably not, and this did not seem the time to ask Bustamente. Medicine Wind saw a section on natural history and field books. He went over and pulled a Peterson field guide of medicinal plants and herbs off the shelf, thumbing through the book carefully, then looking at the price on the back of the book: twenty-two dollars.

"I have an old Peterson book on western birds, but I've never seen one on medicine plants," Medicine Wind remarked. "When I sell my next buffalo-horn knife, I'll come back and buy this." Coe replied that he would put the copy of Peterson's medicinal plants behind the counter and save it for him.

Coe leaned up against the front counter and waited for Bustamente to speak. Bustamente nodded his head in approval of Coe's Bookshop and closed the Phillips art book. Medicine Wind stood at the side of Bustamente, paying attention to whatever the cacique had to say. No one spoke for a moment; Fenster focused on Bustamente, her tail flicking lazily.

"I have seen your bookshop here in Ojo Verde for many years" Bustamente began. "And I have talked with you about the young men that played a joke on you, and you forgave them of their teenage ways." Coe nodded, smiled.

Bustamente continued, "The Tulona who know you in the shop business speak highly and respect you. At the Saint Francis Festival a few weeks ago, I saw you talk with the Hopi, Dan Sinquah, as our Black Eyes climbed the pole."

Coe flinched. How did Bustamente know that? he thought to himself. And why is that important now?

Bustamente went on, "Dan Sinquah is a friend of mine and after the festival was over, he talked with me, and said he had asked you a question. 'Who is going to win in the end, the machine or nature?' And you replied, Sinquah told me, 'The machine in the short run, but in the long run, nature will win out.' Was that your answer, Mr. Coe?"

"Yes, that was my answer. I may have added something like we have cell phone service on the plaza during the festival that contact banks and sell goods during the festival, and that there are airplane contrails in the sky over us. This shows the machine is powerful. But, in the end, nature will win, despite cell phones and planes in the air." Coe wondered what sort of test he was being given?

Bustamente nodded in approval. Medicine Wind, not moving, stared off to the side of Coe.

"We come today to see you about something very important to the harmony of the Tulona Pueblo. You are on the Board of Trustees of the Franklin Deerfield Museum, are you not?"

Coe nodded his head, "Yes."

"Medicine Wind has been observing the inventory of the collection at Franklin Deerfield and knows what has been stolen and what has been returned by persons unknown."

"The cylinders?" Coe said.

"Yes, two wooden cylinders that represent thunderbolts in Navajo thinking," Medicine Wind interjected.

Bustamente went on, "What has been returned is not my, nor the Tulona Pueblo people's, concern. What *is* disturbing me is the theft of a medicine bundle I think is associated with the Tulona, and a dead kiva society that had a bad effect on us many years ago. That bundle of ritual objects may be related to the Hanging Shell kiva, a people that we Tulona confronted long ago."

Coe wondered in what capacity he was being approached: bookshop owner? Board of Trustee member? He knew the Tulona settled their affairs mainly within the pueblo government, a sovereign government. This talk with the cacique was eerily different, unsettling.

Coe concluded that he must go slow, cooperate, and try, if he could, understand.

"How can I be of help to you and the pueblo, Mr. Bustamente?" Coe responded.

Bustamente remained silent. He looked outside at the rain falling more heavily, the headlights and taillights of vehicles shining bright through the gray sheets of rain. Medicine Wind smiled at Coe. Bustamente turned back around to Coe who waited for the cacique's answer.

"The whole world needs help. Not just the Tulona, Mr. Coe," Bustamente replied, gravely.

Coe took a deep breath. He wondered if the "whole world needing help" was related to the museum heist, or climate change, or something else?

"Our tribal policemen, Tafoya and Romero, are investigating the theft of the medicine bundle. We Tulona hope you as a trustee will encourage Director Hornbuckle and the museum to cooperate fully..."

"Of course," Coe quickly replied, overlapping Bustamente's words.

Bustamente continued, "I understand from Lion Walks Night, who comes in here regularly to buy books, that you have a large section of books that you keep behind the purple curtain." He pointed with his chin at the purple curtain at the back of the room. "The books are pueblo books about tales, anthropology, old stories, archaeology. Lion tells me that you are very guarded about who you sell those books to, much less let anyone browse through them." Bustamente paused.

Coe spoke, "Lion is correct. I don't let people go back there without me being present. I sell them to scholars and people I know who are not going to misuse or twist the printed word. I sell maybe one or two of those books a year. Usually by mail to university libraries that place them in special collections. Would you like to see the collection?" Coe asked.

"That isn't necessary, Mr. Coe. Perhaps one day when I have more time, I will. What I am asking you to do for the Tulona is to go through your books behind the purple curtain and find any information on Hanging Shell, or Shell people, associated with the Tulona or nearby pueblos. And, if you do find anything, share that knowledge with me and Medicine Wind. I have knowledge of Hanging Shell from oral stories, handed down from generation to generation. We don't write them down. We Tulona keep them alive in our telling, our ceremonies. But, if someone has informed the *fansaine* or the iron people about the Hanging Shell, and it has been written down, I need to know. There may be something in the books about Hanging Shell that is important. Something I haven't been told. Or, we have forgotten."

"*Fansaine*? Who is that?" Coe asked. He knew the iron people were the Spanish and their descendants.

"The *fansaine* are the snow-looks-like, the white, the Anglo. Like you, Mr. Coe," Bustamente replied, grinning friendly.

"Oh, I haven't heard that term about us," Coe said.

"It's just a description, nothing bad," Medicine Wind inserted.

Coe replied to Bustamente and Medicine Wind that he would comb the books in his possession and would make discreet calls to some friends he had at universities to see if they might come up with anything. He would not mention the Tulona Pueblo, he assured Bustamente.

"I'll keep the Tulona out of it."

"That is good," Bustamente replied.

Coe added he would make sure the museum cooperated with the tribal police to close the case and find the thieves. "I know Officer Tafoya, so I won't have a problem talking to him."

Bustamente ended the meeting with Coe by telling him the sad news about Lance Bernal who had died Sunday. "I must be getting back to the pueblo to handle some matters there, Mr. Coe. Thank you for your cooperation. We will see each other, soon."

As Bustamente and Medicine Wind started to leave, Medicine Wind stopped and asked Coe a question.

"What's the name of your cat, Mr. Coe?"

"Oh, sorry I didn't introduce her. Her name is Fenster, which means 'window' in German," Coe answered.

"Window...window," Medicine Wind puzzled. "That's interesting. You must tell me the story sometime on how she got that name, Mr. Coe. And I'll tell you someday how I got my Tulona name, Medicine Wind."

Medicine Wind and Bustamente went out the door, hailing down a cousin in a pickup on the street. The rain eased up. Cars and trucks stopped in both lanes to allow cacique Bustamente to cross the street and get in his cousin's multi-colored, wooden-paneled, old F-250 with four-wheel drive.

Fenster had come to the door with Coe, sitting on her haunches looking at the two Tulona, both in longhair braids, leave the shop. Fenster turned around and went behind the purple curtain to the restricted book area. Coe closed shop for the second time that day, and went home to Prissy, carrying *Winter in Taos* in his briefcase, and wondering how Medicine Wind earned his name.

30

By Tulona reckoning of time, October is the Month of Leaves Falling Moon. November is the Month of Corn Depositing Moon, the beginning of their winter, the Still Time. Ben Lovato Medicine Wind knew the importance of ceremony, especially the reverence accorded to the end of the earth's growing season that provided corn and harvest food for the pueblo. "Indian" corn was multi-colored corn—kernels red, blue, shades of yellow, gold, and white. Within kivas after the harvesting of corn, prayers were given to the Earth Mother for the harvest and bounty that sustained the people through the Still Time of winter and into the spring, the Beginning Time by Tulona reckoning.

With sincerity and proper respect, Medicine Wind helped perform the ceremony of Harvest Thanks within Old Bow kiva along with his brothers. The ceremony took place at night within the kiva—most kivas had corn harvest ceremonies. Kiva fires were lit and tended, the warmth of kiva fires expelling the Month of Leaves Falling Moon cold air of the night.

At the corn harvest ceremony in the kiva, Medicine Wind sat on a bench along the wall. Unbeknownst to his kiva brothers, he was preoccupied with his role as observer to the inventory of museum artifacts. When the proper time came in the ceremony, he prayed and gave thanks to the Earth Mother for the harvests, but he was worried about the artifacts that they had discovered stolen from the museum. His mind drifted from ritual; he could not help himself.

Taken one by one, each item stolen was valuable. Putting all of the items together, in a medicine bundle, created a concentration of pueblo religious power. "The whole is greater than the sum of its parts," he believed.

Medicine Wind knew it, but McGinnis and Hornbuckle were uneducated in the objects that had been stolen and their significance. Whomever had stolen the items were probably knowledgeable of their significance. When assembled together, thought upon, sang upon, and drummed upon, unconscious and mysterious forces came into being. Medicine Wind ruminated over and over in his mind the stolen objects. The photographs and descriptions on the data sheets alarmed him. The objects had been in a reed bundle tied with belts of conchas, belts of shells.

The drum fell silent. Within the Old Bow kiva, the ceremony was nearly finished. Medicine Wind's concentration turned away from his thoughts about the theft, and he looked upon the designs drawn with white and black natural pigments on the floor of the kiva. The kaolin or white clay brought from Questa graphically outlined Earth Cloud Lake on the floor. All of Tulona were silent, the only sounds the crackling of the fire.

Deliberately, slowly and rhythmically, cacique Bustamente prayed to Earth Mother and Creator that had provided rich soil and rain for corn to grow, nourishing the Tulona people. Bustamente's voice sounded strong, beyond his old age, and what quavering of the voice occurred came from the emotion of the ceremony and not weakness of body, and certainly, not weakness of his spirit.

The kiva ceremony cannot be described for no Tulona has betrayed the secrets, and neither Anglo nor any other ethnic group has been invited to observe. From the Spanish entrada to the inquisitions of modern-day anthropologists, Tulona kiva ceremonies have been and will remain, secret. An observer outside the kiva will hear truncated prayers and singing, smell smoke from kiva fires, and hear and feel the drumbeat, but the substance of ceremony remains secret within the Tulona brotherhood and sisterhood. And, there it shall stay.

The ceremony of Harvest Thanks concluded. The priesthood of Tulona believers, their rituals completed, climbed the ladder to the world above.

"This day, this night, this ceremony of Harvest Thanks is completed and pure," Medicine Wind thought to himself, as he ascended the ladder out of the kiva and into the night air.

He walked deliberately to the feast pole still standing since the Saint Francis Festival, eighteen days before. He stood a few feet apart from the fifty-foot ponderosa pole standing upright in the plaza. He looked up at the crossed vigas at the top, upon which the pole climber had sat and prayed. His cousin, Lion Walks Night, came over and stood beside him, also looking up at the pole and sky full of stars.

"What are you doing, cousin?" Lion asked.

"I am looking at the pole...the stars in the sky....The pathway to the Sixth World for our people, Lion."

31

Earlier in the day before the Harvest Thanks Ceremony, Luis Ortega sat at breakfast with his mother and father to discuss the transport of their Churro sheep to their cousin's pastures near Cimarron. Not an easy task. It entailed driving a large stock trailer eastward over the Cristo Mountains and through the towns of Angel Fire and Eagle's Nest. The three of them agreed the sheep would winter better on the grassy plains than being fed bales of hay and grain at their compound in San Miguel. By telephone, the Ortega's cousins agreed to pasture their Churro sheep for minimal costs—after all it was, "all in *la familia*." From a neighbor in San Miguel, Luis could borrow a large stock trailer and pickup to transport the flock. That arrangement suited Armando.

The Ortega's Navajo-Churro sheep were historic in breed and temperament. Although the breed had been supplanted with other breeds of sheep, Churro remained a substantial stock in New Mexico. The Churro originally came from the Juan de Oñate settlement in the late sixteenth century. He and 400 men with families drove 7,000 head of stock, including 2,900 sheep, from Mexico to settle in the Okay Owingeh area of northern New Mexico. Puebloans were hired and forced to tend flocks as well as digging acequias and building a church.

From the Churro's long and coarse wool, textiles were woven, their meat eaten. The Navajo toward the west, through buying and raiding, adopted the breed and became skillful shepherds, weaving rugs and blankets from Churro wool. For the Navajo, sheep became status symbols. Wealth was measured in numbers of sheep owned, much like the Arab with horses. In the 1930s, due to overstocking and the Great Depression, the Navajo sheep were culled by government edict. Roughly thirty percent of the sheep were slaughtered. It was a sad time, but necessary.

When Armando and Loretta married, they merged their flocks they had inherited from their parents and grandparents. Even into their seventy years, Armando and Loretta spent time in mountain pastures camping out and tending their sheep. The routine of lambing, shearing, pasturing, and tending gave structure to their lives. Sparing his parents from toil, Luis and day laborers had assumed the task of shearing, shepherding, and doctoring. Although Luis was more involved in horses than sheep, he had assured his parents that he would always be a sheepherder first, horseman second.

"The two skills I can manage," Luis assured them. Armando and Loretta prayed for their son's strength and good health.

After their discussion about moving the Churro to Cimarron, Armando telephoned his friend in San Miguel and secured the large stock trailer for transport. He arranged for the trailer to be on loan for several days so that when they unloaded the sheep at Cimarron, they might stay a couple of nights with their cousins and not rush back the next day. Loretta had heard of a *matanza* being held, and if the community gathering of feasting and visiting occurred while they were in Cimarron, she wanted to attend. As expected, the stock trailer would be returned to San Miguel, washed out and cleaned of manure and straw.

"Like I loan the trailer out, bring it back like that," said his friend, in a cordial way.

Once the arrangements for the use of the trailer and the Cimarron cousins notified about the Churro transfer to their pastures, Armando breathed a sigh of relief. As was his style, he laid out the order of battle the next day.

"My son and I will load the sheep. Loretta will come along and look pretty. I'll drive that terrible road over the mountains. You'll help me drive that road, won't you, Luis?"

Luis nodded, yes, thinking he hated that road, too.

32

Wednesday, October 24, Day of Saint Anthony Mary Claret, Month of Leaves Falling Moon

Early the next morning, Armando and Luis borrowed the pickup and stock trailer, leaving behind their pickup for the loaner's use. Armando backed up the trailer to the loading chute of the stock pens on his first attempt. "That's a good sign, to back up only once to the chute," he said to himself. Luis inspected the flock for problems: wounds, hobbled sheep, coughs. The flock seemed well enough to travel. Loretta packed lunches and snacks for the drive over the mountains to Cimarron and French Corner on the plains. She had called the cousins to tell them they would arrive early in the afternoon.

With the trailer full of livestock, the Ortega family drove through Ojo Verde and Taos, turning east on U.S. 64 that would take them through narrow canyons and over the Palo Flechado Pass to Eagle Nest and past Cimarron State Park. The road was an old road that had been a passageway for wildlife, Plains and Pueblo Indians, trappers, traders, military columns, and now tourists and stockmen that skied and transported animals. The Ortegas drove on U.S. 64 that followed Rio Fernando de Taos up to higher altitudes.

"I hear that the Taos Land Trust is trying to reestablish the old Rio Fernando greenbelt," Luis said, as he sat in the backseat while Armando fought the narrow U.S. 64. "They are trying to get rid of the invasive trees like the Siberian elm and Russian olives. Let willows and cattails have a chance to come back."

"That's *bueno!*" Loretta expressed. She looked over at the river on the right side of the highway. The Fernando ecosystem needed serious cleaning up. "Oh, just look at the trash and plastic that is along the Fernando, Armando," Loretta said in disgust.

"I can't look. I'm driving and I just despise this road. It's so narrow," Armando replied as he steered the pickup to the right white line on his shoulder side of the road to avoid an eighteen-wheeler that had drifted partially into his lane. "I really do not like this road."

"Where does the Rio Fernando begin, Luis?" Loretta asked, ignoring her husband's complaint.

"I think it begins at the La Jara Meadows, off to the west near Palo Flechado Pass. Some of meadows are on Taos Pueblo Land. The meadows are beautiful in the summer, and you ski the forest road in the winter," Luis answered.

"So, Rio Fernando begins this high in the mountains, flows through Taos Canyon to Taos, and then somewhere dumps into the Rio Grande, Luis?" Armando asked as he pulled over at a turn out, so a SUV with Texas license plates could pass him. He shook his head as the SUV passed him and abruptly pulled in front of him.

"Fernando meets up with the Rio Pueblo de Taos, then flows on to the Grande," said Luis.

Palo Flechado Pass came to the Ortegas at a height of 9,109 feet. The name, Palo Flechado, meant tree shot with arrows, from a pueblo custom of shooting arrows left over from buffalo hunts on the plains to the east. Armando had his doubts about hunters shooting arrows into the tree and leaving them there, especially after carefully crafting arrows with flint and metal arrow points.

"Luis, ask Lion Walks Night at the Tulona Pueblo if shooting arrows in a tree after a buffalo hunt is true. Would you?" Luis said he would. Armando shifted his pickup into lower gear and carefully followed the curves and switchbacks down the mountain until they reached a mesa near Angel Fire, then turned north to Eagle Nest and Eagle Nest Lake.

Eagle Nest Lake never failed to impress the family, especially Armando who remembered his great-grandfather telling him about working to build the Eagle Nest dam during the Great War. As they drove in the broad Moreno Valley of Eagle Nest, they saw the large herd of elk that was lying down in the pasture toward Wheeler Peak and Taos Pueblo Land.

"Say, Father, you remember that Anglo we met at the *matanza* in San

Cristobal last summer who thought the elk he saw here in Eagle Nest were llamas until he realized better?" Luis laughed.

"Luis, don't make fun of people," Loretta chided hm. "You have been taught better than that!"

Armando chuckled and nodded his head that he remembered the llama-elk story. Another eighteen-wheeler dirt hauler passed him. He looked at the huge and beautiful Eagle Nest Lake to his right that seemed to cover half of the valley floor heading into Eagle Nest. Cabins and houses had been built adjacent to the dirt roads, branching off from U.S. 64. Some were expensive, but other residences were rustic; even some had fallen into disrepair. His great-grandfather had worked as a construction foreman on building the Eagle Nest dam from 1916-1918. Armando remembered the story filled with ambitious and stubborn characters.

The Cimarron River was to be controlled by a 140-foot dam—privately funded. Rich and powerful, the Springer brothers, Frank and Charlie, put up the money and wanted to use the water for irrigation and hydroelectric power for settlements and farms in the area. Because of the Great War and a widow, Mary Gallagher, who didn't want to sell her land for the lake, the dam project had been delayed for years. The Springer brothers were not happy. Armando's great-grandfather worked for Charlie Springer, earning his respect so much that Springer loaned him money to buy a section of land in the Cimarron area at French Corner. That was where the Ortegas were now taking their sheep.

Armando and his family did not stop at Eagle Nest, nor even think about casting a fishing line in the lake, but drove steadily down U.S. 64 through the state park area in the direction of Ute Park and the small town of Cimarron. Ugly and sad, the green of mountainsides had turned black from fire, and highway signs blared, "Warning! Signalman Ahead!"

Before the monsoon rains had come in August, forest fires had broken out. They were the most destructive in decades. The Philmont Scout Ranch had to cancel all of its summer programs and send the staff home. Mile after mile of blackened trees confronted the Ortegas. Large front-end loaders on the side of the road scooped up tons of mud from landslides that had washed onto U.S. 64 from the burn areas.

Between Ute Park and Cimarron, they were slowed down by no fewer than six signalmen and dozens of dirt haulers and frontend loaders. The smell of damp, charred wood permeated the air, coming in through the air vents in their pickup. Finally, after ten miles of devastation alongside the highway, they came out of the canyon and onto the valley floor, a few miles from Cimarron.

The historic Santa Fe Trail came through Cimarron where the Ortegas stopped at a filling station on the crossroads to French Corners. The remnants of the Santa Fe Trail were visible a hundred yards away, the ruts disappearing on the northeast horizon toward Raton Pass and Bent's Fort. As Luis went into the Allsup's filling station to buy chips and soda, Armando and Loretta took Zeke to his own rest stop on a nearby grassy stretch of ground. Armando stood and imagined at what had passed by Cimarron on the Santa Fe Trail in the nineteenth century. Traces of the old trail could still be seen coming from Missouri to the northeast by way of Bent's Old Fort and Raton. Cimarron, with its constant source of water via the Cimarron River, provided Santa Fe-bound caravans much-needed water, green grass, cottonwoods, elms, willows, and welcome relief from the prairie.

This route, the Mountain Route, was the principal route of the Santa Fe Trail. The town of Cimarron was a major waypoint. From the town, the Cimarron River flowed on to the Canadian River about forty-miles away at Rock Crossing. Covered wagons were the vehicles for transport. Modified Conestoga wagons, the Pittsburg wagon, carried 5,000 pounds of freight pulled by five or six pairs of mules or oxen. The total value of goods carried went from $15,000 in 1822, to $5,000,000 in 1855. Goods unloaded at Santa Fe and Taos were often repacked into pack trains headed southward to Chihuahua on the El Camino Real and westward to California.

Armando stood transfixed at the images in his mind, the history of the spot upon which he stood. Shaking his head, he snapped out of his reverie and turned to Loretta.

"Lorretta, those ruts over there," Armando pointed excitedly, "are the Santa Fe Trail. There came packhorses, pack-mules, road-wagons, carts, oxen, and carriages. Some of those pack trains, I bet, went up to

Taos where we just came down from," Armando said with wonderment.

"Armando, you say that every time we stop here. Sometimes I think you were born in the wrong century," Loretta said. She waited for what she knew her husband would say.

Armando shrugged. "Oh, no, if I was born back then, I would never have met you, *mi esposa*. I am glad where I am. With you. *Tu eres la luz de mis ojos*." Loretta had his reply memorized, and loved it every time she heard him say, "You are the light of my eyes."

Armando called Zeke to attention who was ready to jump in the backseat of the cab with Luis who had chips and soda. Luis gave Zeke a chip before they loaded up. Armando had enough of driving.

"Luis, do you mind taking over the wheel? I want a chance to look out the window and see the countryside before we get to French Corner. I'll get back in the seat with Zeke."

Luis took over the driving chore, eating chips and drinking his soda, while Armando looked out the window to see the trail ruts eroded by Pittsburg wagons along the Santa Fe Trail. As the fence posts flew by in his vision, Armando thought of a movie he had seen long ago: *Somewhere in Time*. The main character used a trick method told to him by a psychology professor on how to go back in time. In so doing, the character was transported back to a period in time where he met the love of his life. The movie ended badly for the main character, but that was not what Armando thought about. He knew it was impossible to go back, but if he could go back in time, would he go back to the days of the Santa Fe trade and the life on the trail? It might be nice to get to the end of the trail in Santa Fe at the La Fonda and have whiskey and dancing girls, but the day-to-day travail of driving mules and fighting hostile Indians and rattlesnakes? No, that was not the place to go back to. But, if one could, where would he like to go? What of Loretta?

"Loretta, if you could go back in time, where would you go?" Armando suddenly asked.

"That's crazy, Armando. I was just kidding a while ago about you wanting to live in another century."

"I know you were, Loretta. I'm just curious. Humor me."

Loretta thought a moment…

Luis interrupted Loretta's reflection, and said, "While Mother thinks a minute, I can tell you where I would go back in time."

"And, that is where, Luis?" Armando perked up.

"I would have liked to have been with Juan de Oñate when he first came into New Mexico and settled near San Juan Pueblo. Being the first settlers of the area and building acequias and raising sheep. It would have been amazing to see the area without cities and towns we have now."

Armando thought his son was odd to choose the time of Juan de Oñate. Why not Woodstock or cattle drives that came through in the nineteenth century?

"You are keen on horses, *hijo*, why not something like a vaquero or rider with Poncho Villa?" Armando asked.

"No, I'd rather come with the Spanish and Oñate and settle along the Rio Grande."

Loretta did not speak up. She looked at the flat grassland passing by her window and the far plains in the distance.

"Have you thought where you would like to be in another time, Loretta?" Armando asked again.

"I think this is a silly game, Armando, but if you insist, this is my thinking: I don't want to be anywhere else but here. The here. The now. And nowhere else. I am with my husband and son and going to tend our sheep. Oh, yes, and Zeke is here, too. I am happy with modern medicine and a little TV. I don't like computers or the internet. I choose not to enter that world. I'm happy with the twenty-first century. I go to church and confession and Mass. I have you and Luis and my friends. I want nothing else. Oh, maybe a few kind words and a little more time. But, that's it." She turned around and looked lovingly at him, and he could not do anything but smile and nod and place his hand on her shoulder.

Armando had been swept up imagining a romanticized sliver of history as he had stood at the filling station in Cimarron. Yes, he admired the Santa Fe Trail from Missouri to Santa Fe, the excitement when caravans arrived at destinations, the friendships forged, the battles fought, the animals ridden and driven for commerce. That was all well and good, but the conversation with Loretta and Luis had taken a serious turn. Luis, he could understand wanting to be the lance point of Spanish settlement in New Mexico. But Loretta enlightened him. She was philosophical and seriously religious about life in the here and now. He had always admired her mind, and her critical words about *Somewhere in Time* made him think again. Armando remembered his English teacher at the community college in Española, who taught him Voltaire's dictum: "Tend your own garden."

We may not have a garden at the moment, but we do have a herd of sheep to tend, Armando thought. "That's the here, that's the now," he chuckled to himself. Loretta heard Armando laugh, but decided not to ask what was he thinking. The Santa Fe Trail ruts faded away in the rearview mirror as Luis drove east to French Corner.

Past French Corner, Luis turned off the highway onto a county road and after three miles of bumpy road, turned into his cousins' ranch. Approaching the ranch house, they saw corrals, barns, a full stock tank of water, and bales of alfalfa hay sheltered under sheds. When they stepped out of the pickup, the smell of fresh alfalfa hay and prairie grasses was sharp and clean, the wind light and cool. Their cousins ran out of the house to greet them.

Armando filled his senses with family and land and a cloudless blue sky. He said to Loretta, "I want to be here. No other place in time."

The Ortega's sheep were unloaded through the chute and checked for shipping fever. All seemed fine with the ewes and lambs. Nonetheless, they were quarantined in a separate pasture from the rest of the cousins' flock so a spike in sickness could be isolated, treated, eradicated.

Luis looked around at his cousins' spread. The French Corners' pastures were replete with grass and water. Several protective sheds had been built in the pastures, and the round barn held several hundred bales of hay for the winter. The Ortegas planned to spend two nights with their cousins, attending the *matanza* the next evening near Cerrososo Creek. Luis lamented that Flowers Dancing was far away in Espanola.

As they finished unloading and throwing hay to the Churro, Armando reflected, "When we took the sheep a few years ago up to Quintana Canyon, who was the sheepherder we hired from Tulona Pueblo?"

"Quintana Canyon…that is such a beautiful place. High altitude, but beautiful. I liked having our Churro up there, Armando," Loretta remarked.

"Lance Bernal was the Tulona we hired," Luis answered.

"Ah, that's right...Lance, that is his name" Armando said. "Let's think about getting another grazing permit for Quintana meadows. The sheep did well up there. Maybe we can hire Lance again to come back out and help us."

32

Tulona tribal member Lance Bernal had been buried on Wednesday, a clear day, at the Sacred Heart Cemetery, close to pueblo land along Paseo del Norte before one reached the yellow blinking light. Many Tulona attending the funeral had walked from the pueblo in groups of three, four, or five, according to kinship and friendship. The black robe from the Mission San Francis del Monte performed the rites of burial as mourners stood behind the seated wife and family who were shaded under a tent. Medicine Wind had driven Bustamente and Standing Elk in his old, battered Dodge pickup with high wooden panels in the vehicle's bed. A kinsman in Arroyo Luz had recently repaired the clutch, but the stick shift was still cranky, but by clutching twice, Medicine Wind changed gears with minimum grinding.

Bustamente gave his prayer for Bernal in Tiwa, the melodious tones of Bustamente's speech floating lightly above the mourners. Bustamente flung corn pollen on Bernal's casket. Beatrice, his widow, wept at pollen thrown, but not the sprinkling of holy water by the black robe. She had no issue with the church; she just had no more tears to shed.

When Medicine Wind drove Bustamente and Standing Elk back to the reservation, he told Bustamente he would come for a visit Friday morning at his home for he had something to tell him about Franklin Deerfield. Bustamente replied he had intended to invite him over for talk on Friday, as well.

Medicine Wind provided transport for several of his friends and kinsmen who rode seated in the back of his Dodge pickup. Although he drove slowly, his passengers grasped the lower wooden rail for safety. Time and distance seemed longer and farther returning to the pueblo than going to Sacred Heart. Medicine Wind's kinsmen could not explain why that was so; Bustamente knew why, but said nothing.

Tribal policemen Tafoya and Romero attended the funeral on Wednesday, obligatory first as kiva brothers to Bernal and, second, as officers of law. Knowing criminals often were eager to see the effects of their work, Tafoya and Romero observed as well as mourned. Tafoya was especially interested in Alfredo Dominguez, the mason and flagstone layer, whom he had interviewed.

Dominguez was present at the funeral, standing and staring at the casket on the bier ensconced with flowers. He wore boots with heels. He came alone, but socialized with people. Dominguez's demeanor was plainly sad, appearing to grieve with other mourners.

Tafoya questioned Dominguez's mourning, "How much of his behavior is an act?" But then, Tafoya thought Dominguez may be authentic in his grief. It was hard to tell the difference.

Sergeant Romero focused on Lance Bernal's second close friend, Larry Armijo, who lived within the confines of the reservation. Armijo's emotional affect seemed on the lighter side rather than sad, despite Armijo's friendship with Bernal. He smiled too much, Romero thought. Romero had interviewed Armijo earlier in the week, and Armijo claimed he had seen Bernal the week before. They had eaten at the Farmer's Market Café one morning and had gone for a drive on the road beyond the pueblo toward Earth Cloud Lake. "That was the Wednesday before he was found dead at Quintana Canyon," Armijo said.

Sergeant Romero noted that Armijo dressed in Levi pants, hiking boots, an Indigenous-symbol shirt hanging over his belt line, a bolo, and his hair in a single queue. A tall, young man, narrow-faced, twenty-six years old, with small eyes recessed. Armijo had spent two years at the junior college in Espa and had acquired computer skills he used for contract work for the Tulona Tribal Council. He had set up an excellent website for the Tulona Pueblo, some saying the best of all the Eastern Pueblos. Armijo's family had a house within the old pueblo grounds and a concrete-block house with electricity along Abalone Road near the town limits of Ojo Verde. Armijo rented a small frame house near his parents.

33

Thursday, October 25, Saint Antônio de Sant'Anna Galvão, Month of Leaves Falling Moon

Tafoya slept fitfully. In his dreams, he incessantly walked out of the forest at Quintana Pass and saw the sunshade tent sheltering the body of Lance Bernal. Like a mirage, the tent and Lance quivered, and then disappeared. No sense lying in bed with nightmares. Tafoya dressed and drove to the Ojo Verde Café near the south entrance of the reservation for breakfast. Fog obscured all things beyond two-tenths of a mile, and rain was in the forecast by noontime.

"Yeah, and the Franklin Deerfield case and Lance's murder are all fogged up, as well," he thought, berating himself.

He ordered a breakfast burrito with orange juice and coffee, adding extra green salsa on his burrito. He ate slowly, scrolling through his cell phone and reading emails. Tafoya messaged Romero, inquiring if he was coming to the café for breakfast. Romero replied that he was having breakfast at home with his wife, and would see him later at the station. Tafoya wrote a message to Janet to join him for breakfast, but deleted it.

By the time Tafoya left Café Ojo Verde, the night had lifted, but there were no rays of sunshine. Fog remained so dense that the mountain range disappeared. With no visual cue from the mountains, his sense of place was lost. Tafoya thought he could be anywhere. He drove with his headlights and fog lights on to the stationhouse on the Tulona plaza. Traffic was light; people were huddling around their stoves.

Once in the stationhouse, he started a pot of coffee. Smelling the coffee brewing and looking out at the plaza brought his sense of place back in order. Even so, the far side of the plaza disappeared with thick fog. He could hear children's voices, but he saw no children. Ghostly, high-pitched voices came out of the fog.

"This whole morning is weird."

Back at his desk, Tafoya opened the three data silos at his desk. The tribal department's hard evidence files were slim—not unusual for early in the case of Lance Bernal. His second silo of data was his interviews and reports written from the field, including his yellow legal-pad analyses. The third silo of data was the computer files and links, including F.B.I. and Taos County Medical Examiner reports. Dr. Eli Rosenberg had not filed the final autopsy report. The murder occurred Saturday and this was only Thursday. Rosenberg had promised the final report by the end of the week. The F.B.I. was not deeply involved in the Bernal case.

"Hopefully it stays that way with the F.B.I. I don't need to write a powerpoint report."

Tafoya brought out his field notes and yellow notepad on the Bernal case from the top righthand drawer of his desk. Beneath the Bernal case was the museum case. He set aside the Franklin Deerfield Museum robbery case.

"I'll get to that when I can."

He opened up the file to the interview with the widow, Beatrice Bernal. He checked his field notebook as he read the screen. Bernal's house was on the edge of the reservation, adjacent to Ojo Verde city limits and a half-mile from Tafoya's house. Deputy sheriff Cordova had met Tafoya at Bernal's house to interview the wife.

Tafoya carefully read his notes. Beatrice Bernal was in her early thirties, a few years younger than Lance. She was tall, thin-faced, and wore her hair unbraided. Her eyes were large and set wide-apart, giving her an attractive, exotic, face. She was Zuñi by birth. Her sisters and children had sat on the sofa beside her. Beatrice held hands of her sister on one side, her daughter on the other side throughout the interview, unless she had to wipe away tears with a black bandanna. She had allowed Tafoya and Cordova to go through her husband's workshop and toolshed before she sat down for the interview. They found the usual tools, boxes, and lumber. Reloading equipment for ammunition was bolted to a workbench.

Tafoya had asked questions of Beatrice while Cordova looked on. Her story was that on Sunday, the day her husband was killed, Beatrice had gone to Mass in the pueblo with her sisters, and when she returned in the afternoon, Bernal was gone. She had attended the ten o'clock Mass and had lunch with her sisters, returning to the house at about two thirty. Lance had left no note saying where he went, or when he would be back. Beatrice presumed he had walked next door to visit a cousin or maybe even walked into Ojo Verde. When he had not returned by late afternoon, she became worried and called his cousin. The cousin had not seen him that day. Before nightfall, Beatrice drove the pickup into town and around on the backroads of the reservation, but did not find him.

"I was so upset. I thought about calling the police, but didn't. I decided I would wait for him to return. He never came back.... Lance had never behaved like this before." Beatrice said she did not know of anyone that wished to do him harm. "We had no enemies."

She gave Tafoya names of friends with whom he was close. Tafoya had asked her if Lance might have gone hunting somewhere in the mountains. Beatrice had replied he would have arisen early in the morning, or spent the night in the woods to get an early kill at sunrise. Besides, deer season had not opened. He wasn't hunting, and he never poached.

"Lance would not leave me to go hunting without telling me."

At that point, Tafoya asked an important question, "Would you check your husband's deer rifle and weapons to make sure they are still here?"

Beatrice and her daughter went to the bedroom closet to check on the guns. After ten minutes, they came back. "His deer rifle is missing, officer...I don't understand. He would never loan it out or go hunting without telling me." She had stood in the floor, puzzled, her long arms folded, hugging herself.

One of her sisters arose from the sofa, went to her side, and put her arm around her. Beatrice cried.

"I'm sorry to keep questioning, but I'll finish soon," Tafoya had said, apologetically.

"Do you know the caliber, the kind of rifle Lance had...the deer rifle that is missing?" Tafoya asked.

"Yes, I know. I have gone hunting with him. It's a 7mm Remington magnum, bolt action, with a sling. It's got a scope, but I don't know what it is," Beatrice said.

"Would you look through your files and find the serial number of the rifle? Call us when you find the numbers." Tafoya said. The short interview was over.

Tafoya closed his notebook of the interview and put it back in his drawer. Tafoya remembered the priest knocking on the door when the interview concluded. When the black robe entered the room, Beatrice wailed, "I don't understand, Father, I don't understand."

Tafoya sat back in his office chair, "I don't understand, either, Beatrice."

Tafoya had interviewed Bernal's close friends the day after the interview with Beatrice. Both men were Tulona. Ambrose Vasquez, close to Bernal's age, had not seen Bernal in over a week. On Sunday, the day of the murder, Vasquez with his wife and family had driven to Santa Fe to attend a christening service of his nephew. Tafoya scratched him off the list as a person of interest after he had checked Vasquez's alibi with the church in Santa Fe.

After interviewing Vasquez, Tafoya drove to the home of Bernal's second close friend who lived in Ojo Verde: Alfredo Dominquez. He was in his fifties, shorter than Tafoya and in good shape from lifting, cutting, and laying stone. Alfredo told Tafoya he had not seen Bernal in over two weeks. He appeared upset over his friend's death. The interview took place in the front yard of Alfredo's small home. He lived alone and did not invite Tafoya inside to talk. Tafoya noticed his workshop in back of the house had deer and elk horns mounted over the door. Knowing that Dominquez had been pushed out of the pueblo for failure to participate in ceremonies, Tafoya asked him when he might be returning to the pueblo.

"I don't think it will be anytime soon, Tafoya. I am busy with many things and making good money."

Tafoya nodded, but countered Dominquez, "I'm sorry to hear that, Dominquez, but you still wear your hair in braids, and I notice you cut the heels off your boots. Haven't given up traditional ways entirely, have you?"

"How do you know about my heels?" Dominquez quickly shot back.

"I'm wearing regular boots. Been working all day. See?" He lifted up his right foot to show Tafoya his heeled boots.

"I see what you are wearing," Tafoya said, "but on your porch?" Tafoya pointed at the house's porch overhang, "Your heels have been cut off on those boots." Dominquez turned his head quickly to his porch where his boots were sitting next to the door. The boots had their heels cut off, pueblo-style, traditional.

"Oh," Dominquez said, shrugging his shoulders. "Yeah, you're right. I wear those sometimes," tossing off Tafoya's observation.

"Maybe then, one day, you'll come back to us, Dominquez?"

"Yeah, well...maybe," Dominquez stammered.

Tafoya wrapped up the questioning. "You think of anything that might help us find the murderer, call me." Tafoya gave Dominquez a business card from his front pocket. Dominquez looked at it, and then stuck it in his front shirt pocket.

Tafoya started to leave, then stopped and turned around.

"One more question, Dominguez, where were you Sunday, October twenty first, the day Bernal was killed?"

Dominguez glared at Tafoya. "Why are you asking me that? You think I had something to do with Bernal's death?"

"We ask questions like that to all people in the victim's immediate circle. Just routine, Dominguez."

Dominguez looked at the ground, trying to remember. He remembered. "I was finishing a flagstone project down in Taos at the Martinez House," he answered, not amplifying any further. He stared at Tafoya who was concentrating on writing down his answer.

Tafoya made a note of Dominguez's answer, putting an asterisk beside his scribbles to check out the alibi with the staff at the Martinez House. Tafoya pocketed his notebook and looked at Dominguez's workshop and the antlers mounted over the door.

"You getting ready for deer season? Season starts soon."

Dominquez blinked, not even glancing at his antler trophies. "No, I'm really busy. Trying to catch up on our contracts. Maybe later in the season."

Tafoya left Dominquez's place wondering, "Considering all the elk and deer horns above his shop, I would've thought he'd be more excited about deer season."

Sitting at his desk, Tafoya peaked his hands in thought, reflecting on the interview with Dominquez. "Why would he deflect my declaration that he cut the heels off his boots?" The response puzzled him, but it might not be of any significance.

On his yellow legal pad, Tafoya wrote down Dominguez's deflection about heelless boots, and again made himself a note to check out his alibi at the Martinez House. With that, he rose from his chair and walked to the front of the stationhouse to look out on the plaza. The fog remained; no children's voices were heard for they had gone to school. It began to rain.

34

Director Jennifer Hornbuckle of the Franklin Deerfield Museum called a staff meeting in the board of trustees' conference room. The IT techies had removed the monitors and computers that had been assembled for the robbery investigation; the boardroom looked normal again.

On the evening of October 31, the museum was hosting a Halloween party in conjunction with All Saints' Day and All Souls' Day or Day of the Dead events, November 1 and 2. She wanted to finalize the arrangements and assign duties to the staff for the party. By invitation, the party was limited to staff members, interns, and patrons of the museum and their guests.

Ray Tejada, the Tulona curator of the museum, attended the meeting, but he was self-absorbed in thinking about the robbery. The robbery in the early morning of October 13 had never been far from his mind. He paid attention to Hornbuckle's instructions, but on his notepad, he doodled. She had distributed a handout of hosting assignments and was explaining each person's duty. Tejada was to schmooze and circulate among the guests. McGinnis would give short lectures on the museum's Day of the Dead artifacts, particularly the death cart that would be displayed prominently in the main hallway. McGinnis said he was prepared to give a five-minute presentation to anyone that wanted to listen. Hornbuckle droned on—blah, blah, blah.

Tejada recollected the items stolen from the museum: Child of Water Navajo mask, two wooden cylinders representing lightning bolts, two scalps, and a pueblo medicine bundle of unknown origin. The cylinders had been returned, mysteriously. The value of the stolen items was moderate, maybe $2,000 at most—and that was a stretch. If the thieves wanted to make money, there were rings, necklaces, and bolos of turquoise. Every ring and necklace were accounted for; besides they were in a safe. Why were only Indigenous artifacts stolen? Very strange, mysterious, but not without a reason. But what was the reason? Tejada continued to doodle and ignore Hornbuckle, as best he could.

The rain had begun at noon and continued through the day. Tribal policeman Tafoya and sergeant Romero worked a wreck at the yellow blinking light intersection at noon, and then performed a welfare check on an elder living close to the main plaza who had not been seen in two days. As they parked in the elder's front yard, Tafoya and Romero saw him getting firewood from underneath his shed to take inside.

Tafoya stepped out of his vehicle, drawing the elder's attention. "Grandfather, you haven't been seen in a couple of days. Are you well?"

"I am, Richard," the elder said. "The Corn Harvest Thanks ceremony took a lot out of me. I have been inside eating beans and chili from cans... and sketching things on canvas."

"That's good. The Senior Center had missed you at their meals." The old man waved them off and went inside. Tafoya and Romero were relieved.

Once welfare checks had been made, Tafoya and Romero drove back to the stationhouse and Tafoya went back to his desk. He set aside the Bernal case, and picked up the case files on the Franklin Deerfield robbery. He needed a break from the murder case, thinking he could come back later with a fresh look.

Opening his silo of field books and his personal notes, he turned to a fresh sheet of paper and began to recapitulate. The two thieves that stole the artifacts either had a key to the basement door, or were let in by an accomplice. He opened up the online case notes and found that McGinnis and Tejada had personal keys to the museum and the basement door. The front door lock was a digital pad, not a key lock like the basement door. The cleaning staff and all other people had to check out the keys from the security officer. The keys were in a locked key cabinet behind the security officer's desk. A record was maintained of who checked out what keys and at what time.

Tafoya picked up the telephone and punched the key pad for the security officer at Franklin Deerfield. The security officer answered on the first ring. Tafoya asked her to count the keys to the inventory basement in the key cabinet to verify that all the keys were either stored in the cabinet or checked out. The security officer said she would make the count and call him back in a few minutes.

Within five minutes, his phone rang with the museum security officer on line.

"We are missing a key," she said. "One key. I double-checked the list. We have a total of five keys to the basement. McGinnis has one, Tejada has one, so there should be three on the hook left. There are only two. One is missing."

The security officer said an inventory is conducted twice a year, once in January, once in June, and by the records, the key count to the inventory room was correct. The security office does the count.

"Is the cabinet always locked?" Tafoya asked, knowing the answer.

"We keep it locked, but...," she stammered, "it's sometimes left open when there's a lot of traffic in and out of the office. The director and others need access, and we don't want to keep coming back and forth from our rounds. I can't testify the cabinet is absolutely locked all the time. You know..."

"I understand, officer. Thank you for your candor. I'll be in touch," Tafoya interrupted.

Tafoya hung up the phone and scrolled the online case report, looking for any mention of keys. He knew Tejeda had already assigned someone, an intern, perhaps, to do a key count and look at the museum's guest register.

He found a notation, "Intern Martha Johnson will look at guest register and do a count of keys." Johnson had been given that task the day after the robbery. She had not filed a report for the key cabinet, but had submitted data on the guest register. She had accomplished one task, but why not the other?

His to-do list on the Franklin Deerfield case was growing longer. Interviewing Martha Johnson shot to the top of his list. His talk with her would be in person, not on the phone.

35

Forest Service biology specialist Janet Rael had not seen the fog lift all day. She walked to the front door of the headquarters several times, but the fog held, thinning at times, but always there. At noon, heavy at times, rain fell and the culverts diverted water to arroyos that filled with rushing water. Across the street from the Forest Service headquarters, the New Mexico State Troopers and sheriff's department officers were handling numerous traffic accidents on Paseo del Sur. Fortunately, no lightning struck transformers, nor trees, and Dancing Rock Cooperative Power Company repairmen remained in their offices two blocks away. Power had not been severed, but the day was still young.

Janet and Tafoya texted each other during the day. He was at the pueblo station, then investigating wrecks, and back again to the office working on cases. She had a safety meeting early in the morning, worked on a report of her field survey at Tract A of the Tulona Reservation Land Trust, and examined the topographical maps of the Pot Creek archaeological site near Fort Burgwin. Her supervisor scheduled Janet to examine the site for tourist impact and continue up the Rito de la Olla into the National Forest for a survey of forest roads and wildlife count. She saw that the Olla River originated in higher altitudes near Quintana Canyon and Pass.

Janet had good news to share with Tafoya, but she did not want to send the news in a text message, so she called him and asked him to meet her at Tablita's around six thirty to have an appetizer and a drink. She would not tell him the news, insisting he wait until they could meet in person.

"I'll be there, Janet. Must be really good news for you to invite me out."

At Tablita's, six thirty sharp, Jason Taylor, their server for the appetizer, seated Janet and Tafoya at the window overlooking Paseo del Norte. Rain continued to fall. The lights flickered once, but came back on. Jason lit a hurricane-style vessel with candle at their table.

"Just in case Dancing Rock has a transformer blowout. And we know that always happens! Right?"

They both ordered the house Bordeaux red wine and shared queso, guacamole, and chips. Tafoya had changed into mufti: blue Levi's, a western-patterned shirt, a light brown field coat, and hiking shoes. Janet wore black stretch pants, high-top hiking shoes with Swiss-patterned socks, and a black, heavy-cotton blouse with a turquoise pendant. Her hair was put up in a ponytail with a turquoise clasp. Tafoya and Janet had raindrops clinging to their clothing and hair, but they evaporated quickly.

The wine was good enough, strong on the tannin. After small talk, Tafoya asked, "What's the good news?"

"Richard, I got notice this afternoon that I have been appointed the Liaison Officer to the Tulona Tribal Police. A twenty-eighty split, twenty-percent working with the tribal police, eighty-percent continuing with my standard Forest Service duties. Just like I wanted."

Tafoya reached over and squeezed her hand. "Congrats, Janet! You're the perfect fit!" They raised their glasses in a non-verbal toast. Tafoya knew there were fourteen employees at the station, and she would work with others besides him. She's brave, she's smart; she will help the Tulona, he thought.

Jason had seen the toast as he walked by their table. He stopped. "Celebrating?"

"Yes, Janet is going to be working with the tribal police as a Liaison Officer with the Forest Service," Tafoya said, proudly.

"That's good, Janet. I feel safer already!" Jason exclaimed, walking on with a tray of food for another table.

"Richard," Janet said, "this work with the tribal police broadens me. My uncle Alex at Isleta was a tribal policeman for thirty years. I admired him and his work."

"Is he still alive?" Tafoya asked.

"Oh, yes, he's in his seventies...very much alive." Tafoya nodded at her response.

Janet turned serious. "Officer Tafoya, there are more reasons why I want to work with the tribal police," she said with a smile on her face.

"Oh, what's that?" Tafoya perked up.

"I can teach you how to write a powerpoint, and, second, I can fly in, and fly you out of trouble," Janet said, flirtingly.

Tafoya laughed. He did not want this woman to ever leave his life.

Suddenly, the lights flickered twice in Tablita's, then went out completely. The lamp on their table cast light lambently on Tafoya and Janet. Within a matter of minutes, Dancing Rock Power Cooperative trucks made their way northward along Paseo del Norte, their crane buckets and arms stretched over the driving cabs.

A message chimed on Tafoya's phone. He read the message, looked up at Janet, and said, "Transformer blowout on the road to Questa, adjacent to Tract A of the Tulona Reservation.... Fortunately, Liaison Officer Janet Rael, we are *not* called out to Tract A. At least, not yet...." They laughed, finished their appetizer by candlelight and drove eventually to their separate homes, happily, in the rain.

36

Friday, October 26, Day of Saint Peter of Alcantara, Month of Leaves Falling Moon

Medicine Wind opened cacique Bustamente's screen door and knocked on the solid, turquoise-painted door early Friday morning. He had asked to talk with the cacique, and Bustamente had invited him for an early breakfast on the way back to the pueblo after Bernal's funeral. Bustamente's wife answered his knock and opened the door. The smell of eggs, chile, and tortillas from her breakfast cooking made his stomach roll over in hunger. He saw a place set for him at the table with family-style plates of food already set out. Medicine Wind sat down at the table to enjoy the gift of puebloan generosity.

Following breakfast, Bustamente and Medicine Wind went to a backroom to talk privately. As Medicine Wind entered the room, he saw a large calendar on the wall with red magic-marker circles around October 13 and 21, the dates of the break-in at Franklin Deerfield and the murder of Lance Bernal. The cacique, apparently, did not want to forget those dates. A fire in the conical corner fireplace gave warmth to the interior room; thick blankets and rugs covered sections of the room; and Bustamente's medicine pouch hung suspended from a viga.

The cacique motioned Medicine Wind to sit down in a wooden chair. Bustamente drew up a chair beside him and at an angle so they could converse. A propane gas lamp flickered along the far wall, shinning additional light within the room. Medicine Wind was always concerned about propane fumes within a room, but he set those thoughts aside. "There's the draw of the fireplace and the lamp is low," he said to comfort himself. He still fretted.

The two of them spoke of the good breakfast they had enjoyed, the harvests of corn and other crops, and the approaching hunting season. Then they fell silent. Medicine Wind waited for Bustamente to speak. Bustamente fiddled with his blanket, then stopped and smoothed out the blanket that covered his leg. He cleared his throat and spoke at a volume slightly above conversational level. Medicine Wind knew something important was coming down.

"Grief lies heavily upon our Pueblo, Medicine Wind," Bustamente said, his words coming slowly. Medicine Wind did not interrupt; he would not speak until the cacique was finished. "Bernal's death will stay with us for a long time. He was one of us in all things. As a people, we will be anxious for Tafoya and Romero to solve this case quickly. But even with knowing who took Bernal's life, the grief will not lift quickly from us. I must, we all must, be ready to understand this thing, this life-taking. Until it is resolved, we will be on edge, on alert, our hearts grieving."

Bustamente paused, but he was not finished. "Behind Bernal's death," he continued, "lies a story in the killer's head, and I am certain that the story endangers we Tulona in ways we have not seen since the arrival of the Americans over a century and a half ago. Bernal disappears on a Sunday morning. No one saw him leave. He is killed in the mountains near Palo Flechado Pass, and there is no evidence of how he traveled there. I knew Bernal. He was kiva. And now he is dead. I sense a very bad spirit among us, an evil presence. We must pray. We must stay alert. The story, whatever it is, within the killer must be neutralized. If necessary, the killer erased."

Ben Lovato Medicine Wind had never heard the cacique speak so frightfully. Medicine Wind began to think of powerful spirits to give himself courage to confront what it was that Bustamente feared and sensed walking among the Tulona.

Bustamente leaned back in his chair and stared into the fire. He was finished. Neither man said anything until the piñon fire burned lower. Bustamente's interior room within the Summer House became cold. Medicine Wind stood from his chair and walked to the corner of the room, fetched three split logs of piñon, and placed them, teepee-shaped, within the fireplace. They caught fire, easily. "If only evil spirits could go up in flames so readily," Medicine Wind thought. He stood, his back to the fire, thinking.

Medicine Wind changed the subject. "I have news for you," he said as he sat back down in the chair, "about a medicine bundle wrapped in a shell belt that was stolen from the museum."

Bustamente replied, his voice low, "*Xa axa*," the bear sound.

"The thieves, there were three of them, two in the museum, one outside as a watchman, stole a Navajo Child of Water sacred mask. They also carried off two wooden cylinders representing thunderbolts, two scalps, and a medicine bundle," Medicine Wind said, then fell silent.

"Go on," Bustamente encouraged.

"The bundle had marsh reeds covering a buckskin wrapping. Around the reeds was a belt of shells..."

"Hanging Shell," Bustamente overlapped.

Medicine Wind continued. "Inside the bundle were several sacred items."

"How do you know what was inside the bundle?" Bustamente asked.

"Every item in the museum has a data sheet describing what it is, where it came from, and so on." Medicine Wind paused. Bustamente nodded his head he understood.

Medicine Wind continued. "Within the bundle were several things: two stone Corn Mothers, turquoise necklaces for them, some old Corn Mothers with kernels missing, a retablo of a rainbow, a retablo of bird figures, and a 'world straightener.'" Medicine Wind paused.

"Hmm, the world straightener.... What birds were painted on the retablo?" Bustamente asked.

"Eagle, chokecherry bird, magpie."

"Those sacred items are mainly for kiva business, but also other ceremonies, some of which may not be so good," Bustamente added.

Medicine Wind continued. "The two wooden cylinders were returned to the museum. One of the thieves broke into a curator's house and left them rolled up in a Ganado red rug, along with a message that read, 'The gods roam the hills for scalps.'"

Bustamente laughed. "I'll bet that scared the *fansaine*!"

Medicine Wind chuckled. "McGinnis didn't seem too fazed by the message. He was more upset that someone broke into his home to leave the cylinders and message...."

Medicine Wind rose from his chair and put more wood on the fire. He sat back down.

"What's a 'world straightener,' Grandfather?"

"South of us," Bustamente answered, "the Ohkay Owingeh use the world lengthener or straightener in their Water Giving ceremony for a child in the first year of its life. It's like a folding, carpenter's measuring tool. On either side of the altar ceremony for the child, it is unfolded and waved across the colored sands to ensure a long life for the child.... Now, what a world lengthener is doing in the Hanging Shell medicine bundle is...puzzling."

"The world lengthener must work for the Ohkay Owingeh," Medicine Wind said, "because they have a lot of elders still going strong down there." He and his family often visited Ohkay Owingeh on their ceremonial days.

Bustamente pulled his thin blanket tightly around himself and stared into the fire. Medicine Wind wondered if he should stay or go back home to Quail Looks Away. Finally, Bustamente spoke.

"I must think on these things, Medicine Wind. One of our brothers has been taken from us, and now I know what was stolen from Franklin Deerfield. Both events are troublesome. We Tulona have two events disturbing our harmony. What you have told me about the masks and medicine bundle is more threatening than Bernal's murder...I think."

Bustamente's words hung in the air.

"How so?" Medicine Wind asked, stirring in his chair, uncomfortably.

"The thieves wanted *that* bundle, not just anything in the museum. They wanted *that* bundle. That bundle has power, and when it was used by the Hanging Shell cacique, he brought power and more death into the world. Few know the story, but Wood Quiver was a witch, and with that bundle he brought ruin to the Hanging Shell people. He is dead, but the bundle is now again in the world, and we are in danger."

Piñon wood popped loudly in the fireplace, causing Medicine Wind to look away from Bustamente and gaze into the fire. He took the poker and stirred the coals and straightened the wood to burn evenly. Sparks flared up from the wood, glowing brightly, rapidly escaping up the flue. He sat back down.

"I have a story to tell you, Medicine Wind," Bustamente said. "It is a story whose elements are eternal in the world of humans. I think you should hear it and attend to its meaning as you think you should. Let yourself become a part of story and add to it."

"Yes, Grandfather, I am listening."

From the kitchen, laughter broke out, and voices were raised. Bustamente stood up and walked to the door and gently closed it, sealing off the room from the rest of the house. He sat back down, adjusting his blanket.

"It is a story that began long ago near the Big River. It is a story about the Hanging Shell people and the destruction of their pueblo by Wood Quiver, a man who used witchcraft to pursue power. The medicine bundle stolen from Franklin Deerfield was his bundle…."

Medicine Wind listened carefully and when he departed Bustamente's home, he began to prepare himself to hunt. The hunt was not for deer in the forest.

37

Later that Friday morning, two days after Bernal's burial, Tafoya and Romero were at the pueblo stationhouse. Neither had any outstanding observations at Bernal's funeral two days before, yet each decided to write a report on the crowd and ceremony, noting the behavior of Larry Armijo, Alfredo Dominguez, and a few others. As Tafoya entered his report on the computer, he noticed the Taos County Medical Examiner, Eli Rosenbaum, had uploaded his final autopsy report on Lance Bernal. Tafoya retrieved his yellow legal pad from the desk and began to take notes.

Rosenbaum stated that Lance Bernal, thirty-five years of age, had been murdered. Two bullets, one definitely a 7mm magnum (discovered under the body), the other probably the same caliber, had killed Bernal. One shot fired from at least six feet away (no powder burns on the back of the shirt); the other point-blank from the front of Bernal, the muzzle placed directly on the shirt and body. "No scattered powder residue on the front of the shirt, a direct placement of the muzzle over the heart." Bernal bled out at the scene of the shooting, the ground beneath him saturated with blood.

Rosenbaum added that the compass direction of the initial shot could not be precisely determined. "That's a question for forensics to answer." The angle of entry and exit of the bullet, however, indicated the shot may have come from downslope on the mountain, as the angle of *exit* being four-inches higher than entry. The victim was in good health. The victim was shot twelve to eighteen hours before discovery at nine in the morning, the next day, placing the time of death between three in the afternoon and nine in the evening the day before. Toxicology reports indicated neither drugs nor alcohol in victim's body. Rosenbaum entered into the final report that subcutaneous cuts on the right side of Bernal's cranium occurred within minutes of his death or before. "There was significant bleeding from cuts at the scene which cannot have occurred hours after death. The source and nature of the cuts cannot be determined."

Rosenbaum had taken photographs of Lance Bernal on the autopsy table. One photograph showed a long trocar thrust through the first wound, indicating the entry and exit angles of the bullet, from Bernal's back to the front of his chest. The photograph illustrated the upslope trajectory. The cuts on the right side of Bernal's cranium were three in number and four-inches long, probably induced by a knife. Some attempt had been made to tear flesh and hair away from the scalp. Tafoya quickly scrolled through the rest of the photographs— "Enough." He closed the Rosenbaum report.

Tafoya rose from his office chair and walked down the hall to Romero's desk.

"You read the autopsy report?" he asked Romero.

"Just finished, Richard. What do you think? Anything in there we can focus on...something we can build on?"

"Not a first glance. We need to put out another bulletin, make sure the newspaper prints it down in Taos, asking anyone with information, Sunday of the murder, seeing Lance Bernal in Ojo Verde, Taos, Angel Fire, or back up at Quintana Canyon, to come forward...let us know. Run his driver's license photograph with the bulletin," Tafoya said.

"We need to put out a tracer on Bernal's rifle that is missing. I'll talk to Beatrice and see if she has found the serial number on the 7mm magnum among her papers," Romero added.

"On the autopsy report, Romero," Tafoya added, "the cut marks on the side of Lance's head...they worry me. They can be a lot of things, but I'm thinking intentional branding marks, a signature of the killer...or..."

"Or, what?" Romero asked Tafoya.

"You know the answer, Sergeant. The killer wanted scalp, but decided against it, leaving his brand and tearing of flesh instead."

38

Saturday, October 27, Day of Blessed Bartholomew of Vicenza, Month of Corn Ripening Moon

Luis Ortega loaded Buck into the horse trailer. In the front part of the trailer, where he hung saddles and tack, he stored farriering tools and supplies. Buck's halter was tied with a slip knot close to the front compartment, and Luis stepped quietly alongside Buck and shut the trailer gate. Luis started his pickup and steered toward SH 522, turning south to Ojo Verde and the Tulona Pueblo. The day's forecast was good: temperature high to be sixty-five degrees, winds light, and fair through the day. The sun was already warming the day as Luis departed his home compound at San Miguel. He had left his father washing breakfast dishes for his wife.

On this fair and sunny Saturday, Luis was to give Lion Walks Night at the Tulona pueblo a lesson on trimming hooves. Lion was a good student, attentive, listened closely, and liked to be around horses. Lion owned no horses, but he was looking to buy a horse, perhaps train the horse himself. Luis had committed to helping Lion train his horse, once he found one. Ojo Verde and the pueblo had horses to sell, but Luis advised Lion to go across the Cristo Mountains, and purchase a horse from a rancher near Las Vegas, New Mexico, who had good-bloodied stock, both quarter horses and paints.

Tourist traffic was heavy going in both directions on SH 522; tourists going north to Colorado, and Coloradoans traveling south to Ojo Verde, Taos, and Santa Fe. The road to Ojo Verde from San Miguel was straight, not like the hairpin curves on U.S. 64 that he had maneuvered the day before from Cimarron. The Ortega Churro sheep had shipped well; no problems had developed once unloaded at his cousin's pasture. Luis, his mother, and father had stayed overnight for two nights, attending a *matanza* near the cousins' ranch at Cerrososo Creek.

Luis's mother and father had contributed two lambs for the *matanza* community festival. A domesticated pig had also been slaughtered. The Cerrososo *matanza* had been in the planning for one year, and the slaughter of the animals on Thursday morning had been a somber, almost reverent, occasion. Pits had been dug for the roasting fires. Water barrels were boiling to use in scraping the hair off the pig. Potatoes, onions, beans, hominy, chile, posole, and tortillas were cooked to fill out the *matanza* day.

More than a hundred people attended the Cerrososo Creek festival, a custom that had been brought over from Castile, Spain. Although refrigeration and food markets had brought an end to the necessity of the *matanza* for a regular supply of meat for a community, the socializing function remained important. Luis could do without the politicians glad-handing for votes and money, but he did enjoy the music and dancing that went late into the night. As Luis danced, he pined for Flowers Dancing, wondering if she would have enjoyed the festival.

At the pueblo corral grounds, Lion Walks Night was waiting for Luis. They unloaded Buck from the trailer. Luis attached reins to the halter of Buck, mounted him bareback, and rode him into the pasture for exercise. Coming back to the corral, he gave the reins to Lion, and had him ride Buck a few minutes around in the corral. After exercising Buck, the two of them took brushes and groomed Buck. A few Tulona had come over the corral panels and spoke of Luis and Lion, "riding old Tulona-style," bareback and close to the horse. Luis told the small crowd that Buck could be ridden without halter and reins, "But today is not the day. I'll show you another time." As Luis and Lion began to set up the lesson for trimming hooves, the Tulonas dispersed, murmuring about the horses they had known and ridden.

Luis and Lion put on farrier chaps. Luis brought his tool bag to the edge of the corral.

"You, Lion, will trim the right hoof. I'll trim the front left hoof...to show you how it's done."

Luis used a hoof brush to remove dirt and debris. With the long nippers, Luis trimmed the hoof wall, putting his nippers in his apron a couple of times, looking at the shape of the hoof he trimmed, then finishing the hoof. He used a hoof knife to cut away some inner frog part of the hoof. Luis then placed the hoof on an adjustable farrier's stand and used the hasp to file away some of the sharp edges of his trimming and outside of the hoof horn. Setting the hoof down on the ground, Luis stood back and looked at his work. Buck had lowered his head and was almost snoring with the manicuring.

Luis then trimmed and shaped Buck's left hind leg hoof, repeating the steps and explaining a second time what he was doing to Lion. Luis watched carefully. Then, Luis told him, "Okay, Lion, your turn with Buck."

Luis asked one of the Tulona to come into the corral to hold Buck's lead rope while he instructed Lion standing beside him. Buck continued to adjust his body to allow the trimming to take place, lowering his head, relaxed and pleased he was the center of attention. Buck's iron horseshoes had been removed after the Burned Mountain explosion. When he would be ridden in rough country, Luis would reshoe him. That would be a good time to give Lion lessons to shod a horse.

Lion trimmed and filed with the hasp Buck's foreleg and hind leg, getting encouragement and critiquing from Luis as he worked. He began to sweat and had to stop and put a bandanna around his head to keep the sweat out of his eyes. Still, however, drops formed on his nose and dropped off on Buck's hooves and the dusty corral ground.

When all of Buck's hooves were trimmed and filed, Luis instructed to Lion to apply a coat of hoof conditioner to each hoof. "It's a pine-tar derivative, avocado oil, and glycerin to help restore and maintain hooves. Like a kind of fingernail polish. Buck's a gelding, but he likes nail polish anyway." They laughed. Lion applied the coat of conditioner, and Luis thought about Flowers Dancing's fingernail polish.

Once finished with Buck, they unsnapped the lead rope, and Buck promptly laid down on the ground and rolled in the dirt, then stayed prone in the late morning sun as they put the tools away.

"He may go to sleep, Lion," Luis said. True enough. In two minutes, Buck began to snore.

Buck slept, breathing heavily, as Luis and Lion leaned on the corral panels and gossiped. Toward noon, Luis loaded Buck in the trailer to drive back to San Miguel. Before he started back, Luis asked Lion if he would go with him to Medicine Wind's house on the Tulona plaza and see if Quail Looks Away was home.

"Sure, what for, bro?" Lion asked.

"I want to ask Quail if she will give me Flowers Dancing's telephone number down in Espa. I want to call Flowers Dancing and talk to her," Luis answered.

Lion walked Luis down to Medicine Wind's home, knocked on the door, and Quail Looks Away greeted them at the door. She held Dezba on her hip. Luis reached out and grasped her little pink fingers. Dezba curled her hand around his callused finger.

"I stopped by to get Flowers Dancing's phone number...if you'll give it to me?"

"Sure, Luis, let me look it up on my cell phone. Here, you hold Dezba."

Luis took Dezba from Quail. He remembered he had held her a few days after she was born, when Lion had taken him to Quail's house to introduce Dezba. At the time, Luis wore his farrier chaps and Dezba lay in his arms that day, her legs and bottom resting on his horsy, musky chaps. All of which Medicine Wind, Quail, Quail's mother, and Flowers Dancing approved—there was something about the scent of leather, the horses, the liniment, the sweat-stained chaps that sensually opened the world outside to Dezba. They were happy Luis played a part in that being so.

Luis held Dezba and baby-talked to her while Quail wrote down the telephone number of her sister for him. "Here you go, Luis," she said. Luis reluctantly gave Dezba back to her mother.

When Luis and Lion left Quail's house, Quail turned to her mother and said, "Do you think Flowers Dancing will date him, mother?"

Quail's mother thought for a second, "As sure as the sun rises over Tulona Mountain, she will."

39

As Luis and Buck exited the pueblo, G. Armstrong Coe, the bookseller, passed them in the opposite direction, going into the pueblo. His car was halted. As was the policy set by the Tulona warchiefs to stop unfamiliar visitors, Coe was stopped at the entrance. A young Tulona, hair in braids and wearing sunglasses, walked to Coe's rolled-down passenger window.

"Are you here to see our pueblo?" the young Tulona inquired, thinking Coe another tourist.

"No, I am here to talk with the cacique, Bustamente," Coe replied. "I'll park in the visitor parking lot. I know where his house is."

The young Tulona, kiva-educated, probable warchief in the future, held up his hand, further discouraging Coe from entering.

"I will have to talk to Bustamente first, before you are allowed to walk into that part of our village. Park in the visitor parking lot and wait for me to go see Bustamente if he wants to see *you*! What is your name? And I need to see some identification."

Before Coe could take his driver's license out of his billfold, Lion Walks Night came up to his car and greeted him. The young Tulona looked surprised Lion knew Coe. When Coe explained he needed to see Bustamente, Lion said he would escort Coe to Bustamente's house. After Coe parked his car, Lion walked Coe to Bustamente's house. When the cacique granted the visit, Lion went on his way.

Bustamente and Coe retired to the back room. Sunlight filtered through the skylight; gas lanterns were not lit. The room was a comfortable temperature, but Bustamente started a small fire in the conical fireplace, "To slow us down, as we stare into the flames. We humans get too much in a hurry." Split piñon logs crackled and spewed. After a minute of staring at the fire, Bustamente broke the silence, sensing a restlessness in Coe.

"You have found something in your books about Hanging Shell, Mr. Coe?"

From the inner pocket of his field coat, Coe pulled out several four-by-six-inch index cards with writing on them. He shuffled the cards and began. "I read through the books in my shop, and I called a friend of mine at New Mexico Highlands University who teaches anthropology. He looked through his library for Hanging Shell data. Here's what I found, Mr. Bustamente."

Bustamente held up his hand to stop Coe from proceeding. "I suppose you know, since you are on the board of Franklin Deerfield, what was stolen at the museum?"

Coe said that he did and mentioned the Child of Water mask and the medicine bundle with a leather belt of shells.

Bustamente nodded in agreement. "I just wanted to make sure you knew."

Coe adjusted himself in his chair and was about to start over when he was startled by a loud "pop" from the piñon fire.

"That's the fire talking to us, Mr. Coe. The fire is not happy with the theft," Bustamente said with a straight face, then laughed.

Looking at the piñon fire, anticipating another "pop"—which did not come—Coe began again. Coe informed Bustamente that there were no references he could find—or his friend at New Mexico Highlands University—to Hanging Shell. Shells, however, played a part in pueblo ritual and adornment. Olivella, small conchas, large conchas, scallop, cowrie, and freshwater mussel shells were used in pueblo communities. Clusters of olivella shells were attached to sticks to use as rattles, medicine water was often dipped with a shell to be administered in curative ceremonies and rites.

"The shells attached to the medicine bundle stolen from the museum were freshwater mussel shells," Coe said.

"Hmmm," said Bustamente. "I didn't know that."

Coe continued to report, "Freshwater mussels in the Rio Grande and many rivers in New Mexico are endangered. The habitat for mussels has been reduced and water has become polluted. Today, about the only area for freshwater mussels is down near Carlsbad along portions of the Black River."

"What type of shells were attached to the medicine bundle stolen from Franklin Deerfield?" Bustamente asked.

"They were the Texas hornshell, according to the U.S. Forest Service biology section, who looked at the black-and-white photograph on the accession notes," Coe answered. "They are endangered along with a turtle named 'Rio Grande cooter', a fish called 'gray redhorse,' the blue sucker fish, and the Pecos springsnail." Coe adjusted his notecards and looked up at Bustamente. Bustamente was staring off, looking at the piñon logs burning down in the fireplace.

"And these fish and mussels are dying because of bad water...." Bustamente sighed. His lips moved ever so slightly, as if in prayer, Coe thought.

"So, Mr. Coe, no mention of Hanging Shell in the books?"

"No, Mr. Bustamente, I'm afraid there's not, but I do have a few other things to tell you.... You may already know that among the Navajo, a most revered spiritual figure is Changing Woman. Her sister is known as White Shell Woman, made from the white shell of the ocean. White Shell Woman is considered the younger, subordinate sister to Changing Woman. Some authorities say that White Shell Woman is Changing Woman when she is dressed in white. Among the Apache, they have a figure called White Shell Woman as well. She gave birth to the cultural hero of the Apache, Child-of-the-Water. But what is of interest is the Zuñi Big Shell Rain chieftaincy."

Bustamente looked away from the fire, "Go on, Mr. Coe, this might be interesting."

Coe looked at his note card, "The Big Shell Rain society possessed a big concha they had acquired from the Great Water in the Southwest, the Pacific or Baja. The big concha was altered, like is common to do, so when it was blown, sounds would be made, like a trumpet. You drill a hole in the apex of the big shell and blow through it, using your hand to raise or lower the pitch. In the stories of the Zuñi Big Shell society, when the horn was blown, people were blown back to the east!"

Bustamente laughed, "Sometimes when the tourist traffic is backed up on Paseo del Norte during the summer, I wish we had a big shell. I wonder if the Zuñi tried to blow Oñate away?"

Coe grinned, and then continued, "What happened was that the Big Shell was taken away as a fetish from the society because they were using the power of the Big Shell to kill people that weren't witches. The Big Shell chieftaincy had to learn how to use their power with the shell to do evil, not good. Sort of the old story of power corrupting those that have it, Mr. Bustamente." Coe stacked his notecards and put them back in his field coat.

"That's all I could find. Did any of this help you?" Coe implored.

Bustamente was quiet, lost in thought, trying to make sense of what he had heard. Hanging Shell, Big Shell—the two shells ran together in the narratives. Hanging Shell's chief, Wood Quiver, had used the power of the medicine bundle to bad ends, killing those people he perceived to be his enemies, eventually bringing a lethal invasion to his kinsmen, ending his life and destroying the community that now lay abandoned on the edge of the Rio Grande. Wood Quiver had used shells like the Big Shell chieftaincy, but he had failed to learn a lesson. Bustamente remembered that the Big Shell society changed their ways and earned their fetish back. They had listened to the community, the others, the puebloans around them. Wood Quiver did not listen; he died.

Bustamente turned to Coe, "I want to tell you a story, but you must promise me that you will never write it down or tell it to anyone."

Coe was startled. He realized the gravity of the promise he must give to Bustamente. It was not a kiva secret, or was it? No, Bustamente would never do that.

Coe swallowed hard and said, "I promise I won't write it down or tell anyone, Mr. Bustamente. You can trust me."

Cacique Bustamente proceeded to tell Coe about the Hanging Shell society and Wood Quiver.... At the end of the narrative, Bustamente said he believed the bundle at Franklin Deerfield was associated with the extinct Hanging Shell village.

"That may not be good," Coe said. "Do you think the theft at Franklin Deerfield was committed by Tulonas? You have any suspicions?"

"I think Tulonas are involved," Bustamente replied. "I am talking with

Richard Tafoya and Medicine Wind about these things, but they are not making progress. The murder of Lance Bernal is occupying their time. I am worried, Mr. Coe, that the Hanging Shell medicine bundle has fallen into bad company, and like the Zuñi Big Shell, dangerous things can occur."

"When the Navajo lightning cylinders were returned to McGinnis," Bustamente continued, "a message came with it. 'The god roams the foothills for scalps of his enemies.'" Bustamente looked directly at Coe.

"What god? What enemies?" asked Coe, his thinking that something deep had opened up in the earth, and it might not be such a good thing.

"I do not know, Mr. Coe...I do not know."

Coe and Bustamente said goodbye at the cacique's front door. Coe reasserted his promise to help with the Franklin Deerfield theft and return the items to the museum. "It may very well be the Hanging Shell medicine bundle should be returned to the pueblo."

"We shall see, Mr. Coe. At least the Corn Mothers need to be back among us. As someone once wrote a book entitled, *When Jesus Came, the Corn Mothers Went Away*. Maybe we can get some of the Corn Mothers returned to us."

When Coe walked back to his car in the visitor's parking lot, magpies alighted on the coyote fence. He counted five magpies. He thought he recognized one of the magpies. Was it the one that used to sit on his front porch chair for ten minutes each morning before it flew off to congregate with his chattering mates? All five of the magpies sat on the coyote fence staring at Coe. He started his engine and drove out of the parking lot and down Abalone Road to his home in Ojo Verde. He had many stories to tell Prissy, except for the Hanging Shell story. A promise he intended to keep.

40

Father Jose Padilla walked to the ambo on the epistle side of the Mission Saint Francis del Monte at the Tulona Pueblo. It was time to deliver the homily, the order of ritual before the Eucharist. The mission church of the Tulonas was three-quarters full, a well-attended Mass for a Saturday afternoon at five fifteen. Attendance of the faithful on Saturday met the obligations for Sunday. As always, there were more women than men, and he knew so long as the women came to Mission Saint Francis del Monte, the church would survive. Among all the tugs on the hearts of women, he prayed the church was always tugging the hearts of women.

Father Padilla, on his visitations from Santa Fe, was always enchanted by northern New Mexico. Coming from Santa Fe, past Española, the altitude rose dramatically through Embudo Station, and then up on the mesa past the horse corrals in the small canyon to the east. When he came up on the mesa, he could see thirty, forty miles away toward the Tusas, Tres Orejas, and the Jemez to the west.

Passing through Taos interested him, but Ojo Verde to the north of Taos was the smaller village, reminiscent of Taos in the twenties and thirties—or at least what he had read Taos was like back then. Father Padilla loved taking a drive around the Ojo Verde village plaza that still had a water fountain in the middle, and an open acequia that ran along the southside of the plaza and then underground to orchards and fields beyond the village limit. Towering cottonwoods shaded the plaza, and the town had planted young cottonwoods to supplant the elder trees when they became enfeebled. So quiet was the plaza and its fountain that he often parked in front of the decades-old hardware store on the southeast side of the plaza and sat on park benches under the shade of trees. He usually sat undisturbed, but welcomed a friendly conversation with villagers.

Tulonas sat and conversed with him and read newspapers. One time at his sitting, Father Padilla had struck up a conversation with a Tulona by the name of Albert Walhuime who told him, "I hear good things about you, padre. I don't go to Mass regularly, but I might one of these days if you talk about the Tulona." Father Padilla had thanked Albert and mentally made a note that one Saturday or Sunday when he came to celebrate Mass at Mission Saint Francis del Monte, he would deliver a homily devoted to the Tulona and their place in Mother Church.

As Father Padilla looked out over the laity that morning, he recalled his meeting with Albert. He looked for Albert, but he was not there. That was good because he did not have a Tulona homily. But one day he would deliver the Tulona homily, just not today. He opened his notebook and began.

From the view of the Tulonas, sitting in the pews, staring at the padre, Father Padilla was tall. Tall even for a snow-looks-like. His frame was not thin, but full and powerful. Rumor had it he played rugby in Mexico before attending the Jesuit seminary. The rugby teams in Mexico were amateur, soccer being the most popular sport, but they played a rough-and-tumble game. His face was round, his eyes oval and the pupils dark with flecks of green in them. The well-kept hair of Father Padilla was long, almost to his shoulders. In his early forties, he seemed older, the lines on his face obvious to the congregation. His voice carried accents of Spanish. His English was good, but Spanish was his mother tongue. The Tulonas took notice of Padilla's footwear: high-top leather shoes with the heels cut off. The shoe leather appeared soft, like old-style moccasins.

"In the name of the Father, Son, and Holy Spirit," Father Padilla began, "heed these words, my friends. This day, Saturday, October twenty seventh, is the saint's day of Blessed Bartholomew of Vicenza, Italy. He lived in the early thirteenth century and is honored for preaching to secure the people's loyalty to Holy Mother Church. He was of the Dominican order and spent part of his ministry as a bishop in Cyprus, where he befriended the French King Louis IX, who gave him a relic of Christ's Crown of Thorns. All of that is good, but I want to bring out that he founded a military order to bring civil peace to towns in Italy. A priest founding a military order of knights to establish peace! That may seem strange at first glance, but know this: Bartholomew sought to use the order of knights to secure peace so that the people felt safe and secure in their villages and homes. Where evil needed to be confronted powerfully with swords and lances, Bartholomew's order of knights met fire with fire—so peace would reign, not insecurity.

"So, it is today with civil law enforcement. They are entrusted with protecting us, protecting our society, your pueblo, so that your lives—and mine—may be safe as we grow crops, work in the villages, and travel to other towns to visit our friends and relatives. Where law enforcement officials go wrong—all institutions have their missteps—then they are brought to justice and weeded out. Even the Catholic Church has had to defrock priests and bring its own into line. Being a priest within Holy Mother Church, I am truly sorry.

"Last Wednesday, you buried Lance Bernal in Sacred Heart Cemetery." Father Padilla crossed himself; most of the congregants followed suit in crossing themselves. "His loss of life and the circumstances surrounding it are being investigated by the Tulona Tribal Police and other authorities that reflect the path of justice, much like Bartholomew's order of knights in the thirteenth century..."

At that moment, the entrance door of the nave swung open about quarter-way, and a man set a construction-style, black plastic bag inside the door and, just as mysteriously, closed the door and fled. One of the deacons at the back of the church quickly stood up from his pew and went to look at the bag. The deacon took the bag away from the door to the side of the narthex and looked inside. He looked twice inside the bag, and then from the back of the nave, opened his arms in a perplexed manner, signaling to Father Padilla, "I have no idea what this is." The deacon moved the black bag to the side of the narthex and waited for Mass to conclude. Father Padilla concluded the services, and once the church had been cleared, he and the deacon looked more closely at the contents of the bag.

Inside the large construction bag was a large buckskin mask, the Child of Water Navajo mask, dark red in color, large eyeholes and hole for the mouth, fur and feathers encircling the top of the mask, and hourglass "Xs" in a semi-circle around the face of the mask. A kilt skirt lay at the bottom of the bag.

"That's the mask stolen from Franklin Deerfield, Father," the deacon said.

"How do you know that, my child," Father Padilla asked.

"My cousin is a curator at the museum. He described it to me."

"Go get a tribal policeman at the station. We will have them take this mask. They are like one of Bartholomew's knights," Father Padilla said. The deacon ran off in the direction of the tribal stationhouse.

41

That Saturday afternoon, before the mask was dumped in the mission church's nave, Tribal policeman Richard Tafoya worked on the Lance Bernal case. As his style, he opened his three silos of data: the tribal computer files with links to the F.B.I., the hard material evidence box, and his field notebooks. From his desk, he retrieved his yellow legal pad of jottings, diagrams, and speculations.

Tafoya quickly, but carefully, scanned all three silos. The evidence box held recent copies of pawn shop emails. No hits had been made on Bernal's 7mm deer rifle, but pawn shops would be consistently checking serial numbers of new 7mm arrivals. Bernice had found the serial number for the rifle. Perhaps a hit would be made on a newly-pawned rifle. Other than pawn shop replies, the evidence box held the bullet found under Bernal's body and several plastic envelopes with odds and ends picked up from the murder scene. Once he scanned the silos of his field notebooks and the computer files, Tafoya looked at his list of questions on his yellow legal pad.

Bernal's deer rifle was missing. Was his rifle in any way connected with his murder scene? Had he taken it somewhere for repair...pawned it...loaned it out...? Bernal's two close friends stated they had not seen him in several days. Were they telling the truth? Bernal had gone to Quintana Pass with someone. Why go there? Most obvious explanations would be to scout for deer or campsites. But why would he not tell his wife he was going to be gone? Bernal was responsible to his family and would not likely go for a long ride without leaving behind some note as to his whereabouts. Bernal had no means of travel since his wife had taken the pickup to Mass. So, he went with someone to Quintana Pass. Who was that person? How did Bernal connect up with them at the pueblo?

He either walked to someone's house, or they came by to pick him up. Then they traveled to Quintana Pass. No one had come forward saying they had seen Bernal that fateful day, and interviews with neighbors were unproductive. Of all the snooping and watching that normally went on at the pueblo, surely someone had seen something?

Apparently, not that day. The day of the murder.

Trying another tack, Tafoya turned to the interviews with Ambrose Vasquez, Alfredo Dominguez, and Larry Armijo. Vasquez was not a suspect since he and his family were away the whole weekend of the murder for a christening in Santa Fe. Tafoya had crossed him off the list of suspects. Looking at the interview notes, Dominguez claimed he had not seen Bernal in over two weeks before the murder. Romero's interview with Armijo, the younger friend of Bernal, reported that Armijo had lunch with him on the Wednesday prior to murder on Saturday. They had eaten at the Farmer's Market Café and talked about the ski season coming up—hoping the snows would be good—and other things, including the opening of deer season and Armijo's girlfriend, Martha Johnson, who was an intern at Franklin Deerfield.

Tafoya made a note on his yellow legal pad that Martha Johnson was the girlfriend of Armijo *and* had been responsible for taking an inventory on the museum's keys. She had not completed the inventory. "There are two reasons to interview Martha Johnson," he thought. "Coincidence? Maybe, maybe not."

Tafoya then turned to his interview with Dominguez regarding Bernal. Tafoya had noted in his field notebook that Dominguez was a hunter, but, by his own admission, he had not prepared for the hunting season this fall because of work commitments. Perhaps that was not significant. Dominguez did seem involved in his flagstone masonry work. His craftsmanship was highly regarded in Ojo Verde and surrounding towns. He was probably making good money.

One thing did bother Tafoya. Tafoya sensed that Dominguez had been defensive about following traditional pueblo ways—the cutting off of the heels of his boots. That one pair of boots with the heels cut off on his porch and his attempt to hide it bothered Tafoya. True, Dominguez had not participated in ceremonies, having been exiled from inner pueblo society. Was he still practicing traditional ways on his own, off the Tulona Pueblo? No way to know the answer to that. Why not join back up with the people of the pueblo? Why not come back to the pueblo ways and be traditional with his people? Tafoya made a note to question Dominguez about coming back to the pueblo.

Tafoya stood up from his desk after closing down the computer files and locking the drawer with his field books and yellow legal pad. He walked back to the evidence room and stored the evidence box on Bernal. A few other people were on duty as he went to the front of the stationhouse. It was late Saturday afternoon. Looking through the front window, he saw pueblo Catholic parishioners walking and gossiping their way back home. Being late in October, the sun was lower in the west and dark would soon fall. The fiesta-day pole still stood high—a fifty-foot ponderosa pine timber, stripped of its bark, having been climbed successfully by the Black Eyes.

"Next year,"Tafoya thought, "I'll be helping with Saint Francis Fiesta Day in ceremonial ways, but I'll not be climbing the pole. Leave that to others…the younger ones."

His attention diverted suddenly. From the mission church, the door swung open, and an older man, the deacon of the mission church, came running to the stationhouse. The older Tulona, trotting in earnest, broke Tafoya's reverie about fiesta day.

"Something's going on,"Tafoya said to the officer at the front desk. Tafoya hurriedly stepped out of the stationhouse and ran to meet the deacon. The deacon was panting hard, out of breath.

"Richard," the deacon said hurriedly, "someone dumped the mask in our church."

"Slow down, catch your breath. What mask?"

"You know, the mask stolen from the museum. It's in the nave of the church! Come get that thing! We don't want it there!"

42

Monday, October 29, Day of Saint Narcissus of Jerusalem, Month of Corn Ripe Moon

John McGinnis, Head Curator of the Franklin Deerfield Museum in Ojo Verde, New Mexico, looked closely at the Child of Water mask resting on the main curating table toward the back of the inventory room. Standing close to him, staring at the Child of Water mask, Ray Tejada, the Tulona Curator, shook his head, "The tribal forensic team certainly dusted the mask for fingerprints. It'll take some time to take the powder off, but I think we can do it."

"Hmmph," McGinnis uttered. "We will start with a soft blower, then move on to light sable brushes. Agreed?"

Tejada agreed and plugged in an extension cord, inserting into the extension cord a hand-held blower. He began the process of cleaning that might last a week, maybe two. Both curators were trained to go slow, be patient, proceed with caution, because a curator does not want to correct an intemperate motion or damage the artifact. Whether an Indigenous mask or the stained-glass windows of Notre Dame, careful attention must be paid to the object.

"What is a month or two months of reconstruction compared to the hundreds-year-old material you work with? Go slow!"—a mantra both McGinnis and Tejada learned in laboratory classes at the university. At times, they had worked weeks with dental picks to clean matrix; certainly, the Child of Water mask would be easier than cleaning matrix around a Folsom tool.

On Saturday when the mask was dumped in the nave at Mission Saint Francis del Monte at the Tulona Pueblo, tribal officer Tafoya had first called Tejada about the mask—since he lived on the reservation—and he had then called McGinnis. Once the forensic team had analyzed the mask and taken photographs, Tafoya and Tejada ported the mask to the museum where cleaning would commence on Monday.

McGinnis and Tejada were happy stolen artifacts were making their way back—however strangely—to the museum. Tafoya puzzled over the weird return of the wooden cylinders representing Navajo thunderbolts and now, the mask. Tafoya concluded that one of the thieves, maybe all of them, had a guilty conscience and was trying to atone. But there was no proof to his speculation.

McGinnis noticed the missing shells under the eyes of the mask at the church. "The eye shells are gone, Tejada." He quickly opened the black plastic bag to see if they had fallen off, but no, the bottom of the bag was empty, holding only the kilt—no shells, just some stray fox fur hairs. McGinnis applied his skill to the mask, gently blowing the fingerprint powder off one side of the mask, then vacuuming up the debris. After a half-hour, Tejada took over the cleaning job. They had surface cleaned one-tenth of the mask by lunchtime. Gentle does it.

They took their lunch break in the staff room, overlooking the back patio. Then McGinnis had a change of heart and said, "Let's move outside on the patio. There's little wind and plenty of shade under the arbor."

Tejada agreed, and they carted their lunch boxes and drinks out to the patio where red willows and cottonwoods swayed gently in the noon breeze. Warm and pleasant, it was.

"A fine idea to come out here, John," Tejada said.

Tejada had a homemade burrito, McGinnis a sandwich of chicken and pork mousse he had made himself, accompanied with green chile jelly and pickled okra. McGinnis cleared his throat with pink lemonade—he needed to clear the green chile jelly, very hot—and began to talk.

"I've been thinking about the theft, Ray."

"What about it?" Tejada asked.

"I have no idea as to who betrayed us at the museum, if anyone did. I prefer to think no one on staff did." He took another gulp of lemonade. "So, I have gone back in my memory about people—anyone—that seemed the least bit odd, or asked unusual questions, or wanted information from me out of the ordinary." McGinnis paused and drank more soda to clear his throat.

"Okay, go on,"Tejada said, smiling that the chile jelly made McGinnis's face redder.

"There was a researcher from Boise State I had a conference with. She was quite intense about what we had in our inventory about sand paintings. She had thought we had some weavings from Hosteen Klah here in our museum that had never been made public."

"Yes, the Wheelwright in Santa Fe have Klah's weavings of sand paintings, not us,"Tejada inserted.

"I finally convinced her," McGinnis said, "by opening up Franklin Deerfield inventory list online and running searches for Klah, sand paintings, and Navajo rugs. She and I rummaged through the files until she was convinced that we had no weavings from Klah, and then she went back to Idaho."

McGinnis brought up a couple of more instances, including a visiting researcher from Germany, asking about scalps and whether or not the museum had any in their holdings. "I knew we had those two scalps from way back the way, but I said, 'No, we don't have any significant remains like that.' I lied, but I felt relieved when he finished his interview. He proved to be a fine historian from Stuttgart. He sent me his article on the Taos Society of Artists. Quite good."

The noontime lunch break came to an end. McGinnis and Tejada began bagging their lunch trash to throw in the trash bin. McGinnis's face returned to normal color.

McGinnis returned to possible suspects from the past. "Then there is this guy. Do you remember about a year ago, a Tulona came by, only briefly, and wanted to know about any prehistoric settlements that were between the Tulona Reservation and the Rio Grande?"

"Yeah, I remember you asking me about that," Tejada replied. "You never told me his name. I just figured some college student doing a term paper.... I do remember looking up the site designation of that prehistoric settlement to answer his questions. What was that site number...? I remember giving the data to you."Tejada added. "What seemed odd about him, John?"

"The Tulona was not a college student, but much older. Not an elder, either. He wanted to know if we had any artifacts from the site. After talking to you, I looked up the site as well and told him we have no known material associations with the settlement. That didn't disappoint him. No problem there. But it was his demeanor: serious, supplicating, very intent on something...I don't know...just a strange fellow. I can't remember his name, but I remember the inquiry. Since he said he was Tulona, I gave him all we had on that site data."

The two curators walked back to the basement laboratory. McGinnis started working again on cleaning the Child of Water mask. Tejada logged into New Mexico's Archaeological Records Management Section (ARMS), and looked up, once again, the site designation for the ruins by the Big River. He found the site designation: LA 9976429.

Both museum curators were trained in the state's Laboratory of Anthropology (LA) record management. Since 2018 in New Mexico, site numbers for archaeological and historical sites had undergone revision. The full naming convention included not only the site designation, but also a New Mexico Cultural Resource Information System Number (NMCRIS), and in the case of the ruins by the Big River, the NMCRIS number was 3357888. ARMS in Santa Fe properly listed the site as, LA9976429_3357888. The site had no popular or historic name, but it was located on the Arroyo de Conchas, one of the major arroyos to the north of Ojo Verde, Tract A, Tulona Reservation.

Tejada had given McGinnis the site number. McGinnis had given LA 9976429 with all its details, including location, to the unnamed Tulona. Was it possible the unidentified Tulona was involved in stealing from the museum? But what did LA 9976429 have to do with the museum theft? No matter, McGinnis and Tejada continued to clean the Child of Water mask, dropping their speculations because they seemed unsubstantiated.

43

Janet Rael, biology specialist for the U.S. Forest Service, and now liaison officer with the tribal police, filled the forest green Suburban with gasoline at headquarters in Ojo Verde. She did her "preflight check" on the automobile: a walkaround to check tires, bumpers, antenna connections for radio communications, and any dents before she started on field work along FR 438. The Suburban had high clearance, but she intended to avoid crossing deep arroyos and creeks.

The field mission for Janet that day was to reconnoiter the National Forest Road from Fort Burgwin, southeast of Ranchos de Taos, to Ryan Spring that flowed into Rito de la Olla. Her field supervisor listed several tasks. Janet was to pay a short visit to the archeological sites of Pot Creek (Rito de la Olla) alongside FR 438, determine the status of FR 438 for grading by a maintainer, and perform wildlife counts along the road to Ryan Spring.

From the paved highway SH 518 at Fort Burgwin to Ryan Spring, Janet would drive approximately nine miles on unpaved forest road. Since she would do field work alone, she strapped on her 9mm, semi-automatic, Glock 17 Gen4 pistol. Wearing the black holster with the Glock afforded her insurance in the field, in case of trouble—more than likely a curious bear she might have to scare off by a shot in the air. She preferred a shot in the air than an air horn. Janet also belted bear spray. She packed a lunch from home and departed at eight thirty. Janet's assignment had been given on Friday, and she had the weekend to check maps and weather conditions. The day's weather was to be fair, windy in the afternoon, temperature high forecast was upper sixties. But two days ahead, Halloween, snow was to fall, spoiling trick-or-treaters and other revelries for the holiday.

Driving at the posted speed limit but wanting to push it, Janet drove rapidly through Ojo Verde, south to Taos, turning eastward at

Ranchos de Taos on SH 518. Among adobe houses and trailer houses, she viewed sites that only locals knew about. On her right, she saw the entrance to the El Descanso Cemetery where John Collier was buried. Collier was the advocate for Native American rights who became the New Deal Commissioner of Indian Affairs from 1933 to 1945. He pushed to terminate the assimilation policy of the federal government and close boarding schools. Collier, Janet remembered from her history class in college, sought to help Native American cultures preserve their heritage. She remembered lighting a candle on his grave for All Souls' Day.

Janet's grandfather at the Isleta Pueblo told her of Collier's visit to the pueblo in the 1930s, where he talked with the elders about establishing a public school on the reservation, as well as affirming the pueblo had a right to their ceremonies and cultural identity. She looked at the beautiful blue entrance pillars and arbor over the gate. "I wonder if the cemetery association painted the arbor and pillars blue for the Blue Lake of the Taos Pueblo?" Janet pulled off the road next to the cemetery and with her cell phone took a photograph of the entrance. The cemetery was not on her list of tasks under "Forest Service Mission FR 438" for the day, but she would send the photo to the historian on staff with an attached note.

Another site known to locals lay ahead on the right side of the road. Not far from the Descanso Cemetery entrance, there sat an example of Spanish fortifications: the *torreon*, a castle-looking round structure that provided protection from Indian raids and a lookout point on the road from Picuris Pueblo down Arroyo Miranda to Taos Pueblo. The road was the farthest northern point of the El Camino Real. Janet saw the *torreon* standing alongside a well-kept trailer house. Some of the *torreon* was draped in tarp for repair.

Hurrying past the *torreon*, she saw the Talpa St. Francis Cemetery on her left that had been the foreground of artistic photographs and paintings. Although a vertical water tower had been built that distorted the view of Taos Mountain from the cemetery, the tableau of cemetery with its white crosses and flower adornments remained imposing, even if you drove by it every day to work or school. Solar-powered lights illuminated graves at night. Solar-powered lights on descansos beside the road would be next, she speculated. Soft, touching, but eerie, she thought.

Past Talpa, and prior to Fort Burgwin and FR 438 eastward, Janet turned off the state highway onto the Pot Creek archaeological site to discharge her first task: evaluating tourist impact on the ruins. Since the first of October, Pot Creek had been closed. The parking lot was empty, the trash bins closed tightly with no spillover rubbish. A quick check of the restrooms yielded a favorable comment on her evaluation sheet: clean, winter-proofed, but needing a fresh coat of paint. Walking down the trail a quarter mile, she saw the kiva entrance was sealed with a door, but the kiva ladder arced upward to the sky, despite the seal.

The pueblo had been evacuated about 1320 AD after a short occupation of sixty years. Despite its brief life, the puebloans had built 400 storage rooms and had begun construction on a great kiva, but had abandoned it as the people scattered to Picuris and Taos Pueblos. The great kiva had been burned, whether intentionally or not, by an enemy raid or the departing occupants. May have been accidental. But no evidence had surfaced as to the exact cause of the evacuation.

Standing on the edge of Pot Creek kiva made Janet think of the kiva chamber on Tract A of the Tulona Reservation she had discovered at the Arroyo of Shells a few days prior. Looking at the slender poles of the kiva ladder, she thought, "I wonder if there are archaeological notations on the Tract A kiva? Surely, Franklin Deerfield or at the State Offices have field notes on the Arroyo of Shells ruins. The site can't be that hidden."

Janet noticed a large mound of small pebbles of rocks built up by harvester red ants a few yards from the kiva. Their trails led off into the brush. She saw the ants porting seeds of unidentifiable plants and tiny stones back to their home. Janet thought of the ants' work habits...and then quickly thought of her mission that day. "I need to get back on point... up the forest road."

Janet drove on FR 438 out of the Pot Creek site. She turned eastward on the forest road that meandered Rito de la Olla, a major water source for the vanished Pot Creek people. Janet picked up the radio-com microphone and checked into the Ojo Verde headquarters of the Forest Service.

"Headquarters, Rael here."

"Go ahead, Rael."

"I'm turning onto FR four-three-eight from Cantonment Burgwin and Pot Creek at nine fifty. I finished the eval on Pot Creek. No special notations."

"Copy that, Rael," replied Forest Service headquarters.

"My intentions are to follow four-three-eight along Rito de la Olla past Ryan Springs and Diablo Canyon to Benardin Lake and campsite, approximately nine to ten miles, as per my orders. Over."

The Forest Service in Ojo Verde acknowledged, and Janet signed off.

Janet's route on FR 438 started at 7,500 feet, ascending to 9,800 feet to Benardin Lake. After going two miles, Janet stopped the Suburban at a turnout between the Rito Osha tributary and Diablo Canyon. She hiked into the forest for a quarter mile, noting conditions of vegetation, trees, and evidence of wildlife. Janet donned a flame-red jacket for safety before she hiked into the woods. The dry conditions of the spring season had been alleviated with late summer rains. The Olla River, small stream in any season, still flowed.

The sky was clear. The high altitude cooled the area, and Janet buttoned the snaps on her jacket to ward off the chill in the shade. The conifers did not appear stressed on the trail, and piñon jays, blue jays, and a few magpies called alarm as she hiked in for the quarter mile. She found deer pellets, possible bear scat, and mountain lion scratching on the bark of several ponderosas. The second hike into the forest near Rincon Canyon yielded fresh track of migrating elk. She estimated a herd of fifty, entering the data on her field computer when she returned to the vehicle.

Janet's third and final foray into the forest occurred at Rito Quien Sabe, or the "River Who Knows." At River Who Knows, an altitude of 9,200 feet, Janet attempted to contact the Forest Service headquarters on VHF frequencies, but she was unable to find a repeater being so far in the woods. She switched to a lower high frequency channel. Janet made contact from the River Who Knows.

"Headquarters, I am located at River Who Knows."

"Where are you, Janet? I didn't copy," asked Headquarters.

"I repeat. I am at River Who Knows," replied Janet.

"You don't know where you are? Are you lost, Janet? Have you tried your GPS?"

"Negative, Headquarters, I know where I am. I'm located at the River Who Knows," Janet answered back, thinking that the exchange was getting a little ridiculous. "Who is on first," she thought.

"I advise you to follow FR four-three-eight until you can pick up a land feature and confirm your location," said a supervisor that took over the exchange, his voice alarmed.

Janet did not immediately reply. She was trying not to laugh.

"Janet?" Headquarters asked. "You there? Over."

"Affirmative, I am here at the confluence of the Olla River and the River Who Knows," she answered.

"Copy that. I thought we had lost radio contact. I repeat. Follow FR four-three-eight until you pick up a recognizable landform."

Silence.

Janet thought on how she could end this. Finally, she broke the silence.

"Now listen up," Janet said, with a smile in her voice.

"Get out the topo map. I have my topo map in front of me. It is the Shady Brook quadrangle. Trace FR four-three-eight into the mountains from Pot Creek. You will find a river called, now hear me clearly, it's on the map in clear print, 'Rito Quien Sabe,' translated to English, 'The River Who Knows.' That's my location. Do *you* copy that, Headquarters?"

No immediate comeback from headquarters.

Then Janet heard the transmitter come on; then a voice, sheepishly said, "Well…oh. I, I mean we understand, Janet. Sorry. Check in down the road. Over and out."

"Roger," Janet replied. After she stopped laughing, Janet informed headquarters she would proceed to Benardin Lake campsite, then turning around or proceeding to the Quintana Canyon route and return to headquarters via U.S. 68. Headquarters acknowledged and advised her to check back in at Benardin Lake and inform them of her decision to return via Rito de la Olla or by the Quintana route. The time was two seventeen and Janet's stomach growled in need of lunch.

Deciding to go into the forest alongside River Who Knows for a quarter mile before she ate lunch, Janet followed the stream into the woods. At over 9,000 feet, the air was cold and the conifers' shade made her field hike colder. She noticed on the northside of land depressions snow from an early fall snow squall had not melted. Three hundred feet into the hike at a large clearing, she observed an area where elk had lain down, the grass squashed, flattened.

Having made her requisite field observations, Janet turned around and hiked back to the confluence of the Olla and River Who Knows. She stepped across the Olla on flat dry stones to get to her vehicle. The stream ran fast. Janet ate her lunch of medium-rare roast beef, potato salad, tortilla chips with red salsa, and Gatorade to wash it down. She saved her chocolate bar for later in the afternoon.

As Janet sat under the trees, resting for few minutes, before she checked on the Benardin Lake camping area. She expected to find no campers or recent evidence of camping since it was so far from the main roads. Janet began to ponder the name of River Who Knows.

The name on topographical maps was Rito Quien Sabe. "Had early mapmakers run out of naming rivers, and impatiently ascribed, 'Rito Quien Sabe'? Or, was it possible the stream held a secret? What was its origin back up in the Fernando Mountains, a montane subset of the Sangre de Cristo: a spring, several rivulets of run-off, a lake? Who knows?" She laughed. "Who knows about Who Knows!"

Rael collected her trash and walked back to her vehicle. She started on FR 438 from Rito Who Knows toward Benardin Lake campsite. Turning a curve on the road, she abruptly stopped. Several fir trees had fallen across the road, blocking her way. The flowing Rito de la Olla blocked a go around on one side, the dirt cliffs on the other side. Starting from the highway back at Cantonment Burgwin, Janet had been able to use the winch on the front of the Suburban to pull fallen trees out of the way. But three large fir trees, two dead and one green, completely stopped Janet's progress on FR 438. No way around this time.

The forces of nature, wind, a landslide, and the river decided for her: she would turn back on FR 438 and return to Ojo Verde via Cantonment Burgwin—the same way she came in. Janet picked up the high-frequency com and radioed her intentions to return the way she came. Before then, however, she would walk the quarter mile to the Benardin Lake campsite.

Ojo Verde Forest Service headquarters acknowledged her decision, "Travel safely back, Officer."

Disappointed that she would not travel farther toward Quintana Pass, which was not part of her mission anyway, Janet shrugged and walked quickly around the fallen trees in the direction of Benardin Lake for her final survey. The lake was small, five acres of surface water in total. But before budget cuts in the game and fish division, the lake had been stocked with fish and had proved popular among outdoor persons wanting a deep-woods experience. And they definitely experienced deep woods at Benardin—wild and way far from the city.

Approaching the edge of the lake, Janet stopped. With her binoculars she scanned the shores of the lake and back toward the stand of conifers that sheltered campers. An arbor that had been constructed years before remained intact, only a cross beam having fallen to one side. Close to one side of the arbor, sheep pens appeared functional for another year. FR 438 was one of the historic roads of sheepherders coming from Ranchos de Taos, the other route being Rio Chiquito that terminated at Quintana Canyon and Pass; the Chiquito and Olla rivers had been used as riparian pathways into the mountains since the nineteenth century.

As Janet scanned the far east side of the lake, she noticed blue-gray smoke from a campfire, drifting into the forest. The camper had evidently come from the Quintana Pass direction. Zooming in through her binoculars, she saw an old, dark-green pickup, Chevy it looked like. It had been parked back under a stand of ponderosa, blending into the stands of brush and trees. A man, in squatting position, stood up from the leeside of the fire and waved—a half-hearted, friendly wave. Janet waved back.

As a Forest Service officer, Janet had been trained that in most cases officers leave people alone that are camping and let them enjoy the solitude of the forest. Ten-thousand reasons motivate people to go into the wilderness: hunting, fishing, hiking, meditating, bird watching, intentional solitude from city life, and on and on. Janet saw no issues with the camper; after all, it was close to deer hunting season, and he might be searching for a possible deer camp. Janet decided to leave him alone.

Before Janet returned to her Suburban, she wanted more information about the man. She zoomed in on the license plate of the pickup—New Mexico old-style tags, yellow and red, CGF 894. The tags were a bit dented, but readable at a distance. As soon as she returned to the pickup, she wrote down the tag numbers and called Ojo Verde headquarters.

"Could you run a check on CGF eight-nine-four, New Mexico plates, dark green Chevy pickup?"

Within five minutes, after she had turned around on the road and headed back to Cantonment Burgwin, headquarters radioed back, "Car is registered to Larry Armijo, Tulona resident, twenty-six years of age."

Larry Armijo saw the female Forest Service officer approach Benardin Lake from the southwest. An hour before, he had heard a vehicle growl in low gear from the direction of Cantonment Burgwin. The vehicle stopped and its engine was turned off. He had remained at his camp, hoping nothing further would come of it. When the officer came to the edge of the lake on southwest side, he stood up to wave, signaling awareness of the intruder. From the shape of the officer, the officer was definitely female, wearing a red vest and khaki uniform with a watch cap. A Forest Service Ranger?

"So far out here in our forest and a white woman officer shows up.... Not your land. It's ours," he thought.

Fortunately, she did not come closer, for he had no hunting license, and he was porting a 7mm Remington deer rifle with scope. His knives were sharpened for dressing a kill in the field, although hunting was not his aim for the day. Armijo had built a fire and smudged himself with sage to clear himself of weak thoughts, hesitations, and confusion. The day was approaching when the ancient kiva would be reconstructed, the altar erected, and vigor and power returned to the Hanging Shell people of the Tulona. In preparation of that night of revitalization, he had come down the road from Quintana Pass seeking isolation to purify himself.

After the female officer went away, his ceremony and prayers accomplished, Armijo put out the fire, dousing it with several buckets of water from the lake, and drove back to Ojo Verde and the Tulona Reservation. On his way back, he passed by Quintana Canyon, Valle Escondido, and followed Rio Fernando de Taos alongside U.S. 64, the narrow two-lane highway of countless automobile wrecks.

"May the Creator keep people away from Hanging Shell," Armijo thought, thinking of the kiva over by Big River. And, "May the Creator help us blow the snow-looks-likes back across the sea from where they came."

44

Jason Taylor, Tablita's Restaurant second-longest-tenured server, had been following the weather forecasts eagerly since the first of October. Now, on Monday, October 29, the weather forecasts out of the Albuquerque National Weather Service station predicted snow late Tuesday night and all-day Wednesday. Last winter's snowfall was sparse and the ski season poor in the ski valley. Now, the weather was going to favor him and the ski valley. Snow brings tourists and their credit cards. Snowfall and tips galore—hopefully.

"Snow! Before the first of November! Yea!" Jason had yelled, when he first heard the forecast.

At Tablita's evening serving, the alpha customer at Table 2, beside the window overlooking Paseo del Norte, subtly signaled Jason with a smile and eyebrow arched for him to come to the table. There was no complaint that could dispel Jason's mood—for, "Snow is coming!"

Table 2 hosted a young couple at positions 1 and 3, looking across the table at one another. They had ordered dinner and a bottle of wine. The couple, their origin undetermined but definitely European, had begun dinner hesitantly, first ordering Chili Dusted Rock Shrimp and house margaritas. With a second round of house margaritas, they each ordered the Romaine Hearts with lemon anchovy dressing, shaved parmesan cheese, and fresh croutons.

Jason was proud of Tablita's croutons. Two years before, Jason had harsh words with the Ojo Verde Inn manager over the quality of croutons. He was not alone thinking the restaurant's crouton quality needed enhancement.

Croutons!

Jason, the chef, and kitchen staff had forced the manager to quit ordering croutons off-site. The croutons from some faraway kitchen, off-site, were sending Tablita's Restaurant croutons that were like hard, little bricks that could, if not dunked in water, crack the molars of Tablita's customers.

"We'll make our own croutons, sir," the chef and Jason had argued. "They'll be soft and tasty, and not bring law suits for dental repair!"

The manager eventually bowed to the pressure and opined later, after tasting the kitchen's in-house baking, "These croutons are *really* good! Can we sell these at other restaurants?"

No. Tablita's croutons were limited—just for the restaurant, no other. So said the chef; so said Jason.

"Yes, can I help you?" Jason asked the couple, a little nervous, but no matter, snow is coming. He could handle anything with the cold coming on.

In an accent Jason dubbed as German, the young man asked, "I know we have ordered a bottle of red wine with our steaks, it's still to come, of course. But we are on a tour of the Great American Southwest. We are so impressed with New Mexico and the territory…this town, Ojo Verde… and the Tulona Pueblo. It has made an impression upon me and my wife." He looked at his wife, and they smiled at each other, sharing secrets. "We wish to be more celebratory this evening by changing our wine order to something more expensive."

Jason thought, "Where is this headed? They've already ordered a bottle…."

"May we see your master wine list?" The young woman asked; then, deliberately pronouncing slowly, "*¿Con su permiso, por favor?*"

"Certainly. I'll be right back," Jason said, slightly arching his back in pride reserved for customers that raised the exchange of server and customer to a level of corresponding marriage of food, server, and customer.

The union of food, server, and client seldom occurred. Too often, the customer is only concerned with their meal and other table guests; the server is an appendage to be tolerated and tipped. Yet, during the course of a shift, a unification of server, customer, and food congeals into an experience that remains in the memory of server and customer for all time. Jason thought, perhaps, this may be that rare time: a congruence of the server, customer, and meal with wine.

Jason brought the leather-bound, master wine list to Table 2, the table adjacent to Paseo del Norte, where cars, vans, SUVs, lumber trucks, and Dancing Rock Power Coop trucks passed by, their rumblings and gear shifts to lower and higher muffled through thick adobe walls and double-paned windows. As Jason opened the master wine list, the young German woman stood up from her chair and went to position 2, so that she could peruse the wine list with her husband. Leaving them to look at the wine list—ninety pages long—Jason went into the adjacent dining room to wait for their decision.

The sun had set, the clouds thick in the sky, and cottonwood trees swayed, the lower trunks bending slightly while upper limbs swayed wildly back and forth. A change of weather had started and by the next day, Tuesday, light rain would turn to snow, descending on Ojo Verde and Tulona Pueblo, bringing cold and wind and happiness. "Snow is coming! I can feel it in the air," so Jason thought, standing at the ready for the couple to decide on a new wine. The gesture came.

The young man nodded his head upward to catch Jason's attention. Jason walked to Table 2. He needed no note pad; he would remember.

"We've made up our mind," said the young man, voicing a collaborative decision.

"Yes...what will it be?" Jason asked, attentively.

"We will have the cabernet sauvignon from the Palmaz Vineyard, at Napa," answered the young woman. "I think it will pair *sehr gut*, I mean very good, with our dinner, don't you think?"

Jason agreed with their choice, and it was a true consensus, not a diplomatic assent to a terrible choice. If they had asked him for advice, he would have given them several choices, but as it was, they merely wanted concurrence, not analysis. Palmaz Vineyard? It was Jason's choice as well, hands down.

The young couple from Germany ate slowly and savored their dinner and Palmaz Napa wine. After Jason had run their credit card and brought the final tab, they asked him to take a photo of them at the table. As he took several photos with their smart phone, he noticed that outside the widow, passing by, were several Tulona walking toward the pueblo. Three of them were blanketed.

When the young couple looked at the photos Jason had taken, the young woman exclaimed, "Oh, my! Should we have asked them permission take their picture?"

"Naa, it's okay," Jason answered. "Bustamente, Medicine Wind, and Lion Walks Night would not mind, since it is a coincidence they crossed your background. Take it as a gift to you they were walking by. Course, contact the pueblo if you commercialize the photo, but I'm sure the photo is for your vacation album of the Great American Southwest."

"You know them!" the young man exclaimed.

Jason nodded, yes, and thought of Medicine Wind helping him get his truck unstuck and turned around on the road to Earth Cloud Lake, two months before.

As the couple, holding hands, walked out of the main dining room of Tablita's, Jason stared at them. Not only had they tipped him thirty percent—which would go for ski clothes and equipment—but the business cards they left behind stated: "Prof. Dr. Toby Schwartz, Prof. of Biology, University of Munich," and "Prof. Dr. Louisa Godord Schwartz, Prof. of Germanic Studies, University of Munich."

Jason flipped over the business cards. On the back of Toby Schwartz's business card, he had scribbled, "We so enjoyed our dinner! Maybe we will see you next winter when we come to ski! *Tschuss.*"

Jason Taylor, black-diamond skier and second-longest-tenured waiter at Tablita's, blew out the candle at the Table 2, that, henceforth, in Jason's private naming, would be known as, "The Schwartz Table." After closing and cleanup at Tablita's, Jason went home and slept soundly, awaiting the snow of tomorrow's evening.

Snow *was* coming.

45

Tuesday, October 30, Day of Saint Alphonsus Rodriquez, Month of Leaves Falling Moon

Sharply out of the north, winds blew strong Tuesday morning, and clouds covered the sky all around Ojo Verde with turquoise blue streaks of sky fleetingly seen, never staying long. But no one looked upward or westward, for heads were bowed, stacking firewood and gassing up vehicles for the next day's weather and dark festival—Halloween; plus, checking propane levels in their tanks. As the day progressed, temperatures dropped predictably, so that by early evening, rain fell, transposing later into snow.

At nine thirty, Tribal policeman Richard Tafoya turned into the parking lot at Franklin Deerfield and parked his service vehicle next to the handicapped space, facing outward for a quick departure. He unzipped his leather pouch that contained his field notebook, pens, pencils, and a list of questions he had drawn up for an interview with Martha Johnson, an intern at the museum. She had been in charge of petty, but important, details in investigating the theft of artifacts. Checking his list of questions, Tafoya rezipped the pouch. A sudden gust of north wind blew the car door closed with a noisy slam. He looked northward toward Arroyo Hondo and Questa, the towns north of Ojo Verde, and surmised they were already affected with weather change, and soon it would be upon him and Ojo Verde.

Tafoya's interview with Martha took place in the museum's boardroom. Martha Johnson was in her mid-twenties, but looked like a naïve teenager, just out of high school. A blonde with mid-length hair, her face was one of a thousand forgettable faces lost in the crowd. Her eyes were spaced normal, neither far apart nor closely set, and light brown in color.

Short and light weight, Tafoya thought she could have used some toning up of muscle, but he relinquished that opinion, remembering her work was indoors, not outside. As intern, she had been hired at the museum after graduating from Arizona State University with a degree in anthropology. She had slow-walked her college education because her family did not have a lot of money, and she had to work part time to finance her studies. Pell grants funded a large part of her education. Franklin Deerfield Museum was her first "perfect fit" with her B.S. degree.

As Martha Johnson entered the boardroom, Tafoya rose from his chair and motioned her to sit across the table from him. She appeared nervous. Tafoya began the interview with stating he was conducting a "general" inquiry, and she was in no way under suspicion, but that she might have insight into the theft. She exhaled, losing her rigid posture, and relaxed.

After a few preliminary questions, Tafoya centered on the focal question, the central reason he wanted to interview her.

"You had been in charge of the key inventory?"

She answered, "Yes, that had been one of my duties."

"Did you turn in a report on the key count?" Tafoya asked.

"No, I was interrupted on that assignment and never got around to do it." She did not hesitate answering. Tafoya immediately concluded she could be trusted.

"What was so important that stopped you from counting keys?"

Intern Johnson did not immediately answer, as she tried to remember what diverted her attention in counting keys.

After a few seconds, she retrieved her answer. "I dropped the key count when the inventory of stolen artifacts became the priority. I completely forgot about it. I was hoping it wasn't that important," Martha admitted.

"Okay...." Tafoya was about to ask another question when she interrupted.

"Did the security officer count the *master keys* checked out of the locker?" she asked.

"No..." Tafoya said.

"Well, a master key opens most of the doors in this place, including the basement inventory room," Martha said. "Maybe we need to check the master keys? They are the most important."

"Yes, good idea," he replied, "let's walk down the hall and do a count." Tafoya wondered who was directing the interview—himself or Martha.

Tafoya and the intern walked down the hallway to the security office. The security officer was at his desk, and the three of them quickly counted the master keys and compared the number with keys checked out. Tafoya made a comment that the key locker door was open when they walked in.

"Is the key locker door left open a lot?"

The security officer looked embarrassed and replied that during the day, museum staff needed access to keys, and the locker door is open more often than closed.

"Maybe the museum needs to go to fully digital-locking security. Easier to change the code than collect, distribute, and keep track of keys," Tafoya opined. "Besides, your master keys are colored red. A dead giveaway they are special keys."

The key count for master keys proved significant. Five master keys were listed on the inventory sheet. Director Hornbuckle, Head Curator McGinnis, and Curator Tejeda had each been issued a master key. When they checked the hook for keys remaining, there was only one left hanging. One master key to Franklin Deerfield Museum was missing.

The security officer, without prompting, called Director Hornbuckle. When she came to the security office and verified what she had been told, she called a locksmith from Santa Fe and requested an emergency visit to reconfigure locks and keys. She called a locksmith in Taos to come to Franklin Deerfield and assist when the Santa Fe locksmith crew arrived.

"What a mess! We've got to do better than this!" Hornbuckle said, shaking her head in disgust.

Hornbuckle ordered extra security after closing hours until the locks were changed. The security officer slammed the key cabinet shut and locked it, putting the key to the cabinet in the top middle pull-out drawer of his desk. Tafoya grimaced privately at another problem of security concerning the key cabinet: stashing the key to the key cabinet in the desk drawer in the same room. First place a thief would look.

Back at the boardroom to complete the interview, Tafoya asked Martha if she knew Alfredo Dominguez.

"No. I have no idea who he is. Is he a suspect?" Tafoya ignored her question.

"Do you know Larry Armijo?" Tafoya asked.

Martha fell silent. "Why do you want to know?"

Ignoring her counter question, he asked her again. "Are you acquainted with Larry Armijo?"

"I know him," she volunteered.

"In what context do you know him: boyfriend, casual friend, passing acquaintance?" Tafoya pressed.

Intern Johnson looked down at the table, then back up at Tafoya. "I date him occasionally, and he helps me with my computer problems. He's very smart at computer things."

"When was the last time you saw Armijo, Martha?" Tafoya asked.

Martha paused, "The last time I saw him was…about three weeks ago. He toured the museum again. He likes the pottery section a lot. I showed him the new pots from San Ildefonso on display. Larry loves coming to Franklin Deerfield. He says, 'The museum puts me in touch with the Tulona old ways.'"

Then Martha asked Tafoya, "How did you connect me and Larry?"

"I didn't…until now. It was just a routine question," Tafoya answered. Martha nodded. He did not feel compelled to tell her that her relationship with Armijo had come to light in Romero's interview with Armijo.

Tafoya looked at his notes. He had one more question, "Do you have any idea who might have stolen the artifacts from the museum?"

Martha, the intern, shook her head, "No." She had no idea who might have been involved, nor could she even comprehend any employee breaking into the museum and rifling through the cabinets to steal artifacts.

"Fortunately, the high-dollar turquoise jewelry is in a banker's vault with a combination lock. No key!" she exclaimed.

Tafoya judged Martha's replies credible and truthful—for the time being—and thanked her for her cooperation. He gave her his business card, and said, "Call me, if you think of anything else that might help us."

Immediately after Martha departed the boardroom, Tafoya wrote up the interview in detail, appending the observation that the museum's key management was insecure and needed a substantial make over. In conclusion, he wrote, "A follow-up interview with Johnson regarding Armijo and Lance Bernal is imperative."

Tafoya looked at his watch: it was nearly eleven. He walked to the plantation shutters in the boardroom and opened them to check the weather outside. Clouds had become darker and the ceiling had lowered, so that the tops of the Cristo Mountains were obscured. He checked the weather forecast on his cell phone. The temperature was falling from the fifties, aiming for freezing by midnight with rain changing to snow.

"Happy Halloween, trick-or-treaters," he said to himself.

Since he had an hour before lunch, Tafoya decided to ask Adela Montoya, the administrative secretary to Director Hornbuckle, a few questions if she could spare the time. She was available to talk. She carried two cups of coffee for them to the boardroom. They sipped their coffee while they talked about the Halloween party at the museum the next night.

Montoya was going to dress up as a fortune teller, "I've plenty of long dresses and gypsy-like coats from my past. I need to fashion a Sixties headband like hippies used to wear. You remember those communes, officer?"

Tafoya laughed. "Communes were before my time."

"I was a toddler back then, and don't know much about them," Adela said, winking at him. They both grinned, for she was in her late sixties. She knew about communes.

In the course of their conversation, Adela told Tafoya she had been with Franklin Deerfield for forty-three years, "And, yes, I remember the communes down in Taos with Dennis Hopper, and all the 'Easy Rider' crowd. It wasn't always peaceful with the hippies around."

Curious, Tafoya asked, "What were the problems?"

Adela was quick to answer. "The hippies were outsiders, Richard. They brought in a lot of drugs. You know the anxiety people have of strange, new arrivals coming to town. They were a weird, colonizing, white group. I think all three of our cultures had problems with them, especially the local Chicano youth. The puebloans, not so much. But I had a lot of hippie friends. 'Flower children,' we called them. I even visited a commune, the Blue Lemon, that was trying to make a go of it near Lamy. Down in Taos. The conflict got so bad with the hippie crowd that the summer fiesta was almost cancelled for fear of violence. But at the last minute, the Optimist Club, made up of Anglos and Hispanos, brought the fiesta off for one day, just before the San Geronimo Day at the pueblo."

As a traditional Tulano, Tafoya had heard stories of colonizers way before the Sixties, but not the hippies in that way. The Spanish; the nineteenth-century American influx after the war with Mexico, especially Texans; the art colonizers in the early twentieth; and now he would have to add the Sixties' flower children to the settler-colonizer list. "What next?" he thought to himself; then he remembered a Tiwa old story.

"What you have told me about the flower children coming into town reminds me of a story, Adela," Tafoya said, softening his voice.

"What story is that, Richard?"

"It's a story about a hero among the Tiwa named Point Hill Green. He's still alive and under a lake up north. When he appeared to puebloans, it was said he had the power to point at a hill or mountain and turn it green."

"That's nice. We need him to show up in a drought around here," Adela said.

Tafoya looked out the window of the boardroom at the rain clouds in the distance. The winds had picked up, but no Point Hill Green toward the north. Tafoya continued the story.

"Before any of the puebloans had seen strangers—white people, black people, and so on—Point Hill Green told them, 'You will see different people come to the pueblo, and many of them will make a noise walking in their shoes. More and more noisy shoe-walkers will come and puebloans will become fewer and fewer. After time, all will become white men.' Point Hill Green brought corn, beans, and squash to pueblo people, as well as this story. He was a cultural hero for puebloans. He anticipated many people coming here, including the hippies."

Tafoya finished the story, and looked down at his shoes that were heavy soled and made noise when he walked. "One more thing, Adela, he had the power to fly within a few feet of the stars. He described the stars as bright-breasted hummingbirds."

"Peyote gave him the power to fly?" Adela asked.

"No. He used eagle feathers and turkey wings. Not peyote."

Tafoya and Adela sat silent, sipping coffee. Finally, Tafoya stirred out of his reverie and asked Adela if she had any insight into the Franklin Deerfield theft.

"Do you have any idea who might have helped the three thieves? Some disgruntled employee or former employee?"

She was quick to respond. Adela knew of no one, past or present, who might be responsible. She volunteered that Director Hornbuckle was one of the best directors she had worked under. "She is always applying for grants to help the financial status of the museum, and when I go with her to conferences, she is respected and popular among her colleagues. Curator McGinnis may be a little testy at times, but he is devoted to the anthropology of the Southwest. He wants Franklin Deerfield to be regarded as the best regional museum in America."

Adela added little to what Tafoya already knew. She excused herself to go out to lunch with her husband in Ojo Verde. Tafoya wrote her interview down in his notebook.

Tafoya had an additional query for curator McGinnis. He looked up McGinnis's cell phone number and called him. McGinnis had spare time before he went to lunch, and replied he would stop by the boardroom to talk with Tafoya.

McGinnis came in and sat down at the boardroom table. Tafoya asked the curator if he had any idea why the two wooden thunderbolt sticks and the message were deposited with him at the break in of his home in Ranchos de Ojo Verde?

"The thieves must have known you somehow?" Tafoya asked.

McGinnis said, "Well, I *am* known in the area as the curator and my address is in the telephone book and on the internet, so I'm not hard to track down. Who else might he return the objects to? Easy to explain, I think." McGinnis replied crisply.

"But the note," McGinnis continued, "'The god roams the hills looking for scalps,' I have no idea what that was about, although it fits with the Navajo narrative of Child of Water, as Majerus told us. The message could be a warning. The return of the mask means the thieves wanted nothing to do with it. They knew the mask's power." McGinnis leaned back in his chair and folded his arms, looking at the cloudy sky outside the window.

This guy must be hard to work with, Tafoya thought. Nonetheless. Tafoya felt confident McGinnis's speculation about the motivation to return the artifacts could be correct, "I think your explanation is plausible, but we will only know for sure when we arrest the thieves." Looking at his watch and aware of McGinnis's impatience, Tafoya concluded the questioning.

As McGinnis was leaving the boardroom, he stopped, turned around, and said, "I've racked my brain to come up with any suspicious behavior of people who might want to rob the museum. Now don't misunderstand me, I'm not talking about our staff."

"Yes, what about it?" Tafoya perked up.

"Several months ago, there was this older Tulona that dropped by and pressed me on archaeological sites that lie between the reservation and the Rio Grande.... Sites that may have been related to old Tulona culture. I found only one site with Tejada's help and gave the man the information. I'm sorry but I don't remember his name."

"Would you recognize him if you saw him?"

"I don't know, it was a short encounter here at the museum," McGinnis lamented.

"What was the site designation?" Tafoya asked.

"I don't know off hand, but I'll text it to you. Tejada and I were talking about it the other day." Tafoya nodded in agreement, and said he wanted a quick reply on site designation. McGinnis left the room to find Tejada.

Sitting at the conference table, Tafoya went back over his interview notes he had conducted that morning. "There's a lot of, 'I don't know,' these people are giving me," he said to himself.

Tafoya drove to the newly-opened Pueblo Café on the outskirts of the pueblo, on Paseo del Norte. He texted Janet to see if she was available for lunch, but she was in the field on assignment and unavailable. He would have lunch alone.

As Tafoya finished his jalapeño-sauteed chicken tostadas with sour cream on top for lunch, he received a text from McGinnis, "Site designation is LA 9976429. The museum has a topographical map with the location. It's on Tract A of the Tulona Trust Land."

Re-holstering his cell phone after reading McGinnis's text, Tafoya lapsed into thinking about Point Hill Green again. Yes, Point Hill Green brought knowledge on how to grow corn, beans, and squash. But, in some ways, above all else, Point Hill Green taught puebloans to dance. Tafoya thought of the Deer Dance performed at winter solstice time, the Christmas period. Before the present Fifth World, animals and humans lived closer together, speaking the same language. Tafoya like to think he knew the language of animals.

The Deer Dance represents many things, but one interpretation is that the dance reconstructs the intimacy of humans to animals, the deer in particular. Point Hill Green taught puebloans to dance, and by dancing, humans were praying and giving thanks with their feet.

Tafoya wondered: The Deer Dance this Christmas—who will be the Deer Mother? Reflecting about dancing and Point Hill Green, he knew he wanted to be one of the attendants in the dance with the Deer Mother this year. Quail Looks Away was rumored to be the Deer Mother. Tafoya's conversation with Adela about Point Hill Green had spurred him to dance again. He had not felt that way in a long time.

46

On the cloudy afternoon before Halloween, G. Armstrong Coe sat behind the counter of his bookshop. The street outside, Paseo del Norte, had heavy traffic passing through the village toward Taos and Santa Fe; not so much traffic headed northward to Colorado. Coe walked to his front window and looked outside. Changes appeared: a brisk wind blew from the north, stripping cottonwoods of leaves—no more rattling leaves—the temperature falling.

He opened the door, the overhead bell jangled, and he stepped outside. Turning his face to the north, cold moisture sharply nicked his face. Fenster had quietly padded along with him, sitting on her haunches when he stopped. She stared at magpies across the street on the adobe wall bordering an art shop. The two stood there, Coe with his hands in his pockets looking at the traffic passing by, and Fenster looking at everything, but focusing on magpies. Cecilia, the owner of the women's clothing store next to Coe's, saw him and stepped outside for a chat. Business was slow for both of them that afternoon.

"Hey, Coe, the weather's turning."

"Hi, Cecilia. Yes, getting cold. How ya doing?" Coe asked.

"I'm well." She put her arms around herself, and shivered. "I want snow, Coe, lots of it this winter. I want customers from all over the world to come to our shops and spend their money."

"Oh, boy, do we ever need heavy snowfall for the ski valley," Coe remarked, raising his voice as a loud pickup drove by.

"And, in the evening, have tourists curl up with books they bought from you," Cecilia chuckled, nudging him.

"I hope so, Cecilia." Coe thought for a moment and said, "I wonder if I could turn a profit up in the ski valley with a small bookshop?" Coe knew it took years before a bookshop turned a profit. He had gone through the agony of building up a business when first moving to Ojo Verde.

Coe reversed his opinion. "No, that's a bad idea, Cecilia. I'll wait for them to come down from the slopes and shop with us."

Fenster stood up, arched her back and walked over to Cecilia to rub up against her leg.

"Hey, Fenster. What are you going to wear for Halloween?" Cecilia asked, playfully.

Fenster glanced at Cecilia, mewed, then sat down between her and Coe.

"What are *you* up to for Halloween, Cecilia?" Coe asked. He grimaced as a loud car, needing muffler repair, passed by their shops.

"I'm staying home, handing out treats to the little ones and big ones that come to our door. You have plans, Coe?"

"Oh, I've got a party to attend at the museum. Not looking forward to it with the snow and cold weather coming in. I'm not dressing up. I'm not sure if Prissy will costume or not. She has been talking about going as Wednesday Addams, the "child full of woe" carrying a Marie Antoinette doll.... We'll see, she may change her mind."

The north wind increased, faded, rose again, porting colder air that did not fade away. None of the three moved inside; they stayed outside with wind and chill, for months had passed since the last snow.

Cecilia turned to Coe, "Since you are on the museum board, do you know if there has been any progress on catching the thieves?"

"No, not really, Cecilia. Three artifacts have been turned back in, but several more items are still out there. The tribal police have been preoccupied with the Bernal murder, so they have put the theft down the list of priorities."

"I can understand that," Cecilia replied. "What artifacts came back to the museum?"

Coe explained to Cecilia that the Navajo Child of Water mask and a kilt had been dropped off inside the Mission Saint Francis del Monte while a Mass was going on. Two wooden cylinders symbolizing Navajo thunderbolts were mysteriously deposited at curator McGinnis's house.

"Someone broke in to McGinnis's and rolled the cylinders up in his Ganado red rug," he repeated, incredulously.

Cecilia laughed. "They really wanted to be rid of the Navajo stuff, didn't they?"

"I guess so, Cecilia. The theft forced the museum to revamp security for a second time in less than a year." Coe paused, and turned around to go back inside the shop where it was warm. Then he thought of a question to ask Cecilia.

"What's the word about town regarding the museum's theft?"

"Well, you know how people talk and speculate, Coe. Basically, what I hear is surprise and suspicion. How could the museum be robbed? And, secondly, who helped them from inside? I think the town knows, myself included, that the museum had good security, so there had to be help from the inside. But now, the theft has been largely forgotten. The town is thinking of the ski season and Christmas."

Coe nodded his head in agreement. "There's bound to be an inside connection in some way, but we vet every one of our staff carefully," he lamented. "Ah, well, that's for the police to figure out...I've got to go in, Cecilia, the cold is getting to me."

Coe walked back inside his bookshop, and Fenster padded back behind the purple curtain where Coe kept the Tulona and pueblo collection of books. Coe looked at the purple curtain and contemplated once again about replacing the curtain with a Two Gray Hills rug or a fabric with Indigenous symbols.

Not well acquainted with Navajo rugs, Coe pulled off his shelf, Don Dedera's *Navajo Rugs*. Two Gray Hills rugs came from weavers west of Sheep Springs, New Mexico. Coe read that designs of Two Gray Hills have a border of black with an enclosed rectangle that has geometric symbols of chevrons, zig-zags, frets, and squares. The colors are white, black, brown, tan, and gray. The name, Two Gray Hills, was derived from two gray hills near a trading post of the same name.

After reading about the Two Gray Hills design, he called Tony Rodarte who owned the Silver Concho jewelry shop south of Ojo Verde on the road to Taos. He had seen a Two Gray Hills rug in Rodarte's when he had purchased a silver and turquoise cuff for Prissy's birthday.

"Tony, would you put a hold on that Two Gray Hills rug I was looking at the other day? The one hanging from the vigas."

Rodarte said he would and give him advice on how to hang it at his doorway to the backroom of his shop. After hanging up the phone, Coe had second thoughts about the rug blocking the stockroom, "Is it too heavy to be pulling back and forth?" Despite that, he liked the design, and would buy it anyway.

A customer entered his shop to browse. Coe wondered if the thief that entered McGinnis's house wrapped up the cylinders in a Ganado red rug for a specific reason or message? Were there any connections? Ganado red plus Navajo thunderbolts plus the thieves? Did the thunderbolts and Ganado red mean anything at all?

"And what about the message," he thought. "'The god roams the foothills for scalps of his enemies.' I don't think I'll be going out to the foothills for a while."

The temperature dropped further by the time Coe closed shop at five o'clock. He went home to Prissy to tell her about purchasing the Two Gray Hills rug. Thunderstorms rose over the Tusas and Cristo Mountains by six o'clock, and heavy rain stripped the remaining leaves off cottonwoods and willows. It was the Month of Leaves Falling Moon, after all.

When Coe entered his house, Prissy had a piñon fire blazing in the conical fireplace. He embraced his wife and then went over to the fire to warm his hands. Later, after dinner, they discussed the purchase of the Two Gray Hills for their home. He decided to leave the purple curtains in his shop. Prissy already had a place picked out on one of their walls to hang the rug. She would remove two wall paintings and hang them elsewhere in their home.

47

The Ortegas in San Miguel, north of Ojo Verde, heard rain strike the metal roof of their home. Most of the day, Armando and Luis had prepped the compound for the coming rain and snow. Luis cleaned horse stalls, while Armando restacked wood under the shed and carried in several arm loads of piñon for the fireplace. Loretta drove into Ojo Verde and stocked their larder and refrigerator with canned goods and fresh meat and vegetables. By mid-afternoon, rain noisily pelted their metal roof when the storm line pushed through San Miguel.

When mist changed to dot-like points of snow, Armando and Loretta walked out on their front porch. They saw Luis, doing the same, on the other side of the compound at his home. Luis put on his barn coat and came over to stand with them. The dot-like points of snow turned to heavy flakes. Buck and Monte, the Ortegas' fine-blooded horses who had already begun to grow longer hair with autumn's turn, trotted out from their stalls, raising their heads to falling snow. Buck stuck his tongue out, catching a few flakes; both horses lowered their heads and blew fiercely through their nostrils, then inhaled the fresh scent of snow sticking to the ground.

Armando, in his seventieth year, stepped off the porch, turned into the wind, took off his felt hat, smoothed back his hair, and lifted his face to snow and sky, contented and not lamenting anything in his life, as the cold and snow hit his face.

By three o'clock, Jason Taylor had finished his lunch shift at Tablita's Restaurant. He had no more shifts at Tablita's for the day. He gassed up his pickup at Allsup's near the Tulona Pueblo and headed out to the ski valley. Rain made the highway slick out of Ojo Verde to the ski valley, but Jason switched to four-wheel drive, lowering the risk of losing control. He wanted to drive higher in the mountains, encountering the snow earlier in the day at higher altitudes than the 7,200 feet in Ojo Verde.

"I want to be up there," Jason said, as he ducked his head under the sun visor and looked upward toward the peaks.

As Jason drove higher, 8,000, 9,000 feet, the mist turned to snow pellets, then abruptly into snowflakes. By the time he arrived at the ski slopes, snowflakes were large and heavy, obscuring his vision of Cristo Mountain tops. Parking near one of the ski lodges, Jason walked up a narrow street of ski shops and cafes to a ski lift that in a few weeks would take him to the top of the mountain. Jason stood and looked at the snow coming down, feeling its building intensity, and thought of his good life in Ojo Verde and the bluebird days ahead on powdered slopes.

By the time thunderstorms arrived in late afternoon, Tafoya had concluded his day at the stationhouse. He had missed Janet for lunch, but had called a second time in the afternoon, after catching a cell tower to her phone near her field work in the Columbine-Hondo area north of San Miguel. He invited her to come to the pueblo to have dinner with him and his family. He apologized for calling at the last minute, but said, "I miss your company."

Janet said that she would be there as soon as she checked in the Forest Service vehicle at headquarters. Janet was anxious to see Tafoya, too. Dinner with his family would be the second time she dined with them, the first being on Saint Francis Feast Day, a few weeks before.

At the Tafoya family dinner, the green chile stew was peppery hot and delicious with blue-corn tortillas, the roasted corn dripping in butter, and the non-caffeinated iced tea, sweet and soothing. A bread pudding finalized the meal. Tafoya's parents wanted to hear more about Janet's liaison work with the department, but so far, she had nothing to report.

"Oh, she'll have more than enough work with us, with me, I mean, soon," Tafoya teased.

When dinner was over, Tafoya and Janet walked to the front door and looked out onto the pueblo plaza. A portico overhang shielded the front of the house from the weather. Lightning flashes from storms having passed to the south of Ojo Verde indicated the squall lines had moved south to Taos and Espa.

Saying their goodbyes to the family, Tafoya and Janet stepped outside and stood beneath the portico. Light mist swirled to the ground. Gaslights flickered behind deep-seated windows of pueblo homes, casting a glow on the plaza. Along the ceremonial racetrack, close to Old Bow kiva, a fire had been started and, in the cold mist, Tulonas stood around the fire, parkas over their blankets. The rain was over and a transition to snow was beginning.

Tafoya took Janet's hand, and she gently interlocked her fingers with his as they stood gazing at the fire near Old Bow. The plaza was quiet. The mist cleared even more, and then between the Old Bow fire and Tafoya and Janet, snowflakes fell, slightly at an angle, swirling lightly. The flakes, when they first landed, melted. But soon the snow stuck, congregating in a patina, covering the plaza, drifting in a pile around the sacred pole.

The temperature had fallen precipitously; the ground became firmer and colder, holding the season's first snow. Quietly, subtly, the snow became denser; the fire by Old Bow flamed in Tafoya's and Janet's vision. The men around the fire began to sing softly a prayer of thanks to the Creator for the snow and promise of a good winter, the Quiet Time for the Tulona. Tafoya tightened his grip on Janet's hand, signaling a change of mood. She slightly turned her head toward him. He was staring off in the direction of the fire.

"Our liaison, Janet," Tafoya said, "is more than tribal police work...It is this," he said, squeezing her hand.

Janet thought Tafoya was referring to their holding hands. He was. She thought it was the mist turning to snow. It was. For Janet, the Old Bow fire, the singing, the family meal, snow on the ground, stars in the sky, the seasons coming, the seasons going, all of this brought her closer to Tafoya. More firmly, she grasped his hand.

Around Old Bow fire, singing paused. A few yards away from Tafoya and Janet, Medicine Wind and his wife, Quail Looks Away, warmed themselves beside the fire, their parkas shedding snowflakes. The cacique, Bustamente, cleared his throat from singing and sipped sweet, warm tea in his Yeti cup. Lion Walks Night looked across Cottonwood River to the southside of the pueblo, and noticed three other fires had been built by his kinsmen to stay warm, as they enjoyed the season's first falling snow.

Bustamente looked at Janet and Tafoya standing under the portico of Tafoya's parents; he wondered if Janet, the Isleta Puebloan, would be happy residing among the Tulona. A young Tulona appeared aside Bustamente with a hand-held, shield drum. Bustamente began a song in falsetto as the young Tulona drummed.

*Hey—yo—hey—yo—hey—*yo/ *Heeeey—heeeey...*

Before snow fell that day, he hiked at a rapid pace, almost a trot, up the mountain to the place he had buried the medicine bundle. In his backpack, he carried a collapsible shovel to dig and uncover the Corn Mothers, retablos, and world lengthener. He must find the burial spot before the snow fell and blurred the ground. Cold rain pelted his face and hands. He paused on the trail, fetched gloves from his pack, and fitted them on his hands. The wind soughed loudly through the conifers; the ponderosas especially noisy with their branches spaced far apart.

The higher he hiked, the colder the air, and rain changed to snow. He hurried to the spot he thought the bundle was buried; looking around, he gauged his landmarks as best he could: cliffside of granite behind him—yes; Tusas Mountains toward the west—yes; La Osa Caves to his north—maybe; and the pueblo and Ojo Verde far below to the south—as best as he could tell.

He poked at the ground for loose dirt, indicating a recent burial. After several attempts to find soft ground, he discovered the soft spot and quickly dug up the bundle, stuffing the sacred objects in his backpack. He re-buried the old backpack, and stomped the dirt down firmly.

Snow began to fall. Turning around from the cache site, he doubled his pace down the mountain, trotting around the ash pile on the Winter House side of the pueblo to his pickup. No one took notice of him as he drove out of the plaza area, past the Tulona police station, and to his home on the edge of the reservation.

As he alighted from his pickup with backpack in hand, three crows flew in front of him, crossing between him and his turquoise-painted front door. He was unaware the crows had followed him inflight from the ash pile to his home. Despite snow, they had flown alongside him, and at times, above his vehicle, zig-zagging in the air. The crows alighted on the lowest branches of a bare, dead cottonwood next to his house.

Stopping, he looked directly at the three crows. “Who are you?” he said, pointing at them with his forefinger. The crows looked at him, talked to him, but he did not understand. He stood there, perplexed. At first, he heard nothing.

Then, somewhere he heard a frightening, basso voice, “You are hollow bone. You cannot control me.”

48

Wednesday, October 31, Day of Saint Wolfgang of Regensburg, Month of Leaves Falling Moon

Halloween. Snow fell during the day: heavy at times, continually, without diminishing, and thick, dark clouds blocked sun shafts to mesas. To the eyes, the far range of the Tusas and San Antonio Mountain never birthed during the day, nor did Tulona and Taos Peaks to the east. Before the sun had risen (as far as anyone could tell it rose because of heavy cloud cover) the Ojo Verde Department of Roads cleared Paseos del Norte and Sur. Private snowplow contractors scraped snow from business parking lots and sought clearing opportunities of residential driveways. Before sunrise, Coe's Bookshop parking lot was scraped bare, but snow continued to fall.

At Tulona Pueblo, a few foot trails between houses on the Winter and Summer sides had been beat down with heel-less boots and hiking shoes. Family dogs clustered under porticos, some finding refuge inside conical ovens not blocked with plywood and stone. On the highway to Questa, an eighteen-wheeler with a trailer load of hardware goods jackknifed, blocking the highway to Colorado and Ojo Verde for hours. The local anchor at the radio station in Ojo Verde called the weather, "Pumpkin Snow Day," in honor of Halloween. The temperature never rose above thirty degrees during the day.

He was on a mission. Ben Lovato Medicine Wind knocked on Larry Armijo's family home door on the Winter side of the pueblo.

"Larry is not here," said his mother. "He may be at his home on the edge of the reservation."

Medicine Wind walked back to his pickup in the falling snow, started it, and drove carefully to Armijo's concrete-block house near Abalone Road on the reservation. The murder of Lance Bernal, his kiva brother, had occurred on Sunday, October 21, and here it was, the thirty-first, and no arrests had been made. Yes, it was tribal police business, but Medicine Wind hunted the killer, and, if he did nothing more, he would drive the killer into a box canyon for Tafoya to capture.

Medicine Wind knew Bernal had two close friends, Larry Armijo and Alfredo Dominguez, and he intended to talk to them, regardless of a snowy Halloween Day. "I'll hunt down Armijo, first." He drove from Armijo's family home to Armijo's concrete-block house. Pulling into Armijo's driveway, Medicine Wind observed smoke curling from the chimney. The curtains were drawn, and no footprints were stamped in the snow around the front door, indicating neither exit nor entry. At the back of the house, juniper and spruce trees grew, and a few leafless red willow and cottonwoods stood erect. The bare, dead cottonwood next to Armijo's house, begged to be cut down and spliced into drum barrels or stamping tables for turquoise craftsmen. He knocked firmly three times on the front door.

"Larry, it's me, Medicine Wind." He waited and after a few seconds, he started to knock again, but before he could knock, the door opened.

Armijo did not invite Medicine Wind inside. "What do you want? It's not even nine o'clock," he said fractiously.

"I want to talk to you about Bernal, our kinsman killed at Quintana Canyon."

Armijo's eyes widened. He continued to stand at the door. "What about it?" he asked, this time more frustrated, folding his arms.

"Can I come in? It's cold out here."

"Okay," Armijo said, reluctantly, "if you have to. I'm busy, so make it quick."

Medicine Wind stepped inside, out of the cold. Armijo's propane stove emitted radiant heat. The living room had a dilapidated couch and three chairs, one of them a cloth over-stuffed chair, the others wooden, straight-back chairs facing a new television screen installed on the wall. Occasional tables held newspapers, magazines, and computer textbooks. In the dining room, Medicine Wind noticed the dining table had a large tablecloth thrown over objects underneath—breakfast dishes, pottery? The tablecloth was really not a tablecloth *per se*, but two or three Mexican-style Falsa blankets, gray, dark green, and black. Against one wall, a table held two laptops and a desktop computer. Three topographical maps were spread out on a table against another wall. Fresh coffee and chile smells wafted out of the kitchen on the other side of the dining room. Armijo refused to offer coffee or food, a behavior discordant with pueblo courtesy.

Medicine Wind asked Armijo if he knew anything about Bernal's murder: enemies he might have had, arguments with people, Bernal's disposition the last time Armijo saw him? Armijo had no knowledge of enemies, conflicts, nor did he see a worried disposition on Bernal. Armijo disrespected the questions, giving short, curt answers.

He is giving me nothing, thought Medicine Wind. Armijo was impatient, uncooperative, not interested in helping Medicine Wind. At least he coughed up one informative answer about Bernal.

"The last time I saw Bernal, we talked about elk and deer hunting season coming up soon. We came up with locations for good hunting on public lands as far away as Cimarron to the east and Tierra Amarilla to the west. That was about it."

"Did you happen to see him Sunday here at the pueblo, the day he was killed?" Medicine Wind asked. Armijo looked away from Medicine Wind, turning slightly, gazing at the dining table covered in Falsa blankets.

"No, I left early that morning to go to Tesuque and do some work. I was gone all day." Medicine Wind accepted Armijo's answer—what else could he do?

Armijo shifted his weight from one foot to another. "I need to get back to work," Armijo said. "Can I pour you coffee in a plastic cup to take with you?" he asked, brusquely.

Medicine Wind accepted the offer, and when Armijo walked back to the kitchen, he ambled into the dining room to look at the maps on the table. "Looking for good places to hunt, Armijo?" he asked. Medicine Wind looked at the map designations in the lower right-hand corners: Shady Brook, Arroyo Hondo, Guadalupe Mountain—all in New Mexico.

"Yeah, but with Bernal gone, I don't feel much like hunting this year," Armijo replied. "Here's your coffee. I gotta get back to work."

As Medicine Wind walked out of the dining room, he saw kernels of corn underneath the dining table. They were gem colors, Indian corn colors of blue, yellow, and green. When Medicine Wind departed Armijo's house, he wondered about the gem-colored corn, for Armijo had never started a crop of anything. "A computer guru he might be, but a planter of crops? No way."

Next, he drove to Dominguez's house outside of the reservation, but there was no pickup in the driveway, no smoke curling from the chimney. Snow had clustered on the elk horns hanging over the door of the workshop. Medicine Wind drove back to the pueblo. Armijo's coffee was weak. He threw the coffee away when he stepped out of the pickup, noticing the brown stain of coffee on the snow bank and the melting of flakes around the splotch. He looked up at the falling snow, "Cover the splotch up, Creator, make it whole and white again."

49

Tribal policemen Tafoya, Romero, and the supervisor of the tribal police met in the conference room at the Taos County sheriff's department substation in Ojo Verde. Deputy Sheriff Cordova, New Mexico State Troopers, and a Department of New Mexico Transportation representative also attended the eight-thirty morning meeting. The Ojo Verde City Police Department had been briefed before dawn.

The general purpose of the meeting focused on possible road problems caused by the snowfall and events scheduled for Halloween possibly presenting problems. State troopers and the sheriff's department had been investigating car accidents and the eighteen-wheeler jackknife accident toward Questa. Since snow and wind chill dampened trick or treaters for Halloween, they concluded destructive "tricks" would be minimal.

"Who wants to trick-or-treat with a wind chill in the teens and cold wind blowing up the sheets of ghosts?" Cordova remarked as he presided over the meeting.

Tafoya and Romero frowned, almost cringed, at the coffee at the sheriff's department substation since they had grown accustomed to the pueblo stationhouse's Café Mundo blend of Sumatra Roast from Espa. Tafoya set his coffee aside while he took notes. Romero proceeded to drink the java, but shook his head after each sip—"Not Mundo, for sure."

The New Mexico transportation representatives reported summit passes were snowy, but had been cleared. "Highway sixty-four that goes over Palo Flechado Pass is the worst. We have put up caution signs that only four-wheel-drive vehicles, or those cars and trucks with chains, are to drive over the pass. Despite that, we had three cars stuck near the top of the pass early this morning."

Tafoya thought of Bernal's murder at Quintana Canyon. The turnoff to FR 438 that led through the forest to Quintana Canyon was not far from Palo Flechado Pass. "How are Forest Service roads near Flechado Pass?" Tafoya asked the transportation representative.

"They are passable, at least the major Forest Service roads are. Estimates are about five inches of snow up there, as opposed to two or three inches down here, out of the mountains. You'd have to ask the Forest Service about clearing forest roads farther in the back country."

Tafoya thought of Janet who was now the liaison officer with the Tulona Pueblo. "We have a liaison officer, Janet Rael, who is a Forest Service employee. I'll ask her about the maintenance of back-country roads," he said.

Romero nodded in approval of Janet and mouthed to Tafoya, silently, "She's good."

Cordova dismissed the meeting at the sheriff's substation. As Tafoya departed the station, he looked over at the Forest Service supervisor's headquarters and saw Janet's red Subaru parked under the arbor of solar panels. The snow continued to fall as he drove back to the pueblo to remain on duty and further investigate the Bernal murder. He knew his analysis would be truncated during the day because of the weather.

Sure enough, even before he drove through the entrance of the pueblo, Tafoya was called, along with Sergeant Romero, to the Tulona Casino where the manager was having trouble with a customer who had started drinking early on Halloween and had been banging on the one-armed bandit to give him his "earnings." Tafoya took the inebriated gambler's car keys away and drove him back to his sister in Ojo Verde where he told him to sleep it off.

"And stay off the roads on Pumpkin Snow Day!"

Tafoya drove back to the stationhouse at Tulona Pueblo. Snow continued falling as he backed into a parking slot. Keeping the windshield wipers going to clear the snow off the windshield, he looked across the pueblo plaza. The brown adobe buildings appeared stark with white snow falling like gauzy curtains between him and the houses.

Tafoya listened to radio reports in his squad car, "Accident at Paseo del Sur and Saint. Luke Boulevard, fire trucks and ambulances in route....

Power outage on east side of Ojo Verde, Dancing Rock Coop sending two trucks to blown transformer location.... Altercation at La Mancha grocery store parking lot, city police on scene...."

Tafoya turned his engine off and went inside the stationhouse where Delores, the administrative assistant, stood on a short ladder hanging a garland of Halloween images on the wall behind her desk: skeletons, ghosts, pumpkins, and witches.

"*Hola*, Richard, Happy Halloween! I'm a bit late hanging decoration, but here they are," she said, as she stepped down from the ladder and swung her arm, introducing holiday ghouls on the wall.

"I see them," Tafoya said, shivering in mock fright. "It's cold out there, Delores. Do we have a fresh pot of Mundo?"

After pouring himself a fresh cup of coffee, Tafoya walked back to his office and looked at the Bernal case. He opened up two of his three silos of data: the computer files and his field notes, but not the hard copies and material evidence in the evidence room. He took out his yellow notebook pad and turned over to a new page and dated it, October 31, and on the top line, wrote, "Lance Bernal Murder—Tangents."

Bernal had been killed in the open field at Quintana Canyon with two shots from a 7mm rifle, one shot definitely at close range. The first shot would have taken his life, but the murderer wanted to make sure Bernal was dead. No medical aid was summoned for Bernal. The murderer was intent on taking his life. The murder weapon had not been found. No vehicle remained at the scene. The murderer took the weapon and vehicle, departing the murder scene. The deer season was about to open, so that might explain the presence of Bernal and his killer in Quintana Canyon. But there might be other reasons why they were there—recreational sight-seeing, bird watching, nature observations? It's important to know the motivation as to why Bernal was there with someone, but there was no clue about that. Bernal's wife stated that it was out of the ordinary for her husband to take off without leaving a note.

Tafoya wrote down on his yellow pad, "Bernal going to Quintana—no motivation known. Bernal's wife states, 'Unusual behavior.' Deer season about to open—most logical motivation. Who does he hunt with? Or, carouse with?"

Bernal had three close friends: Ambrose Vasquez, Alfredo Dominquez, and Larry Armijo. On the day of the murder, Vasquez had been in Santa Fe at a christening and that alibi had been checked out. Dominquez stated he had been at the Martinez House in Taos with a construction crew. That needed verification with the Martinez House staff.

What about Armijo? Larry Armijo was in his twenties and was more inclined to books than outdoors, but he was kiva educated and attended community college in Espa. Tafoya looked at the report Romero submitted on questioning Armijo. Armijo had told Romero that the last time he had seen Bernal was at the Farmer's Market Café the Wednesday before the murder. They had discussed deer hunting and Armijo's girlfriend, Martha Johnson, the intern at Franklin Deerfield. So, Armijo and Bernal had discussed deer hunting, raising the possibility that they had taken a quick trip to Quintana Canyon to scout out hunting prospects. They hunted together.

Had Armijo been questioned as to his whereabouts on Sunday, October 21, the day of murder? Tafoya quickly scanned interview reports to see if that question had been posed to Armijo.

A slip up. Sergeant Romero had not asked that question of Larry Armijo.

"Verify Armijo's whereabouts on October 21!" Tafoya wrote down on his must-do list, putting an exclamation mark after the note.

By four o'clock the snow thinned out, then abruptly stopped. Tafoya concluded his analysis for the day and returned to his house on the edge of the reservation, close to the city limits of Ojo Verde. He called Janet and wished her, "Happy Halloween!" He told her he was on duty and would be busy with multiple issues from automobile accidents to holiday parties exploding in violence. Janet said she was going to a party with girlfriends and was not dressing up for Halloween. The party was composed of BLM and Forest Service friends.

"I will come home early, Richard," she said. "Text me or call me if you get a chance. I miss you."

Tafoya laid his cell phone gently down on the dining table after talking to Janet. He had never married, but had had several serious relationships with women. His relationships had either fallen apart suddenly, or died on the vine of neglect. Policing, finding the bad guys, resolving crimes, and tending to the overall health of the pueblo had been the focus of his days and nights. Issues of keeping the peace overrode maintaining a relationship, and he had given countless *mea culpas* to women he liked for breaking dates or being late. He had hurt women wanting more from him—his time, attention, affection—but he had marched to a drumbeat of, "Do your duty."

But it was not just a principle of doing one's duty that had interfered with serious relationships. Tafoya felt and saw the anguish of men and women on the reservation. He felt that he must rescue them, protect them, help them, even save them from themselves. Those tugs on his heart carried him away from women he liked and loved. His relationships fell apart, faded, and disappeared.

Tafoya remembered the women in his life—all of them.

But, now, Janet. She was different. All his intimate relationships were different, but how was Janet different? He did not have to dig deep to understand how so. Just tonight, when he called her, she understood his being on call, the need for him to take care of the Tulona pueblo on a cold, snowy night. He heard no resentment in her voice that he was unavailable to party on Halloween.

And, she told him, "I'm coming home early...call me or text, if you can. I miss you."

Janet understood his attention to duty, the public responsibility to the pueblo. It did not take extended analysis to know he and Janet were compatible. Besides, he thought to himself, she flies a plane and can get me out of trouble.

Tafoya's cell phone rang, ending his musing on Janet. He looked at the caller: Deputy Sheriff Chris Cordova.

"Yes, Tafoya here," he answered quickly.

"We've got a serious problem, Tafoya..."

50

Tafoya and Romero arrived at Tract A of Tulona Land Trust's locked gate at the same time—6:37 p.m. The snow had stopped several hours before; the cold wind, however, continued to sweep down from Colorado, through Questa, Arroyo Hondo, and on southward to Ojo Verde, Taos, and beyond, losing its strength in Old Mexico. Flash bars from New Mexico State Troopers and Taos County sheriff's department flashed intensely over the fallen snow; low clouds reflected the red, blue, and amber lights back to the ground. Tafoya and Romero's flash bars added more illumination to the scene on Halloween night. Adrenaline rose high in Tafoya's veins. He never became accustomed to emergency situations, but he never panicked.

The abandoned pickup at the entry of the Tract A gate belonged to Looking Elk, elder of the Tulona Pueblo and Old Bow kiva. Looking Elk's pickup wore a mantle of snow, indicating several hours of being parked. Approximately one hundred yards beyond the entry gate, on the road to the interior of Tract A, most likely lay the dead body of Looking Elk.

A state trooper had stopped to investigate the pickup and had flashed his spotlight and looked through binoculars to detect a body over the fence and down Tract A road. Luminescent red gaiters on human legs signaled trouble in the snow. The trooper, cognizant of not destroying evidence and foot tracks, had carefully stayed out of the main path to the body. Determining the person dead, he called the sheriff's department who quickly called Tafoya since the scene was located on Tulona Trust Land and technically was tribal jurisdiction.

The wind continued to blow snow and sagebrush back and forth. The black trunks of sagebrush contrasted harshly with the snow. The sun had set too quickly to suit Tafoya, but nothing could be done about that. A small forensic team out of the Taos County sheriff's department arrived a few minutes after Tafoya and Romero stopped on the side of SH 522, adjacent to the gate. Tafoya and Romero walked up to the Tract A gate; Tafoya entered the digital code of the lock, and pushed it open.

The forensic team had taken photographs and video of the gate area. It seemed Looking Elk had climbed over the gate, not unlocked it. The team followed alongside the officers as they walked to where the body lay, avoiding a single set of Looking Elk's footprints in the snow.

Just before they reached the body, Dr. Eli Rosenbaum, the medical examiner, yelled from the gate, "Hold on there, let me catch up!" He trotted to the clutch of officers and, remarkably, showed no signs of being out of breath. Good shape for a man in his sixties.

The body had stiffened from freezing temperatures. Snow had drifted about the body, giving a soft, blanket-like effect to its slumbering position. Rosenbaum stood shivering, surveying the scene. Romero and Tafoya stood back. Rosenbaum stepped carefully to the body and asked for his assistant to take photographs. Kneeling, he brushed snow from clothing on the body. He stood and shook his head.

"Nothing I see shows violence or contortions of murder. He fell. He stayed still. The man died. Let's get him back to the morgue."

More photographs were taken of the immediate vicinity of the body. When a sufficient collection of photographs was obtained, the officers stepped carefully to the side of the body. The dead man lay on his right side, the north wind hitting his back, his head posed westward. He wore red gaiters that came up to his knees, hiking boots with the heels cut off, blue Levi pants, a heavy brown canvas parka, and a black toboggan cap that covered his head. His long-braided hair with colored ribbons and leather intwined hung outside his parka. He wore leather gloves, and a small rucksack had been tossed off and lay a few feet away from the body.

Tafoya and Romero rolled the man over on his back. Tafoya grimaced and looked at Romero. Romero shook his head.

"It's definitely Looking Elk," Tafoya said. "What were you doing out here in this kind of weather, Grandfather?" he asked, sadly.

Romero walked over to Looking Elk's backpack. Inside was his medicine bag, rolled cuttings of sage to smudge, a lighter, and a blanket.

"This is Looking Elk's medicine bag and his medicine blanket. I have seen him many times stand on the blanket to pray."

Rosenbaum continued to scan and search for an outward sign of cause of death. There were no blood splotches, contusions, wounds of any kind. Rosenbaum speculated that he probably had a heart attack, a sudden thrombosis that brought on unconsciousness; the cold and snow finished him off.

"He shows no sign of attempting to turn around and go back to his pickup. He fell and stayed there till he stopped breathing. I'll know more when I do an autopsy. He was alone out here on this mesa with blowing snow…isolated. No other tracks around," Rosenbaum said, shaking his head.

Looking Elk was placed in a body bag and carried by Tafoya, Romero, Cordova, and Rosenbaum back to the highway and ambulance. They each held up a corner of the bag. The forensic team stayed at the scene for another two hours, scanning the immediate vicinity of where the body lay and where the pickup was parked. Nothing significant was found. The team wrapped the gate and adjacent fence posts with yellow crime-scene tape. The team said they may come back the next morning—or they may not. It depended on Rosenbaum's examination of the body back at the morgue.

The sky had begun to clear when all the vehicles had left the scene. Not far away from the death scene, three coyotes crawled out of a den-burrow on the side of an arroyo and trotted up to the place where Looking Elk had died. They sniffed around, scratched the ground, peered around. Their bellies were full from two rabbit kills a few hours before. The mother coyote started back to the burrow for shelter, but then halted, and turned back to where men had stood. She sat back on her haunches, tilted her head upward, and howled. Her two offspring, one a juvenile male, the other a female from the year before, joined in the howling. They did not "yip," but rather drew out their voices in long, wavering, cries—a chorus.

The coyotes sang of death and sorrow unto the stars. For Looking Elk.

51

Tafoya drove by the Franklin Deerfield Museum on the way back to the pueblo. Dr. Rosenbaum followed the Taos County emergency ambulance with Looking Elk's body to the morgue in Taos where he decided immediately to perform the autopsy rather than wait till morning. Tafoya looked at the dashboard clock: nine thirty. Glancing over at the museum, he observed the Halloween party breaking up, but several cars remained in the parking lot. He decided to check-in with the museum staff to see how the party had progressed. The museum, after all, had leased Tulona land for its building, so Tafoya felt justified in stopping by. Besides, Tafoya wanted a different theater of spectacle, far away from Tract A and Looking Elk's death. A Halloween party in a beautiful building, surrounded by art and artifacts, would get his mind off the tragedy at Tract A and his kinsman, Looking Elk. So, he hoped.

Staff people were stationed at the front door of the museum. They recognized Tafoya and directed him to the center of the museum to a lecture hall spread with buffet tables of drinks and snacks. People ambled in the hallways, stopping at exhibits. In an exhibit room, off the main hallway of the museum's party tour, he heard John McGinnis lecturing on one of the museum's popular artifacts, the Doña Sebastiana Death Cart. Tafoya paused at the door to listen.

"Doña Sebastiana, the female skeletal personification of Saint Sebastian, a Roman martyr of the Third Century AD, is seated in a cart, and she has a bow and arrow pointed at human souls. Doña Sebastiana is not associated with Halloween or All Souls' Day or All Saints' Day. I say again, '*not*,' associated with Halloween."

Tafoya looked at Doña Sebastiana seated in the cart. The skeleton was life-size with a head of human hair attached to the cranium. He had seen other Sebastiana skeletons with wash-mop strings for hair, but this was the first human-haired Sebastiana he had seen. He shook his head in disgust.

"And I came in here to get away from death...," he thought. Still, he stayed for a moment more, listening to the curator. McGinnis continued.

"Doña Sebastiana is a part of Holy Week processions, bringing up the rear of the processions. Her arrows are shot at human souls, not in a murderous way, but in the context of a person giving up their life for religion. Here in northern New Mexico, Doña Sebastiana came courtesy of the Penitente brotherhood by way of Spain. The Penitentes conduct public displays of penance during Holy Week that include self-flagellation. The Grim Reapress or Doña Sebastiana symbolizes the Holy Death, the giving up one's life for religion and living a morally-straight life. Penitente brotherhoods remain active here in northern New Mexico. Their acts of self-flagellation and processions, often with a Death Cart, are seen as holy rites, not to be looked at as crazy or weird, although to non-Catholics and tourists, the flagellations and Death Carts are gruesome. All that's relative to your point of view, folks," McGinnis concluded.

Tafoya looked at the people dressed for Halloween in costumes of gypsies, pirates, princesses, kings, skeletons, marvel characters, and ghosts. He stared at Doña Sebastiana in her Death Cart and to himself said, "And, these people in Halloween costumes dare think the Penitentes are weird? A Death Cart? Look at yourselves!"

A young girl, accompanying her parents to the party, said loudly, "Sebastiana is not going to shoot us tonight, is she, Mom?"

Her mother replied, "No, she's a good statue...let's go to the next room, sweetheart."

McGinnis, overhearing the mother and daughter, walked over to the girl and explained the Doña Sebastiana Death Cart in words the little girl would understand. He squatted down to her level, face to face, to explain. Tafoya smiled. McGinnis was a thoughtful teacher.

Tafoya turned around and walked to the exhibit room where food trays had been picked nearly clean, most crackers and dips consumed. Tafoya skipped the food and walked back to the front entrance, looking for Director Hornbuckle and Ray Tejada, the Tulona curator. At a distance he saw Coe and his wife, Priscilla. Costumed as a pig-tailed adolescent, carrying a doll, Tafoya could not make out who she was trying to be—but Priscilla was spooky. Coe dressed as a trustee of the museum: sports coat and black turtleneck to ward off the cold outside. Tafoya saw Hornbuckle, huddling with a group of art enthusiasts from Ojo Verde, one of whom he recognized, despite the witch's costume, as a major donor to the museum. Rather than interrupt Hornbuckle and her fund-raising activity, he waved at her and gave her a positive nod of the head that indicated, "All's okay, no problem."

About to go out the front entrance, Tafoya glanced into the gift shop and saw Tejada talking with Martha Johnson, the intern. Johnson had on her coat, preparing to leave the party, alone. Tejada was dressed as a vaquero with boots, tight pants with conchos down each side, hat with stampede strings, and a paisley shirt with a big blue bandanna. Johnson had not dressed in costume for the party. She was dressed nicely, fit for an evening out, but not a Halloween party at her place of work. To Tafoya, something seemed off balance about her. He walked up to them and passed a minute or two of small talk.

"I like your costume, Martha," Tafoya said, light-heartedly.

"I was stood up for the party. Decided to come like this," she replied, resignedly.

Tafoya glanced at Tejada. Tejada looked away.

"Sorry, hope things work out," Tafoya said, uncomfortably. Martha, grimaced, gave a quick, forced smile.

"Thanks," she said. "I need to be going. I've already told Director Hornbuckle I'm not feeling well and have to go home."

Johnson walked away, buckling her coat as she left them standing in the gift shop. As she opened the large front door to the museum, the strong wind blew the door fully open. Snow and leaves blew down the hallway. The wind ceased abruptly, and Johnson put her head down and walked quickly away from the party to her car.

"Larry Armijo stood her up, didn't he?" Tafoya asked Tejada.

Surprised at Tafoya's identifying Armijo as her broken date, Tejada agreed with him, going on to explain Johnson and Armijo were having problems of late. Tejada did not know what the issues were, and it was none of his business, but Johnson had been depressed lately.

"I feel sorry for Martha," Tejada went on to say. He admitted he preferred to curate at the museum and work on his master's thesis about pre-contact trails and pathways among the pueblos, not pathways of the heart. Tafoya nodded he understood.

"I have sad news, brother," Tafoya said, still looking at the snow that had swirled in through the front doors when Johnson departed. Turning and facing Tejada, Tafoya said, "Looking Elk, one of our elders, is dead, passed into another spirit world."

Tejada appeared shocked, "Where, how, when?" Tafoya told him Looking Elk had been found dead, probably a heart attack, a couple of hours ago on Tulona Trust Land, north of Ojo Verde, toward Questa.

Tejada, tearful, sat down on a large Taos drum the gift shop retailed. Shaking his head, he put his arms around himself, self-comforting, "Tafoya! I just saw him today. He was here, at the museum. I can't believe he is dead…it's awful. Why was he…?"

"Why was he here today, Tejada?" Tafoya interrupted.

"He came to ask me about Tulona archaeological sites out on the Trust Land, near the Big River. He wanted to know if there were any places the museum knew about."

"And…," Tafoya pushed.

"I told him, 'Yes, Grandfather, there are.' I escorted him to the basement where we curate and keep maps, and I showed him on the map where they were. There were several sites, but there was one site that he locked onto."

"Which one was that?" Tafoya asked.

"LA 99, followed by a few other numbers."

"Archaeological site designation?"

"Yes."

"Wait a second," Tafoya said. He pulled up the site designation sent to him by McGinnis. "Is this the site number?" Tafoya's message from McGinnis listed, "LA 9976429."

Tejada looked at the number. "Yes, that's it."

This was the second time Tafoya had been informed about LA 9976429, the first being when McGinnis informed him about a Tulona Indian that had asked about archaeological sites on Tract A.

"LA 99 is located on Arroyo de Conchos. Translated from the Spanish to English, the Arroyo 'of Shells,'" Tejada volunteered. "But you probably know that already."

"Take me to the basement and the map. I want a copy of the data of that site and the topographical map precisely locating the ruins. Let's go, right now!" Tafoya said.

52

Thursday, November 1, Day of Solemnity of All Saints, Month of Corn Depositing Moon

The snow lay two-inches deep on the ground, but with wind, drifts piled up half-a-foot against adobe and stone walls, curbs, and trees at Tulona Pueblo and Ojo Verde. The snow melted quickly. The sun shone brightly upon pueblo and village, the air crisp and chill—fitting, for All Saints' Day, November 1. Clouds and fog of the past few days were distant memories that people gossiped about as they jumped across pools of runoff water and snow-cone slush at village crosswalks and pueblo trails. The community mood had lightened up, for if wet weather and snows continued through fall and winter, water runoff from Tulona Peak and the Cristo Mountains would bring abundant crops and full orchards in spring and summer. The signs were there for a wet and snowy winter. But people had been disappointed before. Yet, on this day, All Saints' Day, hope reigned, and pessimism had no truck among the people.

Father Jose Padilla, the young mission priest from Santa Fe, had driven to Ojo Verde the night before to conduct obligatory Mass at the Tulona pueblo mission church, Saint Francis del Monte. Except for ill health, all the world's faithful were obligated to attend Mass on All Saints" Day. Father Padilla would conduct a Mass at the pueblo at eleven, then proceed to San Miguel at the Chapel of Nuestra Señora de los Delores to officiate a service at five o'clock in late afternoon.

The mission church at Tulona pueblo was crowded. Ex-rugby player, now mission priest, Father Padilla, slowly walked up the aisle to the front of the church, the acolytes and attendants proceeding reverently behind him. He saw a row of Tulona women clothed in Indigenous dresses. He swung the thurible, wafting incense about the congregation. The propane heaters had been lit earlier in the morning and the chapel was warm enough, but not stiflingly hot. As Father Padilla swung the censer and looked at the altar ahead of him, he could not help but notice, out of the corner of his eye, Albert Walhuime standing at the back of the chapel.

Albert had once told him, "I hardly ever attend Mass, preferring the Mother Earth church of the outdoors. I occasionally come with my elderly mother to help her make the service. I might come more often if I knew you were going to say something about the Tulona and the church."

Despite the ritual to be performed and scriptures to be read, Father Padilla decided on the walk to the altar that he was going to give a homily, extemporaneously, on the Tulona and the church—for the sake of the pueblo, and Albert Walhuime. When homily time came, Father Padilla walked to the ambo on the epistle side of the chapel. He saw the Tulona women, clothed in Indigenous dress, and smiled. Albert Walhuime sat down in the back pew beside his mother.

"In the name of the Father, Son, and Holy Spirit. Amen. In 1680, this pueblo and other pueblos revolted, in what is called the Pueblo Revolt. It was not the first, and not the last, revolt of Indigenous peoples in this part of the Spanish empire. Catholic priests and sympathetic Spaniard families were murdered as puebloans forced the Spanish and the church to retreat in panic back to El Paso Norte, the great pass connecting Mexico to the northern frontier, *Nuevo Méjico*."

Albert Walhuime wondered where the tall, robust priest, who spoke English with a Spanish accent, was going to go with this theme? Albert sat straighter in the pew; he was glad he had decided to come to Mass today with his elderly mother.

"Not all Spanish families fled," Father Padilla continued, "in fact, twelve Spanish families stayed, rooted in place with family. In 1692, the Spanish came back, the church came back, under the reconquest of Vargas. The Tulona and Taos Pueblos fled from Vargas's reconquest, but returned under a promise of peace and amnesty a few months later. Still, all was not well in your land for the Comanche, Navajo, and Ute continued to raid and kidnap. Then in the nineteenth century, Spain was deposed, and Mexico, another secular power, took over. Then with the Mexican-American War came the Anglo and their troubling tenure. In all of this, the Tulona stayed, through conquest, reconquest, and the Anglo-American wave. Your grandfathers and grandmothers lived and persisted, holding firm to your values, in spite of the church and political powers."

The congregation breathed more easily with his last few words. Albert remained attentive, not wanting to miss a word.

"The Tulona and other pueblos held fast to caring for one another and sustaining the earth, the mother of us all, the womb from which we all come...and all shall return...."

Father Padilla surveyed the congregation slowly. "Hear me carefully, my children! Before the revolt of Po'pay in 1680, the puebloans were forced into labor, your land taken away, and the church sought to eradicate your kiva practices." Father Padilla raised his voice significantly, "Holy Mother Church erred, and for that we have apologized, prostrated ourselves. The church's apology is delivered in many ways: We no longer seek to abolish your kivas or native rites. We seek to include your words within our words: Mother Earth, Creator, blessings, prayers, Great Spirit, the sacred hoop, the circle of life, and so on. We seek to inculcate your rites with ours. Vespers are held on Christmas Eve in this chapel, and then we take the statue of the Virgin Mary in a procession amidst bonfires about the pueblo plaza while rifle blasts are shot in the air to ward off evil spirits. I do hope those are blank shots, and lead does not fall from the heavens."

The congregants chuckled. Albert knew they were blank, and promised himself he would tell that to Father Padilla. "Or, maybe not—keep him guessing," he thought.

"The Tulona, and other pueblos I visit, have taught me that within your community I see 'loving one another as yourself,' a gentleness of spirit, a caring for one another not constructed upon selfish return, but upon seeing the needs of other Tulonas, and helping them through the day, the year, their lives. I remember the first day I came here at the pueblo, and I was talking with Cacique Bustamente. He said something to me that encapsulated what I am trying to say on this All Saints" Day.

"I was starting to depart from Bustamente's company. We were at the end of the day. I had climbed up the ladder with him to watch the sun set toward Pedernal and the Tres Orejas. It was gorgeous, the clouds layered like ribbons in the sky with reds and yellow and gold. I wish I could climb with him every day of the year. I told him I would pray for him and pray for the Tulona Pueblo, thinking that was all I needed to say. Then he spoke to me, not looking at me, but looking at the arc of the sun sliding to the other side of the earth.

"He said, 'I will pray for you, for our pueblo…and, Father Padilla, I pray for the *whole world*.'"

Father Padilla paused. He looked over the heads of the people sitting for Mass, staring far away, as if focusing on some unknown island on the ocean's horizon that was not on the map.

He gathered himself back in the chapel and his homily at hand. Some people rustled nervously.

"Bustamente said, 'I pray for the whole world.' And, I heard him. I continue to hear him every day. I pray for the whole world in the name of the Father, Son, and Holy Spirit. Amen."

When Albert Walhuime departed the chapel of Mission Saint Francis del Monte, he had greater respect for the church; but more than that, a comforting and warm appreciation for the man, the black robe, the priest, the ex-rugby player: Father Padilla.

Walhuime walked to his home along the race track, toward Earth Cloud Lake in the mountains.

"I will come back, if Padilla is the priest presiding," he promised himself.

53

Before All Saints' Day Mass that morning and Father Padilla's homily to Walhuime, Forest Service biology specialist Janet Rael met Tafoya at the pueblo police station at eight. Tafoya offered Janet a cup of Mundo coffee.

"Thanks, Richard."

The two of them went to the conference room to discuss Looking Elk's death on Tract A of the Tulona Pueblo Land Trust. Janet understood this was her first assignment as the liaison officer with the Tulona tribal police. The Forest Service and Bureau of Land Management had overlapping jurisdiction in managing and supervising the natural resources on Tract A of the land trust. It was pueblo land and the Tulona was the first party of interest and "first occupant" of the land. So, the Tulona were also stewards of Tract A. Of course, from Bustamente's view, the Tulona were stewards and caretakers of the *whole* earth, not just the Tract A.

After a few minutes of small talk, Tafoya set up privileges for Janet on the Tulona tribal police website so she could access files and receive bulletins and email from the department. She had brought in her personal laptop. Tafoya worked from a military-grade laptop used in police vehicles. Rael's official email address as liaison officer with the tribal police was jrael@ttp.tulona.org. "TTP" stood for Tulona Tribal Police. As she opened the tribal police website and clicked on the Looking Elk case file, the autopsy report of Medical Examiner Eli Rosenbaum on Looking Elk suddenly popped up in her folder. She and Tafoya read the report on their respective laptops.

Dr. Rosenbaum wrote that his report was preliminary, but "substantial as to final conclusions." Rosenbaum stated that Looking Elk had died from a heart attack. The severity of the thrombosis was such that even if he had been in an emergency room of a first-class hospital, he would not have survived the attack. The freezing temperature was probably a factor in initiating the attack, but any significant stressor could have brought on the coronary event. No marks of injury were found on Looking Elk, and toxicology analysis would be concluded in two weeks so that a final report could be written. His personal affects and other items could be released immediately.

"I see that Looking Elk's medicine bundle will be released to Bustamente or one of the kiva brothers as soon as today," Janet said, reading ahead in Rosenbaum's supplementary notes.

Tafoya immediately picked up his cell phone and called the Taos County Medical Examiner's Office. He asked to speak to Rosenbaum, and when the doctor came on the line, Tafoya requested that Looking Elk's medicine bundle, backpack, and personal items be sequestered until the tribal policemen picked them up from the medical examiner's office.

"I want to investigate why Looking Elk ventured out in the snow and cold weather on Tract A, and the contents of his backpack and bundle may give me some clues. I'll make sure that his personal effects are passed on to his family and kiva brothers." Rosenbaum said he understood and would lock up the bundle and personal items for safe keeping.

"You have any idea why Looking Elk was out there on Tract A?" Janet asked Tafoya.

"I have one idea I'll tell you about, but first, let's see if Delores has come in with the donuts. I think I heard her come in. I need to introduce you to her, Janet."

They closed their laptops and walked down the hallway to the front of the station. Tafoya glanced into the breakroom and saw that Delores had brought in donuts. Coffee remained in the pot, and Delores had started a second pot of Mundo brewing on the appliance. Walking to the front of station, Tafoya introduced Janet to Delores.

Delores had dressed in a pueblo manta and dress, but without the white buckskin boots because of the mush and snow outside. She wore high-top hiking boots. She was intending to go to Mass later on that morning, if work allowed. Delores' manta was black with dark-red geometric patterns that zig-zagged horizontally on the borders. A white gingham underdress and white leggings kept her body warm. A woven sash of green and white was wrapped around her waist to hold the traditional pueblo manta secure. A multi-stranded white shell necklace hung from her neck, four long strands in all.

When Janet saw Delores, she stopped, and said, "You are gorgeous!" Delores smiled broadly, blushing.

Tafoya had seen Delores dressed in her manta before, but he was still impressed. He made the introductions. Janet confessed to Delores she was from Isleta Pueblo. She said her pueblo manta and accoutrements were stored at her parents' home at Isleta. Janet said that seeing Delores dressed in her manta inspired her to get her dress out of storage and bring it to her apartment in Ojo Verde.

"Maybe you would like to see it?" Janet asked. Delores delightfully said she would.

"What's the occasion for your dressing up?" Tafoya asked.

"My sisters and I are dressing for Mass today at eleven," Delores replied. "Father Padilla needs to see us celebrating, too. And he seems very open to our pueblo ways."

Delores told Janet that she always liked the Forest Service uniforms, especially the style that Janet was wearing: dark forest green shirt and trousers with a light-colored desert yellow jacket with multiple utility pockets.

"Your uniform dress fits perfectly with our tribal police uniforms." Delores continued, "I wish you the best of luck as liaison officer."

Instead of shaking hands with the "best of luck" words, Delores hugged Janet.

Tafoya looked out the front window at thawing snow and bright sunshine on pueblo homes. Though slightly embarrassed at Janet and Delores hugging, he was pleased. Tafoya hoped Janet, dressed in her manta, would be invited to dance on the Tulona Pueblo plaza someday.

On the way back to the conference room to continue analyzing the Looking Elk case, Janet and Tafoya refreshed their coffee and grabbed donuts. Sitting down across from each other at the large conference table, they opened their laptops.

"So, tell me. What is your speculation about Looking Elk being out on Tract A, Richard?" Janet asked.

Janet had a sadness she did not wish to share with Tafoya.

Her sadness arose from reflecting on Looking Elk's last minutes before he died. He had parked his pickup at the gate. Would he have driven onto the trust land had he possessed the gate's digital code? Considering his physical condition, according to Rosenbaum's analysis, it wouldn't have made much difference. The next big stressor was going to kill Looking Elk, be it hiking in the snow or driving on a snowy and slick reservation trust road. But it was dying alone, Janet ruminated, the dying face down in snow that stirred her emotions. What was motivating Looking Elk to take the risk of hiking in the cold? It had to be something huge that drove him into the blowing snow, away from warmth of his pueblo home.

Janet spoke, "Was Looking Elk psychologically healthy, Richard? Had he been acting strangely? Maybe Alzheimer's affected his judgement to go out in the snow?"

Tafoya took a sip of coffee, shook his head, "No, he had no Alzheimer's disorder. He was kiva active and a great storyteller. I'll talk with his family, but there was no indication of that…at all." Janet nodded her head she understood.

"As to my theory," Tafoya started to explain, "there was something that spurred Looking Elk to attend to mysterious business on Tract A. He had met with Ray Tejada, the Franklin Deerfield curator, about Tract A earlier in the afternoon the day he died!"

"What was that about?" Janet asked quickly.

"He wanted to know if there were any archaeological sites on the Tulona Trust Land near the Big River, especially old pueblo structures on Tract A."

"And, if the museum was on top of things and had current maps, they should have known about the kiva," Janet added.

Tafoya stopped; his face puzzled. "You know about LA 99…and a kiva?"

"What's LA 99, Richard?"

"It's an abbreviated archeological site number on Tract A land that Looking Elk was interested in. It's along Arroyo de Conchas, the Arroyo of Shells. There's a longer site number." Tafoya paused and looked at Janet expectantly, "What do you know about a kiva on LA 99?"

"Yeah, there's a kiva," Janet said. "I was out at Arroyo of Shells about two weeks ago, conducting a field survey. I came across archaeological ruins, including a kiva that looked like someone was excavating. But I don't know if it was LA 99."

Tafoya stood up from the table, "Wait a minute, I took a photo of the topo map at Franklin Deerfield with my cell phone. Let me see if I can pull it up." Tafoya found the copy on his cell phone and sent it to the tribal police website site, filing it under the Looking Elk case. They both could open the file on a laptop screen.

Janet opened up the file from her new account link. Tafoya came around to her side of the table and with a pencil pointed at the location of LA 9976429 on the Los Cordovas topographical map.

"There, see it, Janet? And there's the name of the arroyo where the site is located." He pointed to the big, bold lettering for the arroyo on the map. "'Arroyo de Conchas,' Janet, the Arroyo of Shells."

Janet looked closely at the LA 9976429 site on the map. "Yes, that's where I was when I came across the kiva. There were other ruins there, and there were tire tracks in the area. Here, let me see if I still have the photos I took of the kiva." Janet opened her cell phone to her photo album and showed Tafoya the site with the kiva, adobe walls, a few pit houses, and the tire tracks. He looked close at the photos.

"Yes, those are definitely tire tracks…and the kiva." He looked closer at the diggings in the kiva. "There's been digging of the kiva, and I don't think it's a four-legged animal."

Janet nodded her head in agreement. "It's too muddy even to take a four-wheel vehicle out there today, Richard," Janet asserted.

She knew, if necessary, she could conscript a four-wheel-drive vehicle with oversized tires from the Forest Service capable of navigating the snow, mud, and shallow puddles going to LA 99. "You have other cases on your desk, I know, Richard, that you can work on." She really did not want to go out in the mud today.

Tafoya nodded slightly. "Yes, I do. Looking Elk's death is what we are focused on now, but there's also the Franklin Deerfield theft and the Bernal murder out at Quintana Canyon. Looking Elk's death is coming to resolution, but the other two…." His voice trailed off.

Tafoya did not finish his sentence. Of the three cases they had on their desks, the Looking Elk case seemed headed for closure, the museum case was at a standstill, and the Bernal murder remained open and most critical. He needed to shift focus to Bernal. He looked at Janet.

"Janet, let's go over the Bernal murder case. He was, after all, shot and killed on National Forest land. That brings you in germanely, as liaison officer with the Forest Service. Let me bring you up to speed. I need your eyes and brain on this case."

The station conference room was available all morning for them to look at the facts and hypothesize. Tafoya brought in his personal notes and the evidence box from the Bernal case. He and Janet opened up the computer files for the murder case. He had his three silos of data on the conference table: personal notes, evidence box, and reports on the computer for Bernal. If needed, they could utilize the whiteboard with magic markers standing at the front of the room. He had his yellow notebook pad in front of him.

Delores stepped to the door of the conference room. "I'm going to leave early for Mass at eleven, Tafoya, and meet up with my sisters to go as a group to the church. I'll be back after Mass and lunch, say, around one o'clock. All Saints' Day is an obligatory Mass Day for us."

"Say prayers for Looking Elk, Delores," Tafoya pleaded. Delores said she would.

Tafoya began going over the Bernal case with Janet, explaining he was shot twice, one shot at close range. How he arrived at Quintana Pass was unknown. What he was doing at the Quintana Canyon was also unknown. Bernal had left his house with unknown parties and had failed to leave a note with his wife about his whereabouts. His deer rifle was missing from his house, so it was assumed that he had taken the rifle with him when he left that morning. His close friends had been questioned about their contact with him. Only one of his friends had seen him the week of his death, and they had talked about deer hunting. Hence, the supposition he had gone to the mountains looking for deer camp possibilities. But who did he go with? As Tafoya summarized the case, Janet read the reports and interviews on her laptop, jotting down in her notebook names and details she thought important.

One name joggled her memory: Larry Armijo. "Where have I come across that name before?" she thought. She wrote his name down.

Tafoya walked down to the end of the conference table where there was space to open up the evidence box and lay out the few pieces of evidence collected at the murder scene. Janet stood up and went down to the end of the table to see the material evidence. Wrapped in clear plastic and sealed were Bernal's clothes and hiking boots—the heels cut off. The red-checked wool shirt showed dark blotches of blood stains and the powder residue of the close shot in his chest area.

Tafoya laid out the clear plastic bags on the table so the contents could be closely examined. Within the bags were the bullet dug out of the ground, his personal effects, and a bag with a long plastic stick or spoon handle.

The function of the plastic stick or spoon handle was unknown. The forensic notes remitted the item as, "unidentified and purpose unknown. The white plastic item may have no relation to the case." Picked up by the Taos County sheriff's department, its location was fifty yards from the body, on the ground under the first stand of aspen trees as one trekked up the mountains.

Janet picked up the white plastic item and looked at it carefully. It measured about six inches long and appeared to have been broken off from the base of something. She looked at it closely and noted that it had a slight curvature to its shape. Janet unholstered her flashlight and shined it on the item, first one way and then another, pressing her fingers lightly on the stick to determine its shape. She set the item back down.

Tafoya watched her examine the item, and started to ask her, "What do you see?" when she spoke first.

"I think I know what this is, Richard."

"What is it, Janet?" The forensic team had not solved its function, and he sure did not know. "Popsicle stick" was a far as he could go with it.

"It is an airfoil. Aerodynamically, it is a fin that lifts a wing, like an airplane."

"Part of a toy airplane? Its wing?" Tafoya was confused.

"No, not an airplane, Richard, it is a rotor blade or fin. Like on a helicopter."

"I still don't get it, Janet. It's a toy helicopter wing?"

"Close, Richard. It is a blade from a drone. The drone's rotor blade for some reason broke off from the base." She held up the clear plastic bag. "The drone must have hit a tree and lost its blade."

"You sure about that, Janet?" Tafoya asked.

"Yes, Richard. When I am at the airport, I see drones being flown. I've seen them up close, and being a pilot, I know an airfoil when I see one. It's what keeps a flying machine up in the air."

Tafoya entered Janet's conclusion about the drone blade on the Bernal file. He thought it was a disconnect with Bernal's murder, but, then again, there just might be a connection. Did Bernal have a drone? If not him, who had the drone at Quintana Canyon?

Tafoya determined to see *if* there was synchronicity—or not. Who in Taos County possessed a drone? The rotor blade was fifty-yards away from where Bernal was killed. Was there a connection?

After another hour of briefing Janet, she said she had to go to Forest Service headquarters and tend to some matters there. "Let's talk later in the day, Richard." He agreed and put away the evidence box and closed the computer files.

After Janet had left the tribal police station, Tafoya had walked over to Looking Elk's home to pay respects. Looking Elk's widow, Sacred Corn Circle, sat on a couch covered with a Navajo blanket, its black, yellow, and crimson colors reflective of her depressed mood.

Tafoya pondered asking Sacred Corn Circle a vital question, but he had to. "Do you know why Looking Elk was going out in the snow to the trust land?" He respected her grief and asked the question in the gentlest way he could.

Sacred Corn Circle shook head, "No." Then, softly said, "No."

Then she went on to add, "He had been talking with Albert Walhuime.

Walhuime had confided to him the bundle stolen from Franklin Deerfield was the Hanging Shell medicine bundle that his grandfather, Leroy, had possessed for decades. After Walhuime departed our home, Looking Elk grabbed his medicine bundle, stuffed it in a backpack, put on his parka and red gaiters, and told me, 'I'm going to Franklin Deerfield.' Then he left. That was the last I saw of him…until I go to the other world and be with him."

Tafoya left shortly thereafter.

Tafoya stood outside Looking Elk's home on the Tulona plaza, affected by the widow's grief. Standing there in the cold, he replayed in his head the information she had conveyed to him, adding to what he already knew.

From Ray Tejada's information at the museum's Halloween Party, Tafoya now knew Looking Elk had gone to Franklin Deerfield to find out where the Hanging Shell ruins were located on Tract A. After finding out the location from Tejada, Looking Elk had immediately struck out for the site, despite cold and snow. Frustrated he could not enter the gate because he did not know the code to the lock, Looking Elk had climbed over the gate and proceeded to hike to the site, four miles away. He was desperate. The cold and stress of the hike exceeded the power of his heart to achieve his mission. What caused his desperation?

"Why the desperate search? Almost a panic state of mind," Tafoya thought. From Sacred Corn Circle's information, Walhuime had told Looking Elk the bundle stolen from the museum was the Hanging Shell bundle. That information from Walhuime had spurred Looking Elk to immediately go to the Hanging Shell ancient site, determined to stop or investigate the Hanging Shell ruins.

Tafoya repeated, "He was determined to stop something…and someone…. But, who? And what? And why? I need the full story of Hanging Shell…and I don't know the full story."

Tafoya knew Bustamente had answers, or, at least, the story of Hanging Shell and the medicine bundle. He walked to Bustamente's home, and knocked on his turquoise-painted door.

54

Many seasons before Looking Elk's heart failed him in the snow on Halloween, Alfredo Dominguez listened to Looking Elk, an elder he respected. Looking Elk had told him the story of the pueblo people at Hanging Shell one afternoon under the arbor on the Winter side of the Tulona Pueblo. With the exception of Looking Elk, Dominguez had shunned the pueblo, its people, rituals, and other elders. Dominguez had listened intently to Looking Elk's ancient story, and the narrative had grown within him, expanding, dominating his thoughts.

Dominguez, a full-blood Tulona, visualized a resurgence of a lost colony of the Tulona Pueblo, the Hanging Shell people. And, further, he envisioned himself, Alfredo Dominguez, a castaway from Tulona Pueblo proper, to be a leader, a returning prophet of the Hanging Shell colony.

He had questioned the museum curator, John McGinnis, for the exact location of the extinct Pueblo on Tract A of the Tulona Land Trust. It was designated LA 9976429 by New Mexico state archaeologists. At first, Dominguez had kept to himself his thoughts of grandeur—becoming a leader of a new pueblo, the Hanging Shell—for he was a sensible man, making good money laying stone, and carousing with friends in Ojo Verde. It was the medicine bundle, or at least the possibility the medicine bundle existed, that shot him into a fiery fantasy that would not let him rest.

Looking Elk had informed Dominguez that Wooden Quiver's medicine bundle was the source of Wooden Quiver's power, but it had been lost after the raid and never surfaced. How Dominguez discovered that Wood Quiver's medicine bundle existed was serendipitous. He was not searching for the medicine bundle; it fell into his lap, so he thought, from the Creator. Dominguez thought it a sign he was gifted to lead the resurgence of Hanging Shell, his fantasy realized in the flesh.

At a drumming sing one evening at the pueblo, Dominguez had mentioned the Hanging Shell story to Albert Walhuime who was a grandson of Leroy Walhuime. Albert volunteered a family story that his grandfather, Leroy, had donated a medicine bundle to the Franklin Deerfield Museum in the 1950s, and he remembered his grandfather telling the tale the bundle was wrapped in leather, mussel-shelled belts. The bundle was thought to have been associated with the extinct pueblo along the Big River west of Tulona Pueblo.

As Albert finished the story, Dominguez spoke over Albert's words, softly saying, "Hanging Shell." Albert Walhuime immediately spewed that "Hanging Shell" was the extinct pueblo.

"Yes! That's the place! That's where my grandfather said it came from! Hanging Shell!"

With Albert Walhuime's admission, Alfredo Dominguez embarked on a quest to obtain the medicine bundle and use it to resurrect, to revitalize, the Hanging Shell Pueblo. In his muddled thinking, he would be the spiritual leader to bring the dead to life, the dark to light, and power to a place: LA 9976429 on Tract A of the Tulona Pueblo Land Trust. Yet, so, he remembered Looking Elk's cautionary note.

"Ceremonial objects are sacred and to be respected. Do not fool around with them...I hope the Hanging Shell kiva objects are forever lost, for they were very powerful at one time."

Dominguez ignored Looking Elk's warning. Dominguez told the story of Hanging Shell and the museum's possession of the medicine bundle to his closest friends: Lance Bernal and Larry Armijo. At first, they were skeptical of Dominguez's vision.

"Why revitalize those ruins when we could work with the Tulona living along Cottonwood River? Gain influence within the pueblo as it is now?" Bernard asked. Dominguez answered that it was not the ruins to be revitalized, but the *spirit* of the Tulona people. The three of them would be respected and honored for inspiring the pueblo and its people.

When Bernal and Armijo raised the question of how to obtain the Hanging Shell medicine bundle from the museum to implement the resurrection, Dominguez, to their disappointment, stated, "I don't know how." He believed the bundle was not the property of the museum, but was the property of the pueblo. Yet, he had no plan to obtain the bundle.

At that point, Armijo stated they should "liberate" the bundle from the museum since it was rightfully Tulona property. Bernal thought "liberation" preposterous, and Dominguez scoffed at the thought. Armijo forced the two of them to listen to his suggestion. Dominguez and Bernal listened that night, and after a month of back-and-forth discussions, the three of them formulated a plan to bring Hanging Shell back to life. Young Larry Armijo, computer and data guru, had a plan to liberate the bundle from museum control, and they embraced it.

55

Friday, November 2, All Souls' Day, Month of Corn Depositing Moon

Among the pueblos, before the arrival of the European bringing White and Black legends, November 2, as a name of a month and numbered day, did not exist. Come the Spanish, come the iron and horse, come the black robes, there followed names of months and name-numbered days. But whether or not the puebloans had a Spaniard in their Fifth World made no difference. *This* time of the "year" brought harvested crops; drying, shucking, and shelling of corn, and a laying by and storage of crops for winter and coming seasons. It was November, the "month" of Corn Depositing Moon, preceded by the "month" of Leaves Falling Moon, followed by the "month" of Night Fire Moon or December.

Tulona's cacique, Bustamente Bear Standing Fire, nailed a Questa Lumber and Hardware calendar to the wall of his backroom, where he parleyed tribal business with kinsmen, so that he kept track of the European count; but he remembered from his father and mother before him, the Tulona count of Beginning Time, Good Time, Ripe Time, and Still Time. November was the first of four months of Still Time: November, December, January, and February—the Tulona Winter. Though Bustamente endured all of Creator's seasons, he favored and relished Still Time. Nailing the Questa Hardware calendar to his backroom wall illustrated his adaptation: He lived in two *counting* worlds, the European, the Tulona.

Spanish black robes—the black robes being the sartorial manifestation of the Catholic Church—designated November 2 as All Souls' Day, also called Day of the Dead, another term particularly linked to Mexico. On that day, the Tulona remembered their departed relatives and friends in stories and narratives of grandmothers and grandfathers: "She had the sweetest smile...he hunted that season and came back with the biggest buck ever taken and laid him on our best blankets while we gave thanks to the deer."

As time passed after the arrival of the Spanish and black robes, traditions of All Souls' Day and the Tulona blended. Where the Catholic faithful might put food on the graves of their departed ancestors, the Tulona and other pueblo communities performed additional rites, equally as meaningful in their minds.

The Tulona preferred to call All Souls' Day, Grandmothers' Day, which they had adopted from the Zuñi Pueblo. Food and water were carried to the graves; candles were burned at night in houses, on graves, and at Mission Saint Francis del Monte. During the day, Tulona men carried food to Rio Cottonwood and threw it in the water; Tulona women tossed food into the fire.

Bustamente explained, "The throwing of food into the Cottonwood and the fires feed the spirits of the past, so the spirits might help us grow crops, furnish nourishing water, and tell us the wisdom of things past that will keep us fed, secure, and safe. When we offer food to the river and fires, the wisdom of our grandfathers and grandmothers is brought to us. The ritual connects us with our past, as do our stories. We feed the past; the past nourishes us with its wisdom. Yes, the Catholic All Souls' Day is significant. Grandmothers' Day is significant. I see little difference."

Bustamente had given his explanation to a *Santa Fe New Mexican* newspaper reporter the year before. The reporter wrote a lengthy article on All Souls' Day—or Mexico's Day of the Dead—and how it was celebrated in northern New Mexico. The newspaper had been honored with a prize for the article. Bustamente's interview had been buried deep within the article—only seven sentences had been quoted. That was all right with Bustamente, for he had withheld much. He and the Tulona kept knowledge and secrets to themselves, much like Coe partitioning anthropology books with purple curtains in his bookshop.

Bustamente was now alarmed. He was disturbed by the message given to McGinnis, "The god roams the foothills for XXXXXXX of his enemies." For Bustamente knew the "XXXXXXX" signified scalps. And, outside of All Souls' Day, scalps were "fed." Few people outside of the pueblo world would understand "feeding the scalps." The ritual was neither sordid, nor macabre; it corresponded to the courage and event of taking life.

56

Tintinnabulation.

At twelve noon, Father Jose Padilla rang the church bell of Mission Saint Francis del Monte. He rang twice, and every hour from twelve noon to six o'clock the next morning, the church bell would toll in remembrance of the departed souls, the fallen children, grandmothers, and grandfathers. Father Padilla set up a log of tintinnabulation responsibility from Tulona church rolls. Every hour from twelve noon on, a Tulona deacon of the laity strode to the narthex, unlocked the door across from the baptistry font, grasped the rope, and tolled the bell twice.

During All Souls' Day and night, every hour, the bell sounded, "The first toll: *Their time came, they died.* The second toll: *Your time will come, and you will die.*"

The wind is to be believed. It does not, it cannot lie to you. Humans and trickster animals lie; the wind does not. A Spanish *dicho* enlightens, "Believe the wind." The older Tulano, Alfredo Dominguez, and his younger companion, Larry Armijo, stood on the roof of the newly reconstructed kiva northwest of the reservation, on Tract A of Tulona Land Trust. All Souls' Day was sunny and fair, but cold. The wind did not lie; it rested, occasionally variable at eight miles per hour, and the forecast for wind was light for Grandmothers' Day.

Below them, hanging from a pole inside the kiva, two scalps draped down. From their resting place in the museum a few weeks ago, their dryness had gone away from frequent chewing of the scalp hide. The scalps had been "fed" early in the morning and would be fed again in the evening with the kernels of corn from the medicine bundle of Wood Quiver. Blue corn lay scattered on the kiva floor beneath the scalp pole.

When night fell, the full medicine bundle would be unwrapped and ritual objects would be arranged on the bench altar. The Hanging Shell people's spirits, including that of Wood Quiver, would be revived with song, prayer, and drumming. Dominguez and Armijo would become the hollow bones for revitalization. They believed they could handle the spirit power that would flow through them to the Tulona.

As they stood on top of the kiva and looked westward toward the Tusas Mountains, Armijo heard a bell tone. "What is that I hear, my brother? It comes from the pueblo, I think."

Dominguez cocked his head in the direction of the pueblo. Since it was cold, sounds carried tightly, and with merely a breeze, bird songs and bell tones traveled far.

"I don't hear anything," Dominguez said. "Must be your imagination or the wind playing tricks on you."

"The wind doesn't lie, Minguez. There it is again!"

"I heard it that time, Armijo. It's the hourly tolling for the Day of the Dead," Dominguez said, dryly.

"When will it stop?"

"Never."

57

After breakfast at his parents' home at the family compound, Luis Ortega walked to the corral where Buck and Monte, his gelding companions, munched on alfalfa hay in their stable bins. Luis had never quite figured out who, among the two, Buck or Monte, was the alpha horse. Both geldings, lacking *huevos*, never had ferocious stud moments of either kicking or biting one another. One day, Monte might be fractious; the next day, it was Buck. But their disagreements were situational, not temperament. As registered sorrel quarter horses, they shared the same dam in their breeding, but different studs as sire. Buck stood at fourteen hands, Monte at thirteen-and-a-half hands. They had been trained by the Monty Roberts' method. The Circle Diamond Ranch trainer, Marian Augustus Frey, known as "Free," used Monty's method, and no other.

Luis had been championing Free's training and the equine bloodlines of the Circle Diamond remuda to Lion Walks Night. Further, Luis had convinced Free to give Lion Walks Night a discount on the purchase of a mare of good blood from the same lineage of Buck or Monte. Lion Walks Night, sometime in the coming Good Time of Tulona spring, would choose a mare from Circle Diamond and put down money for her. Luis hoped, by spring, that Flowers Dancing, the cousin of Lion, would go along with them when they traveled to Las Vegas, New Mexico, to choose the mare at Circle Diamond Ranch.

Luis' two dates with Flowers Dancing had progressed nicely, and he hoped it would continue. Luis' mother, Loretta, cautioned, "You will have to wait and see." Luis never was pleased when she said that, and she said it so often that he would go away depressed from his mother's opinion.

Buck finished his hay first and walked over to where Luis was standing. Buck raised his head over the top bar of the paneled corral, resting it on the rail, and looked at Luis, expecting a nice rub on his forehead, between his eyes. Luis obliged, and with his fingers combed the hair between Buck's ears downward. Monte, not wanting to be left out of the party—they were herd animals after all, and Luis was part of the herd—walked over and stood next to Buck. Luis grinned, "Jealous, eh?"

"Luuuuisss?" he heard his mother yell from her house.

"At the corral!" he hollered back.

"It's Medicine Wind, on the landline."

What could he want? Luis thought. I trimmed Star and Jess' hooves a month ago, so it's not about that. Flowers Dancing, in some way? He hurried to his parents' house and picked up the old phone, the black, ceramic phone with a rotary dial that, miraculously, continued to be supported by Dancing Rock Telephone Company, not American Telephony Company who had tried a hostile takeover decades ago and failed. Dancing Rock was the company the people supported north of Ojo Verde and on the Tulona Reservation, even though Dancing Rock wanted to phase out rotary phones. Dancing Rock even had telephone lines strung in southern Colorado, all up and down the San Luis Valley.

"Hey, Ben, how's it going?" he answered, after hurrying to the phone.

"The Tulona need your help," Medicine Wind said gravely.

Luis Ortega hurriedly collected every saddle blanket and saddle pad he and the Ortega family possessed and threw them in the front tack room of the gooseneck-stock trailer he borrowed from his neighbor. He ported two saddles, one for himself and one more just in case a Tulona wanted one. The stock trailer was large enough to accommodate eight, maybe ten, horses if they were accustomed to each other and had settled their alpha status.

At Medicine Wind's request and the Tulona, Luis would be hauling four horses, not ten. The horses were acquainted with one another—Buck, Monte, Star, and Sweet Hija. Buck and Monte were his mounts, Star belonged to Medicine Wind, and Sweet Hija was Bustamente's. After loading Buck and Monte, Luis double-checked the hitch and chains to the diesel pickup, jumped in the cab, ignited the big engine, and drove rapidly to the Tulona Pueblo. Zeke, the border collie, had to stay with Armando and Loretta.

"Where we are going, Zeke," Luis said, "is wet, muddy, and snowy. Sorry you can't go. Stay, *perro bueno*, we'll be back tonight."

When Luis pulled up to the Tulona warchief's guardhouse at the entrance to the pueblo, a young Tulona mounted the running board, held on to the door, and waved him through to the corrals where Medicine Wind, Bustamente, Lion Walks Night, and Quail Looks Away stood by the panels. The horses neighed loudly when they saw each other. Quail held the halter and bridle tack to Jess, the packhorse mare she and Lovato owned.

"Looks like I'll be hauling five horses," Luis said to himself, seeing Quail Looks Away ready to ride.

By the directions of the young Tulona, Luis entered the pueblo plaza and circled the fifty-foot fiesta pole to come alongside the corral for a quick loading of the horses. While Medicine Wind threw saddle blankets into the trailer's tack room, Luis led Sweet Hija first into the horse trailer, placing her beside Monte. They neighed a deep, low tone, greeting one another. Then he loaded Star and Jess, in that order, tying slip knots from their halters to keep the horses aligned.

Horses being loaded, Lion Walks Night jumped into the passenger seat across from Luis, while Medicine Wind drove Bustamente and Quail Looks Away in his pickup behind the gooseneck trailer. When Abalone Road intersected the highway, they turned north on the state highway toward Questa. Reaching the gate to Tract A of the Tulona Trust Land on the Questa highway, Luis pulled onto the shoulder of the highway across from the gate and, after checking for traffic, turned the pickup and horse trailer onto the paved entry road and turn-around space next to the gate to Tract A.

After checking the immediate vicinity of the ground inside the gate, Medicine Wind entered the proper code to open the gate, and they drove in and parked their pickups on the semi-dry ground next to the entrance. Farther down the road, it was muddy and impassable for a vehicle. No choice but to ride horses. To traverse to Hanging Shell kiva, you either walked or rode horses. Ride it would be: Luis Ortega on Buck, Lion Walks Night on Monte, Medicine Wind on Star, Bustamente on Sweet Hija, and Quail Looks Away on Jess.

58

Bustamente spoke before they mounted. "We are going to ride our horse people in the old way. I will need your help on mounting and dismounting, but I intend to ride Sweet Hija in the manner that is least disturbing to her balance. Hanging Shell was alive and happy before the horse came. With our colorful blankets, the spirits of Hanging Shell will welcome us as human beings that respect the four-legged ones. We will use reins and bridles and leg pressure to direct the horses."

Luis, standing next to Buck, shifted his weight, uneasily. He had ridden Buck bareback, so that was no problem for him. The saddles would remain in the trailer. What bothered him was the reason for riding to old ruins. Lion Walks Night, on the pickup ride from the pueblo to Tract A, had been quiet and spoke little. He decided to ask a question when Bustamente paused.

When he paused, Luis asked, "Are we expecting to see anyone at the ruins, Grandfather?"

"I think we will see two people at the old ruins. They are Tulona, and we are going there to see if they are doing good or arousing bad medicine for the Tulona. There may be others, I do not know."

Bustamente continued, "Luis, what we are doing involves Tulona ways and because you are trusted among us, what you see and hear today will remain a secret and not be told to anyone outside our circle. We want our ways to remain secret and private.... I have known you since you were a boy and played with Medicine Wind and raced him in high school. You are one of us in spirit, our brother."

Bustamente paused again and then added, "Flowers Dancing likes you very much. That says a lot." Luis's heart soared.

Quail Looks Away spoke up, unexpectedly, "Dezba, Blue Flowers

Springing, sat on your knee and chaps when she was only a few days old. By that introduction with the scents of horse and leather and sweat of you working with horse people, she grows as a child into womanhood that will be strong. *We let you hold our Tulona baby*. That means you are very special. You are one of us, Luis Ortega. The Corn Mother and Creator put you with us, and, here we are, Luis, on this desert mesa, together. You are one of us."

Bustamente, Medicine Wind, and Lion Walks Night all said in deep unison to Quail, "*Heeeyyyy*."

Luis' spirit soared. Was that a drum he heard? He had trouble taking a breath. He could not reply to the words flung from the sky and earth in his direction, "In spirit, our brother...The Corn Mother and Creator put you with us on this desert mesa, together, now."

Something heavy pounded him, pressured him on his chest and back at the same time, and he felt he was going to pass out. "Flowers Dancing... Dezba...Corn Mother...Creator...."Those names, those words were more than sounds...they were incantations to the deep pools of Earth Cloud Lake, the inner recesses of the La Osa Caves. The bare hills of his life changed to a radiant, luminous green of growth and belonging.

What was happening to him? For the rest of his life, he would look back on this moment, the words, his friends, the horses, the mesa, the sky, the wet earth, the little snow patches on the northside of sagebrush, the Tusas and Tulona Peak, a boundless spaciousness, the pressure on his body, the "boundless landscape," the nearness of the little snow patches, the near, the far, the here, the now.

In later years, Bustamente explained the moment, "*It was Point Hill Green, singling you out, Luis Ortega!*"

Horses were not saddled. Their human companions rode close to the withers, their legs hanging loosely down unless pressure was applied to turn them. Mane hair was held and grasped when necessary. The rhythm of the horse became the rhythm of the rider. As much as possible, they—horse and human—became one on the road to Hanging Shell kiva.

59

Earlier, on the morning of All Souls' Day, Tribal policeman Richard Tafoya had arrived at the pueblo stationhouse. At that early hour, seven o'clock, he beat Romero and Delores Rafael by thirty minutes. Not that they were in a race to see who arrived first, but the three of them joked about, "Sleeping in…late night…failed to set the alarm," the usual banter of people that have worked with each other for years. He could best them this morning, he thought, chuckling to himself.

Before Tafoya focused on the Bernal murder, he had made a pot of Mundo and sat down at Rafael's desk at the front of the stationhouse, reviewing the video-security tape on the night of the Franklin Deerfield theft. Then he would go back to his office for the Bernal case. The coffee was good, and he added more cream than usual.

Tafoya knew there had been about a thirty-minute gap in the tape the afternoon before the theft, between 3:56 and 4:32 p.m. He looked at his logbook of the investigation of the theft and read he had stopped viewing the security tape at the twelve-midnight time stamp. He needed to finish viewing the video. Finding the midnight time stamp on the security tape, he began viewing: Security officer making his rounds, security officer checking doors at random, security officer going to front door and looking out in the dark, the usual stuff. The security officer was conscientious.

When the security tape looped to 3:02 a.m., it went blank, then came back on at 3:07. Tafoya set his coffee down and rewound the tape to 3:01 and 45 seconds. Again, the tape blanked out for five minutes, 3:02 to 3:07. Like the previous afternoon, the blanking out of the video occurred on all security cameras. Tafoya made a note of the blank interval and continued to view the tape until the thieves were caught on camera coming out of the inventory room at 4:12 a.m., walking to the rear exit door with one of them performing a dance—the dance the Navajo Majerus from Arroyo Luz said, "It's nonsensical, not important, kind of stupid."

As Tafoya thought about the security video lapses, he realized that analyzing the lapses and the technology for an investigation were beyond his and the department's capabilities and skill set. Romero came through the front door. A cold draft of air followed him.

"Beat you here, Sergeant, you must have stayed up late playing video games,"Tafoya joked.

Romero laughed and claimed he was watching "Law and Order" reruns. Romero poured a cup of coffee and came back to the front of station. Tafoya had shut down the front-desk computer and was sitting in a chair. Delores Rafael would be in shortly, and he did not want to be at her desk, occupying her space. Romero sat down to chat. After a while, Delores came in and went directly to the coffee room to set down a box of donuts.

"I'm going to call Agent Parker of the F.B.I. to help us on the Franklin Deerfield case,"Tafoya exclaimed to Romero. "I've come up with another blank spot on the video at three o'clock in the morning at the museum… about five minutes blanked out."

"So, you think she'll help us, Richard?" Romero asked.

Before he could respond, Rafael came back to the front office and said, "Calling Agent Parker, eh? I hope that gets you somewhere, Richard."

Tafoya explained that Parker had volunteered to assist in the case, and he was going to take her up on it. It was well known the F.B.I. had tremendous resources of technology and computer analysts far beyond the resources of the tribal office or county authorities. Romero agreed, and said he would approve of the alliance with the F.B.I. Rafael added that she would like to get to know Parker better, hopefully finding behind her brusqueness was a likeable person and skilled administrator.

"I worked closely with her on the Saltwater-Blue Lady Mine case. In a weak moment, I invited her to come up for our Feast Day next year," Rafael volunteered. Tafoya and Romero looked shocked, but said nothing. Tafoya kept the fact to himself that he had invited Parker as well.

"Don't look shocked, you two! A pueblo courtesy to do so," Rafael added. Tafoya and Romero shook their heads in agreement.

"Send her a powerpoint about Feast Day, and she'll be happy as a lark,"Tafoya said.

Finishing his conversation with Romero and Rafael, Tafoya poured another cup of coffee in the breakroom and walked back to his office. He opened up his three silos of data about the Franklin Deerfield case: computer files and links to the Tulona Tribal Police website and F.B.I. and his field notes and yellow pages of information. Again, setting aside the Bernal case. He walked to the evidence room to pull the third silo: the evidence box. The evidence box was not heavy, containing museum guest registers and various paperwork that had not been scanned into the department's computer files. The red and black cylinders of the Navajo gods in the Night Chant had been returned to the museum. So also had the mask of Water Child and the kilt had been returned to Franklin Deerfield. He quickly looked over the computer folders relative to the museum case and his personal notes. Tafoya found the personal phone number to F.B.I. agent Diane Parker. He punched the number in quickly.

Parker's phone rang once, then she answered. Tafoya heard no background noise; he imagined her at the office, certainly not at her home at this hour of the morning. He explained to Parker that he and the department needed the expertise of the F.B.I. to analyze two gaps in the security tape at Franklin Deerfield, the gap the afternoon at 3:56 p.m., and, now, the blank in the video at 3:02 a.m. the next morning. Tafoya hoped that some drilling down into the security tape and files associated with the gaps might shed some light on who the thieves were, or reveal the gaps were technical glitches in the security system, not associated with the theft.

Tafoya opined, "Hopefully, recapture what was lost during the blank spaces?"

Agent Parker quickly assented to helping the computer side of the investigation, adding that neither payment nor special funding from the Tulona tribal budget was necessary, for the theft had occurred on reservation land, "Albeit leased to the museum. It's still tribal land and is technically under our jurisdiction as well."

Tafoya had not thought of submitting a special budget request. That was his supervisor's worry. Parker stated the F.B.I. digital investigative team in Albuquerque was experiencing a low volume of tasks, and they would start immediately once certain permissions were obtained from Franklin Deerfield. Nearly all of the digital investigation could be done remotely by computer in the Albuquerque F.B.I. field office.

Tafoya asked Parker, "What permissions were needed?"

Parker went down the list, "Obtain authorization from the museum's director for the F.B.I. to access remotely their computers, servers, and ancillary IT equipment. We need particular access to the security server. Also, we will need the name of the security company that set up their system as well as any other security companies that are being used presently and in the past. To get started immediately, we need the IT and director's passwords to the computer system. We can work on the other angles in good time, but to get started now, get me the passwords and permission to access remotely."

"How soon will I know the results of your investigation?" Tafoya asked.

"Send me that information for access and passwords, and we may have something by early afternoon," Parker answered. "But Dancing Rock Power Coop must keep up the power grid."

As soon as Tafoya put the landline phone back in its cradle, he checked the forecast for thunderstorms. None in the forecast, so Dancing Rock would stay up for the day, unless a transformer blew, or a truck sliced off a utility pole, or the wind farm went dark near Fort Sumner. He called Director Hornbuckle at the museum and immediately received authorization to allow the F.B.I. to access remotely. Within thirty minutes, F.B.I. agent Parker and her team had the passwords and access to all the data and security systems of Franklin Deerfield Museum. Director Hornbuckle was as eager to resolve the case as was Tafoya.

Tafoya returned the Franklin Deerfield evidence box to the lockers and put "lids" on his other two silos of information. He walked to the front of the stationhouse and looked out the front window onto the pueblo plaza. He saw a pickup and a gooseneck horse trailer come onto the plaza, circle the Fiesta Day pole, and presumably, stop by the corrals. A Tulona young man—it looked like Snow Day Spruce—was standing on the running board of the pickup and directing the *vaquero* to circle the pole and go back alongside the corrals. Five horses were tied inside the trailer.

"*Ay*, the *kowenas*," the horses, "are here."

Confident the pickup and trailer were sanctioned by Snow Day Spruce, Tafoya walked back to his office and opened three more silos, all concerning the murder of Lance Bernal. From the evidence box, he lifted the plastic evidence bag containing the broken rotary blade of a drone and placed it squarely in the center of his desk. Tafoya centered his attention on the blade, carefully setting aside all other papers.

"Talk to me, blade. Talk to me now. You talked to Janet; you can talk to me."

60

By mid-morning on All Souls' Day, Coe's Bookshop had seen a slow trickle of customers coming in to browse, purchasing few books. More conversation occurred about Fenster, the cat guard at night for the bookshop, who lounged on the center table stacked with coffee-table art books, than about the latest best sellers in the newly released novels section. To Coe, the morning's slow sales did not bother him, since the day before a high volume of sales left him fatigued by the time he closed shop late in the afternoon.

The phone rang. He answered it promptly and heard Director Hornbuckle on the other end of the line, her voice tense. She called to inform him that the F.B.I. was investigating the case, focusing on the security video lapses.

"Another lapse was discovered this morning by Officer Tafoya," Hornbuckle explained, "and he thought it best to call in the F.B.I.'s data analysis team. They will be accessing the museum's computers remotely. I'm calling all board members. You were at the top of the list since your last name begins with an 'A,' Mr. Armstrong." Coe thanked her, and after a few more exchanges, hung up the phone.

Coe felt hungry, so he called his wife to see if she wanted to meet him for lunch at Tablita's. Despite it being eleven, Coe wished to eat early. Prissy had decided to go to Taos and shop at La Mancha grocery store and do more shopping in the village, so she declined to meet him. She suggested he ask Cecilia, his next-door business friend, to eat with him, as they had done on several occasions.

Coe said, "I might, I don't know," and told Prissy to be careful on the road. He would see her at home after he closed the shop. After Prissy hung up, Coe texted her that the F.B.I. was going to help the Tulona tribal police investigate security lapses in the video. He texted her, rather than call her back, because he did not want the customers to hear the news. His wife sent back a "thumbs up" icon. She must be driving, Coe thought.

Coe told Claire, his part-time help, to watch the store for he was going to lunch early, across the street at Tablita's. He went next door to Cecilia's fashion shop and asked if she wanted to catch an early lunch. She consented, and the two of them crossed the street at the marked crosswalk. By New Mexico state law and the general civic courtesy of drivers, traffic in both directions stopped and allowed them to cross the street. An eighteen-wheeler carrying ponderosa logs, freshly cut from the National Forest, braked nosily for them. The scent of fresh-cut conifers wafted over them as they crossed the street, "Smells like Christmas, Coe," Claire said.

Coe smiled, "I have a feeling we are going to have a good snow season, Claire. The cacique out at the pueblo told me that he thought the snow would be heavy this winter."

"Oh, how so? How does he figure that?"

"Corn husks and onions are the thickest he has seen in several years. And, Cecilia, the Tulona know their maize and onions."

Jason Taylor seated the two of them at the Schwartz Table, beside the street-side windows. Only one other couple was in the dining room for early lunch. Jason was happy. Snow had fallen two days ago, and he had driven up in the mountains after his shift to get the full effect. He took their order for two half-orders of enchiladas and iced tea.

Jason asked them both how business was going. Coe said it had been good the day before, but the morning was slow. Cecilia said that business had been laggard, and that Jason should get a girlfriend and entice her to shop at her place, then go next door to Coe's.

"I'll buy her book on how to save money by shopping wisely," Jason responded, laughingly.

Coe and Cecilia gossiped about town news and the recent list of social discord on the Ojo Verde police blotter: a man was admitted to Saint. Luke's Hospital saying he was hearing voices, a man was trying to camp out on the Ojo Verde Library lawn, someone keyed a car in the parking lot adjacent to their shops, and a man carrying a rifle was walking around the village plaza threatening tourists. They laughed at the gun-toting man threatening tourists and shared the story with Jason. They had theories of why he threatened tourists.

The best answer came from Jason: "The guy was a waiter up at Towngate's Café and mad because tourists weren't tipping enough."

As they split the bill and gave Jason a *very* good tip, Coe told Cecilia that the F.B.I. was coming to investigate the museum heist. "They are not taking over the case, just the security and video parts of it, and they're doing it remotely from Albuquerque."

Cecilia remarked that she had had techies from Taiwan "takeover her computer" to fix a problem she was having at the shop. The computer was crashing too often. It was strange to see techies maneuver her computer mouse from Taiwan.

"And there I was, just standing here, in Ojo Verde, New Mexico USA, and the Taiwanese were moving my mouse around!"

Coe agreed, "Weird."

As Coe and Cecilia stood at the curb, waiting for traffic to stop so they could cross the street, they heard the deep, basso bell from the tower of Our Lady of Assumption church a few blocks away. It rang once, fell silent five seconds, then clanged a second, deep tone. Two tones, one for the dead, and one for those alive that would die. They safely crossed the street.

"Oh, good god, Coe! We'll be hearing that bell from now on till in the morning, all through the night. I won't sleep with my windows open tonight, that's for sure."

Coe responded, "It's old-time village life in northern New Mexico."

As they parted ways to their respective shops, he to his bookstore, she her fashion shop, Coe thought of Hemingway's title, *For Whom the Bell Tolls*, but he also thought of John Donne's sermon, ""No man is an island, entire of itself. Every man is a piece of the continent, a part of the main.... Each man's death diminishes me, for I am involved in mankind. Therefore, send not to know for whom the bell tolls, it tolls for thee."

Coe walked into his bookshop, murmuring to himself, "That's just great! Just great! A reminder every hour from Our Lady of Assumption that we're all going to die!"

He looked at Fenster who was sprawled on the checkout counter, lazily flicking her tail against the cash register. He stood looking at her for a few seconds. Coe took a deep breath and walked over to Fenster. He began to pet her. She purred. He stroked her hair gently…she continued to purr, even louder…and Coe calmed down.

61

In single file, Medicine Wind led the five horsemen toward Hanging Shell ruins. Bustamente Bear Standing Fire followed Medicine Wind who guided them all toward the kiva and ruins four miles away, alongside the Arroyo de Conchas near the rim of the Rio Grande. Bear Standing Fire was riding Sweet Hija who walked carefully behind the pace of Medicine Wind and Star. Quail Looks Away trailed behind Bustamente. Quail's mount, Jess, dutifully paced himself with the remuda and humans riding bareback. Then followed Lion Walks Night on Monte. Bringing up the rear, Luis Ortega gave Buck his head, tying the reins and letting them hang from the withers. The late morning sun and wind of All Souls' Day had begun to dry out the topsoil. Medicine Wind guided the file of humans and horses around water puddles and down and up dry trails across arroyos.

Slung across Medicine Wind's back, a 7mm Remington magnum rifle with scope hung with authority, bouncing lightly. Quail likewise hoisted the same caliber rifle as her husband. Lion had a .30-30 Winchester rifle resting on his legs. It had a sling, but Lion wanted it at the ready in front of him. The Winchester had been his Grandfather Xavier's who had used it hunting elk in Valle Vidal. The file of horsemen echoed a hunting party of old times, traversing meadows and plains in search of elk or buffalo for their families.

Luis strapped his Rueger Vaquero .357 pistol around his waist, teasing the group, "I'm prepared for close-quarter action." Quail responded with a smile, and patting the sheathed knife on her belt, indicated she was, too. The upshot of the group's profile was that they were tending toward very serious business indeed.

Yet, none of the five expected violence. But if shots were fired, they would report in kind.

The cacique Bustamente and Medicine Wind had decided earlier that morning to ride out to Hanging Shell ruins to examine the site. The two had thought deeply, quietly, and spoken after thinking in front of the piñon fire in the cacique's backroom. Bustamente had knocked at Medicine Wind's door at three o'clock in the morning, summoning him for parley. By breakfast, Medicine Wind and Bustamente were of one mind.

Standing Elk had died trying to make it to the old kiva, after discovering the Hanging Shell medicine bundle had been stolen from Franklin Deerfield. Merging the Hanging Shell medicine bundle with the ancient Hanging Shell kiva was a lethal mixture of pueblo spiritual icons and places. The medicine bundle and the spirit of a bygone sacred space needed to remain at rest, not resurrected. Witchcraft might be unleashed, and a place of pueblo spiritual unrest might be revitalized again to haunt the present age. Thus, Medicine Wind and Bustamente decided to act, calling Luis Ortega for help in transporting horses.

Yes, none of the five expected violence, but riding to a powerful spiritual location, possibly occupied by unknown persons who had broken into a museum to steal spiritual artifacts to influence mystical forces at Hanging Shell, was dangerous. The cacique, Bustamente, might fight against the spiritual, but Lion Walks Night, Quail Looks Away, and Medicine Wind would fight physical forces, whether sticks, stones, bullets, knives, or hailstones came their way. Luis Ortega, now an adopted Tulona, stood in attendance for whatever role he was destined to play.

Halfway to Hanging Shell ruins, the bells of Mission Saint Francis del Monte tolled twice.

Luis, at the rear of the column, remarked, "There be the bells for All Souls' Day. Every hour, they toll twice."

"I forgot about the bells, but no matter, doesn't concern us. Besides we will be out of earshot when we reach Hanging Shell," Medicine Wind opined.

"The sound carries in this cold, still air. It is a sign from the black robes," Bustamente said.

"Good or bad sign, Grandfather?" Quail Looks Away asked.

Bustamente rode without speaking for a while. Then, he said, "Quail, it's neither good nor bad. The bells rings truly for those that have passed on, and all of us that will eventually die. A natural process, but it is a sign, a symbol of the nature of all things to live, to die, and others will follow along. The black robes have their way of explaining; we have ours."

"*Ay!!!*" spoke the file of horsemen in unison. Medicine Wind's horse, Star, shook his head, the bit and conchos on the bridle jingle-jangled, metallically, like tiny cymbals among sagebrush and melting patches of snow from Halloween. Star shook his head to readjust the copper roll in his mouth that tasted good and did not pinch his mouth.

Star was relaxed. The single file of horses could see for great distances, and no overhanging bluffs abounded. No lion would be leaping on his back. For now, the surrounds were peaceful, and no flight from danger need occur. That could change, and Star was alert; but for the moment, the tolling of bells and the murmur of human voices comforted him. He shook his head again, and tiny cymbals rang across the desert mesa.

"Look there! Coming our way, Armijo," Dominguez said, standing taller on the roof of the reconstructed kiva to get a better look. "Horsemen…bring me my binoculars! Quick!" Armijo fetched the binoculars from their pickup parked near the cottonwood bosque since the day before Halloween.

Dominguez adjusted the binoculars, focusing on the column. "There are five, some have rifles slung. What are they possibly up to, coming in this direction?" Dominguez let the binoculars down on his chest, then quickly hoisted them back up to have another look. Armijo fretted, murmuring nonsensical sounds.

"Gather the medicine bundle together. I'll get the scalps. We've got to hide them. Hurry, before they get here," Dominguez commanded.

Armijo and Dominguez slid quickly down the kiva ladder into the sacred chamber, repacked the medicine bundle, and put the corn mothers, tableaus, and the world straightener in the backpack. Dominguez cut the buckskin that held the scalps from the pole and stuffed them in his shirt. They ran down to the bosque of cottonwoods to hide the medicine bundle. Dominguez pushed the two scalps into a hollow of a fallen cottonwood that lay several yards from the pickup.

Rushing back to the camp they had set up outside the kiva, Dominguez and Armijo stoked the fire that had been burning for four days. They put on a coffee pot and set it to boil, while they waited for the horsemen to arrive.

As Medicine Wind closed on the camp, he recognized Dominguez and Armijo. Turning around, he quietly informed the column, "Bustamente, it's Dominguez and Armijo at the kiva. They've a fire going, and their pickup is down by the cottonwoods."

As they came within earshot of the campfire, Medicine Wind shouted, "Hail to the camp!"

Dominguez and Armijo shouted back as friendly as they could, nervous underneath about the purpose of four men and one woman armed, riding to their encampment.

The troop of riders dismounted. Luis and Lion aided Bustamente in his dismount. "*Ay*," said Bustamente, "I'm too old to ride bareback this far." He laughed to himself.

Medicine Wind saw the fresh construction of the kiva, but said nothing, allowing Bustamente to take the lead in opening the conversation. Dominguez offered coffee to all. Bustamente accepted a cup of coffee while the rest of the party did not, preferring to drink water from their canteens. Dominguez and Armijo poured themselves coffee, after giving Bustamente a cup.

"I have not seen you for several days, Armijo," Bustamente said. Armijo shrugged his shoulders, offering no explanation.

Bustamente walked over to the old Hanging Shell kiva, now reconstructed with fresh-cut viga timbers jutting out from the circular walls, standing three feet high from the ground. Long spruce poles forming timbers for ladder rungs leaned at an angle against the entry portal in the middle of the kiva. Dominguez and Armijo's reconstruction followed the familiar pattern of pueblo kivas all over the Southwest. The roof consisted of interlaced cedar *latillas*.

"Did you come out here hunting?" Dominguez asked. "You are carrying deer rifles. There's better hunting up in the mountains. Not out here on the mesa."

"Medicine Wind, go look in the kiva. See what these boys have been up to," Bustamente said, ignoring Dominguez's question.

Medicine Wind handed his rifle to Luis who slung it on his shoulder. He climbed up the rock steps to the roof of the kiva and carefully descended the ladder. Dominguez and Armijo stood still. Armijo glanced at Dominguez who was watching for Medicine Wind to come back out of the kiva.

"I didn't see either of you at Looking Elk's funeral," Lion Walks Night said, pointedly.

Dominguez quickly turned his head to Lion, "Looking Elk's dead?" Lion explained to them what had happened during the snowstorm on Halloween.

"He was found dead of a heart attack on the road coming out here," Bustamente added, pointing with his chin at the kiva. "Died just over the gate on trust land coming out to this place. You have any idea why he might want to risk his life for to get out here in a snowstorm?"

"How would we know what was going on inside his head? He was an old man, poor health, *loco en cabeza*, "Armijo snidely answered.

"Shut up, Armijo," Dominguez said. "He may have been old and in poor health, but he wasn't crazy." Armijo glared at Dominguez.

"He told you the story of Wood Quiver and the Hanging Shell people, did he not?" Bustamente asked Dominguez.

"Yes, Grandfather, he did," Dominguez answered respectfully. "Do you know the story?"

"I do. Elders of the Tulona know about Hanging Shell. The story was fading, dying even, among our stories. Other stories and tales are more important to our pueblo ways than Hanging Shell. In a natural way, the story was fading until....," Bustamente's voice trailed off, leaving an intentional space for Dominguez to fill with words.

But Dominguez refused to respond. Bustamente stared at Dominguez. Dominguez looked away. Armijo started to say something, but Dominguez gave him a harsh glance, and Armijo remained quiet.

Dominguez spoke. "We came out here the day before the snow on Halloween. Halloween evening, we saw many flashing lights in the distance, toward the Tract A entry gate. The snow clouds reflected the red and blue and white lights at a distance. The road was impassable for us to go and investigate the lights," Dominguez admitted.

He deliberately avoided talking about the Hanging Shell story.

Suddenly, Dominguez and the others turned around and looked up at Medicine Wind who was climbing out of the kiva. Medicine Wind stepped off the kiva ladder and carefully walked down stone steps to the ground. Luis handed Medicine Wind's rifle back to him. He held it in his hand, not slinging it back on his shoulder. The gesture was not threatening, but Dominguez took a step back from Medicine Wind.

Bustamente spoke. "Hmmph, I know you don't know what Looking Elk was thinking about in coming here in a snowstorm. But both of you know why *you* are out here. And it is obvious to all of us that you have worked on reconstructing the Hanging Shell kiva. I say again, why are you here?" Bustamente said, loudly and pointedly.

Armijo responded. "We have been reconstructing the kiva, yes. We wanted to revitalize the Hanging Shell site, the kiva. There's room for more than two active kivas among the Tulona. The Old Bow and Blue Stone kivas are powerful. Another one won't hurt the Tulona. It might even revitalize the religion of our pueblo. There were three of us that wanted to do this reconstruction...."

"Who was the third man that wanted to do this?" Medicine Wind interrupted.

"Lance Bernal, but he's dead now," Dominguez responded.

Armijo did not continue his explanation. The group fell silent at Dominguez's mention of Lance Bernal.

Very faintly, the bells at Mission Saint Francis del Monte rang—twice. Cold air still carried the hourly tintinnabulation out to Hanging Shell kiva. Luis looked at his wristwatch: two o'clock. Luis thought that whatever was going on out here with the Tulonas should be wrapping up, for the sun set by six-thirtyish or so. He looked at Bustamente who was still engaged with Dominguez and Armijo. Medicine Wind and Quail Looks Away walked over to Bustamente and stood beside him.

Lion had poured himself a cup of coffee and walked a few yards away from the group. He stopped and came back to Luis, "I see tracks down to the cottonwood bosque. Fresh tracks, not old, less than an hour old." Lion whispered the same information to Bustamente.

Bustamente motioned for everyone to come to the fire. Medicine

Wind turned his back on the fire and whispered something into Bustamente's ear. Bustamente nodded his head, attesting he understood. They gathered around the fire near the Hanging Shell reconstructed kiva.

A revered man, a cacique, had ridden Sweet Hija, his sweet daughter, the prima horse, bareback for four miles to ancient ruins on the edge of the Big River mesa. His friend, an elder, Looking Elk, he had helped bury, along with the Catholic ministrations of Father Padilla the day before. Now, cacique Bustamente Bear Standing Fire, stood to talk. And they were going to attend his words.

"Listen, hear me! This place, this kiva, was abandoned! Its principal cacique, Wood Quiver, died when the Tulona-Close-to-Mountains set upon him and his council. He was evil, a bad person, a witch, a destroyer of unity and brotherhood among these Tulona-Close-to-River. The Tulona-Close-to-Mountains helped the people here at Hanging Shell pack their goods and come to the pueblo of the Tulona-Close-to-Mountains. To us. The blood in me, in Medicine Wind, Quail Looks Away, and Lion Walks Night is that of the Tulona-Close-to-Mountains. The people from here, those that came from the Third Light, are within us now!"

Dominguez attended fully, Armijo looked around, stubbing his field boots into the moist soil.

"Dominguez! Armijo!" shouted Bustamente. Armijo stood rigid at the cacique's call, no longer fussing around. "You, both of you, are playing with the Great Power, the Great Spirit that moves in all things. For what? To begin a new kiva that is far away from your people! The Hanging Shell are within you now. You think you can handle the Great Power and be a hollow bone? To what end? To make yourselves respected, worshiped, honored? That way is selfish, un-puebloan, and leads to chaos. Come back to the Tulona by the Cottonwood River, close to the mountains, away from here. Be a part of our kivas. Dominguez! You can move back into the plaza, be a part of us, we want you, and you, too, Armijo." Bustamente paused. "Armijo, stay within the pueblo! Dominguez, come back!"

Cacique Bustamente had spoken, but he was not finished, for what he might say next, depended on Dominguez's and Armijo's response. The wind blew light from the west. However slight and unnoticed, the sun had begun its downward arc toward Mount Pedernal and the horizon. The snow had melted quickly on the southside of chamiso and sagebrush, but on the northside, little patches of sleet and snow remained, a calendric inflection that two days ago, snow had fallen. Bustamente waited for a response from Dominguez and Armijo.

Blue smoke curled from the fire. A hawk flew overhead, its wings flexed broadly and catching a gust, soaring upward, and circling back to the fire and human talk beside the Big River. The hawk cocked its head, seeking signs of dove, quail, or vole among the brush, surrounding the talk of humans beside the Big River. No dove appeared so the hawk sharply whistled and flew down the gorge of the Big River for food.

Bustamente waited for a response. Finally, Dominguez spoke first, "I want to come back, Grandfather. I am truly sorry."

Armijo followed, "I'm already there in the pueblo. I thought a reconstruction of Hanging Shell would be cool."

"Cool! Cool? What sort of explanation is that?" exclaimed Medicine Wind. Bustamente shushed him.

"I understand, Armijo," said Bustamente. "But this revitalization must end. Only two of you and no guidance from elders! Did either of you *dream* of a new kiva? None of your elders at the pueblo dreamed this kiva either. There was no dream from our ancestors to start a new kiva. Looking Elk is no longer with us. He gave his life to stop this aberration. It's over. Stay with us."

Both Dominguez and Armijo sighed relief, Armijo less so, holding back.

As the group relaxed, Bustamente said, "There is more to this than saying, 'I'm sorry.'" Hear me out."

Luis thought, "What now?"

"I need the medicine bundle and the scalps. You have them, and probably stole them from Franklin Deerfield. The pueblo needs them back."

"Medicine bundle? Scalps? What are you talking about?" Armijo shot back.

Medicine Wind stepped forward into Armijo's personal space. "There's a pole in the kiva and blue corn at the base of the pole. You've been feeding the scalps!"

"I don't know what you are talking about," Armijo countered.

Bustamente sighed. "Okay, here's the way this is going to go down. Lion, you follow the tracks to the cottonwoods. Find the medicine bundle and scalps. Bring them here. Dominguez, you and Armijo will follow us back in your truck to the Tract A gate. It's muddy, but you'll make it. If you get stuck, you can walk with us and the horses...get your truck later."

"But, but," Dominguez stammered.

Bustamente spoke forcefully. "Listen! The bundle and scalps came from Franklin Deerfield, a museum that leased Tulona land. The theft is a tribal problem as well as Franklin Deerfield. I will argue before the Tribal Council who has primary jurisdiction in this. The bundle is sacred to the Tulona and will be kept within the Tulona Pueblo. The Franklin Deerfield Museum will, in the end, consent to the Tulona keeping the bundle. We will dismiss any charges against you, Dominguez, and Armijo. It's tribal law, tribal decision, tribal justice. The Hanging Shell kiva will be dismantled. The new vigas and latices will be burned. The Forest Service will be notified that "persons unknown" made modifications to ancient ruins. That will be the end of this and the attempt to revitalize Hanging Shell. Are we clear on that?"

"Yes, Grandfather," said Dominguez, reluctantly.

Armijo nodded his head affirmatively. The gesture was slight, but clear, without words.

"I've got the bundle and scalps!" shouted Lion, running back from the cottonwoods.

"We now have the bundle and scalps. You had them in your possession. The council will decide on your punishment," Bustamente pronounced. "You'll be far better treated with tribal justice than with the police or F.B.I. I will present a case for Franklin Deerfield to dismiss charges against you as well as to our tribal police. The tribal council will prevail in these matters, I am sure."

From afar, a sound came: the hourly bells at Mission Saint Francis del Monte. Luis looked at his watch: three o'clock. "My, how time flies," he uttered, as he helped Bustamente mount Sweet Hija.

The ride back to the entry gate of Tract A went quickly. Dominguez's pickup became stuck only once, but with shifting gears forward and backward, the pickup shot forward out of the arroyo. In front, the column was led by Medicine Wind, followed by Bustamente, then Quail. Behind the pickup, Luis and Lion rode with the medicine bundle of Hanging Shells and the scalps. Luis carried the bundle; he did not want any association with chewed scalps.

Time passes in bells, processes, events.

Two bells at four. The truck became stuck, then unstuck.

Two bells at five. Dominguez and Armijo exit Tract A gate. Luis loads up the horses, and they return to the pueblo. He and Luis circle the Feast Day pole in the middle of the plaza before the horses are unloaded. A young Tulona warchief rides on the running board, attesting to the permissible entry of Luis and the horse trailer.

Between the bells of five and six, tribal policeman Richard Tafoya stands at the window of the stationhouse and looks at a horse trailer circling the Feast Day pole. "Hmmm. Where have they been? Nowhere important, I guess." He walks back to the breakroom and pours the last cup of strong-as-mud Mundo before he strides back to his office and opens three silos: the case of the Lance Bernal murder.

The sun arcs slowly downward to Mount Pedernal; the sky and sun will create an alpenglow, a striking reddish light, after sinking below the horizon. At 7,250 feet altitude, the temperature at Tulona Pueblo falls to forty-four degrees by six thirty; by morning, puddles will have a thin crust of ice, but not for long, for the children will playfully break the ice. This day, Tulona women perform two duties, one is to light candles at the graves of their ancestors, and the other rite is to throw food into Cottonwood River and fires for the departed ones. All Souls' Day is coming to an end. Men play a game of hidden ball in the old churchyard for most of the night.

Before alpenglow gleamed over Hanging Shell kiva, the hawk returns and alights on the spruce poles thrust out of the kiva entrance, a perch from which to see quail. The hawk becomes alert. She hears a wooden rattle and mysterious creaking in the direction of the Big River—a slow, jerky, but rhythmic dry sound.

Pushing off from the spruce ladder, the hawk apprehends a wooden cart coming up the path from the river. No ox pulls it; it propels itself. Within the cart is seated a skeleton with human hair, notching an arrow in her bowstring and letting it fly, notching another in the bowstring and letting it fly.

Then, eerily, Doña Sebastiana stands up in the cart, spreading her bony legs. As wind courses through her vacant rib cage, she twists her head in all directions, looking upward at the hawk, while continuing to string another arrow, and another, and another—never ceasing her shooting of arrows at souls condemned to life. Her wooden quiver is always full, like bread for the multitudes at Bethsaida, always full.

The she-hawk's hearing is keen, like her eyes; she hears the bell at Mission Saint Francis del Monte toll twice. Circling higher by the uplift of desert-mesa winds, she looks back at Hanging Shell kiva. Doña Sebastiana still stands, shooting arrows, shooting arrows, shooting arrows....

62

Monday, November 5, Day of Saint Peter of Chrysologus, Month of Corn Depositing Moon

Tribal policeman Tafoya took Saturday and Sunday off, following All Souls' Day. F.B.I. agent Diane Parker had called him Friday afternoon, informing him the F.B.I. computer investigative team had traced a lead in the theft case to a computer inside Franklin Deerfield Museum. More significant, they had a trace to a laptop of one of their employees.

In order to verify their suspicions, the F.B.I. team had decided to make a quick trip from Albuquerque to Ojo Verde on Monday, the fifth of November, to verify their conclusions. Until then, no new information would be forthcoming.

Disappointed about the delay, Tafoya said he understood it necessary to get a firm grasp of the suspected computers and their users before accusations were made and arrest warrants served. Agent Parker stated that two F.B.I. investigators would be in contact when they finished their inquiry. By early Friday evening of All Souls' Day, Tafoya also decided to set the Bernal murder case aside until Monday. Perhaps on Monday, a fresh look at the Bernal file might show new tangents he had overlooked. He told Romero and the stationhouse he would remain on call, although he was serious about taking Saturday and Sunday off.

"Keep your phone on, Tafoya," Romero advised. "We may not have enough personnel to cover the weekend."

After hanging up, Romero groused further to one of the officers at the stationhouse that the Bernal case was not gaining enough traction. "We need more people on the case. Tafoya needs assistance. With only fourteen of us here at Tulona police station, we're understaffed!"

Tafoya had dinner with Janet Rael on Saturday at Tablita's. On Sunday, the two of them drove up to the ski valley and had lunch at a Bavarian restaurant midway up the slopes. After wiener schnitzel and beer, they spent the afternoon with Tafoya's family at the pueblo. When they went their separate ways after visiting his family, Tafoya told Janet he would need her liaison services sometime next week, in order to follow up on the Looking Elk-Hanging Shell situation.

"I need to find out what is going on at Hanging Shell. What made Looking Elk take off in a snowstorm to investigate? The roads will be dried out so we won't get stuck."

Rael nodded at Tafoya. "Okay, we'll go. I'll sign out the big Chevy Suburban with high clearance and four-wheel drive, if we need to."

Monday morning, eager to get back on the cases, Tafoya ate a large breakfast at Pueblo Café: over-easy eggs with red chile sauce, hash browns, tortillas, breakfast salsa, and two large glasses of orange juice. He was parked outside the café in the police vehicle when they opened at six thirty. Determined to get an early start on the day, he finished breakfast by a quarter after seven and drove to the tribal police station. Coffee Mundo was brewed before Delores Rafael, the admin with a Glock, arrived with a box of donuts and pastries.

Delores did not disappoint. "I went to a new pastry shop over on the southside of Ojo Verde, Richard. I bought donuts, but also eclairs, small custard pies, and fried pies," Delores said proudly. "Here's a menu they gave me. I'll put it in the breakroom. Maybe there's something you'd like for me to get next time."

Tafoya glanced at the menu, took two donuts, and walked back to his office. "Thanks, Delores," he shouted. He had looked at a chocolate éclair, but did not put one on his paper plate. He thought of his physical exam for tribal police proficiency coming up soon, and he wanted to be close to optimum weight, not éclair-heavy weight.

After checking out the Bernal case evidence box, Tafoya once again extracted the rotary blade for a drone from the evidence sack. Janet had defined the white plastic blade as a drone piece. The Taos County sheriff's department had collected the blade at the forest edge at Quintana Canyon. Lance Bernal's body was discovered fifty yards from the blade. Was there a connection? If there was, how could it be proved? Tafoya had his legal yellow pad sheets out and his field notes—his second silo of data. After sketching a positional map of Bernal and the blade, he looked closely at the two factors: Bernal, the blade? Reflecting a minute, he came up with an idea to gather more information.

Tafoya called the Federal Aviation Administration—the F.A.A.—in Albuquerque. After being bumped and ricocheted through departments, Tafoya finally talked to the F.A.A. department that registered drones people purchased in the United States. He asked the clerk if anyone in the Ojo Verde, Taos, Questa, Española areas had purchased and registered a drone. The clerk at the F.A.A. drone department could be heard clicking her keyboard to get into the files. "She must have nice nails, strong nails," Tafoya thought, as he listened to nails against the keyboard. After fifteen seconds, the clerk came back on the phone.

"There are not many registered drones north of Santa Fe. We have only three privately-registered drones in your vicinity: Ernest Adkins at Red River, Jesse Martin in Taos, and Larry Armijo at Ojo Verde."

Bingo! Tafoya thought. Then he asked, "What do you mean, 'privately registered'?"

"I mean registered to private individuals, outside of the government. The Forest Service under Carson National Forest has ten registered drones."

After hanging up, Tafoya surmised the broken rotary blade he held in his hand was probably from a Forest Service drone. He could check with his Forest Service liaison contact, Janet, if one of their drones had crashed. Nonetheless, Tafoya, on his yellow legal pad, wrote the name of Larry Armijo at the site of the rotary blade just fifty yards from Bernal's body. He inserted a question mark "?" after the name of Armijo on his pad.

"Nothing proved, yet," he thought. Tafoya plodded on.

Tafoya opened the interview files on Armijo. Where had he claimed to be on Sunday, October 21, the date of Bernal's murder? Scanning through the computer file to the Romero interview with Armijo, a lot of questions had been asked of Armijo.

A crucial question, however, had not been asked. Reading carefully the report, Tafoya saw Romero had failed to ask Armijo where *he* was on

Sunday, October 21, the day of Bernal's murder. The failure to ask Armijo the question was a slipup. Reading Romero's interview notes closely, Romero had concentrated on asking Armijo about why Bernal might have been at Quintana Canyon on October 21—the motivation angle.

Understandable Romero's focus, Tafoya reasoned, but an incomplete interview. Tafoya would not mention the slipup to Romero. It was now Tafoya's task to question where Armijo was that day. He would contact Armijo, complete the interview, and close the question of his whereabouts on that Sunday.

Tafoya wanted answers to three questions—now. Where was Armijo that Sunday of Bernal's murder? Who's drone blade did the tribal police have? Why was Bernal at Quintana Canyon on Sunday? Tafoya rose from his desk and walked to the front of the stationhouse to take a break. Before he engaged Delores, his cell phone rang. "Janet, I hope." He looked down at the caller: F.B.I. Agent Dominique Suarez, Albuquerque Field Office.

Tafoya walked back to his office to take notes from Suarez's call. Suarez had an alto voice and a commanding manner of speech. Tafoya caught a pinch of New York accent, but not the New York brusqueness he had come across while serving in Afghanistan with fellow soldiers.

After exchanging *bona fides*, Suarez informed Tafoya she and her partner, Angie Clovis, had driven up to Ojo Verde the night before to get an early start at the museum Monday morning. They had succeeded in verifying a sophisticated hack into the museum computer server that included security and video files. Finding and verifying the Internet Protocol address or IP identifying the computer and hacker had proved challenging.

"Our finding this morning indicates the laptop originally used in looking into the museum's server about medicine bundles came from an employee of the museum. The employee's searching appears to be work-related and not suspicious," Suarez reported.

"Who is the employee?" Tafoya interrupted.

"Martha Johnson, the intern from Arizona State University."

"Wait a second, Suarez." Tafoya jotted down the name on a new legal pad, and added beside Martha Johnson's name, "Martha Johnson →

girlfriend of Armijo." He looked at the yellow legal pad he had been taking notes on earlier that morning on which he had scribbled, "drone blade at Quintana Canyon → Bernal's body at Quintana Canyon → Armijo owns drone."

"Go on, Agent Suarez, sorry to interrupt you."

Suarez stated that Johnson's laptop was being hacked into by a *second* laptop whose IP Address was finally identified, after a circuitous routing around the planet, as 194.255.1.77. She informed Tafoya that the F.B.I. team had created a fake server for Franklin Deerfield Museum, so that the hacker, 194.255.1.77, could continue to think he still had access to the museum's confidential files and security. "We call it a masked intercept."

"Do you know the identity of the person who commands the second laptop, and is hacking into the museum?" Tafoya asked.

"We do, Officer Tafoya. We also have the cell phone he has programed to hack into museum security. His name is Larry Armijo, a Tulona puebloan. We will send you by email all the information so that the Tulona tribal police or the Taos County sheriff's department can get a warrant to seize his electronics, when you decide to do so," agent Suarez said.

Suarez added that the F.B.I. computer fraud team would continue to collect information and send it on to the tribal police. "Armijo has not hacked into the museum since before Halloween. He's gone dark. You also need to know that he used his laptop and cell phone to blank out those two segments on video tape, the segment the day before, and the segment at three that morning. We were able to reconstitute five seconds of that three o'clock morning tape, and two men are seen entering the front door. The security guard was at the other end of the building."

Tafoya thanked Suarez for what they had found. She asked for a good place to eat lunch, and he referred them to Tablita's at the Ojo Verde Inn. Before she hung up, Tafoya asked if she was "from back East?" Suarez replied that she was from Queens in New York City. She added that New Mexico was where she wanted to be posted.

"I requested the bureau to send me here to the Southwest, and they did. I want to be in a place where I can see forever across mesas to mountains in the far distance. No more skyscrapers for me—ever. I want to stand on the ground, the earth. And for 360 degrees, all I want to see is the long view, the mesas and mountains, twenty miles, forty miles of landscape. When I resettle, I'm coming here to Ojo Verde."

"To gentrify us, Agent Suarez, from Queens?" Tafoya asked, in a teasing manner.

"No, no gentrification. I want a sustainable home, adobe, natural stone, and I want to be accepted into the community here in Ojo Verde, maybe garden. You know, get into chamiso-earth. Get my hands dirty," Suarez replied, seriously.

Tafoya thought, chamiso-earth...very New Mexico. Desert dry for sure.... Maybe she will come back.

"I hope you do," Tafoya said, "I'll keep you briefed on what we are going to do with Armijo and Johnson. Doesn't look good for Armijo." Tafoya pushed the red button on his cell phone, signing off.

Now what? Tafoya thought. He looked at his notes about the morning of the theft.

The security officer at Franklin Deerfield saw *three* persons jogging away down the road from the museum before he saw the inventory basement door ajar. The video tape showed *two* people exiting from the basement. Not three exiting. Lance Bernal, the murdered Tulona, was close friends with Armijo and Dominguez. Could Bernal have been the third person jogging away from the museum? Or the second person emerging from the basement? The two from the basement were wearing masks, so they could not be identified.

Larry Armijo was most likely one of the three thieves, Tafoya speculated, since he had hacked around into the museum's computer system, but proof was necessary. The other two: were they Bernal and Dominguez? Armijo and the other two thieves stole the Hanging Shell medicine bundle, two scalps, and the Child of Water mask and wooden lightning bolts. The bundle and scalps were still missing.

Now was the time, Tafoya reasoned, that sergeant Romero and deputy sheriff Cordova needed to be consulted about the next step on the Franklin Deerfield Museum heist. A search warrant was needed to seize the Armijo's laptop and cell phone. Then have the laptop and cell phone analyzed by the computer techies with the tribal police or Taos County sheriff's department. If necessary, get agent Suarez back on the case. Tafoya wrote up a report about his conversation with Suarez and posted it to the museum case on the tribal computer so Romero could look at it.

Where was Sergeant Romero? Tafoya had not heard from him. He stood up from his office chair and walked down the hall. Romero was in the front office chatting with Delores Rafael. Seeing Romero with Rafael, Tafoya went back to the breakroom, poured himself another cup of coffee, and walked back up to the front.

"Morning, Sergeant." Romero acknowledged, and Tafoya sat down beside him. After a few minutes of conversation, Tafoya brought up the museum case.

"The F.B.I. reported on the computer and security issues at the museum."

"Oh?" Romero perked up.

"Yes, I think we need to call in Deputy Sheriff Cordova and have a meeting on what to do next. I think…,"Tafoya stopped talking. He pointed out the front window.

Coming to the stationhouse were four Tulona, and Bustamente led them with purpose in their stride.

63

Opening the door to the station was Bustamente, followed by Medicine Wind, Quail Looks Away, and Lion Walks Night. Tafoya and Romero knew Bustamente was the cacique of the Tulona Pueblo, and Medicine Wind, Quail, and Lion sat on the Tulona Council. Everyone stood up in the front office when they came in. Their arrival seemed to be a *de facto* council gathering.

"I thought the council meeting was later this week," Romero joked.

Rafael asked if they wanted a cup of coffee in the conference room. "I have donuts and a pastry box, as well."

"Sure, I know I want coffee," Bustamente replied. "We came here to talk with Tafoya and Romero. Coffee and donuts will be good."

They walked back to the conference room. Rafael and Tafoya carried in the pastries and coffee. Rafael would stay and attend the meeting, while another tribal officer would hold down the front desk and take incoming calls. The seven of them sat around the table. No one sat at the presiding officer's chair. It was left unoccupied intentionally, for no one would preside. As elder, Cacique Bustamente Standing Bear spoke first. He stood up.

From the folds of his blanket, he brought out a sage smudge and safety matches. Tafoya furtively looked up at the smoke detector. It was neither green nor red lit. Batteries had not been replaced. Bustamente Standing Bear lit the sage and smudged the room. The blue-gray smoke of the sage lingered in the air. He laid the smudge down on a ceramic plate at the wet bar on the far side of the room; it continued to smoke. Then, Bustamente prayed.

"*Creator, grant us clear vison to talk. Make our talk straight and make it true. Bendiciones.*"

That was it, short and sweet. They all understood with his prayer and sage smudging, what followed must be serious. Neither Tafoya, Romero, nor Rafael were on the Tulona Council, but what they saw happening was going to be as important as a council meeting. No one sipped coffee, nor ate a donut.

Bustamente spoke. "The Tulona Pueblo has the Hanging Shell medicine bundle. The Tulona Pueblo have the two scalps."

Tafoya looked at Romero. Romero looked at Tafoya. They subtly shook their heads, back and forth, wondering how the retrievals of bundle and scalp had occurred. True to pueblo custom, they neither interrupted Bustamente nor expressed emotion. Tafoya and Romero would hear Bustamente fully express himself. He was, after all, the cacique.

"The Creator has been benevolent to the Tulona and the greater world, for there have been no scalps taken, as was expressed in the message, 'The god roams the foothills for the scalps of his enemies,'" Bustamente said, looking around the table.

Bustamente continued. "The medicine bundle of Hanging Shell has been found. After meeting yesterday, the Tulona Council has, with one mind, decided to keep the bundle within our pueblo, and not let it out of our possession again. Furthermore, those that had possession of the bundle will remain unidentified. The council will punish them accordingly...and in secret. The scalps we will give back to the museum with the promise they will authorize, at their expense, genetic testing of the scalps, and return them to the tribe or tribes, if so identified. We do not want the scalps. Franklin Deerfield, the founder of the museum, would want the scalps returned to their people for them to inter, burn, or do as they please. Those scalps have no business in either the museum or with the Tulona."

Tafoya was thinking fast. He had not informed Romero about the F.B.I. finding Armijo as the hacker into the museum and, probably, was one of the thieves. Should he tell Bustamente now that he knew who at least one of the thieves were? No, he concluded, too many people around the table to expose Armijo and keep the identify secret as to the council's decision. It's tribal police business, and the F.B.I. may have an interest in arresting Armijo. He decided to stay clear of exposing Armijo as the museum hacker—for now. He did, however, have a question.

"Bustamente, do you think that Franklin Deerfield Museum will object to the Tulona keeping the medicine bundle? Did you talk with them about that?" Tafoya asked.

"We have. The council has extracted a promise from the museum. They will not object to us keeping the bundle under our protection. Franklin Deerfield Museum will draw up the paperwork for giving it legally to us. Our lawyer in Santa Fe who handles our legal issues has been contacted, and she will take care of that."

Tafoya already thought of an issue concerning the theft that might be difficult to handle. Armijo had used the internet with all its connections to intrastate and interstate lines to commit a crime. More than likely, if the F.B.I. wanted to pursue charges, they could. But, would they? Again, Tafoya concluded that he would not bring up those conflicts until he and Romero and Agent Parker conferred. Tafoya remained silent. Besides, there's the Bernal murder and he was beginning to think Armijo might be involved.

Cacique Bustamente Standing Bear concluded his remarks and the meeting adjourned. The sage smudge continued to burn slowly. Delores was not going to extinguish the smudge, for the Tulona police stationhouse needed scent to chase evil spirits away.

"It'll take a lot of sage to do that. So, I'm going to let it smoke," she said to herself, as the conference broke up.

64

Officer Tafoya and Sergeant Romero stood watching Bustamente Standing Bear and his entourage walk away from the stationhouse and disperse to their homes on the Winter House and Summer House side of the pueblo. Rio Tulona flowed between the two Houses while residents gathered fresh water for their chores. Delores Rafael settled behind the front desk and began to work at the computer and handle radio traffic with Taos County and the city of Ojo Verde.

From the front window of the stationhouse, Tafoya and Romero looked upon a clear and cool day. Tulona Peak and the Cristo Mountains were sharply outlined by a brilliant blue sky with few contrails flying over the region. Tafoya looked up at the contrails. Jets were compelled to fly 12,300 feet mean sea level over the pueblo and at least 3,000 feet above ground level over Earth Cloud Lake in the mountains. Such buffers were flight rules, so that pueblo heritages would be respected. Tafoya wondered if pilots were ticketed if they broke the rules.

"How I would I know if the planes were below three thousand feet over the pueblo? Probably if they shook the leaves off the cottonwoods. In any case, I'll call the F.A.A. Let them deal with it," Tafoya concluded.

Tafoya and Romero walked back in to the conference room. The smudging continued, its scent wafting throughout the building. Tafoya closed the door and they sat down at the conference table to figure out what they should do about the medicine bundle return. Tafoya explained to Romero what F.B.I. agent Suarez had discovered. Armijo's laptop had compromised the Franklin Deerfield Museum's security, and that Armijo's manipulation had started with his hacking into Martha Johnson's laptop.

"She is an unwitting person in this affair," Tafoya surmised. "Armijo had been snooping around into the museum's accession records for several months, and on the night of the theft, the F.B.I. ascertained two men blocked the security cameras at the front door and entered about three. The F.B.I. had been able to reclaim several seconds of video,"Tafoya said.

Continuing to brief Romero, Tafoya said, "The men were wearing ski masks and could not be identified. The F.B.I. was highly confident that Armijo hacked the computers at Franklin Deerfield. His IP address was all over the intrusions into the museum. The F.B.I. has set a masked intercept of his computer, but he has not gone back into the computer files since the theft."

"Bustamente has gotten the council and the museum to drop the charges, and the council will punish those responsible with community service of some sort," Romero said. "Who are the other two that were in on the theft? Any idea, Tafoya?"

"Armijo had two close Tulona friends, Lance Bernal and Alfredo Dominguez. I suspect they may have been involved, but we can only get a confession from two of the three, Armijo or Dominguez, since Bernal is dead,"Tafoya answered. Romero said nothing. They both fidgeted in their chairs.

Romero spoke next, "We are in a bind here, Tafoya. Bustamente has thrown a cloak over who had the medicine bundle and scalps. He didn't tell us how he recovered them, either. He was very definite that their identities would be kept secret."

"Kept secret by Bustamente and the council, yes, but the word will get out. You know that as well as I do, Romero,"Tafoya interrupted. "We were not asked to *not* investigate any further. Bustamente did not call us off of the investigation. In fact, that's not his call, not his jurisdiction in a technical sense. I think we should get a warrant to seize Armijo's computer and tangential electronics."

"Based upon what crime, Tafoya?"

"Armijo's computer and his cell phone were used in a fraud. He pretended to be an employee of the museum, for purposes of theft. The computer and cell phone involved interstate commerce—the internet, interstate transmission lines, microwave towers—so we can get a warrant based on probable cause."

"I see. And, we investigate the crime and put pressure on Armijo. Maybe he'll give up more information as to the theft, and who else was involved," Romero concluded. "But, listen Tafoya. Bustamente, the council, and Franklin Deerfield are not going to press charges in state or federal court. They are leaving punishment up to the Tulona Council. The F.B.I. may want to press charges against Armijo for using the internet for fraud and impersonation. Send a lesson to other potential hackers. But we don't know if the F.B.I. will press charges, do we?" Romero asked.

"No, not really," Tafoya replied.

"So, what are we doing pursuing this further?" Romero asked. "Merely to get more information on Armijo when it's the F.B.I. that has the issue of fraud using the internet? Sounds like a waste of our time."

Tafoya brought the two cases together. The murder of Bernal, the theft of the medicine bundle.

"We use the investigation of the medicine bundle theft," Tafoya replied, "to find out more connections of Armijo to Bernal. Armijo and Bernal were friends. Armijo was the last person we know of the circle of Bernal's friends that talked with Bernal. They hunted together. They may have planned to hunt together this season. That entails deer rifles. Bernal was killed with 7mm bullets. We need to start focusing on Armijo and check out his alibi which, by the way, we have failed to do," Tafoya explained. "Let's push and pressure Armijo."

Romero nodded his head in agreement.

"And there's one more thing, Sergeant."

Tafoya explained to Romero he had contacted the F.A.A., revealing Armijo possessed a drone, and a fragment of a drone blade has been found near the murder scene a grove of aspens. "We don't know if it's a fragment from Armijo's, but there is a possible association."

"How in the world did we identify a drone blade fragment up in the aspen grove?"

"Janet went over the items in the evidence box and identified the blade."

Romero paused. "We need her fulltime, Richard."

They agreed to talk to their supervisor and get his permission to obtain a warrant to seize the computer and cell phone. After lunch they procured a search warrant for Armijo's home concerning the Franklin Deerfield theft. A New Mexico state judge readily signed the warrant, warning them not to go on a "fishing expedition" in Armijo's house. The warrant extended to Armijo's room at his parent's house on the pueblo plaza.

65

At three thirty that afternoon, Tafoya, Romero, and Deputy Sheriff Cordova of Taos County pulled up in two police cars in front of Armijo's house on the edge of the reservation. Tafoya carried the search warrant for Armijo's house. Beside the house, a dead cottonwood had fallen. The wind and snow of Halloween had blown it over—the snow and rain softening the soil.

Romero remarked the trunk should be cut into drum barrels. "Armijo should do a little physical labor, something Tulona, rather than keyboard his way through life."

Armijo's pickup was gone. Cordova walked around to the back of the house—a matter of routine in case he was home and bolted out the backdoor.

Romero knocked forcefully on the front door, "Tribal police, Armijo, open up! We have a search warrant." No answer. He knocked again and repeated himself. Still no answer.

Cordova came on the radio, "Backdoor is unlocked."

"Standby, Chris, I'll come back there. We'll go in together," Tafoya replied. To Romero he said, "We'll come to the front door, after we clear the rooms."

Tafoya noticed as he was walking to the rear of the house the curtains were drawn. No smoke curled out of the chimney. Tafoya knocked on the backdoor. When there was no response, Chris turned the doorknob, and they entered Armijo's cold house. They cleared the two bedrooms, the lone bathroom, and went to the living room, unlocked the front door, and opened it for Romero. There was no sign of Armijo. A propane heater in the living room was turned on low, so warmth emanated in the front part of the house.

Romero pocketed the search warrant. "Let's search for computers and the cell phone. There's a desktop computer on one of the front tables. We'll take that with us."

They searched for over an hour and failed to come up with the laptop or cell phone. Closets and cabinet drawers were opened; the pantry scanned; mattresses were lifted and examined underneath. In the corner of the dining room, Tafoya found an item that was not on the warrant: a white drone. He looked closely at the rotary blades, discovering one blade had been broken off. Tafoya bent down closely and with his cell phone took several photos of the drone blades, the broken rotary, and the serial and model numbers.

After the three of them were satisfied they had looked thoroughly for the laptop, Romero said, "Leave Armijo a note we've been here and a receipt for the desktop computer. I'm taking the warrant over to his house at the pueblo. I don't expect we will find anything there, but we will look."

At Armijo's family's house on the pueblo plaza, they served the warrant for his room. Armijo was not there. His mother said she had not seen him for several days. She wanted to know what they were looking for and was Armijo in trouble?

Romero assured her, "It's nothing serious, we just need to talk to him about a few things. Have him call us when you hear from him." His words did not pacify her. He apologized for the intrusion, "Don't worry."

Romero hated to give assurances to her when he knew Armijo was in deep trouble—Big River trouble. While Romero finished consoling the mother, Tafoya and Cordova walked out of the house, feeling empathy for Armijo's mother, for they knew her son committed a crime.

The three of them walked to the tribal stationhouse where they had parked their vehicles. Inside, except for Delores Rafael, no one else was around.

"What was with the picture taking of the drone, Tafoya?" Cordova asked, as they set down in the front lobby area. Delores entered data on her computer.

Tafoya explained he had found out from the F.A.A. that Armijo was listed as the owner of a drone, one of a few private owners in northern New Mexico. A portion of a white rotary blade had been found at Bernal's murder scene. Armijo's drone back at his house had a broken rotary blade, and he wanted photographic evidence to compare the F.A.A.'s registration record for Armijo's drone.

"The broken blade in our evidence box may be a fit with Armijo's little drone plaything. We will need another warrant to seize the drone.... We've got two cases slamming together here, the Bernal murder and the museum theft. The common denominator is Armijo, said Tafoya."

"We can't get a warrant to seize the drone because we 'might' have a matching propeller blade, Tafoya," Cordova advanced. "A probable cause warrant for the laptop is one thing, the drone is another case without much substance. I grant you there is a tidbit of substance there, but not enough to seize it."

All three of them stood in the front office without an idea on what to do next.

Delores had been listening to the conversation. "Did you look in the couch?"

"What are you talking about?" Tafoya asked, puzzled.

"Did you look in the couch, behind the cushions or, if it is a hideaway bed, in the bed itself? For the laptop?" she answered. "You know, a thorough search for the laptop?"

"We looked thoroughly enough, maybe not in the couch," Romero answered, puzzled like Tafoya.

"Well?" Delores retorted.

"Well, what?" Tafoya asked.

Delores sighed. "Sometimes you all can be so dense. Here's the situation. You did not look in the couch for the laptop. You need to fully complete the warrant. Second, you have a broken propeller blade in the evidence box back in the locker room. Third, there is a drone with a broken rotary at Armijo's." Delores spread her arms like, "Well?" And, "Duh?"

Tafoya, Romero, and Cordova looked quickly at one another. They all moved fast, "I'll get the broken blade in the plastic evidence bag," yelled Tafoya. "Meet you two out front. Let's take the tribal police car and all pile in. We need to check out the couch!"

Opening the backdoor, for a second time that afternoon, they entered Armijo's house on the edge of the reservation. While Romero and Cordova pulled the hideaway bed all the way out of the couch, Tafoya slipped on latex gloves and lifted the broken propeller blade from the evidence pouch. Placing it carefully against the drone's broken rotary, he fitted the piece against the drone. It was a match. He took photographs with his cell phone and asked Romero and Cordova to verify the fit.

"Looks like a perfect fit, Tafoya," deputy sheriff Cordova asserted. "We will get a search warrant, if necessary, and seize it."

They did not find the laptop in the couch's hideaway bed; in fact, the mattress was stripped of sheets. Folding the couch back to normal, the three of them exited the backdoor for a second time.

Before Tafoya went to sleep that night, he called Janet and asked her to liaison with the tribal police department the next morning. She replied that her schedule could be shifted around, and she would be at the tribal stationhouse at eight.

"I need you earlier than eight." Tafoya said that he wanted to pick her up at her apartment at six o'clock in the morning, so they could go by Martha Johnson's apartment to see if Larry Armijo's dark-green Chevy pickup was parked in front. Tafoya told Janet that Martha Johnson was an intern out at Franklin Deerfield and the girlfriend of Armijo. Janet said she would be ready by six o'clock, and, if necessary, later in the day she could check out the Chevy Suburban from the Forest Service, if they needed to go to Hanging Shell.

66

Tuesday, November 6, Day of Saint Nicolas of Tavelic and Companions, Month of Corn Depositing Moon

Tafoya pulled in front of Janet Rael's apartment on Calle Zacate Verde in Ojo Verde. He had never been there before, so he used the G.P.S. It was five minutes before six. Tafoya sprinted up the steps to the second story and knocked three times on the door. Janet answered, "Come in, Richard, I'm packing my field bag. Do you want a cup of coffee while I finish?" He said yes, and she poured him a cup from a new Cuisinart coffee maker that ground whole beans.

Tafoya walked back into the living room, stood near the fireplace, and looked around. A light-colored leather sofa with matching chairs dominated the space. The color of the leather was dark yellow, a few shades darker than gold. It reminded him of new saddle leather and the smell was much the same. Janet had a bookcase full of hardbound and paperback books; the titles were biology-oriented, cookbooks, mystery fiction, and aviation. Some photographs of Janet and her family filled empty spaces in the bookcase. On the wall were posters of the Santa Fe wine festival and the balloon festival in Albuquerque. In a prominent position on the mantle of the fireplace were sprigs of red aspen, the remnants from Tulona feast day a few weeks ago. Tafoya's mother had given the aspen sprigs to Janet, and Janet had made good her promise, "To put them in a special place in my apartment."

Tafoya caught a glance of Janet's bedroom; she had already made up her bed with a large Navajo blanket covering the mattress. The Navajo design was Teec Nos Pos from the Four Corners area, northwest of Shiprock. Janet came out of her bedroom with her field bag.

"Let's go, Richard, I'm ready."

Martha Johnson, the Franklin Deerfield intern and girlfriend of Larry Armijo, lived in a section of Ojo Verde next to the post office and water tower on Calle Cielo. By a quarter after six, as Tafoya and Janet were driving to Calle Cielo, the village of Ojo Verde stirred. Breakfast cafes were open, a number of cars were parked in front of the exercise gym, and men with construction pickups and trailers filled up their pickups with gasoline or diesel at service stations.

As Tafoya turned onto Calle Cielo, Janet said, "What make and model of pickup does her boyfriend have?"

"It's a dark green, old Chevy pickup, the year is 2005, I think. It has the old style red-and-yellow New Mexico tags, CGF 894, registered to Larry Armijo, Tulona Pueblo." He had glanced at his open field notebook for the license plate number.

Something jiggled in Janet's mind. She thought for a moment as they drove down the street to the Johnson's apartment. "Richard, I think I have seen that pickup. I traced the license plate number a few days ago. I remember the name, 'Larry Armijo,' and the dark-green Chevy pickup. I couldn't recall the tag number."

Tafoya turned his head and looked at Janet. "How did it happen you ran a trace on the license plate? I thought you just worked with trees and bears, Janet," he teased.

Janet told him the story of how she was conducting a field survey on the forest road from Pot Creek to Benardin Lake via Rita La Olla when she saw the pickup and Armijo camped at Benardin Lake. "He was way far up in the woods, Richard."

Tafoya asked, "Where's Benardin Lake?" She told him it was on the forest road from Pot Creek to Quintana Canyon.

Tafoya repeated, "Quintana Canyon?"

"Yes, Quintana Canyon. I had decided to travel the full length of the forest road. Fallen trees on the forest road stopped me from going all the way to Quintana Canyon. I turned around and came back via Rita de Olla."

Tafoya almost missed his turn after hearing Janet's information about Armijo. He snapped out of his daze in time to turn.

"Janet, there's a lot of coincidences going with Armijo." He told her about the broken blade that matched the drone at Armijo's house, the hacking Armijo had done at Franklin Deerfield, and, "Now I learn from you that he was up near Quintana Canyon...we need to find Armijo and ask him a few questions.... No, a lot of questions."

As they drove onto the Calle Cielo Apartment lot, they looked for Armijo's dark-green Chevy. They drove twice through the parking lot, but Armijo's pickup was not there. Tafoya parked—backed into a space—a few doors down from Martha Johnson's apartment. It was still before sunup, but he saw lights on behind the curtain and movement back and forth in her apartment. He sat here, quietly, pondering his next move: knock on the door and ask Johnson some questions, or go to breakfast with Janet and on to the stationhouse. Janet looked at her cell phone and checked her messages. They sat in the police vehicle with lights off. After about fifteen minutes, Tafoya made up his mind.

He called John McGinnis.

John McGinnis, head curator at Franklin Deerfield Museum, called Martha Johnson before she departed her apartment for work. He asked her to meet Tafoya and Rael for breakfast at Tablita's Restaurant at the Ojo Verde Inn. She was instructed to bring her personal laptop computer with her. McGinnis told Johnson that Tafoya and his liaison officer—a woman—wanted to ask her some questions in a friendly manner.

"You're not in trouble. They just wanted a neutral place to ask you about the theft, away from the museum and tribal police headquarters. Besides, it's a free breakfast," said McGinnis. Johnson drove to Tablita's immediately, storing her laptop in the trunk of her Mitsubishi sedan.

Entering Tablita's, Jason Taylor, up early for the breakfast shift, seated Johnson with Rael and Tafoya in a corner off by themselves, away from the front windows overlooking Paseo del Norte. They sat at a table looking out on a patio garden. Despite the early hours, the Ojo Verde Inn gardener watered stands of hollyhock, no longer blooming. Johnson ordered huevos rancheros, Tafoya wanted a breakfast burrito with red chile; Rael settled on blueberry pancakes. Jason brought a large carafe of orange juice and a pot of coffee to the table.

Janet Rael had dressed in her khaki Forest Service uniform and pinned the Tulona tribal liaison officer identification badge on her shirt. Tafoya looked satisfied that Janet took the tension and anxiety away from questioning Johnson.

Rael asked most of the questions, focusing on the dating relationship Johnson had with Armijo. Tafoya had cautioned Janet to remain discreet about Armijo rifling through the museum's files, having first done so via Johnson's laptop. They would tell Johnson about Armijo's hacking when breakfast was nearly finished.

The Arizona State graduate cooperated in talking about the theft. Johnson had not remembered anything more since her first interview with Tafoya at the museum. "I know none of us in the curating department, or any other section, would have stolen our resources."

Johnson admitted that her relationship with Armijo had been strained at times. "He was four years younger than me, and he acted immature… and had a quick temper. He never hurt me, and I tried to get him to lighten up, but didn't succeed." She paused, reflected, "He was very thoughtful, and a whiz at computers. He installed a bigger RAM in my laptop and fixed problems when they came up."

Janet looked at Tafoya when Johnson brought up the laptop. Tafoya scooted up his chair to the edge of the table—a serious move, not caught by Johnson.

"I need to ask you some more questions about your relationship with Armijo," Tafoya asked.

"Okaaaay…," Johnson drawled.

"When was the last time you saw him?"

"A few days before Halloween, he was supposed to take me to the Halloween party at the museum, but stood me up. You may remember me at the museum party? Tafoya skipped over her question.

"When is the last time you talked to him?"

"I have not heard from him since before Halloween. I've called and left messages, but he hasn't returned my calls."

"That's been over a week, Martha. Is it unusual for you to go that long without talking to him?"

"Yes, it is unusual. Since we started dating, we've not had such a long gap in communicating."

"Would you and Armijo have spent a weekend together around October twentieth? That was two weekends ago."

Johnson reached in her purse to get her cell phone and pull up the calendar for the October 20 weekend. "I had a date with him on Friday that weekend, but did not see him on Saturday nor Sunday."

"Does Armijo have a drone?" Tafoya asked.

"Oh, yes! We had such fun with it up in the ski valley and down by the Big River and the bridge. He was very proud of that white drone. He called it, 'White Raptor.'"

"Did you two ever take the White Raptor up to Quintana Canyon, toward Angel Fire?" Tafoya asked.

"No. Just the Big River area and the ski valley," Johnson answered.

Jason came by the table, cleared the dishes, and refilled their water glasses. Tafoya wrestled with whether to tell Johnson at the breakfast table about Armijo's hacking into the museum, or go into the lobby where it was less crowded. He decided to pay the check and then tell her. Tafoya did not like what he had to do, for the results of his telling Johnson would bring self-recrimination. Martha would likely respond, "How could I have been so stupid?" Or, "How could he do this to me? And the museum?" There would be drama most likely.

In the lobby, when told of Armijo's involvement, Johnson controlled herself. Her main reaction was anger at Armijo for using her to steal artifacts. Johnson told Tafoya that the tribal police could have her laptop, "I don't want to ever touch the keys of that laptop again. Use it to get what you need. I don't want it back. The photos and files I need and use are stored in the cloud."

Tafoya told her that Armijo had not set her up from the beginning of their relationship. He began hacking on her computer after they started their relationship.

Tafoya sought to soften the revelations. "Now Martha, listen to me. You presented an opportunity with your laptop. Others manipulated him. He didn't start out using you." Janet put her hand on Johnson's shoulder.

Tafoya and Janet walked Johnson out to her Mitsubishi and took possession of her laptop. Tafoya told her that Armijo had installed malware in her laptop, but had performed the break-in and searching with his own equipment. "Your computer was an initial portal that he compromised. If he contacts you, make up an excuse not to see him, and call us right away. The tribal police and Taos County sheriff's department want to apprehend him. We will be putting out a bulletin to pick him up for questioning. If he comes to your apartment, call us. Don't let him in. If you have any idea where he might be staying, tell us."

"I don't know where he is, and I don't care," Martha said, bitterly.

Tafoya gave Johnson his card with all his telephone numbers. Janet placed her Forest Service business card in Johnson's hand as well. In parting, Janet hugged her.

"Not a good day for Martha," Janet said to Tafoya when Martha was driving away.

67

The sky remained cloudy through the day. Patches of blue did appear quickly, then disappeared with cumulus clouds scudding the sky. The temperature never exceeded the lower fifties; the wind picked up by midmorning, accelerating to gusts of twenty-five in the afternoon from the west, from the direction of the Navajo reservation. The top of Tulona Peak appeared occasionally; the upper slopes and conifers at timberline radiated whiteness, the paleness of ice and snow. The authority of winter rattled the door to enter northern New Mexico from Colorado. Rio Tulona, flowing through the Pueblo, seemed colder than usual, bone-chilling icy to those drawing water for their homes.

At the tribal police station, Tafoya, Janet, and Romero cloistered in the conference room to come up with a plan to find Armijo. Tafoya relayed the information he and Janet had obtained from Johnson about Armijo. All three agreed that finding Armijo had now gone beyond the museum case. Armijo's drone, the so-called White Raptor, had been definitely placed near the Bernal murder site, as the result of the broken blade. Neither Martha Johnson nor Armijo's mother knew where he was. The last time anyone had seen him was before Halloween.

"That may not be true," said Romero. "Bustamente Standing Bear and the group may have seen him on All Souls' Day, out at Hanging Shell. But Bustamente wants to keep it a secret as to who was out there. Armijo was probably out there."

"We need Bustamente to tell us where they found the medicine bundle, and who was involved," said Tafoya. "Where they picked up the bundle may be where Armijo is now, or he is with others that were involved. We need to run down possible locations. Bustamente can help us. We need Bustamente to talk to us."

Romero pursed his lips, shook his head. "I'll go talk to Bustamente now. I'll tell him that we have the F.B.I. identifying Armijo's computer as the hacking computer that hacked into the museum, and the use of the laptop on the internet crossed state boundaries that makes it a case beyond tribal law. I'll stress to him that we have Armijo's White Raptor placed up at Quintana Canyon. What a piece of the wing of the White Raptor means in the Bernal case, we don't know, but we need to talk to Armijo. And we need to know who else was involved. This case is bigger than Hanging Shell. Bustamente will understand." Tafoya agreed. Romero stood up and walked out the door.

In less than thirty minutes, Romero returned. He huddled with Tafoya and Janet in Tafoya's office. Tafoya, while Romero had gone to talk to Bustamente, had composed a be-on-the-lookout for Armijo's green Chevy pickup, and the BOLO had been dispersed to Taos and adjacent counties.

"Armijo and Dominguez," Romero said as he entered Tafoya's office.

"What do you mean, 'Dominguez'?" Tafoya asked.

"Alfred Dominguez and Armijo were at Hanging Shell when Bustamente went out there on All Souls' Day. The two of them had the medicine bundle and scalps. They tried to hide the artifacts, but they were found. They had also reconstructed the roof and walls of the extinct kiva and were probably going to use the medicine bundle to work some magic. They had even fed the scalps blue corn. Bustamente did not know precisely what they were going to do, but he put a stop to it," Romero said.

"We need to talk to Dominguez. Now!" Tafoya said.

Tafoya called Osha Masonry where Dominguez worked, asking if he was on a work crew today. They affirmed he was working on a stone patio porch in Ojo Verde. It was a weeklong construction project, and the crew would break for lunch at noon. Tafoya looked at his watch: eleven forty. Tafoya and Janet climbed in the police vehicle and drove to the site.

At the construction site in Ojo Verde, Tafoya and Janet talked to Dominguez. Tafoya told the crew chief that Dominguez was not wanted for anything criminal. He wanted to ask him some questions about one of his acquaintances. Tafoya and Janet, to lessen the formality of the meeting, bought burritos and soft drinks to eat with Dominguez, while they chatted away from the crew who sprawled under a nearby shade tree. They informed Dominguez they knew about the medicine bundle and Bustamente handling the case discreetly with the tribal council.

"We know Armijo was there at Hanging Shell with you the day Bustamente showed up."

Tafoya's concern was finding Armijo to question him about the theft and his relationship to Lance Bernal, particularly the drone blade found within fifty yards of Bernal's body. Dominguez said he had not seen Armijo since they returned from Hanging Shell. Neither had he tried to contact Armijo for he wanted to get back to a normal life, away from Armijo. Tafoya asked if Dominguez had any idea where Armijo was staying? Dominguez did not know where Armijo could be if he was not with his parents at the pueblo, or at his house on the edge of the reservation.

Tafoya brought out his notepad, and made a point of finding a page. The gesture scared Dominguez."

Tafoya glared at Dominguez. "Did you deposit the Child of Water mask at the church?"

Dominguez hesitated, then answered, "Yes, it was me."

"How about the cylinders at McGinnis' house?"

"That wasn't me at McGinnis'. That was Bernal."

"So, Bernal was involved with the Franklin Deerfield theft?"

"Yes."

"Why give the cylinders and mask back, Dominguez?'

"I don't know why Bernal gave the cylinders back. Guilt, maybe? He wasn't fully committed, it seems, as to revitalization. I think he was trying to put things back into place, before the theft. And, he wanted to scare people off with, 'The god roams the foothills for scalps,' message. For me, when he gave the cylinders back, that took away the power of the mask, neutered its effectiveness, so I gave the mask back. I had plenty to work with by possessing the medicine bundle."

"But we'll really never know why Bernal gave the cylinders back, will we?" Tafoya added. Dominguez stiffened and looked away.

Tafoya could not think of any more questions. "That's all for now, Dominguez," Tafoya said. "I'll want to talk to you later. Don't go on any long trips outside the county…frankly, don't go out of Taos County at all."

Janet decided she should go to the Forest Service station to catch up on some work. She could catch a ride with a girlfriend to get back home. On the way to the station, Janet brought up a suggestion. "Richard, why don't you see if the F.B.I. can give us information on Armijo's location. Surely, with their technology and links to his laptop and cell phone, they might could help us in locating him? He's a computer nerd. He must use his toys, don't you think?"

Before they reached the Forest Service in Ojo Verde, Tafoya called F.B.I. agent Dominique Suarez and asked if it was possible to trace Armijo's location using his laptop or cell phone. Suarez replied that was possible, and she would institute a tracking vector as soon as she hung up. She would call Tafoya with any information as soon as she scored a hit on his location.

Before they arrived at the Forest Service headquarters, agent Suarez called him back. She told him that Armijo had not used his laptop since before Halloween. "He probably has another laptop. Out of luck, but we will continue to monitor."

When Tafoya told her that Armijo may be involved in the Bernal murder, Suarez upped her response. She quickly replied she was calling in agent Clovis who worked the case at Franklin Deerfield to assist. "If he's on the internet, Clovis will find him."

Tafoya dropped Janet off at the Forest Service headquarters, and promised to call her that evening. He thought of the Teec Nos Pos blanket on her bed and the red aspen sprigs on her mantle.

68

Medicine Wind sharpened the *tamahaac*, the straight-shafted battle axe he threw with precision, winning all throwing contests he entered. But he used it in camping and field dressing large animals, not merely winning throwing contests. His axe he called by the old Powhatan name, *tamahaac* with a slightly different pronunciation. The *tamahaac* was an old battle tool of his people. The metal head of the axe gave it durability and sharpness.

Since Medicine Wind had conferred with Bustamente over two weeks ago, he had been on the hunt for Bernal's killer. And, being on the hunt required a variety of tools: rifle, pistol, knife, and, of course, his *tamahaac*. He remembered that on Bustamente's wall calendar, he had circled two dates, October 13 and October 21, one for the Franklin Deerfield theft, the other for Lance Bernal's murder. The thieves had been caught, but Bernal's murderer remained at-large.

"My hunt goes on."

Medicine Wind had followed Armijo on All Souls' Day, once he had returned from Hanging Shell ruins. Dominguez had dropped Armijo off at his house on the edge of the reservation. He also made the decision to spy on Dominguez. Dominguez had hibernated at home for the weekend, but Armijo had skipped out of sight, driving his green Chevy pickup off someplace and not returning.

Medicine Wind made periodic checks on both Dominguez's and Armijo's houses. Dominguez remained in place; Armijo was gone. The tribal police and the deputy sheriff had searched Armijo's home—twice—and taken a desktop computer. Medicine Wind suspected both of them of murder, but of the two, Dominguez seemed most likely. Dominguez had been banished from the Tulona reservation and was knowledgeable of both Tulona and Navajo ceremonies. Rumor had it that he knew Navajo black magic songs and curses.

On Tuesday, November 6, Medicine Wind decided to confront Dominguez. He drove to Dominguez's house. Dominguez was not at home. He decided to wait for him. When Dominguez turned onto his street where his house was located, he saw Medicine Wind's pickup parked in front.

"What now?" Dominguez thought to himself. "I just got through with Tafoya and that Forest Service Officer Janet Rael.

When Dominguez parked in the driveway, Medicine Wind leisurely stepped out of his pickup and waved to Dominguez—a friendly wave. They met up on the front porch. Dominguez did not invite him in. Medicine Wind quickly came to the point of the meeting. He wanted to know if the third thief at Franklin Deerfield was Lance Bernal.

Dominguez answered, "Yes, he was. Why do you want to know?"

"I believe Bernal was killed over the medicine bundle or the masks in some way. Maybe he was trying to walk back the theft at the museum, and you or Armijo took him out?" Medicine Wind asserted.

Dominguez stared blankly at Medicine Wind. "Well, I didn't do it. I was working that day, and I have witnesses to prove it. Tafoya checked my alibi." Dominguez looked away, then asked. "You have any proof it was Armijo took Bernal out?"

Medicine Wind paused. If Dominguez had an alibi that day, that scratched him as the murderer. And, he had no evidence that Armijo killed Bernal.

"I don't have any evidence it was Armijo," Medicine Wind replied. "But I have a hunch you are involved, somehow. You three were together to steal the medicine bundle, and that's proved to be trouble for us all."

Dominguez said nothing, impatient to be done with all of Medicine Wind's questioning.

Medicine Wind probed more. "Do you know where Armijo is?"

Dominguez for the second time that day told the truth about Armijo. "I have no idea where he is.... I gotta go." He abruptly turned, went inside his home, slamming the door.

Medicine Wind stood on the front porch for a moment. Then he walked back to his pickup and drove off, still reluctant to let Dominguez off the hook.

69

Wednesday, November 7, Day of Saint Didacus, Month of Corn Depositing Moon.

Temperatures did not rise above icing until late in the morning. The day had been forecast to be fair, no clouds, but winds increasing by late afternoon with possible clouds moving in again. Clouds did move in again by the afternoon, and the temperature fell back to freezing. After all, it was November, the Month of Corn Depositing Moon.

Tafoya, as was his habit pattern, checked the weather when he arose that morning. When he departed for the stationhouse, he took along his parka, just in case he had to go into the mountains. He decided to skip a big breakfast and munch on pastries Delores would bring to the office. Delores did bring pastries, and Tafoya enjoyed the apricot pastry bread. Tafoya settled in his office with Mundo coffee and the pastry and opened up his silos on the Lance Bernal case.

Recapitulating the Armijo-Franklin Deerfield case, there was nothing to do but wait until Armijo showed up at the pueblo, or was found elsewhere. The broken rotary blade in the evidence box matched the drone at Armijo's house. Tafoya wondered if the drone should be confiscated as evidence in the Bernal case? No, for the time being, because the connection with Bernal's murder was circumstantial and flimsy. If the broken blade in the evidence box had bloody fingerprints, that would be probable cause to confiscate the drone.

Tafoya reread the reports, interviews, and notes concerning Lance Bernal, seeking to summarize the case again, hoping for a new insight. Bernal's friends, Dominguez, Armijo, and Ambrose Vasquez had been questioned. Armijo's whereabouts on October 21, a Sunday, the day of the murder, had not been determined—Romero had failed to ask the question. Where was Armijo that day? Vasquez's whereabouts that day had been verified; he was in Santa Fe with his family. Tafoya flipped through his notebook and read his write-up with Dominguez. Where was Dominguez on that Sunday?

Tafoya checked the interview with Dominguez. His write-up of the interview with Dominguez was correct and detailed—as far as it went. But in his notebook, Tafoya had placed an asterisk beside Dominguez's answer to a question he posed.

"Where were you on the twenty-first of October, the day of Bernal's murder?" he had asked.

"I was finishing a flagstone project down in Taos at the Martinez Historic House," Dominguez had replied.

Tafoya had placed an asterisk beside his statement with the intent to check out his alibi. He had failed to check the alibi. Basic Procedure 101 had not been applied. Tafoya had not followed up to verify Dominguez's alibi.

And, I've been critical of Romero, Tafoya thought. We've both messed up.

He looked up the phone number of the Martinez Historic House, punched in the number on his land line, and immediately was placed on hold while the supervisor was paged. Tafoya doodled on his yellow legal pad, waiting.

Suddenly, Romero knocked on his office door and entered quickly. "Armijo has just parked in front of his parents' home here at the pueblo."

Tafoya slammed the phone back in its cradle and followed Romero out the station door, both walking fast to Armijo's parents' home on the Winter House side of the pueblo. They caught up with him before he entered his parents' home. Armijo agreed to come back with them to the tribal police headquarters and answer questions.

Upon reading the search warrant, issued a couple of days earlier, Armijo reluctantly handed over his laptop that was in his pickup. He had not been to his house in several days, so he was unaware of the search warrant. Tafoya noticed a suitcase in Armijo's pickup bed, as well as *latillas*, fence wire, posts, and digging tools.

Instead of questioning Armijo in an interrogation room, Tafoya and Romero took Armijo into the conference room. The sweet scent of the sage smudge still hung in the air. Sergeant Romero opened the questioning, admitting Bustamente was seeking tribal council protection and punishment for his and Dominguez's theft of the artifacts at Franklin Deerfield.

"The Tulona tribal police will go along with Bustamente and the tribal council," Romero said. Armijo breathed a long sigh of relief. "You're lucky," Romero said.

Tafoya picked up the point. "Yet, the F.B.I. has an interest in the case concerning your use of the internet to hack and perpetuate the theft. Interstate lines were crossed in the using the internet." Armijo shifted uneasily in his chair. Tafoya continued, "We believe they will not pursue the case since Franklin Deerfield is dropping the charges, so that's good for you. But we need to examine the laptop, and we need your cell phone with the password, Armijo. You'll get them back after we analyze how the phone and laptop were used to hack and circumvent museum security."

Meekly, Armijo reached back in his pants pocket and gave it to Tafoya. He had two cell phones; he gave the older model to Tafoya.

"The password to both the laptop and the phone is LA99, the first four digits and letters of Hanging Shell archaeological designation. I have another laptop and this new phone I've been using. They're not relevant to Franklin Deerfield...but if you need them, I'll hand them over."

Writing down the password, Tafoya shook his head, "Armijo...we have a few more questions concerning the theft."

Armijo chose to be cooperative. He verified Lance Bernal was the third person in the Franklin Deerfield theft. He further admitted he had used Martha Johnson's laptop to gain access into the museum, and had used his laptop to continue snooping into accession records, finding the Hanging Shell medicine bundle.

"What about the Child of Water mask and scalps? They weren't part of what you initially wanted, were they?" Romero asked.

"No, they weren't, but when we were looking through the cabinets of artifacts for the medicine bundle, Dominguez took them. He had been out on Navajo land and wanted to use them in some ceremonial way. The scalps were also taken because they were there. All those things have been returned, so we should be off the hook."

"We think so," Tafoya said, "but the case is still being processed and liability is still hanging on you and Dominguez. That is, until the Tribal Council, Franklin Deerfield, and the F.B.I. sign off. Lance Bernal is the only one on this case that is 'off the hook,' and that's because he's dead."

Armijo looked down at the table and shook his head. Tears came to his eyes.

"I've a few questions on Bernal," Tafoya went on, not affected by Armijo's emotion. "Where were you on October twenty-first, the Sunday Bernal was shot?"

"You can't believe I had anything to do with that, do you? Do you?" Armijo said, raising his voice.

"Just answer the question," Romero asserted.

Armijo asked for his cell phone back so he could look at his calendar and refresh his memory. He scrolled through to October 21 and looked at his appointments. He wiped his eyes.

"Yeah, that was a Sunday. I was at Tesuque Pueblo, setting up their new webpage software and teaching their administrator on how to keep it running smoothly. I drove down early that morning and didn't get back until late that evening."

Tafoya took down the names of the people that worked with Armijo and the phone numbers of the Tesuque tribal offices. Armijo handed back his cell phone. Tafoya excused himself and went to his office to make calls to the Tesuque, while Romero and Armijo stepped into the breakroom for coffee.

Tafoya came back after fifteen minutes. "Armijo was there on that day like he said. The systems operator for Tesuque I talked to, as well as the tribal secretary, verify Armijo's story.... I need a cup of coffee."

Tafoya excused himself and went to the breakroom to pour himself a cup he sorely needed, while he figured out a new tack on the Bernal case. When he returned and sat down at the table, Tafoya said he had one more question.

"How is it that your broken White Raptor drone blade was found near the site of Bernal's murder, up at Quintana Canyon?"

"My White Raptor? How did you...?" Armijo stammered.

Romero explained that they had the broken blade in their evidence box, and had matched it when they served the warrant and took the desktop computer.

"My friend, Vasquez, and I were at Quintana Canyon early in October. We were flying White Raptor around and having fun. I was letting him pilot it, and he made a mistake and crashed it into a stand of aspens. I haven't had a chance to repair it."

Tafoya wrote up the report of the interview with Armijo and entered the report on the tribal station server. Romero read it, then called Vasquez to verify the drone crash. Vasquez confirmed the date of the crash. For the moment, that was all Romero and Tafoya needed of Armijo.

"You're free to go, Armijo, but don't leave Taos County without telling us," Romero said.

70

Tafoya and Romero decided to go to Pueblo Café for early lunch. Romero ordered green chile stew and Tafoya, who had not eaten breakfast—only pastries—ordered a Navajo taco of mutton, cabbage, lettuce, and red chile sauce. Sweet iced tea and glasses of water dampened the heat of the chilis. They shared a praline candy for dessert. Tafoya bought an extra praline to take back to Dolores at the station.

"She has a sweet tooth for candies," Tafoya chuckled.

As they drove back to the stationhouse, Tafoya admitted they both had messed up on operations for the Bernal case. "I failed to check on Dominguez's alibi, and you missed asking Armijo's whereabouts on October twenty-first."

"You haven't double-checked on Dominguez's alibi, Richard?" Romero said, looking surprised, side-stepping his own mistake.

"That's first on my list when we get back to the station," Tafoya answered.

Tafoya called as soon as they returned to the stationhouse. The director of the Martinez Historic House in Taos informed Tafoya that on October 21, the historic Martinez House had been closed—a matter of hosting a wedding for a wealthy Taos couple who paid a lot of money to have exclusive use of the house for their wedding and reception.

"A beautiful wedding it was!" There were no workmen at the house that day, the director had gone on to say, "They came out later that next week to finish the job."

After talking with the director, Tafoya told Romero that Dominguez gave them a false statement about his location on the day of the murder. "His alibi does not check out. He wasn't laying stone at the Martinez House that day. The Martinez House was hosting a wedding that day. Dominguez gave us a false statement, but that doesn't make him a killer. Until we talk to him, what other tangents are there surrounding Bernal's case we could pursue, Romero?"

"We have at least two directions," Romero replied. "We have a rifle slug that killed Bernal and we have Bernal's 7mm magnum rifle that is missing as a possible factor in the case."

"Did we ever get a serial number on Bernal's missing deer rifle from Beatrice, his wife?" asked Tafoya.

Romero searched for the serial number in the case file and found Beatrice had turned in the serial number the day after her husband had been buried. She was anxious to help in the case. The serial number had been distributed to pawn shops in Española, Questa, and Santa Fe. Most, but not all, had run a trace on their 7mm magnums, and had failed to report a match. One pawn shop in Española was always slow in reporting, so Romero called them.

Top Mesa Pawnbroker in Española answered in three rings. Romero put the call on speakerphone. The pawnbroker admitted they were behind in entering data on serial numbers in the computer, but the pawnbroker on duty went to the rack of deer rifles, yanked the 7mm Remington magnum from the rack and read out the serial number over the phone. The number matched Bernal's serial number Romero had in the case file in front of him.

It had been pawned on October 21, by Alfredo Dominguez of Ojo Verde, New Mexico. Romero ordered Top Mesa Pawnbroker to hold the rifle, "That's an order from the Tulona Tribal Police, hold it!" until they could pick it up and do a ballistics test. The pawnbroker whined that he was going to lose money. Romero repeated sternly, "Just hold the rifle." Then he hung up.

Romero grimaced at Tafoya who had been listening over the speakerphone. Tafoya knew the next step to take.

"We need to pick up Dominguez for questioning, Sergeant. And I won't be questioning Dominguez at his lunch break under the cottonwood trees, either," Tafoya exclaimed.

Medicine Wind sat in Old Bow kiva. He built a small fire. The kiva for Tulonas, like other kivas in pueblo communities, existed as sacred spaces, apart from the rest of the world. The earth was holy, sacred, the Mother. The kiva existed as a special place. The Tulona had been greatly disturbed in the past month: a murder of a Tulona—still unsolved—and a bad, witchcraft event at Hanging Shell, and a theft of artifacts from Franklin Deerfield. The theft had been resolved and three Tulonas were responsible: Lance Bernal, Larry Armijo, and Alfredo Dominguez.

Still, there remained a question. Why had the three of them resolved to revitalize an extinct kiva that had dissolved in witchery and dissolution? Was there something wrong within the Tulona Pueblo? Medicine Wind thought hard, thought deep, and he prayed. There were no answers to his prayers down in the kiva. His hunt for Bernal's killer was still afoot, even if he could not identify the enemy.

Medicine Wind was not a tribal policeman, but his friends were. Sergeant Romero and Richard Tafoya had clues, perhaps even a suspect. They must share with him, he thought.

"They are, after all, my kinsmen, my kiva brothers." The kiva fire burned low. Medicine Wind arose from the bench in Old Bow kiva and ascended the ladder to the surface of the pueblo. He walked directly to the tribal police station.

He went inside and asked to speak with Richard Tafoya. When he met with Tafoya, he asked for details on their hunt for Bernal's killer. But Tafoya would not share.

All that Tafoya said was, "I'm sorry, Medicine Wind. Stay close, help us when we call. We are still on the chase, but we are getting closer. I may be violating the rules, but know this. We no longer suspect Armijo."

Medicine Wind promised Tafoya he would be close by in the hunt, for the kill.

"Call me. I'll come running." Away from the stationhouse, Medicine Wind concluded, "It's definitely Dominguez."

71

Sergeant Romero and Tafoya drove to Dominguez's house in Ojo Verde, thinking he should be home following work. He was not there. They drove by popular cafes and fast-food places in Ojo Verde and did not see his pickup—a white Ford F-150 with wooden side panels and a tailgate with damage from turning with a trailer hooked when the tailgate was down—damage that happened to a lot of people. After making two rounds of cafes and fast-food joints, Romero and Tafoya drove back to the pueblo. No Dominguez.

The Abalone Creek drummers and singers were drumming that night—a last-minute occasion, celebrating Corn Depositing Moon. Romero and Tafoya wanted to attend, get away from the stress of the day and listen to drumming with their families. Tafoya had invited Janet to come over to the pueblo to be with him at the drumming. He had a special proposal to ask her.

At dusk, the Abalone Creek Tulano Pueblo drummers sat at their four-foot drum. Several fires were lit on the Winter House side of the pueblo where they would drum and sing. Two fires were started on Summer House side. Twelve drummers sat around the drum, wearing jackets. Little girls, six-, seven-, eight-years-old, sat on their grandfathers', uncles', and fathers' laps. One eight-year-old girl stood between her cousin and father, beating the drum and singing loudly.

The Abalone Creek drummers had mostly fast beats on the drum with high tenor, falsetto ranges in singing. An elder would begin the song, followed within seconds by the younger chorus. The Tiwa words derived from special songs had been handed down for generations. Occasionally the beat slowed, voices lowered to baritone, but much of the voice range was in the higher octaves. Overlaying the singing were pitched calls, reminiscent of soaring birds of prey, cries for power, warbles of joy.

The Abalone Creek drummers wore baseball-type caps with brands from New York Yankees to the San Francisco Forty-Niners; one drummer, Lion Walks Night, brandished a white-calico bandana about his head, R. C. Gorman-style. Two of the twelve were bareheaded and their queues of long, dark hair lay prominently down their backs. Three of the twelve drummers were old, in their sixties. Surrounding the circle of drummers, fifty people tapped their feet and sang along.

None of the people danced, but swayed rhythmically in unison.

One song, the calls repeated over and over. "*Yeh-e-e-e-ah—ah—ah-yeh-yeh / / Yeh-e-e-e-ah—ah—ah-yeh-yeh*."

Another song, following a short pause to drink cola or Gator Aide, had phrasing repetitive and hypnotizing, "*Hay yo—hay yo—hay yo---en... / / Hay yo—hay yo—hay yo—en....*"

Bustamente and his wife stayed in their house, listening to the singing and drumming that penetrated through thick adobe walls, recalling previous singings when they were young and swayed to rhythm outside in the cold. But at their age, it was best to stay inside.

Tafoya and Janet stood close together on the outer edge of the audience. His proposal came soon, between songs. He turned and faced her.

"I want us closer together, Janet. Can you see your way to move from your apartment on Calle Zacate Verde to an apartment complex near my home, only a quarter-mile from me?"

Janet looked in his eyes, but before she could say anything, Tafoya rushed, "I'll help you move. Your being close to my home on Tulona land, we'll be able to walk to each other's place."

Janet softly chuckled, then said frankly, "It's about time you asked, Richard. Yes, I say yes." They embraced. The drumming began again.

Medicine Wind's wife, Quail Looks Away held Dezba against her breast, standing alongside Tafoya and Janet. Medicine Wind was drumming. Sergeant Romero, dressed in tribal police uniform, stood with another officer beneath an arbor and close to a fire for warmth. They perused the crowd, not for any reason other than curiosity, dutiful observation. All tourists had been shooed away at four o'clock; only Tulona and kinsmen attended. Some Tulona stood on roofs nearby and looked down upon the scene; they had witnessed races several weeks before from the same spot. Now they saw another sacred event, not a ceremony, but sacred, nonetheless.

The Tulona puebloans around the drummers were as One. There were no metricians or quantitative scientists counting, nor even an anthropologist analyzing the event in categorical, irreducible descriptions. Most observers would not see one body. Most observers would see fifty people and twelve drummers on a cold evening at Tulona Pueblo on the seventh of November in New Mexico, USA. Just a group of people who were watching a drumming event of no particular significance. It was a gathering, an entertaining event to pass the time.

Yes, it was all that, but more. Profoundly more.

The rooftop Tulonas, the people standing around the drummers, and the little girls and boys singing loudly felt the phenomenon of Spirit: the pounding of drum entering bodies, fire smoke wafting over faces, sounds penetrating eardrums, bodies. Scientists could not quantify, nor musicologists describe in the language of musical score of what was transpiring, what was happening, what was alive and circulating with drumming and singing.

But the Tulona felt it: self-loss in a rhythm of beauty. *It began as rhythmic sound in the body the earth faintly trembling, then from plexuses heat arose like liquid churning in the body over and over, a thick mélange of precious elements—gold, perhaps? No, like copper, a warm elemental vein of blood-like vitality first sensed within one's body reaching out to others and others reaching into all connecting the many into One. The heat of the One rose upward into beautiful minds and faces, but heat did not stop there for the mélange of copper liquid rose to the top of the head outward, upward, and throughout all the puebloans singing lost in drum. It radiated out of the crown of the head erupting into air becoming sparks, then floating down the Oneness subsiding gradually and tremble coursed through puebloan blood as self-loss in a rhythm of beauty bowed to earth and starry sky. The puebloans returned again and again with clapping singing drumming, a circularity upon the earth and in the starry sky until the drumming ceased.*

72

Alfredo Dominguez glanced at the Tulona standing around the fires and drummers as he opened Bustamente's door without knocking and walked into his front room, finding Bustamente's wife at the kitchen table, reading a newspaper by the overhead gaslight and electric lantern on the table.

She looked at Dominguez, "You are in the wrong house, please leave!"

Bustamente, who was in the backroom, came through the door to the kitchen, hardening his face at the sight of Dominguez.

"I want the Hanging Shell medicine bundle," Dominguez ordered.

Bustamente shook his head, "You can't have it! The Hanging Shell bundle is not for you. Leave! Now!"

"I'll not go until I have the bundle. Where is it?" Dominguez said, raising his voice.

"Dominguez! Stop it! Leave!" Bustamente shouted.

Dominguez stood still, his eyes searching the room.

Bustamente spoke authoritatively. "Listen to me! The Tulona council is of one mind to disassemble the Hanging Shell medicine bundle. We shall keep the Corn Mothers. The panels and world lengthener will be dispersed to other pueblos. They have greater need for their ancient objects than we do. That is the will of the Tulona Council. Now go!"

Dominguez sneered, insensitive to Bustamente's explanation. He walked past the cacique, brushing against him callously, and entered his backroom. He scanned the room. Two trunks sat on the opposite side of the room. As he started to walk to the trunks to rifle through the contents looking for the medicine bundle, he saw a gray daypack, in the corner. Dominguez unzipped the pack, looked inside, found the medicine bundle, zipped it back up, and slipped the backpack on his left shoulder.

Walking back through the front room, Bustamente stood in front of him, but Dominguez pushed him aside and burst out the front door. As he turned to the right from the front door and ran away, Bustamente's wife came out the door and ran to the Tulona drumming group, waving her arms and yelling.

Sergeant Romero saw Bustamente's wife bolt from the house, but he could not hear her words. The drums and singing drowned out her cries. He saw her waving her arms in a panic. Immediately, he and another tribal officer sprinted in her direction. Tafoya and Janet saw Romero run, and they, in turn, followed Romero. Medicine Wind, seated at the drum, saw them running toward Bustamente's house. He dropped his drumming stick and dashed in their direction. The drumming continued without him, his friends thinking he needed a break.

The Tulona Pueblo consisted of two big houses, apartment-style in form, with outlying alleyways and narrow lanes radiating from the Winter and Summer House sides of the plaza. Within the old part of the pueblo were smaller homes, art shops, the church, and government offices constructed over the centuries. Corrals and stables abutted some of the homes. Rio Tulona flowed through between the Winter and Summer House sides, splitting the pueblo plaza in half. Three bridges spanned the river at the far end, middle, and church end of the plaza.

Dominguez, after running out of Bustamente's house, turned right and darted behind the house. He ran down a lane behind Bustamente's house. The lane was a passageway for people to walk and, in olden days, horse and wagon transportation, not automobiles. Dominguez's intent was to work his way back to his pickup on the west side of the pueblo.

Bustamente came out from his house and told Romero and Tafoya that Dominguez had forcibly taken the Hanging Shell medicine bundle.

"We need to stop him! Get the bundle back!" Bustamente yelled. He gave Romero a description of clothes Dominguez wore.

The Abalone Creek drummers continued singing; that was helpful. If the singing broke up, people going back to their homes would flood the area and interfere with the search. Romero called dispatch at the tribal police office and ordered other officers on duty to commence a search.

"Solitary male, Tulona, blue jeans, gray field coat, black watch cap, and carrying a gray daypack. Use caution, may be armed," stated Romero, over the radio.

Janet said she would circle the plaza area and church grounds, but avoid alleyways. Two tribal officers began searching lanes and alleyways; Romero and Tafoya did the same. Tafoya lacked a portable radio transmitter; he did have a backup pistol he carried, a Beretta Jetfire, 25 ACP; he felt underprepared, but there was no time to run to the stationhouse and get better equipped. He struck out, charging into back alleys. Romero had, at least, loaned him a spare flashlight.

Tafoya reasoned that Dominguez was going to evade capture and flee the pueblo in his pickup. Dominguez had a one-man operation going on: grab the medicine bundle and escape. Then what? Stealing the medicine bundle for a second time would mean loss of freedom—jail time—so that Dominguez was probably planning on leaving the area for good, to go elsewhere, but where? Where he would go in the long run was irrelevant for the present moment. Tafoya's task was to try and capture Dominguez before he left the area. Even if they did not apprehend Dominguez tonight, more than likely he would be caught when an APB was put out for his vehicle. Life as Dominguez knew it, was over.

Dominguez zig-zagged between adobe homes and alleyways, working his way back to the parking lot near the Mission Saint Francis del Monte. His intent had been fulfilled, repossessing the medicine bundle. Next, he would take backroads westward to the Navajo Reservation where he had friends. There was space to get lost in the Four Corners. He would work at day jobs and spend time piecing together a movement, a ceremony, exploiting the Hanging Shell medicine bundle.

"I will become the messiah of a new movement. I will become the new Wovoka, Handsome Lake, Tecumseh. But, for now, I have to escape the Tulona Pueblo...."

Romero and the two other tribal police officers methodically walked and shined their flashlights along every alleyway. Tafoya crisscrossed the walking patterns of Romero and the two officers. He lost sight of Romero and the others. Janet, near the mission church, had made one circle of the plaza, walking across two bridges over Rio Tulona. She paused in front of the church and looked back across the plaza at the Abalone Creek drummers. By the light of fires illuminating Winter House, she saw Tafoya climbing the ladder to the first story of dwellings.

"Is he getting a vantage point above it all?" she whispered. "A good tactical move."

Suddenly, out of the corner of her eye, she saw movement. It was a man, she thought, who darted behind the mission church—carrying a daypack? She could not be sure. Janet walked along the outer wall of the church to investigate. As she turned the corner to the rear of the church, she saw Dominguez.

"Hey! Stop, Dominguez!" she shouted.

Dominguez halted and turned around to face her, thirty-feet away. He looked at her, turned back around, and started walking toward his pickup in the parking lot, away from Janet. Dark places, shadows were at the back of the church, but Janet took steps in his direction, and yelled again.

"Stop, Dominguez! Give it up!"

Just then, from the other corner of the church wall, out stepped Medicine Wind.

Dominguez was caught between Janet and Medicine Wind. He stopped and looked in one direction toward Medicine Wind, and in the other direction toward Janet. Trapped. The cold Cottonwood River boxed him in. If Dominguez ran away from the church and tried to cross the river, he probably would not succeed, but drown in the river, cold and swiftly flowing. And he could not scale the church wall. He was caught between Medicine Wind and Janet on one side, the river and church wall on the other.

"Drop the pack, Dominguez," Medicine Wind ordered.

Dominguez held the daypack tighter. He looked at the river, then at Medicine Wind. He turned toward Janet. She's the weaker, he thought.

Dominguez glared menacingly in the direction of Janet and started toward her.

A thick sound cut the air, not sharp, but solid, of wood and metal, spinning. Dominguez staggered, tried to reach what thudded in his back through his thick coat, and then collapsed.

Medicine Wind's *tamahaac* lodged like a cleaver in his back. The daypack fell aside from Dominguez, and from his coat, a pistol fell on the ground.

Janet rushed to the side of Dominguez, picked up the pistol, put it in her pocket, and grabbed the daypack, leaning it against the church wall. Dominguez groaned and yelled in pain.

Janet called for an ambulance, then she called Tafoya, "I'm over here, behind the church, Ben took Dominguez down. I've called for an ambulance."

Tafoya replied that he had seen her, Dominguez, and Medicine Wind from his perch on the first story of the houses, but when he tried to call her, she did not answer. Janet looked down at her cell phone; she had switched off the ringtone on her phone, in respect for pueblo singing and drumming, and had not turned the ringer back on.

The Abalone Creek drummers continued to sing until the ambulance pulled onto the Pueblo Plaza, and then they disbanded, most of the them walking over to the flashing red and blue lights to see what the trouble was. After stabilizing, Dominguez was loaded face down on the gurney, the *tamahaac* still in his back. At Saint Luke's hospital, the *tamahaac* was removed, and he was placed in intensive care. No vital areas had been penetrated; the shoulder blade bore most of the force and emergency surgery repaired the damage. He was set under tribal police guard, assisted by deputies from Taos County sheriff's office. The Hanging Shell medicine bundle was stored in the steel safe of the tribal council's office, for Bustamente was taking no further chances.

73

Thursday, November 8, Day of Beloved John Duns Scotus, Month of Corn Depositing Moon

The day was forecast to be cloudy, windy, and colder. The wind during the day gusted to thirty miles per hour, and since midnight, the temperature had dropped into the twenties and lingered there. Early that morning, Romero, Tafoya, and other officers assembled in the conference room for a briefing on the Bernal case, particularly Dominguez's pawning of Bernal's 7mm magnum in Española, the day after the murder. After going over the case, the assembled officers, led by Tafoya, drew up a list of questions to be answered.

One major question was: Where was Dominguez on the day of the murder? He had lied about being at the Martinez House on the day of the murder—that had been checked out. There was no doubt he was involved in the Franklin Deerfield heist, and then a second theft of the bundle from Bustamente's home. Since Bernal was killed by a 7mm magnum bullet, might Dominguez have a 7mm magnum rifle in his possession? Or, was Bernal shot with his own 7mm?

"All our leads go to Dominguez," Tafoya said, "and Armijo has been excluded from Quintana Canyon on the day of the murder. Dominguez has not. We need a search warrant to search for a 7mm magnum rifle of Dominguez. We will get a judge to sign off on a warrant."

The Ojo Verde city judge signed off on a warrant to search for a 7mm rifle at Dominguez's. The attorney for the pueblo pushed hard for the warrant when the judge wavered on the Dominguez being implicated in the murder, but in the end, he relented.

"Don't make this a fishing expedition for anything else! Check for the rifle, get it, get out of there, and then go test for ballistics!"

By eleven o'clock in the morning, Dominguez's house was searched, and a 7mm magnum rifle with a Browning scope was recovered. Sergeant Romero directed an officer on standby to take Dominguez's rifle and bullet found under Bernal's body at Quintana Canyon to Santa Fe. On the way, the officer was to stop at Top Mesa Pawnbrokers in Española to pick up Bernal's 7mm. From there, the officer sped southward to Santa Fe to get ballistics testing at the forensic laboratory of the New Mexico State Police compound on Cerrillos Road. As a favor to the Tulona Pueblo, the New Mexico State Police lab promised ballistic testing and retesting within hours. As promised, within hours, the forensic team in Santa Fe attested that Dominguez's 7mm magnum rifle was used to fire the fatal shot into Bernal. Ballistics were a match on the bullet beneath Bernal and Dominguez's rifle. Bernal's rifle was excluded as the murder weapon.

Yes, it was Dominguez's rifle that fired the fatal shot, but did Dominguez pull the trigger? It was all circumstantial, incriminating, but inconclusive. Without a confession or a witness that Dominguez shot Bernal, the case was at a standstill. Dominguez was in no shape to be questioned, but he would be soon. And as Tafoya said, "The questioning is not going to be under shade trees eating tacos."

74

Two days later, Saturday, November 10

Something woke Dominguez from his deep sleep. The lights in his hospital room dimmed. Was it day or night? He had heard the rustling of clothing, maybe blankets? Then, unmistaken, he heard the rattle of deer hooves, a light clacking of a deer-hooves anklet, perhaps the hooves of antelope. He closed his eyes. The rattling ebbed, then ceased altogether. He was afraid to open his eyes. All sound stopped, except for the oxygen tube inserted in one of his nostrils, a steady hiss of cold air pushing on his sinuses.

Dominguez slowly opened his eyes, then blinked twice to clear the film of sleep and to erase the horror lined up in judgement facing him against the wall.

Facing him, as he lay on his left side, stood seven Tulona males, all wearing blankets of different colors and designs. Black dominated the color scheme, and all wore their hair in queues. They stood still, staring at him, blank-faced, deadly serious.

Dominguez did not recognize them, but slowly he became cognizant that beneath their stares they were warchiefs. Two of them carried silver-capped canes of authority. The warchief ensemble shimmered in his vision, like a distant mirage or heat waves arising from a desert mesa. Dominguez thought himself not fully awake. He shook his head to clear his vision, but the warchiefs stayed, shimmering.

"What is it you want?" Dominguez cried out. The warchiefs did not reply.

Suddenly, he heard deer hooves rattle again, behind him, in the direction of the door. He caught the scent of old buckskin, timeless and ancient, the musky cachet of something once alive, now dead.

The god slowly entered his field of vision from the foot of his bed: *To'badzistsini*, the Child of Water. The Child of Water glided to a position between Dominguez and the Tulona warchief ensemble, the deer hooves clacking. The god's mask of sacred buckskin was painted red ochre.

For mouth and eyes, three oval holes in the mask appeared black, deep, ominous. Hanging shells clung beneath the holes. Queue-symbols were painted on the mask, several of which remained opened, signifying scalps to be taken. Fringe of yellow wool formed a crown, and turkey and downy-eagle feathers were fixed to the yellow wool. Fox fur collared the mask. A kilt covered part of the god, his body painted red ochre, the hands white-colored. In his right hand he carried a black-painted cylinder of piñon; in his left hand, a cylinder of cedar, painted red. They represented thunderbolts. *To'badzistsíni*, the Child of Water, wore red moccasins.

Silently sullen, the god and his chorus stood there, facing Dominguez.

Dominguez was petrified. Was he dreaming? What world was he in? "Am I dead?"

Suddenly, taking one step toward Dominguez, Child of Water raised the red and black thunderbolts and shook them fiercely at him.

"The god roams the foothills for scalps of his enemies!" shouted *To'badzistsíni*, shaking the thunderbolts.

Dominguez cringed, expecting lightning strikes.

"*Heeeeeeey*," uttered the warchief chorus in low, basso voice, like a rumble of thunder.

The smell of old buckskin, the blankets, even the red-ochre paint scent was overwhelming in the room. The heat from the god and seven warchiefs suffocated rational response from Dominguez.

"How is this possible," he thought. "I'm hallucinating." Before he could reach for the call button to the nurse's station, the god spoke again.

"Why did you not bring us the scalp of Lance Bernal, my enemy?" spoke the god.

Dominguez took his finger off the nurse's call button.

"I did cut gashes in his head after I shot him! I should've brought you scalp! I'm sorry," Dominguez gushed, as if in a confession booth. "Bernal was going to turn on me and Armijo and stop Hanging Shell from coming to life. I had to stop him. Rejuvenation of Hanging Shell had to be completed. I shot him for us all. Don't you and the warchiefs understand?" The pain from the *tamahaac* injury increased as he spoke to the god.

Child of Water stood still. He began a chant, "*Heeey---O---, O---, O! // Heey---O---, O---, O!*" The god, as he chanted, moved closer to the bed, and raised his black piñon and red cedar thunderbolts as if to hurl them at Dominguez.

Dominguez winced and twice pushed the morphine drip to his IV. He passed out.

75

Santiago Majerus, the Navajo Red Antway singer and resident of Arroyo Luz, drove into the Franklin Deerfield Museum parking lot and stopped. He and Medicine Wind stepped out of the pickup. Opening the rear doors of the pickup, they collected the *To'badzistsíni* Child of Water mask and cylinders from the rear seat and took them inside to the board of trustees' conference room, where Director Hornbuckle and the curators retook possession of the material. McGinnis, Tejada, and Johnson carried the paraphernalia to the inventory room for storage in a locked cabinet.

Tribal policeman Tafoya and liaison officer Janet Rael from the Forest Service stood against the wall, looking on. Majerus walked over to Tafoya and Rael. From his coat pocket, he pulled out a recorder and gave it to Tafoya.

"Is it all on the recorder?" Tafoya asked.

"Yes, Richard, I turned it on before I got out of the pickup at the hospital. I turned it off when I returned to the pickup.... Maybe an hour on the recorder, maybe more. I listened to the critical parts on the way over here. It's all there on the recorder," Majerus replied. "Oh, one more thing. Dominguez babbled about seven warchiefs around me. I was the only one in the room besides Dominguez. Medicine Wind was out in the hallway."

"Hmm. Strange. Thanks, Santiago. We will sort all that out, including the seven warchiefs. The prosecutor will be able to use this in some way. At least, we have a chance of justice. Justice isn't always dealing out punishment. It's finding out the truth. And, by your help, we have the truth, and justice will come. I'll have the department cut you a check in the next few days for your consulting fee."

Santiago Majerus nodded courteously; his hands reflecting speckles of white ochre that had not been washed off, his exposed arms showing red ochre splotches, as well. He wore hiking boots to fight off the chill, having put his red moccasins in the back floorboard.

Majerus was exhausted, the ordeal had drained him in odd and peculiar ways. He would think on his behavior this evening for a long time. He had used mystical powers to achieve a good end—justice as Tafoya defined it. Yet, Majerus knew if he had sought to gain a bad outcome, he would have misused his powers like a Sleep Maker, a witch. As a hollow tube to the incomprehensible-spirit-that-moves-in-all-things, the masked-god spectacle at the hospital had a good outcome. That he knew firmly. But he needed to tell Tafoya something.

"Please, you and Janet, walk with me and Medicine Wind back to my pickup," Majerus asked.

The four of them, Tafoya, Janet, Medicine Wind, and Majerus, walked to his old pickup, one fender colored blue, the rest of the vehicle a beige, and the wooden bed panels stained with weathering from over a decade. The sun had set quickly and the temperature had fallen further below freezing. High cirrus clouds reflected light; alpenglow quickly disappeared into the November night.

Majerus turned and stood in front of tribal officer Tafoya. He put his white-stained hands upon Tafoya's shoulders, firmly and friendly.

"Tafoya, you may cut a check to me, but I wasn't the power that moved Dominguez's confession. I was merely an agent. Behind me, above me, below me, all around me, there manifests a power, an inexplicable force we Navajo call by many names. In this case, the power is *To 'badzistsíni*, the Child of Water, the offspring of White Shell Woman. It was him that extracted Dominguez's confession, and you can't write a check to pay for that." Majerus' hands lingered for a moment on Tafoya's shoulders. Then, smiling, he turned away from Tafoya and Janet.

Majerus and Medicine Wind stepped into the pickup and drove toward Tulona Pueblo, while Tafoya and Janet stood in front of Franklin Deerfield Museum and looked at the fading taillights of the pickup as it entered and crossed the yellow blinking light intersection at the Questa-Ojo Verde roads.

"You know, Richard," Janet said, as she placed her hand on his shoulder, "that intersection no longer has a yellow blinking light."

Epilogue

The Ortegas in San Miguel—Armando, Loretta, Luis—settled into the colder weather of November. Armando seemed strengthened by shorter days, longer nights, although his wife, Loretta, grew concerned about his long naps in the afternoon. Luis took Flowers Dancing frequently to lunch at the Farmer's Market Café near the pueblo when she visited her sister.

G. Armstrong Coe, bookshop owner and trustee of Franklin Deerfield Museum, saw an uptick in business leading into the holiday season. He and his wife, Prissy, began to read Mabel Dodge Luhan's *Winter in Taos*, a few pages each evening with a glass of wine, hoping to finish by New Year's Day. They decided to frame Mabel's personal note in the book addressed to a friend and her sage sprig, displaying both items prominently on their fireplace mantle. Coe presented a motion at the trustee meeting and argued successfully that no charges be brought against Dominguez and Armijo on the theft of the medicine bundle and Navajo mask. The motion carried unanimously.

Martha Johnson, the intern at Franklin Deerfield, resigned and found a curating position at the Ranch Museum in Lubbock, Texas, becoming an expert on High Plains windmills. Before she left Franklin Deerfield, she, McGinnis, and Tejada authorized a DNA multi-factor analysis on the two scalps from the Arizona State University laboratory. The three of them returned the scalps to the Ute Nation in a quiet, reverent ceremony at Fort Duchesne, Utah, the Ute Nation headquarters. The Ute buried the scalps far up in the mountains.

After conferring with his court-appointed defense attorney, Alfredo Dominguez pleaded guilty to the charge of second-degree murder and was sentenced to twenty years in the New Mexico State Penitentiary.

Dominguez had picked up Lance Bernal for a quick trip out to Quintana Canyon to look for deer camp sites. They were to return to the pueblo by early afternoon. Bernal told Dominguez he wanted to stop their rejuvenation of Hanging Shell, and was going to go to the Tulona Council. Dominguez became angry, and when Bernal walked off toward the woods to cool the situation down, Dominguez shot him in anger, and shot him again when he went up to recover Bernal's rifle. He showed remorse at his trial. Dominguez's wound healed, but continued to ache, especially with changes in the weather. The Tulona Pueblo Council banished him forever from setting foot in the pueblo, stating that if he ever was caught on Tulona land, including Tract A of the trust land, the council would find a way around double jeopardy and punish him for Bernal's murder—Tulona-style justice—and there would be no early release.

Larry Armijo continued setting up websites for small businesses and began to perform contract assignments for the cybersecurity investigation division of the F.B.I. The Tulona tribal police department conducted a review of its investigative procedures, finding that basic procedures needed reaffirming and additional personnel needed to be hired.

All of one mind, Cacique Bustamente and the Tulona Council decided to disassemble the Hanging Shell medicine bundle. The Okay Owingeh Pueblo received the world straightener that figured largely in their ceremonies. The painted panels were taken to Earth Cloud Lake the next spring and were weighted down by heavy rocks and placed at the northern end of the lake, so the panels would bleach and decay over time by the effects of water and the kachinas living below the lake. The stone Hanging Shell Corn Mothers remained within the pueblo, becoming an integral part of kiva ceremonies. The Corn Mothers eventually lost their designation of "Hanging Shell" and became just the Corn Mothers of the Tulona. Bustamente spent many hours in prayer asking for the blessings of the Creator and eradication of all things Hanging Shell. Eventually, the Hanging Shell story became a story of the past, as much as any story can become.

Quail Looks Away still wanted to talk with Bustamente about the Tulona concept of the "ancient-present," but there never seemed a good time to do so. But the good time would eventually come, Bustamente counseled. He told Quail they would have their talk at sunrise and at sunset, puzzling Quail even further.

Medicine Wind found no comfort in having to throw his tamahaac to stop Dominguez. In the moment of throwing, he had to prevent Dominguez from hurting Janet Rael and stop the medicine bundle from leaving Tulona control again. Yet, Dominguez was Tulona, and Medicine Wind had lifted his hand against him. He felt his actions just and clear. But, no matter, he felt guilty, sorrowful, regretful to hurt another Tulona. Bustamente told him, in the quiet of his backroom under gaslight and a piñon fire crackling in the corner fireplace, "You will never forget what happened that night; you will remain sorrowful for the rest of your life. But know this, Medicine Wind! You stopped evil from happening, and we, the Tulona, believe you did the right thing for us all. Some humans are not human, but dark formations assuming human form, Sleep Makers, witches. You stopped a Sleep Maker."

Janet Rael relocated her residence closer to Tafoya. Tafoya kept his home on the edge of Tulona land. She moved from her two-story apartment on Calle Zacate Verde to Mesa Sunscape Apartments on Calle Azul. Janet's apartment faced Tulona Peak, and she had a balcony that overlooked the mountain range and onto pueblo land. Tafoya's home was a quarter-mile walking distance. They could see lights turned on in each other's homes in the evening.

Tafoya and Rael celebrated her new apartment with dinner at Tablita's. Jason sat them at the Schwartz Table next to the window looking out on Paseo del Norte where they ate steak with red wine as Jason informed them, "I've earned enough to purchase a lift ticket for the whole season at the ski valley, and, come the first snow, I'll ski the slopes, a bluebird day or not!"

Soon after Dominguez's arrest, Armando Ortega walked out on his porch one morning before sunrise and felt the sharp cold about him. He heard Buck bang his feed bucket in the corral and saw his son's kitchen light come on across the family compound. He sipped black coffee and smelled fir and spruce about San Miguel. Armando's breath rose in wispy clouds to the rafters of his porch. He thought of chores to be done that day; but for now, in the chill of the dawn, he was sufficient unto the day, and that was good enough.

Armando had forgotten about the Santa Fe Trail—that period

somewhere in time's past. Loretta was right, he thought, "The here and now...that's the only place I want to be."

Acknowledgments

Acknowledging the sources influencing *Arroyo of Shells* encompasses an array of people, music, literature, and the seasons of the year. Only a memoir could do broader acknowledgment, and even that would fall short of to whom I am indebted.

Linda Spetter, who teaches literature and is knowledgeable of folklore components, read my manuscript carefully and offered valuable advice that I inculcated. Patricia Quintana of Taos has kindly contributed her expertise on horse and sheep behavior and their relationship to humans. Patricia and her family are historically associated with Quintana Pass. Lyle Wright has given me encouragement and support of my work. He has taught me about gift giving and "trading the old way." Brown's Bookstore in Amarillo and the Taos Book Shop—both now closed—made me aware of how bookstores sell more than books: they are nurturing communities. In law enforcement and constitutional issues, I acknowledge Greg Gullion, Selden Hale, Amarillo Police Department, and the New Mexico State Police. Gentle prompting for a second book in the series has come from Tom Bell, Clay Wiegand, Chris Clark, Mya Coursey, Wally Cox, and Dusty Blu Cooksey. My wife, Brenda, read the manuscript and gave me invaluable feedback from first chapter to my last sentence. My daughter, Wendy, and her husband, Charlie, again provided me space in Taos to write undisturbed. Carl Condit and James Clois Smith Jr. of Sunstone Press, Santa Fe, New Mexico, supported my writing of *Arroyo of Shells*. Their publication, editing, and graphics are superb in every way. I am proud to be listed in their catalog.

The field research and analysis of Elsie Clews Parsons, Esther S. Goldfrank, and Alfonso Ortiz have been invaluable sources. The linguistic analysis of George L. Trager for the Tiwa languages opened up for me the complexities of Tiwa grammar as well as pronunciation. Much is being done now to maintain and preserve languages among the pueblos. The songs and rhythm I write about are derived from Gregorian chant, *The Broadman Hymnal*, my vocal-music history, the infinite songs and instruments of our lives, and my field experience in witnessing pueblo drumming, singing, and dancing.

The Point Hill Green hero story came from the field work of Merton Leland Miller in 1896 for his dissertation at the University of Chicago. George Washington Matthews' work among the Navajo is legendary. Not only did he serve as a medical doctor among the Navajo, but he translated several curing ceremonies for posterity, including the *The Night Chant, A Navaho Ceremony*, published by the American Museum of Natural History in 1902. I also am dependent upon the writings of Leland C. Wyman, Vera Laski, and Sylvia Rodriguez.

I acknowledge an unpayable debt to the literary lights of Leslie Marmon Silko, Tony Hillerman, Arthur W. Upfield, Jorge Luis Borges, Frank Waters, Linda Hogan, and N. Scott Momaday. Borges' "The Anthropologist," in *In Praise of Darkness*, is an essay of how immersion in a different culture from one's native culture can be life changing—at least it was for Borges' anthropologist, and it has been for me.

I met N. Scott Momaday several years ago in the dining room at the Eldorado Hotel in Santa Fe. It was at breakfast, and I saw him seated across the dining room. I walked over and introduced myself and told him that I had required *The Way to Rainy Mountain* for my students, assigning them to write essays according to the form he used in his book: the mythic, the tribal, the personal. It was a brief exchange; he was happy and smiling, and I was glad to have met him.

I have gone my own way in writing, but I often follow Momaday's form.

The National Endowment for the Humanities (NEH) extended to me a research grant to the University of California at Los Angeles to research "Science, Technology, and Human Values." My study and writing under the NEH grant sharpened my vision on the effect of objectivity upon subjectivity and vice versa. As many have said and implied, "Before there was art and language, there was life." Completely focusing on things around us as only "objects" for our profit or use is a little murder, missing the incomprehensible-spirit-that-moves-in-all-things. Thank you, NEH.

Readers Guide

1. In *Arroyo of Shells*, several chapters begin with the day and date of the week, the Catholic saint of the day, and the Indigenous description of the month. What do these three naming categories say about "cultural" time? How does Indigenous naming of the month and season compel a person's behavior?

2. Why did the bookseller, Coe, take home Mabel Dodge Luhan's *Winter in Taos*? He could have reduced the price of the book, but he did not. Why?

3. Tribal policeman Richard Tafoya does not like to compose powerpoints. How does his explanation to F.B.I. agent Diane Parker reflect the Tulona pueblo's position on prohibiting electricity within the central pueblo? Is Tafoya's opinion purely anti-technology?

4. Forest Service officer Janet Rael goes to Tract A alone and also into Carson National Forest to check on forest roads and wild game by herself. She does not show fear or anxiety in being alone in her fieldwork—at least not to the reader. Why is she confident to perform her duty in solitude?

5. What are the processes that help the tri-cultures, Puebloan, Hispano, and Anglo, overcome their differences? Or, at least help maintain a reasonable tranquility?

6. Father Padilla seeks to reach out to Tulona Pueblo in his homilies. How is he successful in achieving amiability with the puebloans?

7. Medicine Wind shows strength of character throughout the book, but there are times he is perplexed at the Tulona pueblo's problems. What were his concerns?

8. Why did the elder, Looking Elk, tell Dominguez the story of the Hanging Shell pueblo? Was he in error to do so? Why or why not?

9. What brings Tafoya and Janet closer together in the story? What might force them apart—if anything?

10. The medicine bundle and Child of Water mask symbolically represent the spirituality of Hanging Shell pueblo and the Navajo. How were these symbols misused for malevolent purposes? How were these symbols used for the good?

11. Despite different backgrounds, cacique Bustamente and Armando Ortega share traits in common. What are they?

12. What was Dominguez's fatal flaw of character?

13. Beneath the mysteries of theft and murder rest several prominent scenes: the hawk soaring above the creaking cart of Doña Sebastiana, Dominguez's seeing shimmering warchiefs, the drumming and singing that brings group unification, Tafoya's march into the woods near Lance Bernal's murder scene, the ringing of the church bell on All Souls' Day, and Luis Ortega's "adoption" by the Tulona at the Hanging Shell kiva site. Of these scenes, which one had the most impactful effect upon you? And why?

14. In conjunction with question thirteen above, what scene would you add to the list? And why?

www.ingramcontent.com/pod-product-compliance
Lightning Source LLC
Chambersburg PA
CBHW010747310726
48980CB00004B/397

* 9 7 8 1 6 3 2 9 3 7 4 7 6 *